Praise for

"Fresh, funny and bi[...]   [...]an
drama!" - Sarah Tur[...]   *The
                            Unn[...]

"A brilliantly relatable read, offering a nostalgic romp through the 90s and 00s. I laughed and cried and completely immersed myself in Louise's story: so much of it will resonate with midlife women who remember their own car-crash twenties and thirties. A must-read for anyone who lived through those decades, loved that music and still have a bucket hat and Adidas Shell-Toes in the back of their wardrobe!" - Sarah Cawood, television presenter, voiceover artist and narrator

"Funny, thought provoking, heart warming and heartbreaking in equal measure. I couldn't put this book down. Sarah perfectly captures the complexities of modern-day love and the irony of how, sometimes, you can be unwittingly chasing the wrong person while your true love is standing right in front of you. This book is a poignant exploration of themes including friendship, self-discovery and forbidden love." - Jennifer Kay Davies, fiction editor and proofreader

"Whitton has perfectly captured the rollercoaster of emotions of being in love with someone you know is bad for you, but being powerless to stop it. I felt every emotion reading this and felt like the characters were my friends. A real page turner!" - Olivia Beirne, bestselling author of *The List That Changed My Life*

"What a guilty pleasure of a book! Set in 2000-2015, this coming-of-age tale offers a candid exploration of love, lust and finding the right partner in the end. Alternately egged on and dissuaded by her loyal group of girlfriends, Louise's journey of true love is, of course, not without hiccups and hangovers aplenty." - Gaye Poole, author of *Edges of Me*

Love listening to music while reading? Why not download the *I Didn't See That Coming* Spotify playlist, featuring all the songs mentioned in the book and more!

Search *I Didn't See That Coming* on Spotify, or scan the link below:

I DIDN'T SEE THAT COMING

SARAH WHITTON

Copyright © Sarah Whitton (2024)

The right of Sarah Whitton to be identified as author of this work has been asserted by them in accordance with section 77 and 78 of the Copyright, Designs and Patents Act 1988.

All rights reserved. No part of this publication may be reproduced, stored in a retrieval system, or transmitted in any form or by any means, electronic, mechanical, photocopying, recording, or otherwise, without the prior permission of the publishers.

Any person who commits any unauthorised act in relation to this publication may be liable to criminal prosecution and civil claims for damages.

This book is a work of fiction. Names, characters, places and incidents are either products of the author's imagination or are used fictitiously. Any resemblance to actual events or locales or persons, living or dead, is entirely coincidental.

First published by Cranthorpe Millner Publishers (2024)

ISBN 978-1-80378-231-7 (Paperback)

www.cranthorpemillner.com

Cranthorpe Millner Publishers

Printed and bound by CPI Group (UK) Ltd
Croydon, CR0 4YY

For my crew,
the Whitton lads

"What a waste my life would be without all the beautiful mistakes I've made in it."

Alice Bag

PART ONE

CHAPTER 1
2005

Third Time, Very Unlucky

I stared at the bride who was gazing at her groom. He was reading his penned love poem – something about different types of water merging into one river of contentment. I'd switched off for a while, but I was abruptly dragged back into the present as everyone stood up. I joined in, raising my empty glass, and slurred my toast. I finished on a bit of a boom, causing people to turn around. My best friend, Heidi, giggled opposite me, and I poked my tongue out at her. I refilled my champers glass, knocked it down in one and slammed my flute onto the table. Most of the guests were supping politely or wiping tears from their eyes, overcome with the romance of the day.

Fucking weddings.

I was on the fence as to whether I liked them or not. As a kid, I loved them: a fancy frock, dancing till late and staring at a beautiful bride and her swish husband. Nothing had changed, except now I wanted to be a bride and I wasn't. This was my third wedding of the year.

Following the boredom of speeches, it was time for the food and we were all assembled in a decorated barn that was never really a barn. I could not be arsed to face another declaration of never-ending love while I was still single. Even catching the bouquet or listening to the speeches could tip me over the edge.

Yet I RSVP'd like the decent girl I was, despite the invitation arriving in an exploding envelope, glittery letters jumping free when I took the card out. I was still finding them down the sides of the damn sofa months later. Equally annoying was that the invitation requested my company along with my hopeful plus one. It began:

Dear Louise and ?

I wasn't sure if I was offended.

Whoever wrote the invitation had heard the rumours – I hadn't met a decent bloke since the late 90s. Was I being unfair on myself? Was it really that long? A tad perhaps, but the last man who did it for me was a Jack Dee lookalike I'd met in the pub. We snogged behind the Aunt Sally wall, smoked fags and he did impressions of the comedian to impress me. It was oddly arousing, and I'd hoped to bump into him again somehow, and then he served me on the till in Homebase a few weeks later, when I was buying a toilet plunger.

I only vaguely knew the bride, but the groom was an old friend of my best friend, Flint. We'd been to festivals with the groom, got drunk with him, and we'd all scoffed down his Thai green curry countless times. Heidi had seen more of the groom than I had; she'd had a wild fling with him a few years ago. It had started one spring evening and fizzled out a few weeks later after he bent her over the barbecue. Yet, here she was, enjoying herself as if nothing had happened at all.

My gorgeous friend, Di, shuffled up and sat next to me,

looking more like Corine Bailey Rae than ever. Her smoky eye makeup was perfect, her short dark curls looking playful while her fringe was held to the side with an antique-looking leaf-shaped hair clip.

'I think if I get up, I'll fall over,' she said.

'Me too. Shall we stay here then?' I giggled, leaning my head on her shoulder. This was the third time this year I'd been pissed before I'd even seen the seating plan.

Di shook her head. 'We need a top up,' she said, picking up the wine bottles on the table to see if there was any left to refill our empty glasses.

Don't get me wrong, I loved seeing my friends get married, of course I did. And this was, without doubt, a stunning wedding.

But it wasn't mine.

I desperately wanted to be sat at the head table instead of slumped here, bored, full of food and starting to see double.

'I'll have to get up; these are all empty.' Di staggered off looking for leftover wine to pinch from other tables.

Flint, my loveliest mate who was also an usher at the wedding, wandered over and sat down beside me, a half-drunk pint of lager in his hand.

'Alright?' I asked, noticing my voice becoming less like my own and more like a younger Miss Hannagan's.

'Nope. I'm pissed off you haven't told me how sexy I am in this get up.' He gestured to his navy-blue suit, looking down at himself.

'You haven't said I look racy either,' I said, jabbing my finger directly at his toned bicep.

Flint smiled; I knew "racy" had amused him.

That was another thing. Because this was the third wedding this year, I was wearing the third dress I'd bought on my credit card, keeping my fingers crossed I'd be able to wear it again. Let's be real: these dresses *would* have more outings – but only to the christenings that would inevitably follow all these bloody weddings.

'Green is a great colour on you, very sexy. You look hot,' Flint said, deliberately glancing down at my cleavage.

I let out a guffaw. 'So do you. You're hot... I mean... I love you in a suit,' I murmured, resting my head on his shoulder.

'I saw that bloke slurping in your ear. Was he trying to take your earring out with his teeth?'

Ugh, yes. The bride's best mate. He had been severely mis-sold to us. Billed as 'an absolute dude', in real life, he was a guy who didn't eat in public, leading you to wonder what the point of inviting him to a wedding breakfast might be. He'd pushed his grub aside, leaning in close to me, and attempted to chat me up. His ill-fitting suit jacket, onyx silver signet ring and ruddy complexion were all big red crosses on my ideal man chart. Even the sight of him, the only single, dismal male here, leering at me with a gormless expression, was enough to put me off my Key Lime pie.

'Don't, Flint. I wanted to meet someone terrific tonight.'

'Was he dull, then?'

'So dull. I even started totting up my bank balance in my head, and you know what a task that is for me.' I demonstrated counting on my fingers.

Flint grinned and whistled knowingly. 'That's boredom right there.'

I let out a sigh.

There were no men that fit me here.

There were no fit men here.

My friends and I were always added to these offcut tables with the oddballs and misfits. We'd only been invited in the first place to offer invigorating conversation and to add a sparky, flighty energy to the dance floor.

Today's table was yet another classic mishmash.

We had the stiff, professional couple. He was eyeing up every female except his uptight wife; she was a colleague of the bride who didn't appear to appreciate Heidi talking with her mouth full, which considering she was sat right next to me, neither did I (but I'd given up pestering her about her manners before we'd left secondary school in the early 90s).

Next up was the middle-aged cousin of the groom. She was in her mid-fifties, single, with a wispy fringe that didn't quite cover her teal mascara. I feared she was my future, although being single didn't seem to bother her. We soon found out why, as she shared a story with my mate Chrissy about how an estate agent came across her vibrator on her bedside table. Chrissy usually liked to have a story to match, to bat back so to speak, but this one stumped her. Chrissy would never leave her vibrator out. She always cleaned up after herself, and everyone else, for that matter.

I sighed again. Third wedding, third dress, third fucking wedding gift. As usual I'd left it too late, and all that had remained on the wedding list were odd bits of posh, overpriced

Denby chinaware, a lovebird salt and pepper shaker set and ten days' holiday insurance for a skiing trip for the dreamy couple. Wrapping those two little birds had been a nightmare.

I rested my elbows on the table and turned to Flint. 'I'm bored of looking for someone. Why can't *he* find *me*?'

'Who?' Flint asked, finishing his pint while glancing around the room.

'The man who will stop me from feeling alone at thirty-three; the one I click with.'

'Oh, *that* man. I dunno, I'm too pissed to think logically.'

'Any girl catch your eye?' I asked, attempting to locate my lippy in my handbag.

Flint rubbed the back of his neck. 'Not sure. It depends.'

'On what?'

He coughed, mumbling under his breath, but I couldn't make out what he said, and before I could ask, Di arrived back at the table with more booze. She poured wine into her glass and mine, emptying the rest of the bottle into Flint's pint glass when he tipped his empty glass at her in a not-so-subtle gesture.

We'd all be ruined in an hour.

♣

Staggering into my bedroom much later, the shrill horn of the taxi beeped as Flint, Chrissy and Heidi departed. Di had pulled someone towards the end of the night, and as *September* blared, we'd laughed at her performance on the dancefloor, gyrating her hips against him and stroking his shoulders.

What if she married him? That'd be another friend hooked

up or hitched up, and she was bloody younger than me.

I whipped my dress off, table confetti spilling onto the floor, and fell into bed, bra, pants and makeup still on.

Just as my eyes were closing, I made a mental note. If Di married that guy this year, I wasn't fucking going.

CHAPTER 2
Fast Forward a Bit to 2006

The Boys From London

I was running late to meet my friends at The Goose. If I'd known what would happen down the line, I may have decided to be so late that I was a no show.

That morning, as I completed my habitual cleaning of my one-bed house, which always took me ages, Chrissy had texted me.

```
How about it, a little night
out, me, you and Di.
```
```
                     Why the devil not?
```
```
Sorted, The Goose, 7 p.m.,
don't be hours late.
Off to Brownie Camp. Would
Nikki and Heidi be in?
```

I texted Heidi but didn't bother with my cousin, Nikki. We'd spoken on the phone last night, so I knew she was saving money before V Festival.

I showered, reflecting that, out of the four of us, Chrissy had the most responsibility, being a single parent, but still always managed to make it on time. I didn't get how she could do it all. I wasn't tangled up in family life like her, but I would undoubtedly be the last to arrive, a fact my friends were all too aware of.

I needed to get a wriggle on. I sprayed dry shampoo in my hair, glanced at my watch, and sighed with satisfaction that for once I wasn't going to be that late. As I cranked up the stereo, my mobile lit up. It was a text from Heidi.

```
Sorry flower no can do tonight
- in London. Work do.
Catch   you   tomorrow   for
essential hangover chat? Xx
```

I applied a quick bit of makeup, ran a hand through my hair and had just enough time to drag on a pair of jeans and a black top, slanting across the shoulder to show off my golden tan. I put my faithful khaki jacket on, then took it off, then put it on, then took it off again. I sighed, deciding to just carry it, before lacing up my Converse boots.

I was ready. I looked okay.

The Goose was a pub right in the city centre of Oxford. I'd lost count of the number of times the name had changed in my drinking lifetime.

I paused outside the vinyl record shop next to the pub and glanced into the window to check my appearance. My face was a bit pink from the rushing about.

Chrissy texted me to report they were in the garden.

```
We've met three men, making
us laugh.
```

Hurry up.

I walked through the main bar area. Voices were loud as people queued for drinks, laughing and chatting to friends or strangers. The Goose didn't have music and relied on its punters to produce and sustain its decent atmosphere. Most of the tables were empty, indicating the garden would be rammed.

I swerved and swished between drinkers in a bottleneck area. As I approached the fresh air outside, the lowering sunlight hindered my view.

I paused as I shaded my eyes and peeked around at my fellow drinkers. I was correct – the garden was jam-packed, the atmosphere thick with loud laughter and the smell of fags, vibrant perfumes and chips.

I didn't see the girls at first glance, but as I looked around the crammed tables I spotted a dark-haired man leaning his chin on his fist. He wore dark-framed glasses and had a beard he clearly kept on top of. He stared at me. It was a little intense, and I checked behind me to see if he was looking at someone else. I was one hundred percent sure I didn't know him, and as I turned back to face in his direction, my eyes reconnected with his, but then he looked away.

Chrissy's shriek stole my attention.

'Oi! Lou Lou! We're here!' She stood up and used her wine bottle to wave at me, her shoulder-length blonde curls bouncing along with her. Chrissy was the only person ever to call me Lou Lou.

As I got closer, I clocked the bearded man still checking me out. What was his problem? Despite being in a place so familiar to me, I felt uncharacteristically uneasy manoeuvring over to my friends' table, and I kept checking the floor for items I might trip up on. I fiddled with my fringe. The man was hot, not my usual type, but there was something and it was making me insecure in a place I knew so well. The other two men were also watching me approach the table, but I couldn't stop sneaking looks at beardy.

'Hellooo. Sorry I'm late, the buses, you wouldn't...' I laughed along to the guffaws and general ribbing about my tardiness that followed.

I needed to catch up on the booze consumption, pronto, so I poured myself a glass of white wine, plonking myself down between Chrissy and a man wearing a Tottenham top.

'You smell nice,' I commented to Chrissy.

'Thanks! Look at your lovely tan,' she exclaimed, stroking my shoulder.

I caught Di's eye across the table and she blew me a kiss. She looked particularly cheeky tonight – her caramel skin was clear; her cheeks flushed from the wine, I suspected. Her hair was in cute pigtails, and I noticed the left sat higher than the right.

Chrissy introduced me to the three strangers, though I instantly forgot the names of the Tottenham fan and his freckly friend. Dan was the beardy one, and he and Chrissy held court for a bit, talking about their kids and passing around photos on their phones. Chrissy was discussing her brief marriage.

'Three years was enough. As I've always said, he is a top chippy, but a shit husband. You can trust him with your skirting boards alright, just not the husband bit.'

Di laughed as she left the table, heading to the bar.

'He's married to his wood,' Chrissy continued.

We laughed as Freckles choked on his beer, spluttering as he tried to wipe up the remains dribbling down his chin.

'He is! He lives to work, and work again, and that wasn't for me.'

'As it shouldn't be. Kids need your attention,' Dan said. He spoke with a soft London-ish twang, as did his mates.

Feeling left out, and nowhere near pissed enough, I turned to talk to the Tottenham fan on my right, scrabbling for something interesting to say.

'So, what brings you to Oxford then?' I asked, hoping he'd bring out my funny side.

'Him.' He motioned to Dan with his thumb.

I liked him pointing at Dan; it gave me a chance to take a quick look.

'Enjoying it?' I pushed.

'Yeah, it's okay. An arse to get to, though.'

'How do you mean?' I asked, digging for more pointless conversation.

'Just the shit roads and that.'

'Oh.'

Bored as he was, I watched the waitress clear the table next to us. She stabbed a pencil into her blonde Amy Winehouse beehive as she walked away.

Di returned from the bar with more wine and murmured something to Dan. Whatever the joke they shared was, it made Di laugh loudly, making me desperate to join in.

The other guys were now looking at one of their phones

together. The chitchat with me was clearly over.

Di and Chrissy left to go to the toilet, and I glanced over to the other side of the round table to find Dan looking at me, smiling. When I smiled back, he looked down at his hands on the table.

'Your friends are a bit mad, and loud.' Dan made headphones out of his hands.

I laughed. 'Yes and yes. But so are yours.' I nodded my head to the two men, engrossed in their phones without speaking.

Humour flickered in his eyes. 'Yep, they're hilarious alright.'

'How long have you been drinking for tonight?' I asked, pouring myself another glass of wine.

'You know what? I've no idea. Might be an indication of how many pints we've drunk. We asked to sit at their table and the rest, as they say…'

I smiled. I imagined Chrissy and Di agreeing to table guests, but one drink in and the men wouldn't have been able to get a word in.

'So, do you guys work together?' Dan asked.

I shook my head. 'We met at a spinning class about five years ago.'

'I'm impressed. Spinning. Hardcore.'

'It is, and Fitzy's class is like folklore around here. He is the demon spinner, the fittest creature I have ever seen, and he never breaks out in a sweat. Not even those little sweaty moustaches.'

'I hate him already.'

'So do I, but his class is oddly addictive, and you'd think after my first session I'd rather peel my own toenails off than go back.'

'What happened?'

Dan was laughing and I was buzzing.

'On my first night as a newbie, he shoved me to the front of the class with Chrissy and Di. They were also new. I can only say I trembled everywhere possible as he plonked me right in his eyeline. My backside was there for all the class to see, and I had literally nowhere to hide. Afterwards, Chrissy, Di and I chatted; we agreed that although he clearly wanted to humiliate and boss us about via the mic, we fancied him. His motto was "We dream to spin". I'm still scared to death of him.'

Dan chuckled.

'I mean, he gets off his bike, prowls around the room, switches up your gears if he thinks you're being lazy. It's the look he has about him – his sharp dark eyes don't miss a trick, and he makes it his business to catch you out resting or chatting, wherever you are in the spin room. That man takes no prisoners.'

'Been caught out, then?'

'Yeah, but I met two great friends there, so there's always a silver lining, even if we do sweat and moan about our numb fannies.'

I was speaking faster than I was accustomed to. I wanted to impress him, and he was smiling, so it appeared to be working.

'Sorry for boring you all with kids' photos. Do you have any?' Dan asked, taking a mouthful of his beer.

'Nope, not yet.'

'Would you like some?'

'Yep, definitely, one day. I do have godchildren and nieces.

I'm close to them.'

We smiled at each other, accepting the slight pause. Dan traced the condensation on his pint with his forefinger.

'I love them to bits. In fact, I've just had my nieces for a whole weekend. Talk about knackering!'

He chuckled again. 'Well, I wish we had one of you helping out with my two.'

'I am the best. I've taught them all the important life lessons: how long to dunk chocolate digestives in tea before they melt; how not to get caught chatting in assembly. You know the sort of stuff. I'm even taking them to this little kiddie festival thing next month in Stapleford. Do you know it?'

'Yeah, I live there. Did I tell you that?'

'No way!'

'I'm taking my kids there, too,' he said, his eyes bright and animated, his cheeks blushing. 'It's not my cup of tea, but my kids love it. Music, stalls, food and all that crap.' He paused to take a slurp of his pint. 'You know, we should meet up. I mean, with your friends as well; it could be a laugh. Have you been before?'

'Sort of.' I winced, a memory working its way back into my mind. 'It's embarrassing.'

Dan moved to sit next to me, bringing his pint with him. My stomach wavered, knowing he wanted to settle in and listen to my story.

'I drove over to see a friend in Stapleford a couple of years ago. I got the timings wrong of the festival and got lost in a temporary one-way system thing and was stuck in the middle of the procession. I was sandwiched between the Carnival

Princess float and the grumpy scouts. I've never lived it down to be honest.'

'I don't reckon you'll be allowed near the floats this year. In fact, I thought you looked familiar, I think I've seen your wanted photo in the pub. People have thrown darts at it, smeared ketchup on it, that sort of thing.'

'Please tell me they've drawn cock-and-ball graffiti over it as well?'

Dan laughed and faked a disgusted expression. 'Not in Stapleford, but it's okay, those Mexican-style moustaches sort of suit you.'

Dan grinned at me, refilling my wine glass. We were soon engrossed in conversation, eyes only for each other. I was taking him all in, every morsel, and his potent stare told me he was absorbing me, too.

But something didn't add up. He was talking like a single dad, looking at me like a free agent, but he wasn't hiding his wedding band. Despite those things, I fancied him. He rubbed his belly when he spoke, like he'd eaten a meal. It was endearing. I was convinced it wasn't a six-pack area but a softer tummy and all I could wonder was what it would feel like if I stroked my hand across it.

Louise, stop it.

Dan got up to buy more drinks for all of us, and from then on, my glass was rarely empty. He was comical and had us in stitches; I found him a natural at performing little scenes and doing impressions. He did impersonations of us all, mimicking not just our voices but also our mannerisms. A couple of times he nudged me in the ribs, targeting the joke in my direction, and I didn't hide my blushes; in fact, I wanted him to know I was, quite frankly, lapping him up, like I was part of a comedy duo with him. This side of his humour was fast becoming *very* alluring to me.

Sometime later, we shared stories about dating in London and Oxford, Chrissy regaling us with stories from a single parent website she'd joined. Dan bowed out of this conversation, but I watched him laughing and listening attentively as we listed the dating strategies we would not attempt anymore. For me, it was online dating.

Chrissy groaned, laughed loudly and flung her head back.

'What?' Dan asked, nudging me in the elbow.

'It's bad, really bad.' I clutched my imaginary pearls.

'It is,' added Di. 'Where do we start, maybe with the bloke that wanted you to blow a whistle when you came?'

'What?!' Freckles couldn't hide his widening eyes.

Chrissy gleefully clapped her hands. 'Or there was Tortilla Guy.'

'Jeez, you two are giving me a bad name. I'm not a lost cause,' I grumbled.

Dan prodded me as he cleaned his glasses. 'I don't think you're a lost cause.'

Freckles interrupted. 'Mate, let her finish. I want to hear about the Tortilla geezer.'

'Okay, so, I met a bloke online and arranged a cinema date at a retail park. First error: no chatting opportunities.'

Tottenham fan interrupted. 'That was probably his plan.'

'Yeah, I think so.'

There were nods of encouragement around the table and

Dan grinned at me.

'But when we met in the foyer, he'd booked the film already without discussing it with me, and worse, he had booked tickets to see *Hulk*.'

'What's the problem?' said Freckles. 'You're sitting with comic book film fans here; I reckon that's not a bad attempt...'

'Wrong,' Di muttered.

'First date, you don't book *Hulk*, alright?' I turned to face Dan; he was shaking his head.

'I love all comic book films, but I'm with Louise on this one.'

I nodded sharply, feeling pleased that he'd agreed with me. 'Anyway, he was quite dishy, so I rolled with it.'

'Dishy?' Dan repeated with a did-you-really-use-that-word look.

'He bought me some Maltesers, which was the best part of the date, but he sat munching his way through some tortilla chips drenched with this buttery, oily sauce, making these little content noises every now and then.'

I looked around the table. Di had her face in her hands. Chrissy was preparing for the laughing tears by holding onto a tissue.

'Halfway through the film, he tapped me on the arm. I turned to face him and there he was, coming in to kiss me. Now, to be clear, dishy or not, I didn't want that, but before I could do anything about it, he kissed me, and it was bad. His mouth was covered in slimy, warm butter.'

Everyone either groaned or shook their head, while Dan scrunched his face.

'But that's not the end. His lips glided away from mine and found themselves sliding over my cheekbones.' I pointed to the apples of my cheeks. 'Then, to top it all off, when he did find my lips again, little bits of rogue tortilla chips flew into my mouth, causing me to cough them up!'

Everyone loudly expressed their revulsion and Dan put his arm around me and gave me a quick squeeze. I didn't look at him, but felt everything.

It was now dark outside, and the navy sky I had stared up into just a few minutes ago was replaced by deep, raven black. The warmth we'd been lucky to bask in during the evening light wasn't leaving us, and Oxford was now at the height of its bustle.

Di had asked the boys to join us at another bar, and I'd mentally crossed my fingers as they nodded. Dan had glanced in my direction, his ears blushing, causing me to inhale and thank the universe as I ran off to the loo.

A few scattered police officers were keeping their eyes on the streets full of revellers: the drinkers, the tourists and those who had eaten juicy ribs at Old Orleans or legendary steak with blue cheese sauce at Maxwells. Dainty fairy lights hung with grace along the windows of Jamie's restaurant as we passed groups of people finishing their boozy dinners. Flickering candles were almost at the nub, indicating it was time to call it a night.

The noisy audience from the New Theatre had clearly enjoyed the show, laughing and talking as they exited onto

George Street. They wandered from the path and into the road, making it difficult to navigate and stay in our little gang.

As we passed Pizza Hut, we all groaned in appreciation of the wafts of garlic and dough; we could have been easily enticed inside. But instead, we tackled the drunk walkers, ignored the bus drivers yelling in frustration and aimed for the new pubs and bars of the city.

Just as we reached the cobblestone path facing the Malmaison, Di collided with another woman, the tassels of her cardigan tangling with the buttonholes of the other woman's royal blue suit jacket. After their initial shock, the pair laughed with each other while Chrissy and I attempted to unpick the mess. I knelt down, separating the tassels in an attempt to prevent more knotting. The lady and her friends were drunk wedding guests, and in between giggles they told us that the wedding was doomed and that the bride was really "one of those lesbians".

Dan pretended he was a news reporter for the local news; he narrated our actions into a pretend mic, even detailing the doomed marriage. Both victims took off their entwined garments; in the absence of scissors, this was the only option. I knelt on the floor, trying to compose myself as the royal blue garment was being removed and wriggled off.

I looked up at Dan, who was smiling down at me. He held his hand out to help me up, but just as our fingers were about to connect, Di grabbed onto my shoulders, jolting my hand away from Dan's.

'Lou, concentrate!' she yelled, fidgeting and worming around.

Dan smiled, shrugging his shoulders. I shrugged mine back, rolling my eyes as Di eventually righted herself.

Standing, I laughed as I watched my friends flapping, giggling and talking to the ladies. A warm, slightly rough hand took mine. I glanced up at Dan. He grinned down at me, winked and gave my hand a little squeeze. I managed a breathless smile back, then let go, hanging on to his little finger.

What was happening?

What was this man doing to me?

Was this a joke? Was I was secretly being filmed for a crappy documentary on Channel 5?

We aimed for Bar Haha and I hung back as the others went inside. I paused as I watched Dan walk inside, hanging out with my friends, laughing with them as if he'd known them as long as I had. He opened the door for Chrissy and closed it on Di as she laughed on the other side. I liked his light-heartedness and impish nature... screw it, there was a lot about him I liked. But it felt established, in a we've-been-around-the-block-sort of way. It was as though I already knew him.

CHAPTER 3

Why Do I Feel Like I Know You?

Dan and I stood alone, the music and our friends' laughter fading into the background.

We were comfortable with each other, talkative and flirty, and though I should've felt the opposite discussing personal things with this bloke, I didn't. The booze relaxed our tongues, allowing the mind to let all manner of things gush out, and here I was, happy to hang onto each and every word he said. I was openly thrilled he liked my banter. He asked me more questions and every now and then asked me to come closer to hear what he was saying. I glanced around to see if anyone had noticed this woman enjoying this married man's company, but everyone else was doing their own thing. Girls Aloud were far too noisy for my liking and singing about a love machine. Dan and I were in our own colourful, animated picture frame and the rest of the room was gradually fading around us.

'Marriage is tough, you know. It's all romance and hope at the beginning. We were young, to be honest. I was twenty-seven. Now it's like, we've grown up but are facing the other way from each other. Does that make any sense?' Dan used his hands to point in different directions.

I nodded, taking a sip of my wine. 'I have divorced friends who say the same thing.'

Dan sighed. 'It's just... my wife, Melissa, and I, well... we don't chat like this anymore. She doesn't ask me how I am, or give a shit about my views and opinions. I used to make so much effort doing all that crap, but I just gave up. I think marriage, kids and not being ready for it has sort of ruined it all." He gave a self-deprecating laugh. "This is making me sound like a bit of a prick, isn't it?'

I grimaced and nodded.

'Ah, do you think badly of me now? What I mean is, we used to be like that, all honest and open, you know? I thought it was gonna be us for life, but it's sort of... gone. Am I making sense?'

'Yeah, I do get you. I suppose she feels the same.'

He shrugged. 'I wouldn't know how she feels.'

Changing the subject, I asked, 'What does she do for work?'

'She's a hospital director, so her job is stressful and hectic. She works mega hours and as soon as we had Ben, we decided she'd return to work and I'd stay at home.'

'Wow.'

'Unusual, right?'

'Yeah, but impressive. I don't even know what a hospital director is.'

Dan laughed, tilting his head nearer to mine. 'To be fair, I'm not sure either. It's like a planning, organisation job, and trust me, she's good at that, especially at home.'

I grimaced; though I was eager to hear more about their

relationship, I couldn't help but think he was being a bit shitty.

Dan continued, 'I know, I know. That was mean. It's just… Melissa knows I want to grow my web design business. I was dipping in and out of crappy jobs and never happy, and it sort of fitted in with us, but I suppose we focused on our kids and work and not our relationship. We just haven't made it back to the pre-kid times. I just want us to connect again, you know?'

I appreciated his matter-of-fact honesty, feeling the need to take his hand as he spoke. Every now and then, our bodies would connect by the brush of a hand or leaning past one another to put a drink down. When my shoulder skimmed his arm, we glanced at each other, as if we had both experienced more than the slight touch of the physical connection.

'Why don't you separate, if it's not right?'

He stared at me. I'd clearly crossed a line. My face heated up and I moved my gaze away from his for a beat. When I looked back, the smile I'd hoped for wasn't there.

Fuck.

'Sorry, that was, um…'

He shook his head and took his glasses off to clean them. 'It's alright. Them kids are everything to me. I love them so much. I can't leave them. They need me, not her. She's always working, and they rely on me.' He pointed his thumb at his chest. 'We're like a little gang, us three. I love it.'

A dude wearing a Hawaiian shirt barged past me, causing me to nudge Dan's shoulder. He put up a protective hand and moved in a bit closer.

'So, you mentioned you're a support worker. Are you happy doing that?'

I shook my head. 'Not really. I mean, I enjoy it and it pays well. I don't worry about money, considering I live alone. The house is all mine – no more crappy house shares – but I feel a bit tied in. I have other dreams.'

'And?' Dan asked, moving closer to listen in.

'I want to be a writer; a novelist. I write short stories at the moment, in the hope I can turn them into novels one day. Impossible, eh?'

Only Flint was aware that I wrote in my free time. Heidi knew I'd kept diaries since I was a teenager, and Di knew I read a fair amount of books, but it was Flint who took the piss and occasionally addressed my birthday cards 'to my own little Jane Austen'. Sharing this vulnerable part of me with a relative stranger was out of character for me, but weirdly, it felt exactly the right thing to do.

'I think that's brilliant. And it's not impossible. Hard, sure, but not hopeless. To be honest, I'm equally impressed you own your own place – now that's something else. You should be proud of yourself.'

'I am, I guess, but I got lucky with timings and I'm a bit sensible sometimes. Owning your own home isn't really an achievement you can shout about though. Like, I didn't go to uni—'

'Neither did I.'

'But I sort of need a degree to help me be a writer and I can't go to university now because I need to work.'

Dan tried his hardest to explain that I didn't need to have a degree, and then I began to regale him with anecdotes of my childhood writing. He gazed at me with a smile that slowly grew, and it was comforting, like he'd wrapped one of my favourite hoodies around my shoulders.

'Don't ever give up. With your writing, I mean. I understand how it feels to be a creative trapped in the rat race; escaping was the best decision I ever made.'

I admired his determination, but I sensed a lot of sorrow in him. I guess you can have some parts of your life in complete check, but if there's a thread running through that's flawed, it can unbalance you if you aren't truly happy. I was missing something from my life; I thought he was, too.

Reality suddenly jabbed me in the shoulder insistently, demanding I ask myself uncomfortable questions. How did I know what was absent in his life? What was I doing, listening to this guy I barely knew, giving his discoloured life a rub down and even sounding sympathetic?

More importantly, where was my loyalty to the sisterhood?

Did he always chat up naive women on a rare night out? I wasn't sure I'd been party to this before; the signs were unclear. Did married men all use the lack of understanding trick to get their way? I started to wonder what his aim was.

Dan disturbed my thoughts by facing me square on. He placed his hands on both my shoulders and said, 'Look, I need to go for a piss, but when I come back, I must tell you something.' He darted off into the crowd.

Whilst he was gone, I recalled encounters with the men I'd hooked up with recently. I shuddered with embarrassment. There was the date where I spent the last thirty minutes locked in a toilet cubicle to avoid any more of his space fantasy theories. There was the Clark Kent lookalike, who in real life was anything but, pulling up in his Volvo and waving a hanky at me. Then there was the farmer I'd met through speed dating. No further information needed.

What united them all was the lack of connection and the clear absence of fizzy feelings. But when I looked at Dan, I felt the mysterious jolts I'd been wanting for years to experience. I wanted to know more about this guy, wife or no wife. He'd captivated me, kids or no kids. I didn't know what the fuck I was thinking. I couldn't explain it, but I knew this whole evening and meeting him was just as it should have been.

When he returned, he looked twitchy and guided me away from the crowded bar. I leant against a padded pillar to relieve my aching feet.

He looked down at me, rubbing his belly anxiously. 'I'm nervous now, but I... for some reason... I can't explain... I've just got to say this to you.'

We looked at each other. His eyes were sage green with amber freckles. I glanced down as he licked his lips, and found myself mindlessly wondering how they'd taste. Dan had been quite determined to tell me something before he disappeared, but now he was a little lost.

In my wine haze, I knew he was going to say something big. I felt it, whatever it was. My heart was stampeding around in my chest and I was sure the whole world could hear it. I gave Dan a brief smile, hoping this might hide my nerves and reassure him to get the hell on with it.

'Thanks for that smile. And your smile, you should know, is cute, so so cute.' He paused, glancing at his feet, then continued. 'Shit, this is weird... crap and weird...' He trailed off and looked away, pinching his lips together between his thumb and forefinger.

I moved closer to him and shouted over the inconvenient music. 'Shall we go outside?'

He nodded, leading the way. Carrying our drinks, we walked to the tables outside, joining a group of drinkers at the end of their table. He pinched his lips together again, looked around him, and took a big slug of his beer. Staring back at me, he took my hand.

I spoke first. 'You can tell me anything you like.'

Dan nodded and smiled. I moved back away from him. I shouldn't be this close to him, but I wanted to kiss him, and it was overpowering my mind. At the same time, my nervousness took charge. He leant closer to me, our cheeks almost touching, and a tiny shiver ran down my spine as his breath tickled my ear.

'I feel the same, you're so funny. But you know that, right? It's everything about you, your accent... you're a great listener.'

I stared at him. I couldn't find a response in my head, so I let him continue.

'It's driving me mad, and fuck me, you're sexy.'

I smiled, twirling the ring around on my finger; I found the idea inconceivable that my Oxfordshire accent could have this kind of effect.

He took a deep breath in. We were still cheek to cheek. 'Look, I want you to know, since I've been married, I've never done this. This ain't normal for me. But whenever I've looked at you tonight, it's like my normal has gone out the window.'

I nodded. 'Same here. You aren't my normal type. I don't

even know if I should go for those types anymore; they clearly aren't doing much for me, but you know what I mean, right?' I drank some more wine and pulled my hand away from his. 'You're doing all sorts of crazy stuff to me too, you know, and I wasn't expecting that tonight, at all.'

'I'm glad it's not just me. I've never said anything like this to anyone. I've never wanted to, you know? I've told you how my marriage is and, well... but it doesn't mean I've messed about elsewhere, because I haven't.' He trailed off, glancing away, then pressed on. 'Look, I feel like, like I fucking know you or something. It's like I've always known you, and it's freaking me out.'

I laughed. 'I know, its mad. I thought something was going to happen hours ago.'

He swallowed. 'Me too, although it hasn't happened yet.'

I raised my eyebrows at him.

'You have something about your eyes that I can't stop looking at, but it's more than just that. I... I... I want to kiss you,' he said.

We stared at each other, and I bit my bottom lip. He took another sip of his drink and shrugged, a cue for me to speak first. But I couldn't. Our eyes were still connected and my heart was hammering in my chest.

I opened my mouth to speak, but Dan did the same.

I laughed. 'Do it, then.'

Half of me was berating my honesty and the other half clapped me on the back for being a modern woman. My speedy response reeked of desperation, but that's because I was, and now he'd be aware of it.

He laughed too and leant in closer. 'Thanks for joking with me; I'm more relaxed about what I've told you now.'

His warm breath heated my cheek, and I didn't think I could take this anymore.

'I wasn't joking,' I said, turning my face to look directly at him. 'I want to kiss you too, right here, right now.'

Dan looked at me, grinning. 'Well, we can't here. I can't let my mates see. They've known my missus for years.' His voice trailed off and he glanced over at our friends.

I nodded, showing him I understood his point.

'If we went to a club and everyone was dancing, and we just happened to get lost for ten minutes...'

I raised my eyebrows and smiled.

Dan picked up my jacket from the tabletop. 'Drink up love, you've pulled,' he whispered in my ear, before pulling away and throwing my coat at me.

It landed on my face, but quick as anything, he pulled it back, catching me grinning from ear to ear.

Rounding up the troops, we marched off to the nearest place I knew that stayed open late. At my age, I wasn't fond of the clubs, especially in Oxford. They'd never been decent, even when clubbing was in. But Jongleurs was open, just around the corner, and the streets surrounding it were perfect for hiding and snogging.

The bouncers took their time, but eventually we were all admitted, and with the club stamps on our hands, Dan and I snuck back out again. I messaged Chrissy to tell her I was a bit woozy and getting some air. Her reply was an army of question marks. She clearly didn't believe me at all.

I led Dan by the hand to a cobblestone alleyway nearby and we stopped at the same time. Dan leant against a wooden gate. He didn't look at me at first, glancing around.

I rolled a stone around with my foot, then moved nearer to him. His hand found mine, pulling me closer. The slight touch from him made me forget my surroundings. I wanted to hit pause; anything to draw out this dizzy feeling I had discovered.

Knowing we were alone made what came next somehow okay. All that mattered was that I could kiss him. He drew me in, maintaining eye contact the whole time. I could have gazed at him for hours.

Still looking into his eyes, my hands circled the back of his neck. His hair was damp with sweat. He pulled me tighter into him, chest to chest, and our lips finally met.

The kisses were soft and faultless, and as they continued Dan moved his hands down my back and then rested them on my arse. When our tongues touched for the first time, I felt as if I could have floated away, taking Dan with me.

Not once did his touch feel out of order; in fact, it was the opposite. I wanted more. My hands were still lost in his hair, gripping harder with every kiss, and my back was pressed against the wall as he kissed me greedily. He flinched when I kissed his neck, and when I glanced at him, his head was tilted back, his eyes shut. Knowing the effect I had on him was turning me on.

What a fit moment.

Eventually, we came up for air. His hair was all over the place, and his dazed expression completed the look. My lips were puffy from passion. Dan fiddled with his crotch area and adjusted his glasses, which I'd managed to knock partly off centre. We laughed at the ridiculousness of it all, and he pulled me in again for a brief, tender kiss. As it ended, I held onto his bottom lip with my mouth and slowly let go. Dan held my head in his hands and shook his head. Neither of us could fathom what had happened.

Still… there was an end, and it was coming fast, and in our case, we both knew this was as good as it would get. In a moment of shyness, I fiddled with the hem on his t-shirt, his hands glued to my backside. We tried to chat but neither of us could seem to get the words out. Kissing was a better pastime.

Dan took my phone from my jeans back pocket and passed it to me to unlock it. I gave it back to him and he called his mobile from my phone.

'There,' Dan said, grinning.

He pulled me back in, draping his arms around my shoulders and placing a light kiss on my forehead.

'We can meet up next month at the festival, remember?' he said.

I nodded.

'Not sure I'll be able to concentrate on anything knowing you'll be around, though.'

I kissed him again to avoid answering. Meeting him in public was never going to happen, we both knew it.

'We'd better get back.'

Dan nodded and we meandered, arm in arm, back out of the alley. Just before the streetlamps came into view, he stopped.

'Hang on a minute.'

He turned to me and pulled me roughly against him, kissing me so powerfully I could only return it with an enthusiastic kiss of my own, one I already knew he liked and had a weakness for. He slumped against the nearby wall, dragging me with him.

'Please tell me you want me as much as I want you,' Dan said, eyes wide. 'This isn't in my head, is it?'

'Honestly, if you didn't have to get back to your mates, we'd be in a taxi right now and I'd be taking you home.'

Dan closed his eyes and covered his face with his hands. His gold band shimmered back at me, like a cautionary "Danger!" sign, warning me away.

Sweaty and with numb lips, we took our fizzing selves and emerged into the hordes of dancers and drunkards. The thumping music hit me and my eardrums screeched for help. I wondered if the whole club sensed what we'd done as we searched for our friends. Someone must have noticed how I kept finding ways to stroke his back and how he ruffled my hair in the crowd. Di and Chrissy provided us with vigorous smiles at the edge of the dance floor.

'Where are they?' Dan asked, a little panicky.

'Waiting outside for you. One's feeling rough, too many shots, and the other one is moaning,' said Chrissy. 'They left quite a while ago, though.'

Chrissy's expression revealed that no one had been rumbled.

'Well, ladies, it's been a blast.'

He kissed all of us on our cheeks, lingering on mine as he squeezed my hand behind my back, before walking away.

I turned to face my girls and we all screamed, huddled and then moved to the dance floor. I had never felt so vivacious and desirable. We stayed dancing to Donna Summer, Goldfrappe, Chaka Khan and essential ABBA with compatible strangers until 1 a.m., when we staggered out of the club, unsteady on our feet, not from drinking but from energetic disco whirling.

Our voices were hoarse and cracked from shouting and singing. I was exhausted and I needed my bed. I filled the girls in about the bits they'd missed as we walked to get our separate taxis home. They wanted to know everything.

'Your "I'm available" sign was on and, as usual, it was a joy to behold,' Di said, putting her arm around me.

'Anything else?' I asked.

'You were doing that thing you do when you laugh and you throw your head back. Dan couldn't stop looking at you.'

Chrissy fiddled in her bag. 'He's married,' she said, frowning. 'You think you'll see him again?'

I shrugged her comment off.

'Do you want to?'

'I've no idea. I'm going to go home, have all the dreams, and thank the lord Heidi isn't here.'

Di laughed. 'Amen to that. And Flint.'

I groaned. I didn't want to depart from the man buzz I was in, but I had an inkling Flint and Heidi would not have supported tonight's lowdown. Flint would consider Dan greedy, having two women "on the go" at the same time, and would assume he was trying to take advantage. Heidi would tell me I should be looking for a better, more stable option.

'Oh, I didn't mean to sound negative. I suppose I just worry, that's all,' Chrissy said, linking her arm through mine.

'I know you do, and I love you for it. Come here.'

We all hugged hard, giggling, before going our separate ways.

As I paid the taxi driver, let myself into the house and stumbled upstairs to bed, I found myself still grinning.

❦

Feeling delicate, feet throbbing, armpits sweaty and with mascara smudged around my eyelids, I woke up the next morning on top of the world. I bounced down the stairs like Tigger. Did that really happen last night? My cat, Bennett, purred as I made a cup of tea, and I talked to him as I poured his cat biscuits into a bowl. I stared out of the kitchen window and touched my lips, remembering. I could almost feel the soft prickle from Dan's beard. My lips turned upwards into a smile, a smile so wide it became quite simple to understand the deal – other men hadn't been quite so victorious at making me feel like this.

I flung open the back door to allow the morning sunshine in and encouraged Bennett to scamper into the garden. I curled up in the living room, switched the TV on and grabbed my mobile out of the handbag I'd dumped on the floor. There were four missed calls from a landline. A local code I recognised to be Stapleford.

Fuck.

Was it the wife?

Dan?

Why not call from his mobile?

There was no voicemail.

I called Chrissy for answers.

She answered after two rings and was, as usual, as cheery as can be. 'Christ, this is early.'

'He's called me.'

'Today?'

'No, last night.'

'Christ, what did he say?' she asked, her voice turned up a notch.

'Easy! My head is killing me. I can't cope with those noise levels.' I frowned, rubbing my forehead.

Chrissy sighed. 'Take some paracetamol. I want to know what he said.'

'I dunno, I didn't speak to him.'

'Eh?'

I explained to Chrissy that while I'd been asleep, someone had called at 2:05 a.m., 2:15 a.m., 2:45 a.m. and 3 a.m., but left no message. Chrissy concluded that Dan must have called from his landline, not the wife, but that it *was* odd and amateurish. My mobile number could be listed on the landline phone bill.

I didn't know what to do. I wanted more. I wanted *him*.

I was lonely.

I'd been looking for something in a man and had begun to feel like it would never turn up, so when it was standing there, wrapped up in a beard, glasses, and a sense of humour, I wanted to grab it. I wanted to take it all, despite the wife.

I needed to respond to him.

'Well, you can't call back,' said Chrissy, crunching toast in my ear.

'I could text him,' I replied, as I flopped onto the sofa.

'What would you say?' she asked.

I chewed on this for a second. Chrissy would be on my side, and I detected her delight at this new romantic encounter, yet I knew she didn't want to see me get hurt.

'You like him, don't you?' she added.

'God yeah. I can't explain why, after just one night. I mean, this isn't me. But not seeing him ever again... well, I can't even consider it. I know he's married, but our connection last night...'

'Hmm, I saw. Di and I kept kicking each other under the table. The way I see it, you're single and haven't done anything wrong, but you must remember two things. If you leave it today, the memory will always be unforgettable.'

'But?'

'But, if you send a text and something follows, you must accept that you get what you're given. He'll never be fully yours.'

I gulped. Chrissy had perfectly and perceptively nailed the situation I found myself in, but I was hooked, a goner, and I planned to ignore her sound advice.

After we'd hung up, I took a deep breath, then set up the delivery report facility before typing out a message with a velocity that could only be matched by Heidi. Making sure the text made sense with the limited characters my mobile allowed, I hit send before I could change my mind.

```
Hi, it's Louise, I've seen
    some missed calls from
Stapleford, they were from
you? I won't call back but
```

```
            wanted to say thanks. We had
                a great time, didn't we?
```

The text was not delivered or read.

CHAPTER 4

A Phone for the Family, and A Phone for the Fucking

'Okay, here's the thing. You know he's not read your text, because *that* phone is for the fucking and he has a normal phone for normal life, family life, whatever that is. Thus, he'll read your message on his next night out when he switches the "fucking" phone on. He'll either hit delete or keep you on the back burner for bit of sex texting.'

A week had passed, and I was sprawled on the grass after what had loosely passed as a Race for Life training session with Heidi. She was giving me one of her looks.

I'd known Heidi since I was nine. We'd sat on different tables at school, and it hadn't taken long for me to become her number one fan. I remember admiring her dark brown plaits, which she'd chewed when she was concentrating. My mum wouldn't plait my hair, complaining that they didn't stay in. Instead, I always had variations of bobs: with fringes, without fringes and, of course, the Lady Di side fringe. I still wore a recycled version of that style, but so did Heidi; her dark hair was in shoulder-length plaits that even now I marvelled at.

I'd found out Heidi was a good'un when I'd forgotten my PE skirt, meaning I'd have to do PE in my pants. I remember crying, my lip trembling at the thought of showing my pants to the boys.

'Don't cry. We mustn't cry about small things, my mum said so.' Heidi had wagged her pointy finger at me, imitating her mum. 'If you like, I'll pretend I've forgotten my skirt and we can both wear pants.'

That's exactly what we did, and it was the best PE lesson we ever had.

From then on, we were joined at our rucksacks and pencil cases, but our friendship could sometimes be laced with spectacular disagreements. We'd fallen out about most things, from who could do the best handstands on the school field (always her), to who most resembled Wendy from *Transvision Vamp* (neither of us), to who Darren Hilton fancied more (again, neither of us), and, more recently, who would do better on *Big Brother*.

I knew everything about her and loved that she knew everything about me. She was my sounding board and was one hundred percent honest with me, which was why I loved her so much. But honestly, thank fuck Heidi hadn't been free to join us on the night I met Dan.

'Look, I don't mean to be cruel,' she continued, ignoring my squirming. 'You know I'm up for connections, attractions, meant-to-bes or whatever the shit that was last week, but he's married. With kids. And he's bored at home. I take zero pleasure in being the one to remind you, but there you are.' She took a swig from her water bottle.

'Thanks.'

Heidi had been trying to touch her toes to stretch out her hamstrings, but her protruding belly prevented her reaching her feet. She gave up, giving me another direct stare.

'Don't be sulky. He's approaching middle age and not getting sex. End of. I don't want you to be his fuck buddy.' She shook her head at me to emphasise her last point.

I looked down at the grass, unable to answer. Lunchtime was looming and kids screamed with happiness in the nearby playground and splash park. Heidi and I sat in a strained, forced silence as two kids zoomed past us on their scooters, their screams filling the break in our conversation.

'I know you've got my best interests at heart, Heid, but this is not the same. You'd love him. There's so much to like about him. Yes, the wife and kids and marriage are big issues...'

Heidi started to interrupt me, but I cut her off.

'Shoot me now, but I don't think I'm going to feel settled unless I see him again, or something.' I picked handfuls of grass, waiting for her answer.

'So, how will that work?'

'What do you mean? Finding time to see him?'

'Yeah.'

My mouth was dry and I wanted to say something that wasn't going to sound defensive. 'I don't know, I mean, we haven't arranged anything yet—'

'And you haven't spoken to each other since.' Heidi rooted around in her backpack for something, avoiding eye contact.

'Um, no, but I mean, he called me and I texted him, but we haven't actually spoken—'

'So wouldn't it be better to think of it as a one-off then?'

'Um... maybe? But I don't want to.' My face reddened. 'I... I think he's busy with the kids and work and stuff. I'm sure he'll text me back soon. Or maybe he's run out of free texts or hit his call limit?' I crossed my arms in full support of the excuses I'd made for Dan.

'Sure, he has a lot to be busy with, doesn't he, including his *wife*.' She spat the last word at me and it landed between us on a patch of buttercups.

How had I rationalised this in my head? Why didn't I care about his wife? He was married, for fucks sake. I *should* care. Heidi did, so why didn't I? Was it my desperation for a connection? My loneliness? My inability to let go of the fact that Dan and I had understood each other in a way I hadn't felt about anyone for years? What was wrong with me?

Heidi scoffed at my silence. 'Well then, guess there's no hope for you,' she grumbled as she stood up, pulling me with her. 'You'd better ride this out and see if he ever calls. In the meantime, I'll be doing everything I can to distract you. Now get running.'

She smacked my arse and we returned to our training. I wondered if she understood the size of the job ahead of her, diverting my attention away from him.

🌷

A few days later, I was hiding in the most depressing place on earth: the work tearoom. There was a lightbulb that blew about three years ago, never to be replaced. Even the fluorescent yellow Local Authority paint couldn't cheer this place up. The room housed three fridges, mostly containing gone-off lunches, and the walls were covered in flyers, posters and announcements that were not only curling at the edges but were all out-of-date. Nobody took ownership of this area. It was too depressing to eat any food here, but as we were only allowed fifteen minutes for our tea breaks, unfortunately this was where we hung out.

As the water boiled, I opened my diary and spotted a note I'd made. Two months today and I'd be on holiday, in the sun, with Nikki. I sent her a text.

> Two months today!!!!!

The kettle clicked off and jolted me from my excitement about a week in Spain.

I'd made my afternoon cuppa and was praying I wouldn't be disturbed. It was a lottery as to who would interrupt you when you wanted to be left alone: the deaf caretaker, the mardy Internal Processes woman who never spoke to me, or worse, the fanatical cyclist who came in to rinse his Lycra. I was standing next to him at the sink once when he leant over me and a droplet of sweat from his arm landed in my tea.

I stared into space, enjoying the serenity over the humming of the fridge, when my boss, Jasmeet, entered. Dammit. I was in trouble: I'd taken seventeen minutes. She'd probably ask me to lock up tonight now.

'Whatcha,' Jasmeet said as she noticed me in the corner, staring into space.

'Hi, you alright?' I asked.

'No, I need coffee, a gallon of the stuff.' She poured hot water into her cup, already filled with one of her little café latte sachets, and stirred at high speed, her tongue resting in between her teeth.

'What's that smell?' she asked, turning up her nose.

I tried to subtly sniff my armpits.

'Not you,' she laughed. 'That sort of off-cabbage, cheese smell.'

'The bins?'

'Urgh, probably. You okay? You look a bit vacant.'

I laughed. 'Isn't that my normal expression?'

Jasmeet chuckled.

'I'm alright, just daydreaming.'

'Name?'

'What?'

'His name?'

'Ah, obvious, is it? Dan, and it's complicated.'

Jasmeet perched on the edge of a sofa opposite me. 'Is he worth the complications?'

'Too early to be sure, but I'd like to find out.'

'Well, go for it, have some fun, and you know where I am, right? For detail sharing, I mean. I'm old and married, remember.'

I nodded. 'Course.'

'Good. Right, have you got any chocolate in that bag of yours? I'm desperate.'

She sat down next to me as I searched my bag. I must have something in here for her; then she might leave me alone. Jasmeet quoted calorie targets and sugar contents as I sifted through receipts, a tampon, hairbands, a bookmark and an empty packet of chewing gum. The recognisable sound of my mobile phone in my bag grabbed my attention: the sound of the read receipt.

Dan had read my text message.

CHAPTER 5

Fourteen Years Old or a Middle-Aged Dickhead?

The next three hours and twenty-two minutes dragged by in the office. Despite reading my text, Dan hadn't replied to it. This turned me into a manic border collie, human type. I stared into space as the reception phone rang, my colleagues tutting at me. I scanned documents numerous times in error, freezing the scanner into a sulk. I couldn't concentrate on my work. I have no idea what advice I offered my clients; I daydreamed throughout my interviews and every now and then found myself cackling in a style that wasn't my own. I didn't behave like that at work; my clients craved secure, safe people to share their stories with, not me staring into the distance one minute then hooting the next. I kept imagining various scenarios of Dan walking into the busy reception to take me away from all this, and it was sending me round the twist.

I logged off my PC at record speed, collected my stuff and waved as I exited the office. I inhaled a deep breath of contentment as the hot August air greeted me: my companion to the bus stop.

I swiped my bus card and said hello to the driver, who

favoured turning a page of his tabloid to returning the politeness. Finding a seat at the back of the bus, I plonked myself down and noticed the recognisable whiff of long-gone sweaty passengers. I smelled McDonald's meals snuck onto the bus by teenagers; body odour mixed with the sweetness of wet wipes. The windows were open, but I needed the breeze blowing in as the bus departed to reduce the stink. Not that I *really* minded the aromas; I was too excited by the buzz around me. The thrill of something happening. I knew everyone around me couldn't know, but it felt to me as if everyone could sense an adventure was pursuing me. Like it was chasing me down the street. I placed my bag on the seat next to me and pulled my phone out to send a text to Heidi. I tapped on her name and started to type.

```
           He has read the text. I
           repeat, he has read the
                             text!
```

An incoming call blocked the text screen, not allowing me to send it.

It was him.

'Hello,' I answered.

'Hi, you.' His voice croaked a bit and he coughed. He sounded unsteady. I hoped he was as nervous as I was.

'Well, this is a surprise, are you okay?' My voice sounded unlike my own, a little deeper, like a Silk Cut smoker's voice. I mirrored him, coughing and sorting the gruffness out.

'Yeah, um, we've just got back this afternoon from our holiday.'

The faint London edge to his voice took me back two weeks and my belly flipped over. I suddenly became aware of the quietness for 5 p.m. on a Thursday, with just a few passengers dotted around the bus at the front. I took a moment to understand what was happening here. I wanted this conversation so badly it was disconcerting.

Dan explained he'd left to go on his annual holiday to France with the family the evening after we'd met.

That explained a lot.

He and his wife took one phone away on trips and because her job was the more demanding, she took hers. His mobile was placed in a draw with my text tucked inside it, awaiting opening. He made me laugh telling me about his hangover the night after we met.

'Yeah, I was still mashed up on the ferry. I had to run to the deck and throw up.'

'Eugh.'

'I know, what a mess. My mates didn't get up early, the kids were running around, Melissa went out. I can't remember much of that day; I was in a bit of a trance.'

'Me too.' We paused, then I asked, 'Was it all worth it? I mean, did you have a nice break?'

'Yeah, I mean, the kids loved it. The weather was boiling. I've a nice little tan going on and I even read a whole book.'

'Relaxing, then?' I switched the phone from my left ear to my right.

I noticed my palms were clammy. What was he building up to? Reports of happy families and reconciliations over baguettes and frogs' legs? Or worse yet, regretful memories of him and me with our hands up each other's tops in an alleyway as he sailed home, holding his wife's hand from St Malo?

If that was the plan, I was not his target audience.

'No, not really,' he said.

I held my breath, my heart upping its beating to a ferocious level, causing me to place my hand on my chest to diffuse the sound. I was sure the bus driver could hear it. I waited for him to inform me that everything I'd been reliving the past fortnight had been nothing more than a fantasy in my head.

'How come?' I tried to sound confident and ordinary. Like I was booking my next haircut.

'You,' he replied.

'Oh.'

Good *you* or bad *you*? I wondered, holding my breath.

'Christ, not like that. Shit, I mean, I couldn't stop thinking about you. What happened and what we did.'

The bus driver started the engine and we moved away from the stop.

'Oh, right.' My laugh came out skittish and odd. I congratulated myself for introducing a new, weird laugh now of all moments. 'I thought you were about to say the exact opposite.'

'Shit no, you were...' – he paused and took a deep breath – 'you were all I thought about for two weeks. Shall I leave it there? If it's making you uncomfortable—'

'No, carry on, it's fine. It's been the same for me to be honest, but I didn't hear from you, so I gathered that was it, you know, where we left it.'

'I worried you might think like that.'

He went on to explain that he couldn't remember much of his taxi ride home with his mates that night. He was pissed, we all were, but the drink wasn't the reason for his dizziness. He said his mind was crammed with what he wanted to do with me and hadn't had the chance. He recalled setting his mates' beds up in the living room. They'd all had more to drink in the garden, smoked, and eventually his mates had crashed for the night.

Dan hadn't been able to sleep, and as soon as his mates were out, he'd called me. He'd needed to tell me he was going on holiday and the absence of any contact from him didn't mean he regretted what we did; that he felt the exact opposite. The battery on his was mobile low, and he hadn't wanted to fetch his charger from upstairs in his bedroom.

'So I took the landline, went into my kids' playhouse in the garden and I called you.'

'Seriously?'

'Oh yes, I'm dead serious. There I was, crouched down, leaning against the kids' kitchen sink, trying to see your number on my mobile screen in the pitch black so I could dial it on the landline. My knees were killing me.'

'That's bonkers.'

'Well, I wasn't in my right mind. In a good way.'

'I'm glad – I think.'

'I didn't want to leave it like we did. I was shaking when I dialled your number, but I couldn't give up. I wanted to be respectful to you. I know it wasn't the right thing to do in many ways and the significance of calling you might bite me on the arse, but the idea of saying goodbye properly, not just a peck on the cheek, wiped all the sense out.'

'I think what you're saying is you knew what you were doing.'

'Yeah, you got it. I'm waffling. I'm nervous, but basically, I tried your number like ten times and then just gave up.'

'Why didn't you leave me a message?'

'Because I'm a prat.'

We burst out laughing.

'I love hearing you laugh,' Dan said. 'I've imagined you laughing for the last two weeks. Over and over. I remembered your accent, your giggle, your lips. I would catch myself thinking about you and I was really bloody happy about it. I couldn't stop smiling. Then, an inflatable killer whale would hit me in the face and I realised I was in the pool with one of my kids. I ran off for showers to get away from everyone. I felt separated, like I wasn't in the same place as them and instead I was in the same room as you. I feel terrible about that.'

'I'm sorry. This is a bit shit, isn't it?'

'Yeah, it is,' Dan replied. 'But at the same time it isn't. It's fucking mental, insane, and I've no idea what to do about it.'

My bus journey was halfway complete and the bus was now full and boisterous. Fellow passengers were listening to music, chatting to friends, while I stared out the window talking to a married man who I fancied the pants off. Something I'd never imagined I would ever be doing. I'd already repositioned my bag on my lap as a tall, lithe guy with the longest twirly ginger beard sat next to me.

'I'm going to leave it to you to decide. You are way savvier than me,' Dan continued.

'What do you mean?'

'Oh shit, that didn't come out right either. Fuck's sake, I'm so crap at this. I feel like I'm fourteen years old again, saying all the wrong stuff to Marie Simms down the rec.'

I smiled inside, picturing a teenage Dan, working his arse off to impress a stroppy girl.

He took a deep breath and continued. 'I have to see you again. I can't not ever see you again...' He hesitated; it was clear he wanted to say more. 'I mean, there is a but. We talked about my kids and how I can't leave them at the moment, but you and I...'

I stayed silent. I was so desperate to leap in, say yes and throw caution to the wind, but Heidi's comments kept rising up in my head.

'What do you think?' he continued. 'I mean, you could think about it if you like. I wouldn't blame you if you said get lost to a dickhead like me.'

I laughed. 'A married dickhead like you, you mean?'

'A married, middle-aged, fucked-up dickhead. God, when you laugh you have no idea what you're doing to me.' Dan's voice became husky and faded out.

I'd never felt so horny on public transport.

'I want to see you again, and I get you can't promise things. I've thought of little else, you know,' I said.

'I hoped you were thinking about me at the same time I was thinking about you.'

'Yeah, me too, and honestly, I want to see you again too.'

'God, I've got like a world of butterflies taking off in my belly. You don't know what effect you have on me,' he said with a quiet laugh.

The conversation rolled on effortlessly. Through the window I marvelled at the cyclists of Oxford weaving around the parked cars, avoiding their own deaths as Dan and I nattered. It was like we'd stored up all the chats we'd missed out on over the past two weeks. We laughed, we talked about our forthcoming weekends, mine a music festival, his cutting the front garden Leylandii because he'd bought a new trimmer.

Dan said he felt older and more uncool than me. I told him I felt alive and fizzy. I wanted to see him right this minute, but instead I navigated getting up from my seat with legs that didn't seem to be attached to my body. As my bus approached my stop, I suggested hanging up as we'd have nothing to talk about when we met up. I wobbled off the bus, balancing phone, bag and my mental state.

'I don't think that'd ever happen, do you? I'd sit up all night talking shit with you,' Dan replied.

I fished my keys out of my bag and we said our goodbyes. I was feeling hollow already. I opened my front door to Bennett meowing, and my phone bleeped. A text from Dan.

```
I   feel   alone   without   you.
After  just  one  phone  call.
```

I sat down on the sofa, holding my phone, and absorbed this brand-new feeling that had landed flat in my stomach. It was like my gut had specifically reserved a place for this feeling to arrive, and now it had.

The sense of anticipation was thrilling but scary. I remembered feeling the same thing as a kid about to go on the log flume at Alton Towers, not sure if I could handle it. I had stood at the front of the queue, taking deep breaths. I'd so wanted to do it, and I couldn't go back down the stairs, so instead, I'd swallowed the scaredy feelings and embraced the rush.

Dan was like that log flume.

Taking a deep breath, I texted him back, arranging to meet. I didn't have to go into work for a few days after the festival, and I didn't have any plans apart from packing away camping equipment and getting the dirt out from under my fingernails. Dan figured he'd plan a fake client appointment and arrange a playdate for his kids.

So, there we were, our first date planned. We were to meet at 12 midday in the only pub he knew in Oxford – the one we'd met in.

Now I just had to get through the festival.

CHAPTER 6

Lilly Allen or Chips?

V Festival, Stafford, 2006 looked pretty fine to me. All my girls, together with Flint, my favourite man in the world... well, perhaps until Dan had come along.

We arrived late Friday evening, put up our tents with no efficiency, drank a lot, danced a bit and crashed at midnight. My tent was organised, and most things had their place. I was sharing my tent with Nikki, and thankfully she was also semi-neat and tidy. I loved camping, but I couldn't live the three days like Heidi did. She partied hard, smoked too much, flopped and zonked out, whereas I always had a wee before bed, took my contact lenses out, put my glasses nearby and got out of my clothes. Heidi never changed her outfit much when we went camping; she'd switch hats or add a bangle, and I would bet large amounts of money that she had packed a pair of the velour tracksuit bottoms she was really into, but that was it.

The smell of bacon wafted into my tent and I sniffed, my mouth watering. I spotted Flint wearing his favourite khaki combat shorts, no top, tossing crispy bacon on a ridiculously small frying pan, already sweating from the morning sunshine and the heat from the meat. He flipped, caught the rashers, looking as proud as punch with himself, until he encountered a problem. I laughed out loud as he navigated tying his knotty brown hair back from his face without putting the pan down. That would be too easy and mean defeat. What would he drop first? Pan or hair?

He pouted.

Flint's pout, frown, or any other outward shows of confusion always reminded me of when I'd first spoken to him, back when we were seventeen. I'd already known him from secondary school, but we had different mates. We didn't hate each other or anything like that, but we didn't have time for each other either. No real mingling. I remember Flint sort of nodding hello at me, and I would shrug back, but our first real conversation was when I ran away from home after a row with my mum.

I'd fled to the local park.

I can't even remember the cause for the argument, but as I sat on the swings sobbing at 3 p.m. on a Sunday afternoon, I remember hating everything about my teenage life, and before I could acknowledge what was happening, Flint appeared from nowhere, leaning against the frame of the swings. He'd stared at me as I'd attempted to wipe my face with my hand. He'd offered me a rhubarb and custard, not saying anything. I shook my head, snivelling, and he repeated his offer by shoving the bag almost under my dripping nose.

'No thanks.'

'Ah go on, it might stop you crying.'

'Doubt it,' I'd added with a whimper.

'Boyfriend?'

'No, Mum row.'

'The worst.'

'Uh-huh.'

Flint had shoved the white paper bag of sweets into his coat pocket and taken a seat on the swing next to me, stretching his long legs into the sky as he leant back. His head had almost scraped the ground. I'd smiled at this teenager, grinning into nothingness with his eyes shut, swinging back and forth with glee. I'd rubbed my face with the cuffs of my jacket and then copied him.

We'd giggled. He was going higher, but I'd caught up and he'd turned to face me.

'See, the tears go away. They always do.'

I had known nothing about Flint, the stranger, but in that small exchange he'd managed to show me a stability within him; a confidence I admired. It had never left him. I was ever so glad I knew him, even if he was a bit of a know-it-all, passed his driving test on the first attempt and stole pints of milk from my fridge.

I could hear his cogs whirring; he'd rumbled me.

'If you're laughing at me cooking your breakfast while you sit looking pretty, that's one less bap for you,' he told me, now with a hairband between his teeth.

'I'm laughing at you multi-tasking, and as usual, I'm glad there's not a third little job you're trying to do.'

'Stop interfering and come and get it, or I'll give this to someone else.'

'Me,' Heidi responded from her tent.

She held her arm in the air towards Flint, in case we weren't able to make out her mumbles. With flour on her cheek, Heidi had already wolfed down bap number one, and spoke with her mouth full. Lucky for her, Chrissy was not here to witness the lack of manners, or there'd be trouble. I squeezed ketchup onto the mound of bacon and licked my fingers. The festival didn't start until lunchtime, so we enjoyed a slow breakfast.

'Hmmm.' I appreciated the salty, greasy taste.

Flint looked over and bowed before the gas hob, while Heidi arranged the drinks area. She'd brought the largest tent for one occupant and had offered to stockpile the booze there.

As Nikki walked in, I glanced at Heidi, who was busying herself placing and replacing cans and bottles of wine. I smiled as she took a sneaky swig out of a cider can. Nikki nudged her in the ribs, flicked open a lager and they giggled mischievously. They were starting early.

After all the bacon in the world was consumed, we drifted off, getting our stuff together. I listened as Flint talked to a group of girls camped next to us. One asked him where his name came from.

'Well, as you asked nicely, my name is Owen Flint. I hated it as a kid. Kids would make up rhymes about me "owing money" – that sort of stuff. Fast forward a few years, I went raving, got into dance music, pills and The Prodigy. Keith Flint was the man. So, I switched them around, Flint Owen. Never looked back. Only my nan calls me Owen.'

He stood back, his arms folded across his chest, waiting for it. He knew what was coming, and so did I – the chorus in shrilled unison.

'Awwww, that's so cute!'

Flint glanced over at me and shrugged. Shaking my head, smiling, I clocked Chrissy coming back from the loos with a face like a wet weekend, Di trailing behind like her maid in waiting.

'You alright, love?' I asked.

'No, I am not,' said Chrissy, her pale face looking grim. 'They are worse than last year. Most of the loo roll is all over the floor and the soap wasn't even put in.'

'And the smell?'

'Don't. We've just got over our gagging,' Di warned.

'Yeah, don't. Gonna check how much hand soap I have.' Chrissy stomped into her tent.

These were strong reactions, but stuck here now, what could we do? Chrissy – party animal she might be – was a prissy when it came to peeing. We'd learnt over the years that the solution was to get her drunk, locate a bush to pee behind and provide her with ample coverage and a diversion while she pissed. Apparently, she always popped a pill to block up the number twos.

I sat down with Flint, Nikki and Heidi, waiting for Chrissy and Di. A shriek came from their tent.

'Christ almighty, I've forgotten my bloody pants, my lashes, and where the hell is my bumbag?' Di came out, fixing her hands on her hips, scowling.

'Who cares about that stuff?' Flint replied. 'You need money and booze, that's all.'

'Says you, Mr Bucket Wash. I don't pack like you, but I have packed a new bra, some posh cheese crackers and a corkscrew.'

Di waved the evidence at Flint.

Heidi picked at her nail polish. 'Well, that's alright then, your boobs will be perky, and you'll have superior munchies, but I have to say, if you can forget such fundamental items, there's no hope for the rest of us.'

'Someone update me; I want to get going – has Chrissy located her wet wipes, and Louise, do you have your top-of-the-range sun cream?' Nikki asked.

The day was already heating up. The weather in August was not always reliable for music festivals and there had been times when we didn't wear vests or little floaty dresses, instead shivering in our hoodies and standing on people's toes getting into a comedy tent to hide away from the rain. This weather was a thankful improvement, and I was prepared for it: SPF50, sunhat, and a reliable spare. I was well known for being organised in the sun protection department.

Flint stood up and grabbed my shoulders from behind.

'Yes, have you packed sun cream, after sun, sick bowl and all that malarky in there? We don't want you in the first aid tent throwing up all day, again!'

'Piss off, you'll be begging me later to rub some sun cream on your shoulders.'

I went to slap him round the head, but he grabbed my arm and wrestled me to the floor, laughing. As I stood up our heads collided, and I felt the soft bristles from his cheek brush against the skin on my face. I caught his eye and looked away, like I'd seen something that I wasn't meant to.

Not quite ready to move, we sat, chatting, and cracked open some cider. The faint sound of dance music played in the distance, a male voice shouting into a microphone somewhere, the laughter of other campers surrounding us and the numerous food smells wafting around.

Flint had been telling us about a new girl, Jeannie, who he'd met online. She was cool, had a neat peroxide bob, but her job was shit, which was big for him. Apart from her job in Starbucks, everything else was great.

As Flint put it, 'She likes *The Fast and The Furious* films, wears wigs in bed and the sex nearly blew my cock off.'

But Flint was a grafter, though Jeannie seemed to be as well, to me anyway. She earnt enough to pay her rent for her flat and have fun, and that was where her aspirations at the age of twenty-eight ended. I admired her. Flint didn't. He worked for the university in Oxford and his 60k income was a big deal for a thirty-ish-year-old bloke with no degree. All of us agreed he was being unfair to Jeannie.

'Oh, I can't debate this anymore.' Flint flopped onto his back, putting his hat over his face. 'Can we talk about your married cheating geezer? He needs some discussion.'

Who'd told him? I glared at Chrissy and Di.

Chrissy shook her headful of blond curls. 'Nothing to do with me.'

I glanced at Nikki. 'You?'

She shook her head. 'Nope, but someone's blushing there.' Nikki hugged Di tight around the shoulders.

I turned to Di, her cheeks turning pink.

'I told him. I couldn't help it, none of us are exactly getting a lot of action and it was romantic,' she said, standing up.

'You were the one who lectured me as soon as he took his

tongue out of my mouth!'

Flint sat up, drained the dregs of his cider and shuffled up next to me. 'Look, we'll talk more over the rest of the weekend, I'm sure. It's huge – I get that.'

Was his support ending there?

'I know how you lot love to analyse it all,' he continued, 'and I'll participate one hundred percent, but let me say this. He'll never change his life for little ole you, never mind how much he wants to bone you.' Flint screwed his face up as he said the last bit, as if he couldn't begin to think of me as shagable at all. 'Enjoy him while he lasts.'. He stood up, pulling me up with him. His chocolate brown eyes were focused on mine as he tweaked my nose. 'He's doing what he can with you because you're letting him.'

'That's what I said,' yelled Heidi as she went back into her tent.

Rubbing my nose, I glared at the tent Heidi occupied.

'But regardless of what advice we offer you, especially while we're wankered, we all think this will end in tears, just like...' Flint frowned, clearly thinking.

'Who?' I asked.

'Carrie and Mr Big?' Heidi suggested.

'Ross and Rachel?' Di said, plaiting her hair into pigtails.

'More like dirty Sharon and Grant from *Eastenders*,' said Flint with a smirk.

'That wasn't horny, it was horrific,' Di scoffed.

'Um, hello, I am here you know,' I said.

'I think what I am trying to say is, affairs, flings... they all end badly, but yours isn't a fling, it's just a fuck,' said Flint, fiddling with his man-bun.

'Not yet, it's not,' I mumbled.

'Sorry, I meant headfuck,' he added, glancing at me.

Flint's honesty frazzled me. I sensed he wanted to add even more, so as a distraction, I inspected my fingernails. He gave a shrug and pulled out his V Festival lanyard with the line up on it and started to read the first page.

'Lilly Allen or chips, everyone?'

The whole crew collected whatever they needed, grabbed their drinks, and I wondered, as we walked away from our tents: when the fuck did Flint get so wise?

The sun sat high in the sky, and we were all in the full festival chilled out vibe, relishing in how little decision-making we had to do.

Toilet or tequila?

Knowing these were the biggest choices to be made for forty-eight hours made everything okay, and I was more than happy to be swept along to enjoy the festival. Except, this year, I also had Dan on my mind, meaning I floated around with the biggest grin stuck to my face, content to follow everyone else's plans.

'What about Starsailor?' suggested Chrissy.

'Nope. Boring,' said Flint.

'Well, Lou Lou and I will go. We love them, don't we?' Chrissy said, poking her tongue out at Flint.

Flint tugged at my arm. 'Nope, we're off to see Beautiful

South, the others are there already. Come on, we love singing to Paul Heaton.'

'Oh, I don't know. I fancy the singer of Starsailor, and I've seen Paul Heaton loads. I'm going with Chrissy.'

'Shallow, you are. Shallow,' Flint said as he kissed me and Chrissy on the top of our heads.

Chrissy and I walked off, arm in arm.

Flint yelled after us, 'You're all about the sex this weekend. You've changed. This is a music festival, for mates and drinking. You should probably book onto that dogging weekend you told me about.'

By mid-afternoon, our group had mutated. Heidi was last seen feeding her churritos to a man with a gingery shaved head, his skinny jeans hanging low. Di was sat on the floor cross-legged, chatting to some lads, while I joined Chrissy, Flint and some random strangers. We ate nachos and discussed Fat Boy Slim and debated why people needed to use the phone-charging booths at festivals. Flint and I disagreed.

'I don't see why people can't relax and enjoy the moment. I do. I don't run off every hour to top up my battery.'

'It's the future, Louise, progression. In less than five years, you'll be doing the same.'

'Nope, I'm not the prime minister or a heart surgeon. I'm not that important.'

As I watched my mates and our new friends linking arms, swaying, singing, wobbling and spilling drinks, I rooted around my bag for my phone. While my phone switched on, I loaded a tortilla chip with guacamole and sour cream. When I glanced down at the phone, the text alerts were going berserk. A blob of guacamole dripped down my top. Four, five, six texts, and seven call catchers. One from my mum asking me to call her when Keane came on stage, and the rest from Dan.

```
Is it wrong to miss you
already?
Well, I do.
I wish I was with you, in the
sun, drinking and snogging.
Can we speak this weekend?
I'm not sure I can hang on
till Tuesday.
I've checked the line-up - go
and see Gomez. They are the
dogs.
I wish I could kiss you. What
have you done to me?
```

My god. The last text was sent just seventeen minutes ago. I wanted to reply to him, but I didn't think it would fall within the undiscussed rules of how and when our communication would be. But I was pissed, lusted up and, well, he'd started this rule by asking to speak to me. Plus, being outside and texting didn't count. I hit reply.

```
            Jeez, leave the girl alone,
                will you? I have serious
                          cider to drink.
```

The text was pending for a bit. I hated that. I stood up, waved my phone around above my head, looking back at the screen. Delivered.

```
What    does    happy-go-lucky
cider taste like, I wonder?
That  was  a  shit  joke.  I'm
alone if you can talk?
```

My phone connected to him in six seconds.

It was divine to chat to him again, normal and ordinary. He did little impressions of my accent, and I found myself mesmerised by his London edge and vocabulary. I'd never in my life been so satisfied by a conversation with a man. He asked me question upon question and added more after my answers. We chatted about what bands I'd seen, who I was spending the festival with and how I knew these friends.

Then the chat took a turn.

'Have you been chatted up by, you know, a lot of men?'

I laughed in surprise, frowning at the question. 'Pardon?'

'Gordon Bennett, that didn't sound right.'

'It was a bit odd.'

'I just meant I'd be all over you, if I met you at a festival.'

'Look, if you mean have I pulled another bloke, no. If you want to know if I've flirted and laughed with other men, yes, of course I have. But if you're trying to find out if you've crossed my mind at all, the answer is yes. A big fat yes. Ever since we met. You fill my mind, Dan, and I like you being there.'

Dan sighed.

What kind of sigh was it? I couldn't tell over the phone.

His question left me feeling fifty percent thrilled that he wanted me so much and fifty percent wishing he didn't have to wonder about me and other men. After all, he'd been down on one knee, had a stag do and walked down the aisle with another woman. It was hardly reasonable.

'That makes me happy, relieved and aroused. What the hell is happening to me?' Dan's voice was no more than a whisper.

'Dunno. To throw cold water on the subject, shall we talk music?'

'Yeah, go on then, but only if you swear we can talk about missing each other before we hang up.'

'Of course.'

'Okay, promise me you will go and see Gomez.'

'Deffo.'

'Tell me what you can see right now.'

'Is that a trick question? Are you here?'

He laughed. 'No. I just want to imagine I'm there with you.'

'Okay, I'm sat cross-legged in front of the Channel 4 stage and all around me are my sort of people: music lovers, sweaty, sticky and smiley. Right in front of me there's a couple, sitting down waiting for the stage to erupt. She has brown hair in pigtails and is leaning her head on his shoulder. I can see a group of girls to my right all dressed up in white. Maybe a hen do.'

Our chat lasted for the duration of The Feeling set. The band left the stage and the crowd started to move around me. I was lying on my tummy, and people were stepping over me while I continued the call, drops of what I hoped was cider landing on the back of my neck. Dan said his family were in London to visit his in-laws for the weekend and I could call him anytime.

Hmm.

I reviewed his update. He was available to chat only because it suited him, yet I was occupied with my friends. I knew I should remain unavailable with my phone begging for a burst of charge in my rucksack. I mean, I'd argued with Flint about those charging booths and the point of them not long ago. But Dan... I should grab his availability whenever I could, *right*?

As my friends were all choosing what to do next, I made a decision of my own. I chose to see more of Dan flash up on my phone. I chose flirty and filthy phone calls and making him laugh softly, over remaining true to myself. I snuck off to the silly little phone booths, feeling a twist in my gut. And as hard as I tried to ignore it, there was not a hint of it leaving me.

CHAPTER 7

The Theory of Dirt

Day two – second round of getting wasted, eating carbs on top of carbs and dancing until my feet sobbed for help.

Flint's advice from Saturday morning had unsettled me, as did my reaction to squeezing Dan into my mates' weekend. I guess these were the dilemmas of my new future, but I'd worry about them next week.

I sat cross-legged on the grass, ignoring the bloke from Manic Street Preachers on stage, imagining Dan visiting my house and us cooking together, except we didn't eat, instead progressing to stripping on a blanket in my garden.

Chrissy snapped me out of my daydreaming. 'Come on. You need a distraction. I'm taking you off to chat up men with me, do some crap dancing, and if you're lucky, you can cover me while I have a wee.'

I did participate in all of that, and after the weeing, we went to watch the Richard Hawley set. Separated from Chrissy, I spent the gig with a group of lads from Dudley. A lookalike of Remi from the Stone Roses asked me to meet him later if I fancied it. I explained that I was sort of taken.

We clinked our paper cups and he replied, 'Well, isn't he a lucky bugger?'

Leaving the tent, I wiped the sweat from my forehead and searched the area for Chrissy. I spotted her sitting on the floor near a hippy clothes stall. Two men were watching her, beaming as she animatedly chatted with her mouth and hands. As I approached, Chrissy spotted me and waved me over.

'Hey, I lost you in there,' I said.

'I know, sorry, but he was soooooo good, right?' She took a swig from her beer. 'This is Pete and Swift.'

I smiled as I sat down. Pete wore usual festival attire, shorts, t-shirt, hat, and his head was shaved. He turned his face to the sky after smiling back at me, absorbing the sun. Swift wore a paisley shirt, the buttons undone to his belly button, with shorts and hiker boots. He was rolling a fag, nodding to a dance beat I couldn't hear. Chrissy finished a story about scars and a pedicure experience and both men laughed at the ending. I watched as Pete undid his trainers and pulled off one of his socks.

'I've got a scar on my big toe. Look.'

He lifted his foot closer to Chrissy's eyeline, and she recoiled, moving backwards. An onlooker might have wondered if Pete was waving a dead mouse in between his toes.

'Did you see? It's right across the toe.'

'Yep, yep, saw that, you can put it away now.'

Swift chuckled, took a brief drag on his roll up and nodded in time to the absent beat.

Pete frowned as he put his sock back on, but cheerfully added, 'Anyway, what you guys doing later? Who are you planning on seeing?'

Chrissy stood sharply. 'We'd better go actually; we've lost all our mates and one of them was throwing up.' Yanking my arm and pulling the rest of me with her, she added, 'Hey, Louise, shall we?'

'Um, yeah, bye guys, might see you later maybe?'

Chrissy speed-walked, taking me with her into the crowds.

'What was that all about? Pete really liked you. You like the shaved head look.'

We stopped walking and stood facing each other.

'Did you see his toenails?'

I burst out laughing. 'Not really. He was showing *you* his feet.'

'Well, I did, and it's a no from me. A big fat no.'

Chrissy always made a full assessment of men's teeth and feet to assess their potential, and they needed ticks in both departments before they were a consideration.

'What a shame. He could have been a bit of something this weekend.'

'Not with toenails like that. You know my theory – if they store dirt there, what the hell is backed up in the arse-bollock area? And no, I don't want to know the answer to that.'

♣

Later that night, we sat back at our tents, knocking back ciders and chatting. I loved this part of a night out, the dissecting and reliving the hours previous. Heidi, Nikki and Di had watched Radiohead, while Flint, Chrissy and I watched Editors and

Kasabian. I was happiest at a festival when I could hear the out-of-tune men around me singing their little hearts out with their eyes closed. Although, the Kasabian crowd was, as always, rough as a badger's arse. Flint resorted to escorting us from the front mosh area to the respectable midway section, avoiding the risk of being trampled on or having piss thrown in our faces.

There was a leftover hint of the warm day lingering in the air, but most of us had located hoodies and blankets to cosy up with. Di nibbled at her posh crackers and every now and then she shivered playfully after she took a sip from her cider. Heidi laid out a fleecy blanket and sprawled out on it, and Chrissy joined her, popping on her bed socks. Nikki was texting a bloke she'd met earlier in the day, smiling as she typed furiously. Flint was still wearing his tatty straw hat, perched on his head, shielding his eyes. He sat on his camping chair, and as I unfolded mine, I remembered when Flint had arrived at my house unexpectedly a few weeks before.

Shouting through my letterbox, he'd said, 'I've got you a present. For V. Please don't make me try to post it through your letterbox.'

I had raced downstairs.

'I'm so excited, hurry up,' he'd added.

I'd opened the door and there was Flint on my doorstep, sitting on a camping chair, holding out another one to me in his hands.

He'd grinned. 'For you, madam.'

I smiled at the memory, relaxing into my new camping chair, and as everyone chatted, I switched on my phone. There were more texts from Dan.

> How is it going?
> I'm off to bed, can you talk?
> Never mind, here's a goodnight kiss.
> And another.
> I've been planning my outfit for Tuesday. It's all laid out on my bed.
> That was a bad joke.
> I'm not thinking about clothes, just you. Told you I'm new at this and nervous.

I typed a reply, but caught Flint staring at me. His judgemental looks hadn't gone unnoticed.

I switched the phone off without sending the message to Dan and threw it down onto the floor, like an empty sweet wrapper. I wanted to appear as an independent, wild and spirited woman in her prime, when in truth I was a woman frantically falling head over heels for Dan and craving his attention. I could get used to feeling this happy, but with the elation came guilt, embarrassment and Flint's disapproving looks.

'More texts?' Flint asked.

'Uh huh,' I replied.

'You've been irresistible this weekend, Louise,' Di said.

'Eh?'

'I noticed you were getting loads of male attention – your taxi light is on.'

'Not this again. Why do you and Chrissy believe that crap?'

Flint said with an eyeroll.

Di threw an empty cup at him. 'We read it in *Heat* magazine, some celebrity swears by it. You won't change my mind. The facts are: when you're taken, you're more irresistible.'

Flint murmured something under his breath.

'What?' Di and I asked in unison.

'Is Louise taken?' he repeated.

'Of course she is, and she's oozing *something* this weekend,' Nikki replied supportively.

'Well, that's her, the way she is. It's not what's-his-face – the married tosser – making her ooze stuff.'

'We didn't say it was Dan. It's infectious. I reckon that's why we're all getting lots of attention. It's your sexual energy.' Di pointed her finger at me.

I glanced over at Heidi, who was shaking her head. Flint got up, went over to his tent and zipped it up. He didn't say another word.

※

It was morning.

I wasn't clear on the time, and I didn't know if it was bright outside of my tent, my eye mask providing much-needed darkness. I slid the mask onto the top of my head and rubbed the crusty bits of mascara from my eyes, sitting up in my sleeping bag. I stretched my arms, aiming for the top of my tent. Where were my glasses? I spotted them, sitting on top of yesterday's dress, not folded up as they should have been.

I wriggled out of my sleeping bag and reached to open the

zip. The heat inside needed to be replaced with crisp air, but in flew the smell of bacon and sausages frying. I could hear someone clattering plastic plates. My belly awoke and gurgled, reminding me to feed it. My friends were chattering, giggling. I heard out of tune singing and some faded Faithless in the distance.

I crawled out of the entrance of my tent and came face to face with Flint, preparing for his bucket wash. It was his version of singing in the shower, I guess. He was on his knees, wringing a flannel, until he noticed me watching him.

'Are you okay if I take my shreddies off and squat for a wipe down?' he asked.

Morning pleasantries were seemingly not a priority, and before I answered, he whipped his pants off. I was regretting our choice of pitching our tents near the back against some bushes. It was fine for the urgent-night-peeing, we all agreed, but not so fine for early morning male scrubbing.

'Go for it, love,' I replied, facing the other way as quickly as I could.

I plonked myself down next to Di.

'Tea?' she asked.

'Yeah, please.'

I fiddled with the eye mask I was still wearing and tried to untangle it from my fringe. It was going to take some work for me to look desirable for Dan tomorrow. I noticed already my armpits were sweaty. I wanted a warm shower. I watched Nikki with envy – her chestnut brown pixie cut looked exactly the same as when she'd crashed out last night.

We eventually cleared up the debris of our weekend,

chatting as we went along. I tried to get Flint on his own. I felt something needed to be talked about. It was like he'd bumped into me and not said sorry, and he didn't normally slope off to bed like that. I was realising my two best friends, Flint and Heidi, were not going to cheerlead Dan's appearance in my life, but it was probably best to worry about that *after* my date.

We reluctantly hugged farewell, this part always leaving me gloomy and empty, wishing the ending didn't have to come around so quickly. Our festival bubble life was over and the sight of the rucksacks and packed-away tents was like sticking a pin in our high-spirited weekend.

Chrissy drove Flint and me home. I sat in the back, trying to nap. They were chatting about the weekend and Flint turned up a Bloc Party track on the radio. I switched on my phone. The battery was almost out. Dan had texted me.

```
I want to go to bed already.
```

```
                                                Eh?
```

```
Because when I wake up, I will
be seeing you again.
                                                Ah.
```

```
You okay? You've only said Eh
and Ah.
```

```
                        Hungover, tired, but very
                            excited about tomorrow.
```

```
Me too, I feel like a boy on
Christmas Eve.
```

CHAPTER 8

Christmas Day

I woke up to a text from Dan, wishing me Merry Christmas. I laughed so hard I coughed my tea all over Bennett.

Our plan was to meet at midday so that we could have the whole afternoon together. He had to be home by 6 p.m., but apart from that, 'I'm all yours,' he'd said.

Those three words had produced quivering everywhere, predominantly in my fanny, and I predicted I would need to make a considerable effort to calm the fuck down when I met him.

At least I was happy with my appearance. I wore a pretty blue and white sundress, showing just enough cleavage. My legs were looking toned, as were my arms, but my tummy? Well, I hoped it was concealed enough. I popped on some mascara, covered up any blemishes with concealer and added lip gloss. I sprayed my scent, Issey Miyake, grabbed all the things I needed, then walked with a skip to the bus stop in a swirl of joy.

The sun blazed in the sky. The busy bus took me from my street along Cowley Road. Every time the bus door opened,

I caught a hint of where I was on the route. Cowley Road housed many pubs, florists, a respectable stationery shop, banks and bicycle repair shops, but also a host of restaurants and takeaways supplying Turkish, Indian, Chinese and Caribbean food. I could shut my eyes and my nose would report which stop we were at based on what it could smell. It was the only place in Oxford where you could have a reiki appointment, buy a washing up bowl and a fountain pen, then see a band, all in one day.

The bus slowed down at each stop and introduced a passenger, each one reflecting the diversity of the city. I would expect nothing less; I loved this place. It was home.

The distracting sights were needed as my guts bubbled all the way to town. At some point between The Swan Pub and The Zodiac I shared my seat with a young student, and as he sat down, he balanced books on his lean thighs. The bus set off and the pile wobbled, forcing me to offer my hand at catching them. He blushed, smiled and stared out of the window on the other side of the bus. A girl with lime green twisted dreads grinned at me as she stood, holding onto the handle dangling from the ceiling.

My home turf always looked superb to me, but some would disagree. Cowley was smelly and dirty and needed updating, but I'd grown up knowing that the place I called home cared for new university students and housed the local community, two groups who, most of the time, fitted well together, until *The Oxford Mail* reported a clique feud involving the usual – drugs, family or love. My Oxford life was nothing like an episode of *Inspector Morse*.

As I stepped off the bus, I saw a harassed colleague on his lunch break. He waved and I nodded back. I couldn't even think about holding a conversation right now. What if seeing Dan in the flesh brought out babbling and devastating communication skills? What if he lost his humour and we sat in front of each other, wondering why we'd bothered? What if he didn't find me attractive without a Saturday night buzz surrounding him, and what if he wasn't fit at all and I'd embellished the romance of the past two weeks?

Ping. Text from Dan.

```
I'm near the bar. Nervous as
fuck. Where are you?
```

I didn't answer; I was already there, peering through the window. I saw him as I entered the pub, staring at the bar, flipping over a beer mat. His dark wavy hair was just as I remembered it, and he wore a navy polo t-shirt with jeans. He was wearing his glasses and appeared thoughtful. I could have stayed looking at him till the menopause.

I made my way over to him, stood beside him and tapped him on the shoulder. He turned quickly to face me and smiled, his eyes glistening. I leant in and kissed him on the cheek. I could smell a faint trace of an aftershave and the soft bristle of his beard took me back to the night we'd kissed. My tummy overturned, reversed and overturned again.

'Hi,' I said.

'Hello to you,' he replied. He shook off his formal greeting with a grimace and a shrug, adding, 'Pint?'

'Please.'

Dan's hands were shaking when he handed the note over to the bar staff. I attempted to sit on the bar stool next to Dan, but using the bar for balance and holding onto my dress hemline activated a clumsier me and I gave up. I settled for standing by his side, accepting the nerves were going nowhere, and fiddled with my jacket buttons.

I took a bossy lead as the drinks arrived. 'Shall we find somewhere to sit?'

He nodded and climbed down from his stool.

'Follow me.' I winked.

Dan's luck was in. I knew this pub, and that the sunny weekday afternoon would encourage most of the punters outside. We found a table upstairs just for us, tucked away in the corner. We both sipped our beer at the same time before he took my hand. My tummy flipped, and I felt like my hand was about to melt like butter before my eyes. I could practically hear my heartbeat quickening.

'Can we start again?' Dan asked.

I frowned. 'Have I got to walk back in? To be honest, I'm not sure I could do that again.'

We both laughed and I squeezed his hand, stroking his fingers, the action reflecting how I was feeling.

'Look, I'm nervous. This is massive and I'm feeling all sorts of things.'

'I agree,' Dan said. 'The last few days have felt like the longest foreplay of my life.'

I grinned. 'You know, what would really put me at ease is if you kissed me before we go any further. That is, I want you to kiss me. If you want to kiss me? I just reckon there's a lot of tension and...'

Before I could finish, his lips met mine. I could've collapsed and slid into a heap on the floor. He was exactly as I remembered; his taste, his everything. The shape of his lips, slotting together with mine like a key in a lock. Everything clicked into place. Kisses with other men had often required a mutual tutoring, or suggestive move in a certain direction. I had come to expect all that. But when Dan and I kissed, we didn't need guiding; it just worked, and it blew my mind.

We spent the next few hours talking, gazing at each other, drinking beer, running off to the loo and hurrying back, so we could do it all again. Later, Dan suggested a walk outside; he wanted to hold my hand and sit in a park like teenagers.

I took him to University Parks, and on the way there we held hands or walked arm in arm. Dan said he hadn't been this happy in years.

I pulled my sunglasses down and looked at him over the rim. 'That's nice and all, but I don't believe you. What about your kids?'

Dan took his glasses off and rubbed his eyes. 'That's different. They do bring me happiness, despite being a pain in my arse every day, but this, with you... I'm feeling so good about this. Whatever this is.'

As we lay under a lime tree, we listened to Dan's iPod and talked about music we liked, and he played some Michael McDonald I'd not heard before. Dan said he'd been listening to lots of music recently, and often found himself in a sort of trance thinking about me.

'Is that creepy?' he asked, inspecting his nails.

'Yep,' I teased.

He looked away. Sensing his awkwardness, I placed my hand on his cheek, stroked his face, then gave him a deep kiss. When I finished, I glanced at him. His eyes were still closed.

'No, it's not creepy at all. I'm not used to men doing such romantic things, but I'll take it.'

Dan then told me all about his childhood. He had an older brother called Tim. They didn't seem close, but Dan said he wanted to be.

'He's eight years older than me and the coolest brother. I loved getting his hand-me-down clothes. People always said we looked alike, and when teachers compared me to him, I was so happy. But when he was about eighteen and I was ten, we were rowing in his bedroom once and Tim shouted something like, "You're always just an annoying little prick, now piss off." I bawled and bawled.'

'Oh, that's awful.'

'I think Tim has always seen me as his irritating little shitty brother, even now.' Dan cleared his throat after a pause. 'Can I tell you something?'

I nodded.

'Tim and I had to be better mates in a hurry, cos my mum died.'

'Oh my god, I'm so sorry.'

Dan shook his head and continued. 'It's alright. It was years ago. I was nineteen and she had a stroke. Like one minute there she was, then boom, she was gone. I don't think we ever got over it.' Dan swallowed, looking away into the distance.

'I can imagine... although, I can't really. I mean, my parents are here and I'm not nineteen. Sorry, this is coming out wrong.'

'It's okay, it's a heavy thing to talk about. I shouldn't have brought it up so quick. I just want to know everything about you, and vice versa.'

'Tell me about her, your mum.'

Dan looked at me with an intense, perplexed expression. Was he wondering why I was asking more about his saddest life moment after five bloody minutes? Possibly, but I sensed he was glad that someone gave a shit at the same time. He smiled with a warmth that confirmed I'd pitched it right.

Dan told me how he'd ambled home from the corner shop one afternoon to find his dad hysterical at the foot of the stairs and his mum dead. Twenty minutes before, she'd sent him out with a list and shouted, 'Don't bother coming back until you have everything on the list, especially custard powder, or I'll never talk to you again.' She'd laughed, waving a spatula at him on his way out the door.

'She never spoke again.'

As Dan shared these private and intimate details of his youth, I intermittently stroked his hand. He didn't cry or anything, but the cracking in his voice and his minimal eye contact told me how much this still affected him.

He took off his glasses and rubbed his eyes. 'I ran to my house and Dad was sitting on the stairs, head in his hands. He grabbed me and held me so close to him I could smell his fag breath, his snot and tears smearing all over my cheek. I tried to escape from his arms as I couldn't fucking breathe. The police were hovering in the hallway, watching us. I remember them speaking, but everything went weird, as though I were underwater and I couldn't hear what they were saying.'

I squeezed his hand.

'Of course, I remember her funeral, the wake, the family, the laughter, the memories, the photos and then the drink. And to be honest, booze sort of took over and I thought it would take me to the place where my mum had gone. But of course, it never did. Mum was gone and we never even knew she was ill. I remember feeling so fucking sad that none of us had helped her, took care of her or even took her to the doctors. She'd done all of that for us when we were kids. Every day she picked me up from school with a biscuit and a smile. Never cross, just cuddly.'

'How's your dad now?' I asked.

'He's okay, but he's kinda blank, if you get me? They laughed all the time, my mum and dad; he'd pull her chubby cheeks as he kissed her, pretending to ruffle her hair, but he knew better than to mess up her do. If I had a bad dream and nipped downstairs to tell them, I'd always find them on the sofa, Dad rubbing Mum's feet. He told me at the funeral that he'd hated her feet, the corns, the little hairs she trimmed on her toes, but he'd do anything to rub them again. That's real love, I thought, and I want that.'

'Don't we all?' I replied, lying on my back.

Dan joined me. We lay in a comfortable silence for a few moments. I questioned how this sudden death must have affected Dan, and I couldn't help but wonder how I would feel, losing my mum so suddenly.

'I didn't know my mum and she never got to know me,' Dan murmured.

I gulped back my own emotion. My parents knew me as a woman and I'd never been thankful until now. I squeezed Dan's hand, both of us looking up into the cornflower blue sky.

'But hey, I don't want to ruin today.'

'You haven't.'

I had no relevant experience or anecdotes to part with, but I was overwhelmed with affection for him already. A surprising need to care for him washed over me. To be right there for him when everyone else had left him to it, in one way or another. Heidi and Flint would say it was odd for him to share so much so soon, and to a certain degree, they were right. But I wanted him to know that it was okay to be bold and brave. None of us knew what we were doing in life; we were all making it up as we went along, weren't we?

We were joined by a variety of strollers, joggers and dog walkers that afternoon. People passed us, glancing at us as we held hands, our legs intertwined, engrossed in each other. An elderly man walked by just as we'd stopped kissing. We were sitting facing each other, cross-legged. The man smiled and I relished that we looked like a normal couple in the early stages of a relationship.

Why did I have to let him go? I wasn't ready. As we lay side by side, our shoulders touching, I knew I would feel the shape of him glued to me long after we said goodbye.

'Would you like to meet up again?' I asked.

Dan rolled over to face me. 'Are you kidding? Course I do. Though... are you sure you want to see me? Haven't I been, like, too intense?'

I laughed. 'Not at all! Of course I want to see you.'

'God, I want to see you every day, but... can I let you know? When I can?'

I shrugged and rolled onto my belly. Something stabbed my insides. Somehow, I'd moved on from his "want to see you every day" comment and skipped straight to "can I let you know". That was the cause of the knots in my tummy. When would I see him again?

He wriggled over to me, our shoulders touching. 'I'm sorry, our timing is unreal, isn't it? As much as I want you, it has to be like this for a while. It's all about my kids, you know that, right?'

I nodded.

'Look at me.'

I turned to face him – his magnetic, green eyes locked onto mine with a soft expression, but then his brow frowned with worry.

'Can you do this?' he asked.

My heart plummeted; the answer should be no. I should get the fuck out of this.

'Dunno. Can you?'

'I can't not do this with you.'

I threw myself at him, kissing him deeply. Then we kissed some more.

We had our answers.

CHAPTER 9

Bingo Balls at the Ready

'Do you have plans for the Bank Holiday? Please say no.'

Dan called a few days later and couldn't seem to hide his enthusiasm. I pictured him crossing his fingers.

As it happened, I did have plans. Di always hosted her August Bank Holiday barbecue, and this year I was on pudding duty. I'd already been sent a flurry of regular and insistent emails from Heidi and Di containing their recipe suggestions.

I told him my dilemma. 'It's been planned for ages. Let me get back to you.'

'You don't have to cancel your plans, it's just that I was so excited when Melissa said she was taking the kids out for the day; I immediately thought, bingo.'

'Nice that you associate me with bingo. Is that on the agenda?'

'Yeah, if you like,' Dan teased.

'Sex bingo – that's a new one for me,' I replied, giggling.

Dan laughed. 'Man, I miss you.'

I mulled over the conversation and my comment about sex. It was forward, but I was all about throwing it out there to see where it landed. I decided right then to cancel the barbecue. I dialled up Di. As I expected, she was cool and understanding and even invited Dan too, but shit-friend news travelled fast with my girls, and Heidi soon got in touch.

```
What are you playing at????
```

I ignored her attitude, and texted Dan back instead. He replied with:

```
Yes! Result. I can't wait.
I'll get my bingo balls ready.
```

I later called Heidi to smooth things out with her, and though she was a bit frosty at first, she soon helped with my preening checklist.

'Exfoliation, arm pits, muff trim, and have you been using Dove's tanning body lotion?'

'Yep to all of them except the tanning lotion. I can't reach everywhere, and I don't want to look like a patchwork quilt – not a sexy look.'

'Good point.' Heidi turned on her electric toothbrush and left me to do the talking.

'I'm nervous. What if it's rubbish? What if he can't get it up, or what if he sees me naked and walks out of the room shaking his head?'

Heidi spluttered in my ear and then coughed. 'Hang on.' When she reappeared, she said, 'You've lost the plot. Of course his pop up will pop up. You've felt it already, right?'

I giggled at Heidi's names for sexual organs. 'Yeah.'

'Well, there you are then, and he won't walk out of the

room, that's mad. It's not an appraisal or a filling appointment at the dentist. Besides, how would he get home if he walks out? He doesn't have a car.'

'Thanks.'

Heidi laughed. 'You know what, love, it might be rubbish, it might not be all dreamy, but that'll just mean you'll both have the next time to look forward to.'

'Yeah, I guess.'

'Shitting hell, what am I doing sounding supportive? I don't want you to have sex with him, that's when the trouble starts.'

'Heidi, the trouble has already started.'

'Shite.'

'Yep. Shite.'

🌷

As agreed, I picked Dan up from a bus stop, deciding against meeting in central Oxford for our second date. Instead, I'd invited him to my place. There was an unspoken desire in both of us. We wanted to have sex.

I parked up three minutes before his bus was due. I hadn't slept well – I'd woken up a few times and enjoyed sex daydreams. I wondered what he liked in bed, how he liked to be touched. Fast fucking or slow and slurpy. It was a given he would like blow jobs, but mine? Was he used to everything in a certain way?

I checked my rear-view mirror to see if a bus was approaching, willing one to arrive. I wanted to look distracted, mentally occupied, but inside all I wanted to do was jump out of the driver's seat and wave madly when I spied Dan walking towards me. I took a deep breath and changed the CD I was listening to – removing Athlete and selecting Cherry Ghost – and as the first track started, a tap on my passenger window startled me. Dan flashed a lopsided grin through the window, and my planned self-control vanished.

He stood outside, fumbled with the door handle and pointed to it, as if to ask if he could get in. I leant over and opened the door for him, smiling at the civility.

'Don't be shy, get in. I don't bite.'

'That's a damn shame.'

Dan gave me a kiss that made me want to nibble him and be nibbled. He sat back and put his seatbelt on, leaving me staring at him.

I wanted him.

'Drive woman, move it.' He slapped the steering wheel, and I jumped more than necessary, just for entertainment value.

Then we set off.

The short journey took us away from the A-roads of the Oxfordshire countryside to the suburbs. Soon after leaving the bus stop, the buttercups hiding in the high grasses mixed with poppies bid us farewell. We stopped at some temporary traffic lights, and I glanced at Dan, who was looking out the window, his arm resting on the frame. Out of my window, I noticed the lofty daisies and violet wildflowers. Dan's other hand stayed on my thigh, except when gear changing got in the way, when he'd move his hand to the back of my neck. I shivered when he applied pressure – did he know how erotic this was? Well,

I did. The blood flowing straight to my groin confirmed how much I wanted him.

He smiled as I clicked the handbrake on and parked in my driveway. 'This is nice.'

We passed my pots of summer flowers in the front garden, the geraniums, begonias and marigolds now withered after a dry summer and their keeper forgetting to water them. I opened the front door and Dan followed me in, took his trainers off, walked through the living room doorway and paused. He flicked the strands of my beaded door curtain, turned back to face me and grinned. He meandered around my small living room, taking in the view of my garden through the windows that needed cleaning. The sunlight forced its way into the room, emphasising the dust on the coffee table. He checked out my CDs and books and then picked up the unrequested *Hello!* Magazine my mum had given me. I couldn't watch this anymore; Dan looked like an estate agent valuing my home.

I went into the kitchen. 'Drink?' I shouted.

Dan appeared behind me. I whipped round to face him and he pulled my hands towards him, securing them around the back of his neck. The kisses were soft and hypnotic. His hands moved around my waist and then stroked my back as our kisses became deeper. As our tongues met, I pulled away. I'd never encountered this amount of sexual eagerness so early on. I wanted to hold back and savour this feeling, but at the same time, I was overwhelmed and needed to breathe.

'You alright?' he asked, his throat strangling the words.

'Hmm.'

He frowned. 'What?'

I flicked the kettle on and dragged him by the hand into the living room. We sat on the sofa and I sat facing him, cross-legged.

'I'm okay, I'm fine. But can I be honest about something?'

'Please.'

'You'll get used to me being honest, it's the way I am.'

'I hope I do.'

'Hope you do what?'

'I hope I do get used to you being honest. Look, can you hurry up and spit it out? I'm a bit nervous here.'

'Sorry.' I took his hands. 'Look, I didn't want to stop kissing you just then. I just wanted it to go on and on and on until it gets dark outside, but I had to stop.'

'Why?'

I took a deep breath. 'I'm scared by how much I loved it, and how I wanted more, and more of everything, and more of things we haven't done yet. And then more again, all the time. This hasn't happened to me before, well not for years, well maybe not ever. I don't know. I think what I'm trying to say is... *fuck*.'

He smiled. 'Fuck indeed.'

'Don't take the piss, I'm deadly serious.'

'Sorry, I'm certainly not taking the piss out of you. I'm in awe of you for being honest.'

Bennett scratched at the back door, so I got up to let him in.

'You see, I'm the same,' Dan continued. 'I think about you all the time. I wonder what you're doing, where you are, what you're wearing, and the other day I counted the freckles on your nose in my head as I remembered them. I think about you, then I forget where I am and what I'm meant to be doing. So I hide away a lot in the office, and because I can't always call you, I sort of talk to you in my head. Like Flash Gordon did.' Dan's cheeks flushed and he looked away.

I got it; I'd seen that film too many times to not remember when Flash communicates with Dale via telepathic methods. I sat back down, grinning.

'I know what you mean. But your powers didn't work, mate. You'll have to repeat it all.' I moved closer and kissed him on the cheek.

Dan looked at the ceiling, exhaling. 'You see, every time you touch me, every time, something happens, in here, you know?' He tapped his chest.

'I know, same here.'

'So, let's take our time.'

'Yes, let's. I mean, I've thought about marching you upstairs right now, and getting the first time out of the way, like ripping off a plaster, but...'

'Even when you suggest ripping off plasters you manage to turn me on,' Dan teased.

'Come on, let's go for a walk.'

He raised his eyebrows.

I stood up and pulled at his hand. He was going along with my idea, or standing up at least.

Looking down at me, he added, 'I can't resist you. I'll do anything you ask me to do.'

'Well, get your trainers on, then.'

Dan saluted and we left.

We walked through the wooded area at the back of my house, our arms wrapped around each other. I loved how we laughed at nothing and everything. We stopped to kiss against a tree. His lingering looks made me appreciate our isolation, with no risk of bumping into anyone, as we talked about old school days and how we felt like teenagers skiving off.

We chatted about my disastrous dating life, and as cringy as it was for me, I wanted to explain how he was different to other men.

'Remember when I told you all about whistle guy? Well, as funny as it was, there are some weirdo men out there. And I'm so sick of not feeling that *thing* with a guy, that mysterious stuff that you can't explain. I've had a stream of shit dates and it feels like my last boyfriend was before Tony Blair was elected.'

Dan chuckled. 'Was it?'

'I'm not saying, but I don't even think he was the proper thing. I'm not even sure I've experienced it. It's tiring, you know, and when you meet someone who ticks all the boxes – sometimes twice over – you can overlook some added extras.'

There was a slight pause.

'Like a wife and kids?'

'Yeah. I mean, it's far from ideal, but if you were happily married, I wouldn't even...' I stopped walking, and Dan followed suit. 'I just mean, it's so bloody nice to be with someone who I actually have feelings for.'

'I know. I understand. I mean, if you flip this onto the b-side, and look at my situation, I'm massively into someone who isn't my wife, risking everything because that someone has got something.' Dan sighed and put his arm around my shoulders as we started walking again. 'You know, although I'm not into whistles in bed, I do have a little flag I'd like you to wave.'

I loved hearing the smile behind his deadpan voice. 'Now you're talking, flags all the way. The whistle guy had me wrong.'

I pulled Dan by the loop of his jeans into a shaded area, the warmth from the sunshine leaving me, his kiss heating my body in seconds.

'Want to go back?' I asked, my voice husky.

Dan covered his head with his hands and spoke to me through his fingers.

'Gordon Bennett, course I do. What's happening here? We can't even be normal. I feel like I'm exploding.'

'What do you mean?'

'I dunno! It's moving so fast I feel like I have whiplash, but because nothing has happened, it feels like whiplash in reverse.'

He flopped his head onto my shoulder as I laughed. We held each other for a few moments, then Dan tugged at my hand, indicating that we should leave.

We returned to the house, made tea together, our hands touching as we passed milk and spoons, making my heart hammer, screaming to get out. We sat close together on the sofa, the back door wide open, eating Hobnobs and watching Flash Gordon. When my landline rang, Dan answered it in a Russian accent. I laughed so much I didn't want the mad moment to end.

After the film finished, I collected our mugs and took them into the kitchen. I returned to the living room, where he was sat petting Bennett.

'You alright over there?' The catch in his voice gave him away.

I nodded. I toyed with my watch strap. Something needed to happen. I remembered this tenseness from our first date, and as soon as we'd kissed, normality resumed. Maybe I should take the lead? We needed to have sex or the whole house would erupt with a sexual bang.

I walked over, sat on his lap and kissed him. He immediately allowed me to take control, until I pulled back. He remained motionless, with his eyes shut for a moment. Then, Dan leant in to kiss me. I put my finger to his lips and added a hot kiss to his neck. He let out a groan and nestled his face into my chest, murmuring something into my boobs, before gazing up at me.

We made our way upstairs to my room, then stood facing each other, almost touching. I don't know who took the first step to close the gap, but suddenly we were kissing, panting, and mumbling words that would never be selected as a *Countdown* conundrum. We fell onto the bed, causing my head to bump on the frame. Dan ruffled my hair, laughing, but then we found ourselves facing each other. Dan kissed my neck, and in between these prolonged kisses, he ran his hands up and down my bare thighs. Each time he reached my underwear, he tugged them down a little. As he stroked my arse, my need for him was dancing deep inside me. I didn't know what to do with myself.

I pulled him close, clutching at his t-shirt, regarding his sweat and liking it. In our haste, we sat up together. Dan steadied himself and just avoided falling off the edge of my bed.

'Shit, this isn't what I planned,' Dan said, his smile crumpling.

'What do you mean?' I cupped his face in my hands.

'Well, this is more like a Carry-On film, not, you know, you and me.'

I laughed. 'This *is* you and me. Get used to it.'

I wrestled with his shorts, trying to remove them, and he watched me, cracking up until I sat on the bed and crossed my arms in a make-believe strop. Chuckling, he undid them, spun them around his head in a whirl, and threw them across the room. I stood up, taking my dress to hip height as Dan appeared behind me, kissing my neck. I stumbled as his hot breath neared my earlobe and he found my nipples, my weak spot. Then my bra clasp pinged – the bra was off and flung away in seconds, landing on the lamp beside my bed.

We searched each other using hands and mouths. Dan positioned his face between my legs. My mind was exploding and I felt his moans as I quivered. I was noisy; I grabbed a pillow to hold on to.

'Am I too loud?' I gasped.

Dan lifted his head. 'God, no, don't stop.'

We gripped each other, my body warm everywhere as Dan pushed himself inside me, everything noisy, fizzy and fast. Then it was over, and I wanted to start all over again. My head was spaced out as Dan muffled things into my hair as he came.

'Sorry, I couldn't hold it in anymore,' he said, panting and clinging to me for a few seconds as I huddled into his chest.

'Better out than in.'

'Did you really say that?' Dan grinned and raised his eyebrows.

'Yeah, I'm afraid I did.'

CHAPTER 10

You Fancy Alan Davies?

Dan called me to say he could meet me after work if I fancied it, but he would have to get the 10 p.m. bus home.

'That's okay,' I said.

'No, it isn't, but it's all I can manage.'

'I know, but... look, let's not get down about it. I can't wait to see you.'

We returned to Oxford for a quick evening out. Dan said he wanted to wait for me in a pub, with a drink, and I would walk in, the sexiest woman in there. It was a lot to live up to. I didn't feel that attractive after a day in the office, but following a quick dab of powder, an extra slap of mascara and a spray of perfume, I legged it to meet him. When I noticed him sat at a table, reading a newspaper, my belly flipped over and I couldn't care less about the possibility of smudged mascara.

We'd agreed to meet in a new pub – Far from the Madding Crowd; it was bookish and it served great ale. It was rare for Oxford locals to drink there, unless, like me, it was an after-work choice. The regulars were current students or those lifelong students remaining in Oxford, living out their lives in a post-graduate way – refusing to end the way of life they loved so much.

The pub had what I imagined to be the feel of a university tutor's office: faded, ornamented wallpaper on some walls and racing-car green painted on others. The pub was dimly lit with high lampshades in the corners and chandelier-style lights fixed to the low ceiling. The bijou round tables faced a small stage, hosting a maximum of four seats. These were cushioned with dark red and green velvety material but included the inevitable stains of pub life.

Dan leant on his elbows. 'Another pint?'

I nodded.

It was open mic night and a young man performed on the stage. He was about twenty but dressed like an elderly academic, wearing a tweed jacket, chocolate brown cords and a mustard waistcoat. He attempted humour, slurring his words, holding his ale glass high and spraying his spit as he told us anecdotes of upper-class life that I would never understand.

Dan returned with drinks and snacks, grinning. 'I've got a game. Spot the most attractive people in here, apart from us.'

I chuckled. 'Okaaaay.'

'Well, look, I'm not fancying myself too much here, but look around. We're the fittest here.'

I glanced about. He kind of had a point. There were a few contenders. I clocked boys who could still be teenagers smoking pipes; there was so much wrong with that.

Dan asked me to pick a fanciable male, and bar staff didn't count. I located a young Alan Davies lookalike going into the toilet. I pointed him out, but Dan missed him.

'You fancy Alan Davies?'

'Yes, I do. I like his dry sense of humour.'

'Anyone else weird you fancy?'

'Sean Hughes and Mark Lamarr.'

Dan raised his eyebrows.

I jabbed him in the arm. 'There he is!'

Dan looked in the direction of the toilet, shaking his head. 'Sean Hughes, Mark Lamarr...' At my look, he raised his hands, concluding, 'No judgement.'

He looked around, trying to spot a woman he could call fit, struggling until a couple walked in and sat on the table next to us.

He moved closer and talked into my ear. 'Now, don't think I'm on the pull here, but that woman who just walked in is kind of interesting.'

I looked over his shoulder to take a look, trying not to stare, and kissed his cheek to prolong my viewing. She was magnetic. She removed a black fur jacket, and her male companion took it from her and placed it on the back of her chair. She went to the bar and sauntered past our table. She wore paisley dungarees and a white t-shirt, her dark red hair in a 40s updo, rolled at the front. She could have been about fifty but as she ordered her drinks and laughed with the bar staff, I realised I admired her confidence.

'She's incredibly watchable, isn't she?' I said.

'You're incredibly watchable.'

I turned to look at Dan, and he was staring back at me. He raised his eyebrows. I copied him and we both leant into each other, elbows on the table.

'We've learnt a bit about each other tonight,' Dan said.

'You know what, I want to know who your crushes are next. And you know what else, I reckon my Alan Davies guy is better suited to your dungaree girl than her current boyfriend, do you?'

Dan nodded. 'I'll have a think about crushes, and yep, her bloke fits in with the crowd here. This is where the ugly people come to drink, apart from us, of course.'

We smiled as we clinked our beer glasses.

︎🌷

A few days later, it was ladies' night at the leisure centre, and Heidi and I met up for a girly swim. We hadn't spent much time together since I dropped my Eton Mess off at the barbecue and left to meet Dan. I wanted to see her and not let anything fester between us, but as it turned out, Heidi was preoccupied with work and concerned about an urgent appraisal the next day. As we swam up and down next to each other, attempting breaststroke but swallowing words and water, Heidi confessed she had been passing off some work projects as complete, when they weren't. I stopped and swam to the edge.

'Over here,' I said, and she followed me.

We were at the deep end, and she held on while I treaded water next to her.

'I need more information.'

'I've been signing tasks off when they aren't done and trying to get the admin assistants to do them. It worked for a bit, but I think someone has dobbed me in.'

'Christ, love, what made you do that?'

'Dunno. Bored, too much work, and you know, since Di left, the new manager has been a bitch on wheels.'

I imagined an over-efficient manager, yelling and whooshing around an office with wheels for legs.

Heidi explained her new manager, Katharine from Hull, had been looking forward to meeting her. She'd sent an introductory email alluding to her being "salt of the earth" and "one of them". Heidi hoped they could talk about Beautiful South together and she'd even hoped Katharine might have known Paul Heaton.

'Hull isn't that big, but all she's done since she arrived is micromanage, poking her nose into our projects in front of each other, and it turns out she doesn't know anyone from Beautiful South; in fact, she doesn't even like them.'

'Bring back Di, eh?'

Heidi nodded and ducked under water, popping back up again. 'I need a scheme to get me out of the shit.'

We swam back and forth for a few more lengths and discussed a plan of action for her appraisal, and when Heidi dropped me off at home, she squeezed me tight as we said goodnight.

'Thanks, love. I can always count on you, and I will definitely mention I'm a member of the union tomorrow. I'll feel safer then and think of you.' Heidi looked at me as I started to undo my seatbelt. 'Hey, I know we haven't seen each other much lately and you're in the sex zone, but don't forget us.'

'Oh my god, Heidi, never! Who do you mean, us?'

'Well, Flint and me mainly. This is the first time in ages I've seen you, and Flint said you haven't had an old film night for months. I know how you two like to do all that together.'

Flint was a snitch, but she had a point. From early on in our friendship, Flint and I had watched old films together, sometimes musicals, taking it in turns to choose the next film. We never shared this with anyone else. It was our thing. Our Flint-and-Louise thing.

Heidi interrupted my thoughts. 'Okay, let me be blunt. I'm a bit worried about this Dan dude.'

'Heidi, he's not a dude, he's my boyfriend.' Man, it felt lush naming him that, but as quick as my heart rose, it sunk into the pit of my gut. He was not *my* anything.

Heidi clocked it. 'This is tough, I know; he's everything you want, and I think it's getting to you that he isn't yours. I knew this would happen, but don't bottle it up.'

'Maybe you would feel better if you met him.'

She winced.

'Oh, come on, I need you and Flint to suss him out, we always do that sort of thing, right?'

'Louise, love, we've already sussed him out. We're just waiting for you to catch up.'

'What do you mean?'

'Look, it's late, your hair is getting all frizzy, and as much as I could talk to you for twenty-four hours on the trot, I want some cheese on toast.' She shooed me out of the car and sped off, whacking up Aretha Franklyn as she reversed out of my close.

Flint was also hot on my heels. He texted me that night and asked me to meet him for lunch the next day at our favourite place for soup and tortilla chips, and made it clear he wasn't happy with me either.

After he'd wolfed down his lunch and started pinching my chips, he blurted out, 'So, Heidi and I are wondering how you've been.'

'I know, we met up last night.'

'Good. We know where you're hanging out and can imagine what you've been doing, but there's no need to piss off completely.'

'I haven't pissed off completely, I spoke to you last week! And Di popped round.'

'Yeah, yeah, phone calls and popping round – that isn't you. What's he done to you?'

'If you mean Dan, nothing apart from make me happy. Happier than I've been in ages.'

'Look, all I'm saying is, we're still here, your real people, and we love you, all the time, whether you're being a prat or not, even when you pretend to know what a posh ingredient is but have to secretly ask that stuck-up girl in your office.'

'Liza.'

'Yeah, her. We even love you when you whine about being single and finding no-one to click with; we love that you went line dancing with your mum and enjoyed it, and I personally don't mind your driving, despite what Heidi says about it. Does what's-his-face love all that mad stuff about you?'

I touched my cheek and the heat beneath. 'Shit, I told you about the line dancing in secret,' I hissed, looking over my shoulder. 'My driving is alright, I know I need to practise my reversing, but jeez. And as for my man drought, I like sharing my worries with you.'

He reached over the table and offered my hand a tight squeeze. 'It's alright. I like that we chat – you and I, I mean.' Flint winked at me.

I sighed. 'I know you both care. I'm just loved up and fluffy, that's all. It's like that at the beginning of relationships, isn't it?'

'Relationships.' Flint raised his eyebrows, but didn't add anything further, getting out of his seat to go pay the bill.

When he returned, I tried to pay my half but he batted my fiver away.

'Don't forget us, yeah? Especially me.' Flint grinned cheekily. 'I'm the friend who buys you lunch.'

♥

Dan and I slipped into our pattern of office-hour dating. It was the new thing.

I didn't know all the excuses he gave to Melissa – I didn't ask – but it did seem Dan managed his work schedule effectively. My friends questioned why it was my schedule that had to be jiggled about. They were right, of course, but what choice did I have?

Remembering what Heidi had said about the lack of film watching with Flint, I invited him round to share fish and chips one evening. We settled on *Some Like It Hot* as, oddly, neither of us had seen it. As we unwrapped the steaming salty chips, Flint asked me to explain the premise of *Desperate Housewives* in detail. As he dished out the chips onto separate plates, he shoved a few into his mouth, nodding, yet giving zero input. With the fish now unwrapped, he changed the subject, catching me off guard.

'So, he, like, never takes you out for dinner, or to see a musical?'

I followed him into the living room. 'Um, where did that come from? Didn't you want to know more about Teri Hatcher?'

'Not really. You wanted to tell me about that show. But I've been having thoughts about your dates with what's-his-name. Look, I know you love live shows and all that stuff. So why isn't he taking you to London? No one will see you there.' Flint did his usual thing of getting to the point, making me squirm.

'I mean, it's an issue with time, isn't it? His time.'

'Hmm.'

'What do you mean, "hmm"?'

'Oh, I dunno. Seems like it's all about him. I want more for you.'

'So do I!'

'Seriously, though. I mean, it's just not proper, is it?'

'When did you get so chivalrous with women?' I laughed, throwing him the kitchen roll.

Flint smiled back at me, throwing the kitchen roll at my head. 'Hey! I can do the romance, be the manly hero, sensitive and romantic. I *am* that kind of boyfriend. I think I might have done quite well with Jeannie.'

'Yeah?' I stuffed another chip in my mushy peas. Jeannie having everything she wanted from Flint made the emotions tug in my belly.

'Absolutely. I might like Jeannie. Quite a bit, actually.'

After we finished eating and watching the film, I detected an oddness around Flint and me. Things were changing, I guess. New beginnings, new lovers – was that it?

Or had Flint seen the bigger picture with Dan and me? One that I'd conveniently tucked away as if it wasn't really happening?

Although Dan and I didn't have many proper dates and there was no talk of cinema trips or weekends away, I loved my new normal life. Anything I heard, or laughed about, I reported back to Dan with glee. He felt the same – and called me numerous times a day to tell me things he had discovered; things he had seen on the news or in the paper. The gaps between seeing each other were taken up with extensive phone calls, giving us the opportunity to laugh more and talk intensely.

But I learnt Dan was restless about losing me already and it was alarming how insecure he was. If I didn't call him back as quickly as he wanted, or respond to his text messages, he'd totally stress out. He was also anxious about my mates putting me off him. One Saturday night in September, he was family bound and I was out in the pub. He sent me a text.

```
I've snuck off to the toilet
to text you. I hope your mates
aren't telling you to get rid
of me. I don't know what I'd
do if they encouraged you to
meet someone else, someone
who could be yours.
```

Then there was a voicemail he'd left me while apparently nipping to the shop to get milk.

'I'm missing you like crazy, please don't meet anyone else tonight. I know this is hard, but, well, I'm hard just thinking about kissing you. Well, actually, I'm not. I'm outside the Co-op and that'd be weird, but... fuck, just don't forget me.'

Later that week, we had one of those balmy summer-like days in autumn when you talk yourself into making the most of being able to hang clothes out on the line. Those days where the sun seems washed out and blurry. Gone were the dazzling cornflower blue sky days, and although the heat was still with us, there was a promise of new temperatures looming as the sun hung lower in the sky to prepare for its predictable change.

I was based in one of our outreach offices and we were run off our feet. At lunchtime I had enough time to eat, sit in the sun and check my phone. Knackered, I sat on the grassy area at the back of our building. A couple argued directly over the top of their child in a pushchair, and I was thankful I wouldn't be the one interviewing them.

I switched on my phone. Dan had texted me – a lot.

```
Morning you, how are yah?
I miss you darlin. Are you
busy?
I can't stop thinking about
you, I'm getting zero work
done
```

I dithered over calling him. I'd always wanted this level of attention from a man, so why was it troubling me that he was needy? Previous boyfriends hadn't shown their vulnerabilities so soon, if at all, and that was what made Dan stand out in a good way. Or did it?

I called him back, listening to his domestic news and waiting for the right moment to have my say.

'Actually, I wanted to have a word about something. Please don't worry about my friends talking me out of seeing you. I am strong enough to know my own mind, you know. And for the record, some of them have tried, but I've ignored them. They just want to look after me.'

Big lie. My friends would never be one hundred percent on board with this relationship.

'I just worry every time you don't text me back that it's because you've seen sense, because you probably will.'

'It's not that. I'm either at work, sleeping or, you know, getting on with life. Maybe you could take a step back and think of all the times I can't call or text you, cos that's against the rules. It's tough for me. I miss you, and it's hard when I'm alone knowing you are with your kids or her.'

'I'm sorry,' he replied, considering his words. 'I'm such a twat. Of course it's bloody harder for you, and by the way, I'm only ever like that with you, you know? Not with her anymore.'

Was he talking about sex? I wish he hadn't made me think of them shagging. Now all I could see was Dan having sex with a headless wife, because that's how she appeared in my mind.

'We put the kids to bed, she works on her laptop and I read. I'm like an old git at thirty-five.' He laughed, perhaps anticipating me to laugh with him.

I wanted to ask if they still had sex; they must have. I wanted to think he didn't want to go near her since I'd come along.

I suppose stopping altogether could rouse her suspicions, so it must have continued in some form. My lunch suddenly weighed heavy in my stomach.

'Can we not talk about Melissa, please?' I asked, noting that it was the first time I'd spoken her name out loud.

'Sure, course. I want to add something though.'

'Alright.'

'I don't think I was clear just now. You and me is all I think about. Sometimes I feel so happy that you're in my life. But then I worry I'm being too happy in front of Mel, sorry, *her*, and that she'll suspect something. I'm sort of acting and being different versions of myself. Then I worry about how you are, and I never really know.' He sighed. 'Am I making any sense?'

'Yeah.' I paused for a moment. 'Although, I called you today to talk about your texts – which can be a bit needy, but I sort of like you needing me – but I wanted to reassure you, to make you a bit more relaxed about us. I want you to be happy in this.'

'I am.'

'Yeah, but what's happened is I'm feeling insecure. I'm now worried I'm not the only woman you kiss like you kiss me, and because I go crazy when you kiss me, I don't want another woman to feel like I do. And this doesn't make me calmer about our relationship; in fact, I just want to see you right now and I can't. I have three more hours at work and a team meeting.' My voice shook. I stopped and pursed my lips together.

'I'm sorry, shall I see if I can get someone to pick up the kids and get a taxi over—?'

'No, it's okay, I'm meeting some friends later. We have to get used to this, I suppose.'

'I know we do, but I'm invested, yeah? I want to get used to us. You know that, right?'

We ended the call after I lied and said I was needed back in the office. Instead, I lay on my back, wiped a few tears from my eyes and wondered how anyone got used to this kind of relationship.

CHAPTER 11

Payday Sex with The Wife

Later that night, Di invited Heidi and me around for her superb moussaka. Di lived alone like I did, and loved inviting friends round every couple of weeks to feed them her countless specialities. We always accepted enthusiastically and, of course, supplied the wine.

Di was the other grownup of our group. She loved DIY and would spend weekends avoiding us all, building a bookcase or putting in original style shutter windows in her bedroom. Then she would emerge and invite us round to see her clever grafting, putting us to utter shame. I could hardly manage an IKEA bookshelf, unless Dad or Flint were there to supervise.

Di's house was pretty and dainty from the kerbside view, and elegant throughout. Her hallway flooring had brown, white and turquoise tiles, and to the left a marble-top table with a retro landline and a cheese plant on top. My favourite room was the dining room, with homemade bookshelves fitted to the walls, her unsteady wooden table with six unmatching chairs in the middle. As soon as I was inside, I could exhale; Di's strength along with her promise of solace brought a calmness.

We'd all thrashed out worries, dramas and plotted boyfriend abductions at this table, and Di would always sweep up the debris and get the kettle on.

After we'd scoffed dinner, we sat out in Di's garden. Heidi was meant to be working and had brought some files with her, but I could see her laptop from my seat, and she hadn't yet started. She had a photo of Danny Dyer semi-naked on her desktop. The Pixies were playing from the kitchen and, as it was warm, Heidi was sprawled out on a sun lounger, shades on, nestled under a blanket pulled up to her chin. Di and I sat on the metal vintage chairs with our feet up in front of us on a matching table. Half of the sky was dwindling into a pale blue. Intermittently, the clouds eliminated more of the blue and turned the other half a stunning pink, like those little shrimp sweets.

Di turned down the volume on The Futureheads and asked me the latest on Dan. I wanted to talk about him, of course, but Heidi tutted.

'Urgh, can we have one night where he doesn't come up?'

'No,' said Di. 'We listen. That's what friends do.' She clinked her glass to mine.

I told them about his worries and me putting him right. Then I approached the sex between Dan and his wife.

'Course he's still fucking her.' Heidi sat upright as she spoke.

'Heidi!' Di exclaimed.

'What? I mean, it's obvious, isn't it? He has to keep both motors going, so to speak.'

'I know that.' I didn't, actually. 'It's just... how do I deal with it? How do I cope?'

'Well... can you handle it?' Di asked, massaging in her vanilla-scented hand cream and chucking me the tube.

'What do you mean?'

'If he is still sleeping with her?' Di clarified. 'Though maybe he isn't in that kind of relationship with her anymore.'

Heidi chipped in. 'Well, obviously you'll never know, because he's a liar, but do you want to know what I'd do?'

'Go on, enlighten us,' I said.

'Find someone else to date but don't end it with Dan. Get a free agent, fit and everything. Have sex with them both. See how he bloody likes it.'

I rolled my eyes at Heidi. 'Really? I have a boyfriend.'

'Do you? He's *married*, Lou Lou. You can't really call him your boyfriend. What you should be doing is calling it a day.'

I sighed but didn't answer. How could I? How could I say that what we had was addictive? That Dan had hooked me in? Tears began to prickle at the corners of my eyes.

'It's just... I just can't see a way out that would result in me happily existing. I don't want to not have Dan in my life, even if the time spent with him is on his terms.'

Heidi rolled her eyes. 'You've got to be fucking kidding me.'

'No,' I snapped, trying desperately to keep the wobble in my voice at bay. 'I'm happy. Bloody happy, thanks.'

'Are you, though? All I hear are problems; you're barely spending any time together outside of fucking, and then there's this whole issue of you only being able to call at certain times. That's not a relationship, Louise, and you know it.'

'It's *our* relationship.'

'Well, I can already see what's going to happen and you're only a month in. You aren't glowy and radiating love anymore. It'll be the questions next, the wondering, and I don't think it's right.'

Heidi's words had winded me and I blinked to stop the tears getting out of hand. To cover my feelings, I sat myself upright.

'Heid, I know you're saying this because you care, but I'm okay.' My chin automatically dipped, my gaze following. 'I would be the same if you were in my shoes, but I'm okay. I love him.'

'But even if he loves you, you and him, it can never happen,' Heidi said, softening her voice.

'Why not? Things can change. I've not met a man in ages that has it all. What if I pass up on this being something in the future just because I'm afraid?'

'But he will always have met you by cheating. He'll always be the one in your relationship that could bugger off when things get shitty at home. I don't think you'll ever trust him, not really.'

'Look, can we leave it, this isn't making me feel—'

'Alright, but you know where we all are when things go Pete Tong.'

'When things go wrong... are you saying you've all been talking about me?'

'Yep,' Di and Heidi said in unison.

For fuck's sake.

Incoming tears made my throat ache, so I swallowed a large gulp of wine to try and push the sadness away. Di tidied the wine glasses, not looking at either of us, while Heidi stared off into the garden with her arms folded.

'You know, if you want to do one better than her, you could perform every sex trick in the book,' she said into the night air. 'Every dirty, fantasy type thing, every time you see him.'

Di stopped what she was doing.

'Princess Leia outfits, sex in the shed, all that jazz. Then he'd never be able to go back to payday sex with his wife. Or whatever it is they do.'

Payday sex? Where did she pick up these phrases from?

Di laughed. 'She can't do that, Heid, she's not a hooker. And lower your voice – my neighbours think I'm alright.'

'How do you know I haven't done some of that stuff already?'

'No wonder he's keen then,' Heidi snapped back.

I shuddered. 'I just... I hate the idea of him doing anything with her.'

Di smiled reassuringly. 'He probably doesn't. I'm sure it's very perfunctory with his wife. You must get all the best sex.'

I appreciated where she was going, but something else was on my mind. 'I want to know what she looks like.'

'Why?' they both asked simultaneously.

'I just do.'

'Why?' they asked again.

Heidi scoffed. 'It'll be the kids next, or the family gerbil.'

'I just want to see if she's like me or not. I want to know what he sees in her. He's never described her to me. All he's said is we're quite similar and both have big boobs.'

'Wanker,' Heidi muttered.

Di sighed. 'I reckon it's best not to know. I'm not sure what good it'll do you. If you saw her, you'd agonise that she's prettier, thinner, bigger, has nicer skin, or better teeth. I'm not sure seeing her will help. It's not important, is it? He is, after all, choosing to be with you.'

'And Melissa,' I added. I'd jumped ship; joined Heidi's team in the dismantling of Dan's merits.

'But he's not choosing to stay with her because of who she is. He's staying with her to be with his children,' Di continued.

'How do I know for sure though?'

'You don't,' Heidi said, shrugging.

Di looked up at the sky. Night-time was fast approaching. 'Think of it like this: he's risking it all to be with you. How about that? Isn't that special?'

'Special, huh? Special *needs*, more like. But hey, here's what she looks like.'

Di and I shot up from our seats and crowded around Heidi's laptop.

There she was. The wife.

While we'd been chatting, Heidi had casually searched up her name; we knew she worked for the NHS and Google stored everything, including a grainy photo from the *Oxford Mail* when her team had taken part in a charity abseil down the side of John Radcliff Hospital.

Dan had lied. Melissa and I were not alike at all. She was mid- to late-thirties, with shoulder-length light brown hair curling from root to tip. Her skin was warm and natural, her blue eyes genuine. She was pretty in a I-wouldn't-mess-with-her kind of way, which was ironic because I'd already messed with her, and she had no idea.

I couldn't believe Heidi had found her.

As we packed up to head inside for a cuppa, I felt neither above her nor below her in the attractiveness stakes. We were equal. But as I removed my mascara that night and cleaned my teeth, I hazarded a guess about her bedtime routine; did she wash her face, have a bath or a shower? Was she taking her makeup off with Dan standing next to her? Was he making the same jokes she'd heard a zillion times before, but because of the comfort of their relationship and to keep things simple, did she laugh anyway? Or maybe she didn't laugh, but rolled her eyes instead.

Or maybe, worse yet, did she laugh because he was still witty to her, and after all these years she still loved him and he still loved her?

I wasn't qualified to question the merits of a successful marriage and how the racked-up years, mixed with familiarity, could wring out the passion. But what was left when the impulsiveness and getting-to-know-you bits had faded and you didn't bother anymore? It was what Dan and his wife had now: loneliness, boredom, and a redhead on the side. But surely, if I was to ever be in a proper relationship, or even a marriage with Dan, wouldn't that be my future? To saunter along the same path as Melissa was walking down right now, even though she was ignorant to it?

I didn't feel so equal now; she had it all. She may not have known about me, but she still came out on top in my eyes. She had all of him and, while they could climb into the same bed, sex or no sex, I was getting into my bed alone.

CHAPTER 12

Show and Tell

Dan called to ask me some random questions. He'd been writing them down as they came into his head.

I didn't really have time to chat to him – Heidi and I were meeting at the gym – but the thing was, any conversation Dan and I started could never be called brief. One of us would go off on a tangent and drag the other down a road of digression. Before we knew it, an hour had passed; he hadn't unloaded the washing machine and I'd missed the gym.

'What kind of questions, can you be more specific?' I asked.

'Okay, let me have a look at my list.'

'You actually have a list? What, is it stuff like the name of my first pet? Why I have the scar above my eyebrow? How many times I've taken a driving test? Because I will not reveal that to anyone.'

He just laughed.

The next morning, Dan bounced himself into the passenger seat of my car with the cheekiest grin. He'd started to wear hoodies now as the sun was making less of an appearance, and today he wore a bright red one, with some green writing on the front.

I flashed him a smile and he unplugged my seat belt to get closer as our kisses progressed, fast for 10 a.m. on a Wednesday morning. The parked bus beeped its horn from behind my car. I waved an apology to the driver as I pulled away, while Dan's hand massaged the back of my neck. This minor movement produced sensations between my legs that shouldn't happen when you're responsible for a moving vehicle. I felt wayward, sexy, rebellious, aged fifteen but with a mortgage and a Tesco Clubcard.

At my house, we couldn't stop snogging in my hallway. Dan was sending my head up into the clouds with his slow kisses and I was contentedly secured against the wall – like one of those American teenage girls in high school films pinned against a locker, trapped by her boyfriend's mouth.

Bennett was meowing and ambling around our feet. My arms were around Dan's waist, holding on; any sudden movements or slowing down of his kissing and I'd hit the floor in a heap. He paused and ran his index finger down my neck and stopped between my breasts. He moved in and kissed my neck three times in the same place.

'Have you been swimming? I can smell chlorine.'

'Uh huh,' I murmured.

'I like it, it's one of your smells. Let's do the list,' he whispered. 'I want to know everything about you. I want to know it all.'

He wanted to talk.

I just wanted him inside me.

I moaned in a do-we-have-to fashion.

'Humour me, I thought this was romantic. It's all the things I've wondered about you since we met and, well, look.'

Dan produced a handwritten list from the back pocket of his jeans, like a proud little boy about to do his Show and Tell.

I stifled a laugh and tried to hug him.

'You can laugh all you like, but this list took some work. Are you ready?' he said, fiddling with his hard-on.

'Um, not really,' I said, my hand heading down the front of his jeans.

Dan rolled his eyes, grinning. 'Do what you want with me then, I can't resist you for long.'

We didn't move far from my bedroom. Naked, Dan twirled my hair around his fingers, then sat up with a jolt. He'd remembered the list and located it from his jeans pocket. I sat up, smiling as he jumped back into bed, paper in hand.

We cracked up at the questions and answers that followed. We were more alike than we knew.

1. Dan did stand-up comedy – once.

2. He had NOT heard of *Anne of Green Gables* – I showed him my collection of books to prove my love for her.

3. When talking about our 80s crushes, I guessed he fancied Belinda Carlisle and he did.

5. He was a busker in his twenties and hid this (and all the cash he made) from his dad.

6. He wanted to write a book.

7. He read to his kids every night and sometimes made up the stories. Once he called the lead character, a long-suffering princess, Louise, by mistake. His kids noticed. He'd squirmed his way out of that one.

He learnt about me too.

1. I wanted to be Anne of Green Gables.

2. I sometimes ate hummus and Doritos as my dinner.

3. I loved swimming, especially outside.

4. I used to perm my hair in the 80s and pretend I was Molly Ringwald.

5. I fancied C Thomas Howell after watching *The Outsiders* and Dan needed evidence to prove their existence.

6. Mags was the fittest in A-Ha.

We ate cheese and pickle sandwiches and snack-size Milky Way bars in bed, and as the afternoon disappeared, our new item on the agenda was clock watching.

I picked up my phone; there was a text from Flint. I didn't open it. My mood dropped with every glance at the time. The eagerness to drag the date out by five minutes halted when Dan decided it was time for him to go. I wasn't finding this any easier or habitual; it was shattering my hopeful nature every time he left.

He climbed out of bed, located his clothes and started to get dressed. He could remove his clothes quickly when he wanted to. Earlier, Dan had removed his jeans at the speed of light, but looking at him putting his socks on was pitiful. He went to the toilet and came back into my bedroom, drying his hands on the towel. He perched on the edge of my bed and turned to face me.

'I have to go.'

'I know.'

'I'm finding it impossible today.'

I nodded in agreement. I tried to locate the words in my

head to say the opposite of what I felt, which was: *I think you should fuck off, as I'm falling in love with you and you're leaving me for your family.*

Instead, I left the words hanging there, got dressed and went downstairs.

Dan appeared, standing in front of the doorway, and watched me lock up the back door of my house, close the windows and appear as if I was in charge of my life. I caught his eye looking for the car keys and then his arms found me. We held onto each other.

I inhaled him as he placed his chin on top of my head, whispering, 'I'm sorry.'

The car journey to his home was silent, but despite the lack of talking, our communication was crystal clear. We sat at some traffic lights, both staring ahead. I'd fallen for this guy in a hefty and swift way and I hadn't expected to. I could watch him watching me for hours, in the way he did. I could see he was torn; he was happy, but troubled.

We arrived in Stapleford, and I pulled into the street where I always dropped him off. As he turned to say goodbye, I could see in his expression the absence of quips and banter. Was he as scared to death as I was? What were we doing?

🌷

Flint sent me a text asking if he could pop in after work with Jeannie.

> What for?

> Er, do we need a reason?

No, he didn't, but I didn't reply. I hadn't met Jeannie properly yet. Our first encounter was on Flint's doorstep. She was leaving Flint's place as I arrived one Sunday morning. She looked gorgeous, with her ruffled morning-after-bonking bob. Clearly lots of dirty wig-wearing sex had occurred – she had that sheepish glow. I had zero radiance about me and wished I'd changed out of my tartan PJs. Flint was dying to show Jeannie off properly to all of us, but I was last on his intro list.

Heidi and Di had been to the pub with them, and Chrissy invited Flint and Jeannie round to meet Alice, Chrissy's little girl. Chrissy called me after they left with the lowdown.

'Oh, they are so sweet together. I'm happy for them. Alice painted Jeannie's toenails, Flint brought cakes and we all played Junior Monopoly.'

'Junior what?'

'You heard. It was fun. Alice was in charge of the cards and Flint let Jeannie win.'

'Let her win? Flint never lets anyone win, even at Snap. You've seen him. And as for letting Jeannie win, did she need help with Junior Monopoly?'

From what Flint had written in his text message, I noticed he was a "we" now, and at 6 p.m. there they were on my doorstep, love's young-ish dream, all smiley, full of sex vibes. A streetwise version of Jehovah's Witnesses.

I gestured for them to come in as Flint walked past me. I smiled at Jeannie as she hovered in the hallway.

'What's up with you then? You've got a face like a slapped

arse,' Flint said to me.

'Flint,' Jeannie warned softly, grimacing apologetically at me.

'It's okay, she knows I love her really.' Flint tickled my waist as I passed, then he sprawled on my sofa.

Jeannie perched on the arm next to him.

'Spit it out, then. Tell your ole mate Flint you've finally dumped what's-his-face.'

I placed my hands on my hips. 'Do you really want to know?'

'Yep.'

I gave him a blow-by-blow account of my day with Dan, but as I started to get into the details of our sex life, Flint put his hand up,

'Urgh, skip that stuff, would you?' he'd groaned, rolling his eyes at Jeannie, who was now kneeling beside Bennett, stroking him as he rolled around in the sunshine.

I noticed her nail polish needed removing as she tucked her hair behind her ear.

'Honestly, I don't know what to add that hasn't already been said,' Flint continued. 'I don't ever want to meet this utter prick.'

'I want you to though, Flint. I think if you actually met him you'd see what I love about him.'

'Nope. He wouldn't want to meet me – trust me. All you need to know is he's a serial cheater; he'll repeat it all over again with you years down the line, and you, my dearest, do not deserve that.'

I changed the subject and offered them a drink, but they

declined. They were going to see a film.

'It's a flying visit,' Flint explained.

As they left, Jeannie said she wished they could stay longer, and Flint rumpled up my hair and glanced down at me. I lowered my eyes to my feet, smiling as he gave me a Flint-style, tight, brief hug. I wanted it to last longer, and for him to stay around – preferably without Jeannie.

As I shut the door, I wondered was the purpose was of their visit? To rub my nose in their new, fresh relationship? Or to remind me how shit mine was? Or a combination of both?

Dan called me later that night, just as I was about to turn in.

'Sorry for calling so late. I have news.' There was excitement in his voice.

I stroked the back of my neck, took a deep breath and prepared to fake things up. I couldn't be all teary, clingy and emotional. I would have to go for robotic until I knew what I was going to do about him.

'What's the news?' I asked.

'Are you okay?'

Holding things together didn't last long. I started to cry big, gloopy tears, hating myself for it. Wiping them away, I gave up on the robot façade and started to tell him about my conversation with Flint.

He listened without interruption.

'I wouldn't blame your friends for protecting you from a married prick like me,' he said once I'd finished. 'If I wasn't with you, I'd protect you from someone like me too.'

I sniffed. 'Ironic.'

'I said this wasn't going to be easy or normal. I knew you were unhappy, normally when we're chatting you barely pause to breathe, but tonight...'

My silence answered him, but he continued anyway.

'Are you crying?'

'What does it matter?'

'It matters to me. Shit, now I want to come over and hold you.' He paused. 'This is all my fault, isn't it? Do you think we should call it a day?'

My heart stopped. The blood pumping around my veins yanked on the emergency break.

'No, no, I'll be okay. It was a tough conversation, that's all. Flint can be like that.'

'*Fuck.*' He took a deep breath.

'What?'

'I thought for a minute you might say we should knock it on the head. I wouldn't blame you. Christ.'

'Don't be dramatic.'

'Alright. I've got something to tell you. Two things, actually. I can make that Embrace gig with you and your mates. Maybe if they see us together, they won't think I'm a total twat. Also, I can stay over as Melissa is taking the kids to their aunt's house for the night. I'm not needed here.'

'That's fantastic.'

'We'll have our first sleepover. I've been planning it. I'll even make you breakfast. It'll be a top night. We can lie in, have a shitload of sex. I don't think I can wait. I'll even bring my pyjamas.'

'Do you have a dressing gown?'

'Leave it. Actually, there's something else I'd like to say. I was going to tell you when I saw you at the gig, but after this conversation, it makes more sense to say it now.'

I gulped, my mouth producing an elated, dorky grin. I was thankful he couldn't see me.

'I've been rehearsing this in the mirror like a knob. I assumed I'd be with you when I said it.'

I smiled wider, imagining him talking to his bathroom mirror, changing the angle.

'I even practised facial expressions as well.'

I laughed.

'Ah, now I wish I'd waited, I'm feeling a bit weird here.'

'You sound it.'

He took a deep breath. 'I've fallen in love with you.'

My heart stopped, this time with joy. 'I've fallen in love with you too, Dan.'

CHAPTER 13

Dan's Library

After the "love" conversation, Dan and I barely existed in our real lives, living in our own romance novel written by us. I didn't tell my mates about *that* word being thrown around. I'd tell them soon, but for fear of any lectures, I kept it between Dan and me – it felt more intimate that way.

A week later, Heidi, Di, Chrissy and Dan all traipsed to the student union gig hall to see Embrace. I'd loved them since '98 and Dan had no idea who they were. We shared a bit of common ground on the music front, but we'd introduced each other to all sorts of music. He made sure I would always love Bob Dylan and Gomez. I made him listen to Beautiful South, The Proclaimers, The Streets and loads of indie bands I'd seen at festivals. Dan said his mind was spinning from all the long-haired lead singers from bands like The Fratellis, The View, The Pigeon Detectives and The Kooks.

I met my friends in The White Horse pub, located on the busy main road near the venue, and Dan agreed to meet us there. The White Horse was only as hustling as it was because of its location near the football ground and the Student Union

Hall. The Brookes students didn't socialise here, as there was always a match on, volume loud, lots of lads and often arguments between them about the match. On gig nights, the vibe shifted and the place was filled with music fans, but the landlord switched the TV off in favour of indie music, and tonight, Franz Ferdinand roared throughout the pub.

I got pissed too quickly. I was necking my drinks because Dan was meeting Heidi. She'd quite clearly brought her teenage glares out of retirement. As soon as he walked into the pub, her bitch button was pressed, and I was worried for him; she wouldn't hold back. As introductions were made between Heidi and Dan, she cut me off.

'I don't think we need to be so courteous, do we? I know who you are.' She turned her head the other way and flicked her hair in time to the music.

'Heidi!' I protested.

Dan was smiling.

'Seriously?' she said, holding her hand up. 'I'm not sure I'm up for all this yet. I need to make up my mind about you first. I need to be convinced there's more to you.' She wrinkled her nose at him, got down off her bar stool with style and went outside to smoke. God, she was good.

I stared after her. Dan kissed me on the cheek.

'Hello, by the way. I reckon I can handle her, and if I can't, I'll just run home like Forrest Gump.'

Embrace were on top form and, feeling sentimental, I wished it was the 90s and I was hanging out in one of my favoured venues. Reality soon shattered that dream; I remembered it was a pain in the arse to get served in this place.

My mind wandered as I queued for beer. It was weird not being on the pull at a gig, or at least chatting up men while I hung about in the endless bar queue. I caught Dan staring at me as I laughed with my friends. His expression shimmered over me and left me wired. I nodded to a couple of blokes I knew from gigs. I waved at a girl I recognised from school. She blew me a kiss, displaying her flamenco pink lipstick, and then carried on with her conversation.

Dan and I stumbled through the door of my house around midnight, and we flung open the back door, made cups of tea and sat outside in my garden.

'I enjoyed tonight. I could be myself around you and your mates. I was like a normal bloke for a change,' Dan said, stretching his hands behind his head.

'Even with Heidi?'

Dan laughed. 'She loves her mate, and I can see why.'

'Shucks.' I looked down at the table as we carried on chatting.

I sensed the anticipation of sex wrapping around us, electricity passing back and forth every time we touched, and it was enough to keep the intensity bubbling and sparkling.

We sat in silence for a few moments, looking at the sky and sneaking shy looks at each other. I loved this part of a new relationship; gazing at each other, neither of you looking away. Above us, the sky was all so black and there were heaps of glittering stars pin-pricked about. They'd switched themselves on for us, and their brilliance was everywhere in the sky. With other men, I might have tried to pretend I knew the names of the stars or comets, but I didn't need to talk for the sake of it with Dan, let alone attempt to impress him, get the facts all wrong and then regret trying. I understood this quietness. Dan did, too. He held on tight to my hand across the table and kissed it. I appreciated the complete absence of any conversation and not needing to balance it out.

Eventually, I broke the silence.

'At least Flint wasn't there tonight. He's... well... let's just say I think you should win over the girls first.' I smiled. 'Flint is very protective of his hareem.'

'Do you think your friends will ever accept us?'

'Who cares?'

'You do, and I think I do, if I'm honest. Meeting the mates of the girl you're in love with is a great thing to do. I'm good at it normally, but this isn't like that, is it?'

'No, and I'm sure I will never meet any of your mates, or family.'

Dan sighed. 'The sad thing is, they would love you. I know my kids would adore you, especially Izzy. She would show you her room and line up her dolls for you. My dad would love to hear your chatter about council life, and I think in another world you and Melissa would get on.'

I wasn't expecting that. 'Back up. Do we have to talk about her?'

Discussing "the wife" wasn't what I'd ordered from the boyfriend shop. Was it too late to get a refund or a like-for-like exchange?

Dan cleaned his glasses in a hurried fashion. 'Sorry, yeah, that was a dick thing to say.'

'Yeah, just a bit.' I fiddled with the beads around my neck.

We sat in silence again, but this time the quietness strangled the atmosphere.

'Look, this is weird, all sorts of weird for both of us, and it's your call,' Dan said. 'Whenever you want this to stop, we'll stop. I'll never be able to end it.'

'Hang on a minute.' I stood up to have my say. 'You call the shots about when we meet, how we meet, where we meet, and I get to choose when it's over?'

'Hey, you knew it would be like this. I can't change things.'

'Ever?' I asked, biting my lip.

'Not unless my situation changes. I can't make the promises you want.'

'Or the promises *we* want?'

'Yeah, exactly.'

There was silence again. I drained the remaining cold tea and took both mugs into the kitchen. He locked the back door and followed me upstairs. This was our first proper night together and I wanted to send him home.

I drew the curtains and clocked him in the doorway of my bedroom. I couldn't take my eyes away from his stare. This was the first time since we'd met that he didn't look entirely self-assured. I swallowed instead of speaking. I should have said: let's leave it. You go home, ask Melissa how she feels about being my mate, big me up, will you, and arrange for us to have a girly night with face masks.

But I felt the pull towards him, and I knew he couldn't resist me in the slightest. It wasn't just written all over his face; our need to fuck each other filled the room with static.

We tore and tugged at each other's clothes as we kissed,

absolutely no skill in the messy flinging of t-shirts, socks and a bra. Dan couldn't remove the condom from the wrapper quick enough with his teeth. We toured and revisited our bodies, tasting each other with slow tongues, then with arousing small bites. One made me yelp; they were so good and wicked, and we tried them again.

How could I ever end this? How could he delegate that task to me and equate it to something humdrum and routine? Like deciding if there was enough garlic in a chilli con carne, or whether to wear my parting to the side or in the middle? How was it fair for me to have the sole responsibility for something so big?

♦

Dan texted me a few days later.

```
I need to see you and your
freckles. Can you call me
later so we can hatch a plan?
```

When I called him, he picked up sounding like a harassed Little Chef café worker. I could hear the smoke alarm in the distance, radio blaring and his gruff hello.

'Shall I call back?' I asked.

'No, no it's okay. I'm busy sorting fish fingers, chips and peas out before Beavers.'

I chuckled; I liked this domestic side of him. His kids were screaming and shouting in the background and the washing machine was on its final tilt. Dan added something I couldn't make out.

'Pardon?'

'Hang on a minute, Louise. What did you say? Can't you find it in your bedroom? I think it's under your pillow,' Dan said to one of his kids.

'Who's Louise?' one of the kids asked.

'Daddy's friend. Now, look, can you go and find that book or we'll be in big trouble with Mummy.'

'I want to say hello to Louise.'

'Um...'

'Please!'

Dan sighed. 'Louise, are you okay to say hi to Ben while I go upstairs and find a book?'

'Um, okay.'

I was fine with kids and didn't mind talking to him, but weren't they little motormouths? Couldn't Ben get Dan and me into trouble if he snitched to Mummy about "that Louise lady Daddy talks to"?

'Right, here you go, don't touch the buttons and just say hi.'

Dan vanished and a confident little boy spoke up.

'Hello, Louise.'

'Hello, Ben.'

'How did you know my name?'

'Your daddy told me. He tells me lots of nice things about you.'

'My daddy hasn't told me about you at all.'

'Oh, what would you like to know?'

'Who are your children? Is it Nathan?'

'Nope.'

'Is it Ollie?'

'Nope.'

'Okay, Ben, time's up.' Dan was back and breathless as he retrieved his mobile phone. 'Here's the book, now skedaddle. Louise, can we chat later please?'

When Dan called back, he apologised for ending our conversation so bluntly.

'It's okay, I thought you were getting twitchy about Ben asking me questions.'

'No, I'm not worried about that. I've talked about you to the kids before, and also, remember when I mentioned you in a story? Well, that's not the issue, it's that your call got in the way of the kids' section.'

'The kids' what?'

'The kids' section.'

'I need more information.'

Dan offered a heavy sigh, 'Don't take the piss. I get quite busy and stressed, and you know men can't multitask, right?'

'Uh huh.' I didn't like the stress seeping into our relationship.

'So, hear me out. I've been trying to figure out how to explain my mind to you. How I think. I don't want to describe you as a section, you're so not a section kind of girl. So here goes. I can only handle one book open at a time. Like, if I'm working, I'm working, and I focus on that book. If I'm with the kids, I can't read my work book at the same time. You get my drift?'

'Sort of.' Trying to picture the library in Dan's head was

messing with my own mind.

'You must have noticed I never check my phone much when I'm with you. That's "us" time. It's your book and I want to read it all the time. It's valuable to me.'

'I have noticed that, but also I've noticed you do send some texts when we're together.'

'Ah, you see, that's Melissa saying "can you get the bread out" or "don't save me any dinner", that sort of thing. We don't communicate all that much. But this is about books and we're getting away from the point. I don't have Melissa's book open anymore. But if the kids were ill, and it was the school calling, I'd pick up.'

'Hmm. I think what you're saying is you need more defined boundaries. If I call when you have another book open, you can't talk to me. Is that it?'

'Something like that. It's easier explaining about the books. One book at a time.'

Something entered my head. 'Here's a question. When you've finished the Louise book, what happens then?'

'I'm not sure, I've not been in this situation before. I mean, all of my books are ongoing. Don't read too much into it.'

'Okay.'

'I wanted to mention it because I'm getting a bit anxious these days, and I realise these odd requests sound strange, but it helps give my attention to whatever it is I'm doing.'

It bothered me that Dan was using the words "anxious" and "stress" in this conversation. It also made me wonder what would happen to the Louise book when he was done with it. I wasn't liking the visual of Dan's library.

I twisted my silver ring on my finger. 'Would you like to talk more about your anxiety?'

'Ah, no, don't worry, it's not reached that point yet. You'll know when I'm unwell, I'll be rocking at your bus stop.'

'That's not funny.'

'Sorry. Seriously, I'll share with you. Hang on, let me go outside and lay down.'

The line became clearer. Kitchen noises faded out.

'By the way, not sure I like you referring to me as something you are doing,' I told him.

Dan exhaled. 'Ah, you know what I mean.'

'Of course I do, don't worry about it. I'll try to lay off any spur of the moment contact, okay?'

'Alright. I feel like a dick making all these rules. New love should be easy.'

'I'm not telling you it's going to be easy; I am telling you it's going to be worth it,' I said. 'I read that somewhere in a magazine.'

He laughed. 'I'm not sure the quote made things better. But you are worth it, that's a fact. You've made me feel better already.'

'I didn't know I'd helped, but now I'm the one pouting over here. I think we are both finding this tough.'

'Well, here's a kiss for that pout, okay?'

I took a quick breath in. 'Thanks, I needed that. Would like more. Are you still in the garden?'

'Nope, in the utility room now wishing you were here. I'm always turned on when you're around, or not around. Just knowing you has made me the horniest I've been in years. I now have an erection putting towels and flannels in piles and I'm not sure that's normal.'

I went to bed that night aroused and bewildered. I was allowed to feel like that in my own home, no book restrictions here, but as I got into my PJs, I questioned if all these add-ons were right for me. And more importantly, would it last? I wasn't the kind of girl to be packed away and then whipped out for someone else's pleasure. I wanted to be free and spontaneous in love and the last thing I wanted was to be held back.

I loved him, though, and these were the compromises, it seemed.

But they were his compromises, his bloody books. Not mine.

CHAPTER 14

Flint Is What I Need

I called Flint. I needed his cynicism. I needed his outspoken critical, sarcastic, distrusting point of view. He was the only man for the job.

I drove to his house. I'd left him a voicemail saying I was on my way and it was urgent. He opened the front door in his pants after a few loud knocks, and gestured for me to come in. His housemates were asleep and he told me in no uncertain terms that he should be tucked up in his bed as well.

'This had better be worth me getting up for, my little gingernut.'

I could detect last night's dinner from the smells lingering in the hallway – something garlicky and gingery, mixed with the rubber of the bicycle tyres stacked by the downstairs toilet door.

Flint found some joggers in a wash pile – clean or unclean, his or not, I couldn't be sure. He popped them on, made us coffee and we sat in the living room. Finding somewhere to sit was an issue. I tidied the sofa and tried to find an area not covered in newspapers, phone chargers, laptops, or oven gloves.

'So?' Flint said.

I told him about Dan's library, and he didn't interrupt. His bleary, sleepy little face stared at me with a careful gaze, and he nodded and took a few sips from his coffee. He could be so forceful and annoying sometimes, and he often pressed his opinions into unwanted ears, but today he showed his gentlemanly side. He sensed that he needed to shut the fuck up and so, just like that, he did.

'We're in love, proper love. I'm worried I'll never feel like this again. It's like I'm on fire all the time.'

Flint nodded.

'Also, I don't care about Melissa and I don't care if she's hurt. Same with the kids. I know that's beyond fucked up, but I don't know these people, so in my mind it doesn't count.'

'Okay...'

'No eyeroll? I am a horrible person.'

'Yes, but keep going.'

'I hate that my morals and my humble upbringing is buried under huge quantities of oral sex, an introduction to minor spanking and ribbed-for-her-pleasure condoms.'

Flint burst out laughing, his cheeks reddening.

I met his gaze. 'And? I now need you to do your magic. Make this make sense.'

'Sorry, I think someone has done their magic on you already. Intro to spanking? Christ almighty, Louise.'

He sighed, putting his coffee cup on the table. I noticed his bicep muscle twinge as he folded his arms across his chest.

'I'm not sure what to say.'

Not an inspiring start.

'You must have an opinion,' I pleaded. 'Help me.'

'Look, we warned you right from the start, and you ranting like that, well, that was always going to happen. You were always going to come to your senses, but hey, this guy, he has something, some sort of wizardry.'

'We both have something. It's us, together.'

'But do you? You must know there is no "us"?'

This was more like it.

'It's different.' I found myself folding a pile of washing next to me.

'Look, I could say that about Jeannie and me,' Flint said, his eyes glistening, 'but I'm pointing out that Dan has definitely performed some kind of hypnotic magic on you or something.'

'Behave. You haven't even met him.'

'And nor do I ever want to. However, you have two options. You end this shitshow now, text him, tell him it's over, you can't do it anymore and then delete his number. Or you just carry on, knowing nothing will ever change.'

'I know all of that! I do. I just... I need someone to tell me what to do.' I grabbed his hands and shook them. 'I need someone to tell me to get out.'

He stared at me, pulling his hands away. Flint hadn't seen me quite so passionate or desperate before. A bluebottle zoomed away from us and flew to the other end of the living room.

'What would you do?' I asked.

He ignored the question. 'Look, here's a review. He's married; having a crisis; is never going to leave his family to shack up with you, until maybe it sort of suits him, by which point you will be too old to have kids; he will need a hip replacement *and* Heidi will still hate him anyway.'

I laughed. 'Basically.'

'But,' he continued, 'you have this connection, whether it's right for you or not. Plus, you've been on your own for so long, it makes this married waster look half decent. You love the shagging, the laughing, you like the same stuff, and I recall you saying he makes a fine cup of tea? Right?'

'Uh huh,' I replied, chewing my lip.

'Fuck it, I wouldn't end it then. You asked what I'd do. I'm weak, I'm a bloke. I'd enjoy the ride and await the almighty fucking explosion, then get out.' He paused. 'Cos there will be one.'

He looked away, and I stared at him. I noticed a twitch in his jaw. The friend I assumed I could bank on for hardcore boyfriend bashing had bailed on me. Had I tapped into Flint's deeper, softer side? He'd always been a bit squidgy, but maybe I'd discovered he could be envious of my love with Dan. I never thought in a million years that Flint would advise me to see the relationship out. Now more than before, I wanted Flint to meet Dan, but that would take some work.

'Bacon sarnie?' he asked.

He pulled me up out of my seat and smacked my arse as I walked into the kitchen ahead of him. I was more confused than ever.

Flint woke up his housemates, cranked up The Prodigy and we ate the most glorious breakfast: eggs, bacon, sausages, toast, butter, beans and copious amounts of tea. During breakfast, my phone beeped. It was Dan.

'No texting knobhead, please, not in my company.' Flint seized my phone and placed it on top of the fridge, out of my reach.

As he washed up, I dried. My mobile rang this time. Flint and I both glanced over at the fridge. I moved, but he stopped me by flicking soapy water in my face.

'Hey!' I giggled, wiping the sploshes from my nose.

'Remember, no more talk of Dan in my house or I'll do this.' And with that, he came behind me, tickled under my armpits and around my waist, knowing it would have me on the floor, screeching with laughter.

I landed on my bum.

'Are you just going to leave me here? Help me up.' I wiped the happy tears from my eyes.

Flint held his hand out, pulling me up in front of him. We shared a look; something travelled to my belly, but we didn't say a word.

He grabbed the tea towel I was using and flicked my arse with it, saying, 'You still have work to do here. Get on with it.'

🌷

At around 4 p.m., my landline rang. It was Nikki. Bonkers, lively and much needed Nikki. She was the perfect distraction.

'Hey, how are you?'

Apparently, she had called to plan the driving, discuss suitcase contents and provide a countdown for our holiday in September. We were due to fly in nine days.

Nikki had been dumped in April by her boyfriend, Dave.

He woke up one morning, made her marmite on toast in bed, left for work and texted her at lunchtime to say he was going to live in Scotland. By nightfall, he was living in Glasgow and Nikki wasn't sure if she would ever leave her bed again. I'd gone to stay with her for a weekend, wanting to look after her. I'd liked Dave, but I've never forgiven him for leaving Nikki in pieces. While drunk and making plans for her future as a single girl, we'd planned a holiday to get away from all the shit.

I'd known the holiday was coming up – it was marked on my calendar and in my diary – but I'd become so preoccupied, I'd forgotten about organising euros, booking a bikini wax and asking for my sarongs back from Di. What was happening to me? I had to get a grip.

'So, you're okay if my parents drive us to the airport then?' she asked.

'Oh, yes of course, I'd love to see them. I'm sure Dad will pick us up after the holiday. I'll check and text you, is that alright?'

'Sure. So, any other news?'

'Oh yes, I have news and it'll take a whole seven days to tell you the tale, dissect it, spit it out and start again.'

Nikki chuckled. 'I can't wait.'

🌷

Dan was not so impressed with my holiday plans. He was happy for me, but he showed little interest when I filled him in about sizes of suitcases, the books I'd packed and what time Nikki's parents were picking me up. Amid our blooming romance,

I'd mentioned I was going away, but it always seemed weeks away, and thinking about time apart from him was something I didn't want to bring up.

'Christ, I need to see you before you go,' Dan said a few days later.

We were chatting on my lunch break and I was sat in an unappealing garden area near the city centre office tucked away at the back of St Aldates. There were three benches all dedicated to academics or researchers who had passed away, and I'd hit the jackpot: a bench all to myself. Normally, I'd be joined by colleagues or shouty local drug users on their way to the police station, the county court building, or the Tesco Express.

'I don't think we'll manage to meet up now, but I'll try to fit in with whatever you can do, you know that. I'll miss you while I'm away, but it's only seven days.'

'I know seven days doesn't sound like a long time, but in my world, with you in the middle of it, it's like a hundred years.'

'Same here. I'm sure you have enough horny memories to keep yourself occupied.'

He laughed. 'Oh don't, please don't say horny, not now. I won't be able to think of anything else. I've got to call a client in eighteen minutes.'

'If we were together, we could do so much in eighteen minutes.'

'I know…'

'What are you imagining? Doggy style?'

'Stop it.'

'How about going down on me in the back garden?'

'What are you trying to do to me?' he asked.

'Well, if I haven't turned you on, then I haven't done very well.'

'I'm changing the subject before I have to go off and have a wank. The joys of working at home, eh?'

I smiled. 'Okay.'

I peeled the last bit of my nectarine as Dan told me he'd made me a CD to take on holiday.

'You mean like a mixtape?'

'For god's sake, this is serious. I've made two CDs for you. One has some softer, acoustic stuff on it, basically a bit slower, and then the second CD has rockier, bluesy stuff. You'll love it.'

'I don't think anyone has ever made me a mixtape before.'

'It's not a tape. It's a CD.' He sighed. 'Do you have something to play it on? Like an iPod or something?'

Now it was my turn to be embarrassed – as the biggest Luddite of my peers, I didn't know how to get music onto these gadgets. The iPod my parents had bought me for Christmas a year ago was still in the box – if I wanted music, I just used my CD player. I made a mental note to ask one of my friends what to do, maybe Flint or Heidi.

'Yeah, sure.'

'Good, it's music that makes me think of you – you and me. Stuff I've listened to since we met, when I should have been working.'

'But were wanking instead?'

'Absolutely, now bugger off so I can go and finish the job.'

'Okay, love you. Have a lovely wank.'

I smiled to myself, staring into space, picturing Dan carrying out what I'd started. I sat smiling to myself for a few moments, until I sensed someone watching me. I turned around; leaning on the iron railings were two cheeky builders grinning in my direction. They were on their lunch break, drinking tea from a flask. One of the men raised his mug to me – a toast to the sex chat they'd been in earshot of.

CHAPTER 15

Are You My Boyfriend?

It was a bad day in the office.

We were so busy; our organised rota flew out the window before 10 a.m. and Jasmeet could be heard stomping around, the sound of her heels on the carpet a clear giveaway that she was in a shitty mood. She marched up and down the passageway interrupting interviews, gesturing with her made-up sign language. She favoured this way of communicating if there was an unnecessary queue: to alert us to any trouble looming or to inform us that we needed to hurry up and "go on your bloody lunch break".

One of our regular clients had been kicked out of her rented temporary accommodation with her baby. Reading the initial report, it was clear that the landlord was acting within the law, but understandably, she was a mess, and the situation she was in was a bigger mess. She would only deal with me, and as soon as I spotted her stumbling into the reception area wailing, I knew it was going to take most of the day to reassure her, calm her down and find her a place to go.

As soon as I became free, I took her and her baby into a

private interview room. The baby, called Tia, five months old, was crying her eyes out, and resembled a ready-to-burst glacier cherry.

'Meecha, you must feed her. Do you need to heat a bottle up?'

'No, I breastfeed most of the time, but I can't do it here.'

Meecha attempted to soothe Tia by rocking her. I couldn't stop looking at her pointy shamrock-green nails.

'Oh, please Meecha, how long have I known you? Anyway, I can't concentrate with Tia like this. I'll log onto this PC while you have a go.'

I manoeuvred the screen to give Meecha privacy. Tia began to whimper and wasn't latching on. I typed away and then a relieving silence joined us, followed by a quiet contented snuffle from Tia.

Meecha told me how things in her newly acquired flat were at the beginning. She was spending a lot of time alone with Tia and not with the group of destructive mates that were part of the cause of her bad luck. She was eighteen and I'd known her on and off for a year. We'd built up a strong professional relationship and I'd dedicated time charming numerous landlords to secure her a place to live. Eventually, one caved in and offered her a one-bed flat in a suitable area away from the friends that had distracted her. She wouldn't be lucky again – I couldn't keep bigging her up – but she had a reputation and landlords in Oxford talked. A lot. Meecha could be in trouble. I needed to know what went wrong.

I didn't mess about. 'Is it Mason?'

'What do you mean?' Meecha jutted her jaw out in defiance.

'Is he back?'

Meecha looked down at Tia, who was now fast asleep in her arms. Tears plopped onto the sleeping baby. Her nose twitched as a tear landed square onto it.

'Ah, I can't talk about him now, I can't wake her. Look, she's waking. Louise, what shall I do?' Meecha's voice went up a notch and was almost at screeching point.

'Here, let me take her while you talk, is that okay?'

She nodded and handed me Tia, who thankfully hadn't woken fully.

Meecha explained that Mason had returned to her and was on probation. He'd disrupted her nice, secure home, and told his probation officer he lived there. When he'd turned up, Meecha said no way, but as usual he won her over, and this time he had an additional string to his bow: Tia. He said he'd help with caring for her, offer money and buy Tia things she needed.

'He is her dad though, ain't he? He does love her; anyone can see that.' Meecha wiped her snot on her hand and continued. 'He started off okay, coming back with nappies, little bits and bobs, but I said I had to tell the council and Income Support. I didn't want to be in any trouble. He just kept saying no.'

'Meecha, you should have called me, or your social worker. Anyone.'

'Pah, not that old biddy, she hates me anyway. I'm trying not to call her these days. I could have tried you but I wanted to prove I could get rid of him, go it alone and that.'

'You can.'

'But I didn't, and then he'd go out after I put Tia to bed,

saying he was getting me a bar of chocolate and come back three hours later, stoned, with some geezers I didn't know and no pissing chocolate.'

'Well, that's not on,' I joked.

Meecha offered a flat smile and then tears started rolling down her cheeks. 'Louise, I love my little home, but he's trashed it, smashed holes in doors, he's broken the hob and only one ring works, he's hacked off my neighbours, who liked me at first. The lady next door made me and Tia a moving-in cake. It was coffee and walnut. Mason emptied her rubbish bin out in her garden because she asked him not to swear in front of her grandson. I've lost it all.'

I sat there, quiet. Bloody men. They really had a hold on us all. I'd still fight for Meecha and Tia, but first I'd lock horns with Mason's probation officer and then I'd tackle the landlord. I handed Tia back to her mum and explained the plan.

'If we do this, and I hope we can, I recommend you move away. If you can't do that, every time he contacts you or turns up, do not think of you, or him, but her.' I pointed at Tia. 'She is the priority, the priority of us all, and you can do this.'

'I don't know.'

'You can.'

'I just want to be loved by him. He's all I've wanted since I was fifteen. I'd wait for him to grow up, you know, if he'd ever get there, but you know what? I don't think he will. But I'd still wait for him, I'd wait years for him. I want him to love me. Pathetic, ain't I?'

'No,' I said, patting her arm. 'You aren't at all.'

Who would have thought: Meecha and I, leading the same

crappy love lives. We were both waiting for and wanting a man who would never deliver.

I sent Meecha off, not wanting her to just sit in our reception area stewing over her life choices, before calling the probation officer and asking for Mason to have restrictions on Meecha's address. I asked the old biddy social worker to cover the costs of the repairs as a one-off, and after a lot of nagging, she agreed. Finally, I drove to the landlord's office – he was a solicitor in Headington. Of course, he said a flat "no" to cancelling her notice to quit, but I showed him the evidence I'd collated that morning to demonstrate we were trying to help her. This was her last chance and I had faith she'd come good. He took his metal framed glasses off and placed them on the table, then walked over to a filing cabinet, pulled out a brown file and buzzed his secretary to come in.

'Tanya, could you retract the Section 21 issued to Ms Meecha Brown please. Could you also write to her confirming she is no longer under notice, but the next time I am forced to act in this way, I will not be forgiving etc etc...'

The whole time, he held my gaze.

I smiled at him. 'Thank you. I'll leave you in peace.' I stood up and added, 'I am going to speak to Meecha's neighbours and reassure them that things will be okay again. And once again, thank you.'

I shook his hand and he offered a firm reply.

'Well, life is somewhat perplexing sometimes, isn't it? These young kids get into all sorts of messes. I see it a lot. But I must say, with you in Ms Brown's corner, she could achieve better things.'

I sped to Meecha's house. The neighbour was frosty at first, but when I offered her my card in case of any future concerns, complete with a smile, it evened things out for her and we parted on amicable terms. I called the office and Meecha was there, having returned from moping about town. They put her onto the phone and I explained everything as I ran back to my wonkily parked work van. She didn't say a word except thank you, then hung up.

Emotionally drained and starving from having had no lunch, I returned to the quiet and now closed reception. Jasmeet was hovering – she wanted to lock up. When she spotted me, she put her chained glasses on and squinted at me as I walked past her desk.

'I've just dug out my sleeping bag.'

'Sorry, it's been a long one.'

'But it's all sorted, well done you. You can go home knowing you've helped.'

'I hope so.'

'You have helped. Look.'

She handed me a bit of A4 paper folded up, and there was something inside. It was a bar of Dairy Milk and a note from Meecha.

You were well shocked when I said Mason never gave me chocolate. I hope someone buys you chocolate often, cos you're great. And if he don't, he should. Here you are.

Love Meecha and Tia xxx

I'd nearly forgotten about my night out with the girls. I needed this: no Dan, and no talk of him. I wanted to do normal things, like nipping to the beer garden after work, even if it was early October, talking about the best new mascara while wearing scarves and fighting for the outside heaters.

I ambled into The Old Tom on St Aldates. I slid into a chair next to Di and hugged her, then all the other girls, one by one. I squeezed them tight; I wouldn't have my fix of my mates for seven days. I'd miss them. I'd miss Chrissy's bouncy hair and the fact she ironed her spinning towel. I'd miss the smell of Di. She used rich body creams I'd never heard of and always made me want to sniff her. And when Di signed off a text, voicemail, or phone call, she always said "love yah". I'd miss Heidi's thumping music blaring in her VW Golf, her pride and joy. I'd miss the chaos in her car, the carrier bags and the empty lunch boxes.

I'd miss everything about Flint. There was a lot to miss there.

Three pints in and the only sustenance consumed was dry roasted peanuts and some very posh salt and vinegar crisps. The current landlady of The Old Tom had recently vamped it up. There were polished tables and a chalkboard menu hanging from chains on the wall, detailing the specials. Behind the bar, carefully crafted bespoke shelves housed the spirits, and there were wine racks at either end like bookends; red wine at one end and white at the other.

The bricks of the interior walls were made visible everywhere, but above our table in the bay window, dated and distant beer mats covered the ceiling. I feared one would become unstuck and hit me on the head. We were lucky to nab this position, but it came with a minor snag; the landlady's dog, Tempo, was sat at our feet, sniffing for leftovers until she was discovered there and shooed away.

We left the pub to head off to the Malmaison. As big fans of the bar there, we also raved about the quirky drinks and furniture.

Dan had sent a few texts since I'd clocked off work. I wasn't going to be one of those girls that dumped their friends to fluff his ego, so I wasn't replying with any speed, but he was nosy and persistent.

```
Where are you?
Is it busy?
Who are you out with?
Are you eating?
```

My reply was fuelled by booze and bluntness.

```
                    Can't chat now, off to
                             Malmaison XX
```

We caused a fair amount of annoyance to the staff in this posh boutique hotel. We sat downstairs at first in the bar area, making a bit of noise. After a few grumpy stares from the staff, we relocated to the games room lounge. It reminded me of a gentleman's smoking room in a period drama. Somewhere, Mrs Peacock would be flirting with Professor Plum. The carpet was a blue and mustard tartan pattern, and the lighting was dim, luring us in. The limited illumination came in the form of tin flowerpots, dangling from the ceiling like little bungee jumpers, and two large Cadbury-purple lampshades high up on the ceiling.

I noticed a billiard table surrounded by a group of men in formal gear, playing and chatting. Most of their ties were undone, their sleeves rolled up; they meant business. Chrissy waited at the cocktail bar. The male staff member was leaning over, not assembling drinks but focusing on her and a brunette seductively twirling her hair around her finger as she talked.

Di and I sat on a leather multicoloured Chesterton sofa, talking about a garden project she had on her mind that she couldn't afford.

No one had used the lift since we got out of it, and about thirty minutes later, when it made its little ding sound and the doors opened, I glanced up.

Dan walked out.

My friends shrieked and Chrissy ran over to him like he was a superstar. He grinned with an awkward grimace and followed her as she draped herself over him.

'What a surprise *you* are! Louise, look!'

Cue more oohing and aahing aimed at Dan and his "declaration of love", as Di called it.

'Have you come to collect her and take her away?' Di asked, beaming and nudging me in the ribs.

I scoffed. 'Where to? The asylum?'

'Oh come on,' she replied, splaying her palms.

'Yeah, but anyone would think this is that scene from *Officer and a Gentleman*. He isn't going to carry me out and put a hat on me, just so you know.'

Dan winked at me. He took it all in his stride, sitting and smiling as the women around him bigged him up. I thought I even caught Heidi smiling.

Eventually, they let us be, squeezed into one of the more intimate booths in a corner of the lounge. We sat facing each other on the same side of the table. I could smell his soft aftershave and noticed his eyes were shining. I didn't know what to say after his entrance; how could I? This was love, in my book. A small gesture maybe, but he'd planned this surprise with the best he had, and I loved him for it. It wasn't a weekend in Brighton with a hot tub, nor was it the announcement he was leaving his wife, but he was thinking of me when I didn't know he was. That was monumental.

Dan explained that ever since he knew about my holiday, he'd been planning an escape. He earned escape points at home, said he was meeting some old work colleagues for a pint, and all was good.

I looked into his eyes as he stroked my cheek.

'I couldn't stand not seeing you,' he said. 'It was killing me.'

I shifted my gaze away from his. Of course I'd miss him while I was gone, but when was he going to say something positive about my holiday? I certainly needed a break and had worked hard for it; where was his "hope you have a nice trip" or "you deserve a week in the sun"? I'd love to go away with *him*, but when was that going to happen?

'Shit, the other reason,' he said, his cheeks flushed as he took something out of his jacket pocket. 'Now, don't laugh, but here are the CDs. I wanted you to have them before you went on holiday.'

I placed my forehead against his. 'You are getting better and better. What the hell am I going to do with you?'

'Your place, now?'

I stood up, tilting my head towards the lift before making my way over.

He followed.

As soon as the doors closed, I shoved Dan against the wall, kissing him greedily and whispering drunk silliness in his ear. Dan's deep laugh echoed in the metal box as the lift completed its one-floor journey.

We hunted down a taxi, sitting side by side as I stroked his thigh. He smiled as he looked out the window, fidgeting with his jeans.

I couldn't wait to get him inside, but failed spectacularly at opening my own front door. Dan lifted the hair from my neck and kissed my flushed skin. The warmth from his mouth made me to drop the key and I gave in. Instead, we kissed and moaned on my doorstep, with Bennett meowing at us to let him inside. Our kissing intensified, and Dan pushed me with his hips. I was fixed to the spot. My head butted the doorbell.

We jumped, I screamed, and Dan picked up the key to go inside.

We didn't get far, quickly accepting that sex would be on the stairs. Afterwards, we hung out in my bedroom, listening to the CDs Dan had made me. I was forced to admit my lack of technical confidence while Dan transferred the tracks onto my iPod. Watching him, hoping to learn a thing or two, I sat in silence.

Dan asked if I was okay.

I filled him in on my day and he sat with me, watching me intently. He was kind to me; he didn't speak, but when I told him the bit about Meecha saying she'd wait for Mason, he looked down at our hands, which were now entwined.

'I wish you'd told me earlier; I was going on and on about missing you. You should've called me after work.'

'I don't know what you could've done. I wanted to switch off, I guess.'

'But I'm here for you. I want to be, you know that, right?'

I nodded, sucking on my lower lip.

'I never knew your job could be this hard; this draining.'

I nodded again.

'You're an incredible human being. Wise, brave and way stronger than I am. I'm proud to be with you.'

I sobbed a little, not caring that he was seeing the real me. I wept for me, for Meecha and for baby Tia.

'Come here.'

We lay next to each other and he stroked my hair. I didn't feel brave or strong, and certainly not wise.

'I'll miss this,' I mumbled.

'Me too. I want to take care of you, but I keep having these thoughts that you won't come back.'

'Why? I have to come back; I've got a cat to feed.'

'Haha.' Dan coughed and then added, 'You won't sleep with a Spanish hunk, will you?'

'Is hunk back in?'

'I'm serious. I'll worry all week that you'll realise I'm a waste of time.'

'Hey, that's my boyfriend you're talking about.'

He sat upright and looked me straight in the eye, not hiding the alarm in his expression. 'Am I your boyfriend?'

Um. I thought so. We'd eaten Revels off each other's bellies, guessing the flavours; wasn't all that enough?

'Clearly not.'

Dan frowned at me.

Hot tears burnt as they escaped, my voice cracking. 'I didn't think I needed to ask your permission.'

Dan was fiddling with his wedding band.

Suddenly, I didn't want to be near him anymore. This was too much. The man I'd started to think about having kids with was with another woman. How stupid was I to think I could call him anything? I didn't have that right.

I paced my bedroom while Dan stared deep into space. He was so beautiful. In his head he'd planned a romantic spontaneous night, something I'd more than hinted that I'd wanted, and now I'd trampled all over it and waved the boyfriend word about. The exhaustion of my day and acknowledging the true level of intimacy we shared was crushing me.

'Can you come here?' He gestured for me to sit next to him.

Blowing my nose, I joined him.

'Look, I'm sorry, okay? I am your boyfriend, and I love it. It was just a shock to hear the word after all these years. I haven't been anyone's boyfriend since the 90s.'

I couldn't help but smile.

'I may even have pants from that era, but I didn't think you minded.' He nudged my shoulders with his. 'That's better. I hated seeing you so sad a minute ago, even though it's my fault. Do you get why I was shocked?'

'Yeah, sure. I mean, how can you be a husband, a dad and a boyfriend?'

'Yeah, but it's a massive compliment to be your boyfriend.'

I wanted to cry more with him. I wanted to tell him I desired a future, kids, him – forever. All I wanted was for him to tell me everything was going to be okay. That's what boyfriends did, wasn't it? They didn't develop an eye twitch when you uttered the word "boyfriend". Decent men took care of their girlfriends. The name, the label, or whatever the fuck it was, was immaterial. He could say he was my boyfriend a million times over and we would both know it was bullshit.

He was a spouse, and not mine.

'I don't know what to say,' I replied.

He looked at me, and I knew what he was thinking; the rest of me was too tired to care. I was shrinking and taking my dignity with me.

CHAPTER 16

Listen to Your Elders

The next evening at 7 p.m., I was sitting by the pool with Nikki in my swimming costume, Mai Tai firmly in hand. We were watching the last few minutes of a hilarious water aerobics class. Nikki and I laughed at the teacher and his very revealing shorts. The ladies were all smiles, sticking out their boobs and barely getting any of the moves right at all.

Yesterday had been a headfuck day and yet I'd escaped it all, relaxing in another time zone, breathing unusual air and listening to incomprehensible chatter. This was Majorca, and although it was October, it was warm enough to brave the pool; Nikki and I planned on spending a lot of time swimming in the clear, turquoise waters we'd seen nearby.

Our journey had been sweltering and exhausting, not to mention my sexual hangover. Dan and I had been awake the night before until dawn, shoehorning in as much sex as possible. As I'd waited for Nikki to pick me up, I'd received a text from him.

```
You've made my head feel like
one of those fizzy headache
```

```
tablets, my limbs feel like
my bones have been removed,
and don't get me started on my
actual boner.

              I can't move, I ache all
         over. I have sex stiffness.

I don't think I've made anyone
have that before.
I don't want to have a shower.
I can smell you in my beard.
```

I'd wanted to hit the sack early, but Nikki had zero sympathy for me and proceeded to natter for England. As we'd waited for our luggage, I'd told her I would be going to bed early.

'No, no, no, no. First up, we'll have a shower, check out the pool and then have dinner.'

I didn't have the energy to argue with her. Nikki was just like her mum, my Aunty Anne, only without the blue mascara.

We'd arrived at our stunning hotel at around 3 p.m., hot and bothered. There was a lot of huffing and puffing. Our apartment was on the fifth floor and although we were missing the sea view I'd longed for, we had a direct view of the pool, and if we leant over the corner of our balcony, we could just about spot the waves.

'Ah, this is the life,' said Nikki, stretching her arms above her head. She lay flat on a sun lounger and grinned into the sky.

'Damn right,' I replied.

'Remember when we booked this holiday and everything was a mess for me?'

'Yep.'

'You'd come to stay with me that weekend and I didn't even let you take your coat off when you arrived. I dragged you straight to the pub.'

'I know, I couldn't keep up with you. I remember texting Flint, giving him the heads up to feed Bennett as I might never make it home in one piece!'

'Good ole Flint. Do you remember busting me?'

After a boozy afternoon, we'd stumbled back to Nikki's flat. She'd gone straight onto her laptop while I sorted the takeaway out. I'd snooped at the screen when she'd gone to the toilet, and she'd typed into the search engine "train tickets to Glasgow". I'd asked her what she was planning.

'I'm gonna get a train to Glasgow and pour beer over Dave's head and come straight home.'

Don't get me wrong, I'd have laughed a lot seeing it in action, but she had needed telling off, so we'd called Flint for drunken reasoning.

The days that followed our first day at the pool were blissful. We read books, talked about them, ate scrumptious food, sampled all the drinks we fancied on the menu, and I remembered what a laugh Nikki was – batty and fun. In my current state of mind, though, I was worried I wasn't on top form. There was something off with me.

'I haven't noticed really,' Nikki said when I asked her, as we prepared for another day swimming in the crystal waters.

She had her suitcase laid out on the bed in the hotel room and was throwing items of clothing out of it, searching for her missing bikini top.

'Thank god for that.'

'I know Dan is a big thing in your life, and you need a few days to relax a bit. It's like that with holidays.'

Later, on the beach, we took some time away from the high sun and slurped slices of melon under a parasol. Nikki thanked me for coming away and I pointed out how much better she was these days, even without Dave.

'I didn't know I needed this holiday,' she said.

'I know. I needed a break too, not just from the Dan mess, but from everyone else.'

That's what I loved about Nikki and our relationship: there were no judgements. We were both strong-minded and always voiced our views, but I had to confess, I was enjoying a break from Chrissy's disapproving eye glances, Heidi's bad mouthing and Flint's bluntness. Instead, Nikki was chipper for me, and when my phone bleeped with a text from Dan, she did little claps or hugged me. I'd set one rule while away and I was determined to stick to it. My phone was to stay off – I had made it clear to Dan (and my mum) that I couldn't afford to use my phone in Spain for chatting – but I'd agreed to switch it on once a day to text them.

One afternoon, we visited a local market, mooched about the jewellery stalls, pissing off the owners by trying on and not buying much. We sent postcards to our parents, swapping the addresses over. It seemed hilarious three or four bottles of Estrella in, writing them on the balcony of our apartment before dinner one night.

We also signed up for a boat trip around the bay of Alcudia and were the youngest on board by far. We made all the senior citizens laugh with our tales of modern living, as we sailed out on the placid sea for an hour, stopping for a swim. Entering the warm crystal sea offered a welcome escape from the captain and his euro-trash tunes.

When we arrived at the secluded beach, the destination of the boat trip, we couldn't dock there, so we swam the short distance, floating to the shore on our backs. I glanced over at Nikki as I admired the startlingly blue cloud-free sky, and I noticed something – the worries and stresses I'd arrived with were leaving me. I found myself smiling into the sky and realised that this was happiness; this was me.

I could be happy without Dan.

The captain and the other staff began to hand out lunch, Nikki and I helping them to wait on the oldies. When everyone had what they wanted, we sat on the sand, chatting about our home lives. I wasn't sure if it was the exercise or the sea air making me so ravenous, but my god, everything tasted so good. My usual M&S prawn sandwich could not compete.

I adored chatting to these older people; they were all so wise and free of the insecurities that I carried. The men were a little flirty and silly, and the women were sharp and witty, whilst also being motherly. I was especially drawn to Elsie and May. They were with their husbands, and when their men went off swimming, Nikki followed them into the sea, challenging them to a race. I feared I'd drown from the weight of my lunch, so I remained with my new friends, looking out at the view and getting to know them for a bit longer.

As we chatted, I spotted some parasailers drifting overhead, their voices clear to me, even from the sky.

The ladies were telling me about their grandchildren, who

were near my age. They had a mixture of girls and boys between them, and they agreed the boys were fun, and the girls were a headache. I spoke about our nan, who'd died five years before. She'd also been keen swimmer – it was a family trait – and she would have been so thrilled to see us enjoying ourselves, together, without any men.

Elsie asked me if I had a fella. I grimaced; I wasn't sure I wanted to share Dan with them. Would they judge me? Possibly. My nan would have. I imagined her dark green eyes that I'd inherited, looking at me as she paused, making me a cup of tea in her kitchen. Turning to face me, her expression full of questions. Wondering about this man, Dan, and what he would bring to the table.

'Oh, you don't need to tell me, love. Sorry, that was nosy of me,' Elsie said as she patted my hand.

'Oh, not at all. I wasn't pulling that face because I don't want to talk about Dan. I guess you could say he comes with some troubles.'

'Oh, there's the start of a story if ever I heard one,' May said, her interest cranked up a notch. She smiled. 'I had one like that, he was a naughty one.'

'Well, mine is a naughty one too.'

'All fur-coat-and-no-knickers type of chap,' May added, her eyes shining.

The ladies laughed and I joined them, though I didn't really get her point.

'She means, is this Dan all style and no substance?'

'Ah, I see. No, nothing like that, that would be too simple.'

'Most men are,' May concluded.

We chuckled and I told them the whole story, anxiously awaiting their verdict. In their seventies, they reminded me of my nan and suddenly I craved their wise approval, not their disappointment with me and my bad choices.

'So, you see ladies, I've some decisions to make,' I concluded.

'You do,' said Elsie. 'Do you want children? Will you wait for him? Can you see anyone else matching him?'

'Those are the sorts of things I'm trying to figure out.'

'I think another chap will come by and swish you away. Pretty thing like you. Your smile is there for a good reason,' May said, grinning.

'The thing is, I don't think I want to be swished away yet, and I'm shocked I feel like that, to be honest.' I paused. 'I've even thought about forfeiting my chance to have my own children, if it meant I could have him.'

'And be a stepmum?' May asked.

'Yeah, I guess.'

May shook her head. 'No, you don't want to do that.'

'It's a tricky one, but it sounds as if he's got you good and proper,' Elsie said, tutting, adjusting her boobs in her dandelion swimming costume.

We talked a bit longer about options, divorce and houses. They told me a story about their friend, Marg, who'd separated from her first husband and married her divorce lawyer.

I noticed we were alone on the beach. Everyone else was swimming.

May got up and took her sunglasses off. 'I'm heading in. Come on, we can't waste swimming time. If I were you, I'd go back to Oxford, suntanned, smiley and all seductive.' She shimmied as she said "seductive". 'Give that chap of yours an ultimatum. It's me, now or never. See how quick he snaps you up.'

She grasped my hands and I offered her a weak smile. I sensed Elsie had more to say as she attempted to get up. She was a little more unstable than her friend.

I helped her steady herself as we walked towards the sea.

'I wouldn't listen too much to her, duck. There isn't a year that goes by she doesn't mention that ex of hers. I think she's forgotten him, then every now and then, he pops up again. Sometimes I think she's a little doolally, but she told me the full story when I met her over forty years ago. Do you want to hear it?'

I nodded.

'Tommy was her best friend's husband, you see, and they had a fling. Caused a terrible mess, all the families were dragged in. She was single, he was married. They were only kids, about twenty years old. Everyone called her the tart of the town.' Elsie rolled her eyes and shook her head. 'Tommy made plans to run away with her, to escape the gossip, so she packed her bags and waited for him at the back of the butchers, but he never came. She lugged her suitcase back home in the snow and prayed her parents didn't notice. The ratbag never spoke to her after that. Broke her in two, she said. But he moved away with the family, his wife and the kiddies. Who knows where he is now. In the gutter, I hope. She loves her Paddy, I know that, but she always talks about that naughty Tommy. I've often wondered why she thinks about him and mentions him. I'm not sure she ever got over what he did.'

Elsie and I reached the sea and she turned to face me.

'What I'm trying to say is, you'll meet someone else, and this bloke will be your naughty boy. We all have them, but we must forget them. There's not a happy life with a naughty boy. And remember, he'll always be a cheater. He started you and him off being a cheater. And I promise, that will eat you up.'

Elsie's deep brown eyes were tender as she met my gaze. I spotted a little mole on her cheekbone. This scratchy, flustered feeling she'd left with me wasn't intentional, but it lingered all the same. Lucky for me, the vivid sunshine masked my expression of anguish. There was a jet ski in the distance, getting closer, snapping our silence.

'When you see him, you tell him this: "You can't have me now, but in another life, you can have the whole of me, for your whole life". Just see what that does.'

I blinked back the emotion and took Elsie's arm.

'Now, come on, get yourself in this lovely sea,' she said, gesturing at the beauty before us.

As she began to wade in, I remained at the edge of the sea for a minute to calm myself. I stared into the aquamarine water and waited for a few rounds of gentle waves to pass in the distance. I chewed the ends of my sunglasses, wiping the tears with the back of my hand. Elsie was wise, and absolutely spot on.

CHAPTER 17

Payphones and White Bits

Day four of Spain.

We'd been by the pool, watching the water polo match in the glorious sunshine. We'd ordered cocktails that arrived in coconut shells, then after lunch with a beer, I'd nodded off midway through a conversation. Nikki informed me of this after my shower later that evening.

I listened to her singing as a text came through from Dan.

```
Can you call me tonight?
```

It was unusually short.

```
            Is everything okay? I
    can't call from my mobile,
                    remember?
```

The text sat pending.

What was up? Despite feeling unsettled, Nikki and I went for dinner as planned, but I took my phone out with me and left it switched on.

Pink-faced diners, grumpy from hunger and too much

sun, paced from buffet cart to table, their plates over-filled in my opinion. There was limited conversation, just serious food selection – especially in the paella queue I was in. I'd plated up mine on a dish the size of a small dustbin lid when Dan texted me.

```
Can you get a phonecard and go
to a box? I'll pay you when
you get home. Please?
```

'Everything okay, Lou?' Nikki asked, squeezing lemon all over her plate.

'Hmm. Not sure, Dan wants me to call him.'

'That's okay, we can go for a walk after dinner and buy those phonecard things. I'll call my mum.'

I blushed, embarrassed. 'I think he wants me to call him now. Something's up. I'm sorry. I'll eat mine later.' I packed up my bag, unable to look her in the eye as I prepared to leave her at the table alone.

She placed her hand on my arm. 'Would you like me to come? Shall I get this in a doggy bag?'

I smiled at her practical support. Food was a priority – another family trait.

'I'll be fine.' I kissed her on the cheek and made my way to the reception to buy the phonecard.

I was forced to spend ten quid – they didn't sell them in smaller denominations. I hoped this call was worth it as I leant against the wall next to the phone booth, texting him.

```
              I'm calling now. Please pick
                                        up.
```

He picked up after one ring.

'Thank god you called.' His breath was heavy down the phone. 'Thank you so much, you've no idea how happy I am to hear from you. Oh, and hi by the way!' He laughed.

'Are you okay?'

'Yeah, I am now, so happy to hear your voice. So, how's Spain? It's pissing it down here and I've spent most of the afternoon daydreaming about you and me going skinny dipping. I've never done that, have you?'

I think he'd have maintained this sunny, relaxed dialogue had I not interrupted him.

'Have you asked me to call you just to chat?' I asked, irritation building up within me. How dare he interrupt my holiday with my cousin like this?

'Yeah, is that alright?'

'No, not really,' I said, my voice laced with anger. My heart was pounding; my free hand had formed a fist.

'How come?'

'You worried me! I thought it was urgent, like Melissa had found out about us, or the kids had guessed, or you'd left home or something.' I wouldn't have sped off and left Nikki all alone like that just for a chat.

'God no!' Dan laughed, then cut the laugh short, like I'd said the most absurd thing to him.

I couldn't believe he was laughing at this.

'I left my cousin in the restaurant on her own. I didn't eat my dinner, I had to buy a phonecard that I don't have the money for, I walked around the streets looking for a sodding phone box, worried sick, and all because you wanted to chat!'

There was a silence on the line.

'Don't you think that's a little off?' I asked.

'Not impulsive and romantic? You said you wished we could be more like that.'

'Yeah, but this is at my expense, and I don't just mean the cash. I dropped everything because you worried me, but it turns out you just had an opening for romantic twaddle.'

I took a deep breath to try to calm myself down. He thought he was being romantic, which *was* what I'd asked for... I just didn't necessarily mean while I was on holiday with my cousin.

'So, I take it you're alone in the house right now?'

'Yes, and did you just say twaddle?'

I didn't answer. The cash it had taken to make the call continued to evaporate fast before my eyes. I had £7.40 left.

I broke the silence. 'Look, I don't want to fight. You scared me, that's all. Plus, I had a teeny tiny hopeful thought on my way walking here that maybe you'd left her, and do you know how happy that made me?'

'And now you aren't because I haven't?' he replied.

'Well, yeah.'

More silence.

'I love you, Louise.'

'I love you too.'

'I'm sorry I fucked up. Look, I'll hang up. I can't do anything right. We'll chat when you get back.'

'No, don't.' I sighed. 'Let's at least spend the £6.10 I have remaining on making up. Quick, say something funny.'

It took a few quid, but we eased into something less spiky. I talked about my holiday, and he told me about a work project. I did manage to wrench one laugh out of him when I relayed a tale of Nikki having to go topless since she'd lost her only bikini top on day two.

'We have a quid left.'

'I doubt you'll say yes, but can we speak before you fly back, please?'

'Course, how about Thursday, two days away. Can you cope?'

'Nope, but I'll text you tomorrow. That'll have to do. Look, before you go, can you go back and play the CD I made you? Start with track four. I'll do the same. It'll be like we're in the same room or something.'

'Okay. Will do.'

There was a bleeping sound – a countdown. We had seconds left.

'I can't believe how much I miss you,' he said.

The line went dead.

Arriving back the hotel, I took a sneaky look at Nikki, perched on a stool at the bar by the pool, chatting to the staff. She was laughing and flicking her hair. She was happy. I thought about Dan's request. It might be wonderful to be alone; to play the track in my room knowing he'd be doing the same. I could even text him while the track was playing. That'd be romantic.

But I wanted to be happy, like Nikki.

I walked up to Nikki at the bar, plonked myself down and vowed to spend the rest of the evening chuckling, drinking wine and not giving Dan a second thought. And I did.

Sometime after 1 a.m., Nikki and I staggered to our room. Shattered from dancing barefooted to Spanish hits we didn't recognise, we lay on our beds, unable to move. Nikki started wiping her face with a wet wipe.

'You know, Lou, don't let that Dan break you. I know you're stronger than that.'

I nodded as I locked the door of the bathroom, intending to clean my teeth. Instead, I sat on the edge of the bath and cried over the crack in my heart.

Once we arrived home a few days later, I had to pick myself up and get on.

There was a thirtieth birthday party in town and, despite my exhaustion, I dragged my tired arse out to meet Di and Chrissy in the pub, only intending to stay out for a few hours. I had no plans to see Dan, but we'd spoken that afternoon, mainly about my white bits.

'Well, I hope you get to inspect them before they fade,' I said.

'Me too.' He sounded flat and not at all like he wanted to inspect anything of mine.

'Are you sure you're okay? You don't sound very chirpy.'

'Yeah, I'm alright.'

'Well, please perk up or I won't give you your Spanish holiday gift.'

'I'm okay, I just missed you and I'm learning to accept holidays without me are part of your life. Please tell me it isn't a fridge magnet?'

I banished Dan from my mind and tried to match everyone's high spirits in the pub. Chrissy, Di and I were gossiping about the week; so much had happened.

Chrissy had been given a promotion for a year and Di was offering free massages at the Town Hall next week. Di was mixed up in a publicity event to sell good living, and lots of alternative medicine types were selling their wares.

'Terrific, I could do with one of those,' I said.

'Can't Dan assist?' asked Chrissy, winking.

I filled them in on his moodiness, the phonecard fiasco and how it made me feel.

'You haven't been yourself tonight,' Di said as she put her arm around me. 'I'm sure he'll be back to normal when he sees your tan.'

Chrissy remained silent, straw in mouth, staring at us.

'What?' I asked.

She took the straw away. 'Do you think it's getting too much for him? Maybe his wife is suspecting something?'

I shrugged. It was possible.

Around 9 p.m., I was done. I wanted to call Flint and Heidi from my bed, with tea and Dairy Milk. Sat in the back of the taxi, my mobile buzzed. It was Chrissy.

'Hello!' she shouted.

'What have I forgotten?'

'Nothing, someone wants to talk to you.' The pub noise bled into my ear. I pulled the phone away. Chrissy's cackle stopped and another voice spoke to me.

'Where are you?'

It was Dan.

'In a taxi.'

'Get that fantastic arse back here.'

He hung up.

'Excuse me, could you go back into town please?' I asked the taxi driver.

He mumbled as we went back around the roundabout, quite understandably hacked off, and spent most of the journey muttering at me.

I sighed, looking out of the window, watching the journey I'd just taken in reverse. Back I went, to meet Dan. It seemed he wanted to plonk romance in front of me and I didn't get a choice. It wasn't just the taxi that was going backwards; my relationship with Dan was hardly moving forward, except when he whipped out the impromptu romantic gestures.

Outside the pub, Dan waved as I pulled up. He paid the driver and thanked him for returning his girlfriend.

'Hi,' I said, looking up at him.

'Hey you. Looking hot,' he replied.

'Thanks.'

He kissed me deeply. 'I missed doing that. Let's go inside, I need a beer. I want to show you off.'

'I've already shown myself off, thanks.'

He took my hand and started to walk inside. When I resisted, he stopped and turned around.

'What's up?'

'Look, I wasn't planning on a late night. I'm tired and want to go home.'

Dan kissed the top of my head. 'Whatever you like. Just

one, then? I can't stop looking at your face, you've got new freckles.'

We went back in. Dan was bright and chatty, but I was feeble and felt pulled in a direction I didn't want to go. Dan was a tryer, alright. Quips galore, smiles and yarns for everyone. By 10:45 p.m., and near to crawling home, I was temporarily stunned away from my exhaustion when I noticed his wedding band was not there.

'Where's your ring?'

He looked down to his hand. 'I took it off. I thought you'd like that.' He smiled down at me.

'Why would I like that?'

He moved me away from the group. 'Well, we're out with friends of yours. It's not that I'm trying to impress Chrissy or Di, but I thought... well, I thought you might appreciate me taking my ring off.'

'But why? Plus you have a tan line underneath, and that gives away quite a lot, don't you think?'

Dan rolled his eyes. 'Blimey, I can't get anything right.'

'What's that supposed to mean?'

'I mean, anything I do with anyone these days is wrong. I hoped I could mainly get stuff right with you, though.'

We stared at each other. He was talking about pleasing Melissa and me at the same time, and what man could? That wasn't within the template of married life and it sure wasn't covered in the wedding vows.

'Shall we go home?' he asked.

I walked off to find my friends and say goodbye. Chrissy frowned at me as I picked up my jacket and waved farewell.

For the first time since we'd met, Dan walked by my side in silence and with the absence of touch. I'd pissed him off. The feeling was completely mutual.

I relented and took his hand. He squeezed mine back and I stopped walking and stared at my trainers. He turned back to look at me and we both smiled, a little too unconvincingly.

The night had a whiff of freshly lit fires floating around, a smell that meant Bonfire Night would soon be here. Dan and I kept our coats done up as we sat in my back garden, with mugs of tea and my Dairy Milk for company. Our breath crystalised in the air in front of us as we attempted normality, but it was anything but. We didn't mention the wedding ring conversation, but the undercurrents were there, like another person at the table we hadn't invited.

'While you were away, I realised I hadn't told you something.'

'What was that?' I asked, picking at a flake of wood that was slowly detaching itself from my table.

'When we first met, as soon as I saw you, I knew I needed to talk to you; that our meeting wasn't some accident. We were meant to meet that night.'

'Agreed.'

'I thought you might think I was a nutter if I told you that.'

'Hardly. The reason we met isn't clear, far from it, but there must be a point to it all.'

'To fuck up our lives?'

'Exactly.' I shivered and went to grab a blanket from inside.

We sat for a moment in silence, before Dan came around to my side of the table and leaned his head on my shoulder.

'You know,' I said softly, 'my nan told me once: "we're always the best version of ourselves when we're loved by someone, especially someone we want to love us".'

Dan looked up and stared at me. He didn't speak. I shifted my gaze away, feeling myself blush in the dark.

'Wise women must run in the family. You understand everything.'

'What do you mean?'

'I don't think I've met anyone like you, you feel stuff and say it.'

'I'm a woman.'

'You know what I mean.'

'It's not a bad thing, is it?'

He secured his arm around my shoulders. 'No, it makes us fit.'

I offered him a withering look, attempting to swallow the grit in my throat. 'Talking to you is like talking to a girl anyway.'

He ruffled my hair and I snuggled into him.

'I've never been so happy, you know that, right?' I murmured. 'I know we were arsy earlier, but couples row and move on.'

'Course they do, and when did we row anyway?' He tickled underneath my arm.

'Stop it.' I wriggled away from him. 'I don't want this good stuff to ever end. Even though I've started to think lately that I know it will end.'

'Eh?'

'It will. I'm trying to prepare us for that.'

'Why, do you know something I don't?'

'Just that these days, I'm thinking about life without you, because that's more sensible and likely. But I feel sick at the idea of it. Unless...' I took a deep breath. I was going to go for it.

'Unless?' Dan repeated.

'We could make a plan.'

'Tell me more.'

'Do you think that if we're together in, say, a year or so, like this, could we change it?'

'Like how?'

'Could we think about your family life, how the kids are and discuss you splitting up?'

'That's a hell of a plan.'

'It's been on my mind; I don't know if I can do this forever.'

'I know, and by the way, ending my marriage is something I think about a lot.'

'Do you?'

'Yeah. It's been discussed, just not carried out.' Dan took a deep breath. 'Please don't think I don't imagine a life with you, at this house, and what that would be like. I mean, it'd be such a happy place and I want that. When I met you, I felt so much in one night but didn't think past the first kiss, the first date, and it went on. But, when you were away, I thought about our future too.'

'Do you want to end it?'

'I thought about how I'd cope, and it isn't something I can do. I can't end it with you, ever.'

'So we carry on?'

'Yeah. Listen, how about, if we make it to a year together, I move out? We can do that. You'll help me, won't you?'

I smiled at him. 'Well, I am quite the master at unpacking.'

'You know what I mean, the heavy stuff, the kids, the divorce.'

'I'll always have your back.'

We sat outside until midnight. Dan wasn't able to stay over, so he called a cab.

'You know, when I say I'm off home... can I tell you something?'

I nodded.

'This is crap, but I'm more at home here, with you, than at my home. Especially after that chat. That makes me a horrible dad, right? My home should be with the kids, but I don't feel right there anymore.'

What could I add to that? I wanted him to move in here – fuck the family home, we'd sort all that out. Melissa's heart might be shattered, and the family routine would need readjusting, but in time, it would all sort itself out. Melissa might want to slap me in the face at first, or she might see him leaving as the best option. Remaining with a partner with no mutual love was surely preventing one or both of them from living a happier life with someone they preferred. There was nothing wrong with that, surely?

Except that, as I was discovering, none of that was on the cards yet.

Could I realistically wait another eight months?

CHAPTER 18

Man Maths

Life passed routinely into November, and I started to understand and come to terms with the straightforward facts: despite my desperate need to cling onto the promise we'd made together, Dan and I were drifting towards the edge of a cliff.

Even our phone calls were dwindling. The conversations were the same as always, and I still felt everything for him, but chatting was all we had. I hadn't seen him in two weeks, and no dates were pencilled in. There was no tangible reason why, but I could sense there was something big going on.

I noticed his lack of urgency to spend time with me. His desperation to know me was vanishing before my eyes. There was a definite withdrawal at his end, but I dared not face it, let alone speak to him about it. If I vocalised my worries, they'd materialise into reality, and I wasn't ready for that. I couldn't fathom a life without Dan in it.

During our phone calls, I'd find myself closing my eyes, hoping he'd announce a plan to visit me or the promise of something – *anything*. But he always left me with nothing, just the monotone ringing that signalled he'd hung up.

I was frustrated that we weren't moving forward. Did I not deserve a bit more of him now? Of course not, I would constantly remind myself. He was married, and I had no right to ask him for any more of himself then he was offering me, even if it was just leftover scraps.

I attempted to throw myself into work, without any luck, and upped the exercise. The girls and I attended Groove FX aerobics classes, attempted running and swam a lot. We tried a circuit training class in the diving pool, wearing little life jackets and these silly flipper things. It was a tough class, once a week. We were in fits of laughter at not only how foolish we looked, but how impossible the class was. For those hours, when I sweated and giggled with my friends, I was simply Louise, accomplishing abundant laughing episodes that brought tears of joy.

Yet, the moment I arrived home, unpacking my swimming costume, towel and goggles all alone, the euphoria subsided, and I was left feeling like half of me was missing. It wasn't enough for me right now, and it never would be.

I wanted a messy house, with kids' toys everywhere, scribbles on the walls, the racket of cartoons on the TV while I cooked for my family in the kitchen, condensation gathering on the kitchen window. I wanted a weary husband to come in through the door, offer me a familiar, loving, meaningful smile before entertaining our children. I wanted chaotic Easter egg hunts and Christmas mornings and adults fuelled by caffeine. I wanted to look at a child who resembled me but, when she slept, she looked like her dad. I wanted a child of my own, one that resembled Dan.

My friends didn't ask much about Dan anymore. I think they were anticipating the finale, the dramatic picking-up of the pieces they'd often mentioned. I imagined them talking about me, and pictured them almost ready on the starting blocks in a one-hundred-metre sprint race. They were equipped, alright; they'd been making plans to mop up the mess right from the start.

Flint called a few days later, interrupting me making a "for and against" list for remaining with Dan.

'Isn't that a bit tragic? I can't believe a clever girl like you needs to write all that shit down. The mathematical sum is quite simple. Man + wife + marriage + kids + mistress = total fuck up. Anyway, I called to ask if I could borrow your cat box, please?'

Flint was getting a cat with Jeannie. I couldn't help feeling a little jealous. They weren't even living together – not yet, anyway – but Flint loved her and she wanted a kitten, so he had produced a kitten. It was doubtful I'd even get a Christmas card from Dan.

When Flint arrived to pick up the cat box, I assumed Jeannie would be with him, but I opened the door to just Flint, standing alone. He was beaming and giddy.

'Where's Jeannie?' I asked, watching him head straight for my living room.

'I'm surprising her. She thinks the kitten is arriving tomorrow, but I'm collecting him now.' He crossed his arms. 'Am I cute or what?'

'Yes, you are,' I said, hugging him.

Flint was a good boyfriend, and he should have known

that. I'd seen all the evidence. Yet, I couldn't praise him. It felt strange, looking at his proud-as-punch face, knowing it was because of something he'd done for another woman.

I recognised my jealousy. Flint had someone; I didn't.

Sure, I liked Jeannie, but there was something not right about her – for Flint, I mean. Something I couldn't put my finger on.

I had voiced my concerns with Nikki as we browsed HMV one Saturday morning. Nikki had yet to meet Jeannie, but she had an opinion on what a steady woman would do for Flint.

'Yeah, but I worry she isn't quite right,' I'd said.

'What do you mean?' Nikki had shoved a Hard Fi album in front of my eyeline.

I had shaken my head.

'Carry on, you said Jeannie isn't right.'

'Well, he had reservations himself at the beginning. I suppose I've not forgotten that.'

'He needed someone to calm him down a bit, you know?'

'I agree, I mean, he's not wild, but he needed someone to pull on his reins every now and then.'

Nikki had laughed. 'I say, let them get on with it. No one is getting hurt, and speaking of relationships, we'll get to yours in a minute. You aren't getting away without discussing it.'

'I'm sure. But back to Flint. I just worry, you know? He's a real sweetie.'

'Hmm, he's always been so good to you.'

'Yeah, I mean, he can wind me up sometimes; be a bit too blunt. But I wouldn't have him any other way.'

'Hmm.'

'He's quite clever, you know, and handy around the house.'

'Hmm, yeah.' Nikki's eyes had widened.

'What does that face mean?'

'Nope, just had a thought.' Nikki had power-walked to the Country Music section, assuming I wouldn't follow her.

'What?' I had matched her speed as she turned to face me, with Keith Urban between us.

'Just that I always wondered if Flint might be the man for you.'

'What!'

Nikki had quickly selected a CD and covered her face with it. 'Don't shout. Have you never considered it?'

'Absolutely not! And why've you never said anything?'

'Dunno. It just pops into my brain sometimes. But why not? I reckon our mums would like that.'

'Really? There's too many reasons why it wouldn't work. We're too close as friends to be together. He knows the whole shebang about me.'

'And doesn't judge you for it. Even though there's a lot to judge.' She had looked away. 'Sorry, I ought to keep these thoughts to myself.'

'You should.'

Back in the present, I hunted for the cat box in the cupboard under the stairs and was thankful Flint couldn't see my face, nor the tears looming. I wouldn't normally be happy about my backside being in Flint's view, but on this occasion, I was relieved.

There it was: the red cat box. I yanked it out and wriggled out backwards.

'There you go. Happy kitten collecting,' I said with a false brightness, my hands on my hips.

He looked at me with concern, then opened his solid arms. I couldn't think of any other place I'd rather be.

I went in, comforted by the feel of Flint's light stubble flickering across my forehead.

'Come on you, hold on tight. Wanna come and collect a kitten with me?'

'Yes please,' I sniffled.

CHAPTER 19

The Birthday

I wasn't permitted to celebrate Dan's birthday with him.

He told me bluntly via text.

```
We can't. I mean we could
celebrate, but not on my
birthday.
```

I was looking for gift ideas on my laptop when the text came in. I slammed it shut and covered my face with my hands. I couldn't give him a birthday present. He'd have to throw it away as soon as he opened it. I pictured my carefully chosen wrapping paper, humorous birthday card and my name with kisses underneath. I imagined my effort and love screwed up in a bin outside Londis... it was nauseating.

The day before we were due to meet up, he called. I informed him I'd take him out for lunch, and we'd have a nice long walk afterwards.

'Can you wear or bring wellies please,' I asked.

'Wellies? I'm from Pinner,' he replied.

'Yeah, but you live in the countryside now.'

'But I don't fork hay for a living.'

'Are you saying you don't go for family rambles?' I'd noticed I'd become rather good at sneering these days.

'We don't do that sort of thing.'

'Well, wear old trainers then.'

'You're bossy today.'

'I know.'

'I like bossy, in fact, are you wearing your glasses right now? You need to, if you aren't already.'

'I'm wearing my glasses, but please don't start any randy talk. I'm far too busy to chat now, we can discuss my spectacles and short-sightedness tomorrow.'

He chuckled. 'Randy?'

The call didn't go half as well as I'd planned. I'd wanted huffy and sullen, but he liked that, texting me seconds after we hung up.

```
That call was arousing xxx
```

It pissed me off. In fact, the way our conversations always travelled and launched us in other directions was really starting to grate on me. One upon a time, it had been cute; a turn on that we would be chatting about Dan and his GCSE Drama show one minute, then talking about my hair colour the next.

'I've always wanted to have a redhead for a girlfriend,' he'd once stated, when we were lying in bed one summer afternoon.

'Um, why?' I'd asked.

'I don't know, they're exotic and naturally pretty,' he'd said, twirling my hair around his forefinger. 'I mean, I love how your hair glistens.'

'I'm just stuck with it, I guess.'

Dan had been on top of me, heading towards my nipple when he'd paused.

'I'd like to add here that redheads seem to know where they are in life. They get teased at school, I know I did a fair bit of that, but I think redheads have to stand up for themselves a bit more, and I like that. That's all I'm saying.'

'What I'm hearing is you've fancied redheads, but never had one.'

'Spot on, but seriously, you're naturally pretty. By far the prettiest girl I've ever kissed or laid my hands on.'

Back in the present, on our non-birthday date, I parked in our usual layby and waited for Dan. I did a double take, seeing him wearing winter clothes. The first chilly day of this December and I'd worn jeans and a V-neck black woollen jumper. My hair was losing its golden tint from the sun.

Dan sat down in my car and put the seatbelt on, offering a feeble smile and no customary kiss. 'What were you thinking about?'

'Just you... us,' I replied as we pulled out of the layby. 'I was remembering that time you said you'd always wanted a redhead for a girlfriend.' I laughed. 'I thought you were so weird.'

'Did I?' Dan stared out of the window.

'Um, yeah, yeah you did.'

I was crestfallen that he didn't seem to remember this. Even so, couldn't he at least appear a little sorry that it had slipped his mind?

We drove in a sombre silence, permitting the views out of our windows to entertain us. I glanced at Dan. He'd just finished cleaning his glasses and was staring at rubbish clinging onto gangly branches on the side of the road.

'Louise, can you pull over please?' Dan asked, breaking our silence.

'Do you feel sick?'

He laughed. 'No, just pull in quick here for a minute.'

I pulled the handbrake and turned to face him.

'I'm sorry, really sorry. Can we start again please? I've had a shit night, shit morning, problems that I can't solve, but none of that is your fault. Can we start afresh? Please?'

I nodded. My emotions were struggling to dissolve. He was asking to start this day again, to smooth things over, but I didn't feel it. Instead, I had a bubbling in my tummy that unsettled me.

'I'm feeling pulled, stressed, pulled again and pushed everywhere. And of course I remember saying about wanting a redhead girlfriend, and now I have one.'

He leant over and kissed me, soft at first, then it evolved into a determined kiss that removed all sense of how crap I'd felt a minute before.

After his apology, Dan showed no signs of the shit start to his day, if his appetite was anything to go by. He chomped his way through whitebait, crusty bread and heaps of butter, scampi and chips, and he didn't even seem to care that the peas were shrivelled up. He'd have ordered pudding if I'd not suggested he should keep an eye on the time a bit more. We wouldn't have had time for the walk I'd planned if he'd ordered the bread-and-butter pudding and custard he mentioned at least three times. In contrast, just about managed my soup *du jour* and steak sandwich. Dan pinched most of my chips and still managed to chat in a way I couldn't; he'd unknowingly passed his bad mood baton onto me.

I was unable to concentrate on him. I was distracted by how he could switch from good cop to bad cop in a flash. I paid the bill and we started our walk down to the river.

The sun joined us for our stroll and showed off by shimmering along the water. The sky was a startlingly bright blue. Empty cans of beer and faded crisp packets were stuck to the edges of the bank. Conkers and dried out leaves led the way as we ambled together. Being outside with nature at its best helped me to mentally thaw out as we walked arm and arm. This was our ordinary; this was right and good. I believed that he was enough, even with one leg in our camp and one leg in the family camp. When we were together, with the sun shining, the river glistening with approval as we walked past, we could do this. I could still do this. But I wanted to talk to him. What had happened this morning that was so shit?

We approached some benches facing the water and the entertaining geese and ducks flooded towards a mum and her toddler. We watched and winced at the child wobbling near the water's edge.

We talked about the books we were reading. He told me about some music he'd discovered. Then he shared what his kids were doing for their nativity plays at school. My heart quivered when he spoke of them, and I hated this ongoing feeling. I'd never have those tender family moments with him; we'd never be parents together.

I snuck a look at him, talking about his children's outfits, the songs they had to rehearse and the ridiculous disagreements between competitive mums. He grinned from ear to ear, this part of his apparently bland life bringing him alive. I'd seen the evidence all laid out, and him telling me about it made me feel more excluded. I'd always been detached from this part of him, and the door to enter this section of his world had always been locked to me. I resented Melissa for having access, and then I hated myself for facing the facts square on. I was the outsider; this part of his life was never for me.

We made our way towards a wooded area, sandwiched between the meadows and the river, and sat on some established-looking logs. It became a rare silent moment – painful almost. We were all about the chatter and I had nothing to say, but the lump in my throat bobbed back and forth, proving otherwise.

Dan nudged me in the ribs.

'Hey, remember our first date? We laid on the grass in short sleeves, no coats; now look at us. You had that dress on and I couldn't stop staring at you, wondering when it'd be appropriate to touch you.'

'Yeah,' I mumbled.

'Are you cold?' he asked, doing up his own coat.

'A bit. Let's warm up and walk over there for a bit.' I pointed to the fields visible through the trees.

I zipped up my grey parka, pulled Dan up to stand and, as I searched for gloves in my pockets, I found a packet of Jelly Babies I'd forgotten about. We struggled to walk through the gluey, thick mud that we hadn't seen from the comfort of our seats, barely making it a quarter of the way around the circuit I'd planned before Dan's left trainer got stuck in the mud. I bent down to pick it up, while he stood on his right leg, holding onto a branch. We were both in hysterics. Dan wobbled as he attempted to slip his trainer back on, pulling at my coat.

'Stop it, you'll pull me over,' I yelled, giggling.

'I'm trying, but my other foot is slipping.'

'Yes, I can see. How have you got mud in your beard?' I couldn't contain my increasing laughter; neither could Dan.

I had a slight upper hand wearing wellies. Dan managed to get the trainer on and, as he stood secure, we clung onto each other and walked like pensioners back the way we came.

Arriving back at the logs, still laughing from the sight of one muddy trainer, we turned to face each other, the longing in his eyes clear to see. My breath caught at his grin.

'How're you going to explain that trainer?' I asked.

'Dunno, not thought about it.'

Reality was lacing its way into our moods.

'Earlier, when you talked about it being summer when we met... do you think we've come a long way or something?' I asked.

'Not sure what you mean.'

'I'm not sure I agree that things have moved on, do you?'

'I didn't say they'd moved on. When I said "look at us", I meant, look how happy we still are, from then until now.'

I didn't answer.

Dan hummed. 'I think, in one way, what we've got is the best I've known. It's that simple.'

I remained silent, waiting for the "but".

'But we haven't moved on.'

There it was.

'Not because we don't want that,' he added, 'but rather because we can't, can we?'

'*You* can't.'

'Yeah, I can't.'

I pulled out the packet of Jelly Babies in my coat pocket, opened them and ate one. This conversation was turning my insides mushy. I needed to remove the bitter taste from my mouth.

'You know I hate the fact that I'm preventing you from doing all this with someone decent, someone who deserves you.' Dan gestured to the outdoors with his hands. 'You should be with someone who can give you all the great stuff I can't. I literally have fuck all to offer you.'

I considered my reply. 'You have you. I want that and I don't want to do this with anyone else.'

I was pathetic. I was laughable.

'What about in the future? Your future?' Dan asked as he stared at me.

I looked away from his gaze and up to the tops of the trees. If he expected an answer, I had nothing to give. Nothing that made sense.

'I think,' I said, hesitating, 'I want to carry on till the end, whatever that might be. Please don't think I'm shit because I can't let you go.' A tear I'd been repressing escaped and trickled down my cheek. I wiped it away with the back of my hand. 'You might think I'm a drip or sad or both, and I agree with you. I am those things. I've lost a bit of my mind and I know I need to be strong or something, and end this, but I can't, and I've no idea why.'

Dan shuffled closer to me and wiped the additional tears away with his thumb. Then he held both of my hands with a firm grip. He lowered his gaze, unable to look at me. I sensed the gloom that was wrapping around him – the spark, joy and fun I'd seen earlier was gone. He released his grip on my hands and, as I faced him, he stroked the side of my head, his fingers looping around my hair. Then he swept my overgrown fringe to the side with his finger. He repeated this tenderness as the quietness continued between us.

I couldn't look at him anymore. I leant my head on his shoulder as he held me tight. I didn't hide my tears as they poured onto Dan's coat.

A minute or so passed. I offered him a Jelly Baby.

He held his hand up to say no. 'You know I hate Jelly Babies, right?'

I shook my head, putting my gloves on. Dan nudged my shoulder with his, repeating the action, and I copied him. He prodded me a bit harder and we laughed at this new game. I looked up at him and he kissed me.

It was tender at first, but then as the heat grasped us, we shuffled around and eventually I mounted his lap, the logs quivering. Dan attempted to get his hands under my jumper and I gasped as his hands touched my back.

'I love your skin. It's so soft,' Dan murmured as he placed soft kisses over my cheeks.

He was taking a shot at undoing my bra. I wanted that. His hand found my breast, and he was taking his mouth up to my nipple when he wavered and fell backwards. He secured himself by putting out his free hand, but it landed on a thorny leaf and he howled. We gave up and took ourselves away from our seats, and as I pinned Dan against a horse chestnut tree nearby, he grinned at me.

That grin.

I was ready for sex with him. Christ, I always was, and I would have stripped had it been summer and we'd been in my back garden. With nobody around, we *could* fuck, and I wanted him. Outside sex was clearly on his agenda as his hands undid my jeans and he slid his fingers around me.

'Oh my god,' Dan whispered. 'You're so wet, I can't...'

His erection was digging into me. I pulled his face to mine, our lips touching, eyes locked on each other.

'We can't. We better get you home.'

Dan placed his forehead to mine and kissed me. 'Not yet.'

Once again, another kiss induced something more. I pulled him towards me, holding onto his arse, wanting to feel his dick against me.

His hands were already under my jumper again, and this time, he found my nipples.

'Come on,' I said.

I pulled my jumper down, one boob in my bra and the other roaming free. I started to walk away, but I turned back to grab his hand and caught sight of him.

My boyfriend, Dan.

Did he wonder how we'd got here, like I did?

He stood, leaning against a tree at 4:32 p.m. on a Wednesday afternoon, complete with a full-to-capacity erect cock, dishevelled hair, his lips parted in shock and inflamed from the energy of our kisses, his expression bewildered.

What were we? Respectable people almost fucking under a tree in winter. It wasn't about the sex. It wasn't about my boob being out and his hard-on trying to escape the confines of his trousers. We were shady and dirty.

As we walked back to my car, arm in arm, I noticed that every few moments Dan would squeeze me a bit tighter, checking I was still there. I had experienced something, a new shift. I sensed there would be further changes coming, and I would be powerless to stop them.

CHAPTER 20

I'm Not Ginger, I'm Auburn

Dan had gone mute.

After our day of snogging on logs, I hadn't heard from him for a week, apart from one vague, and obviously hurried, text.

I imagined awful scenarios: he'd been in an accident and was now in a coma. I imagined the nurses asking him questions as he woke. "Who's your wife?" Dan would call out my name. Cue me running through hospital corridors, tears flowing as I entered his hospital room, and we'd embrace.

Extreme, I'd agree.

After our Monday night spinning class, on day eight of no contact, I asked Chrissy for her advice.

'Well, you don't know with him, do you? Is this normal?'

We were in the leisure centre car park, hanging out by Chrissy's car. I'd cycled to the class and stood next to my unlocked bike. I didn't want to go home alone; I needed someone to calm me down. Normally, I'd call Heidi, but she was the other person in my life who I didn't understand these days. I stood with Chrissy, looking like a sweaty tomato, ripening by the minute. I needed to know what to do.

'No, I'm sensing something is up.'

'Read your last few texts again,' Chrissy said, throwing her sweaty towel into her car via the passenger window.

I read out the text after our date in the woods.

'Is that unusual?' Chrissy asked, putting on a hoodie.

'Well, yes. I mean, he might not respond straight away, but he'd always reply later, apologise and make me laugh.'

'Hmm. And do you still have this rule about no texting unless he texts first?'

'Yeah.'

'I hate to say it, but maybe he's got caught.'

I'd thought that, of course I had, but hearing it said out loud prompted a warm syrupy tear that rolled down my cheek.

Chrissy put her arm around me. 'Go and get changed and come round for dinner at mine. We can thrash it out. Okay?'

I nodded, zipped up my hoodie, put on my beanie, and then another bike skidded in front of us – it was Flint, fresh from the gym.

'What's going on?' he asked.

'Dinner at mine?' Chrissy shouted as she got into her car.

'Spot on, what's the occasion?' he said, not taking his eyes off me.

Chrissy started her engine. 'Lou Lou will fill you in. Can you text the others while I'm driving?' She blew a kiss and sped off.

We stayed silent. Flint was sat on his bike, carrying a rucksack. Recently showered, he smelled of fresh, minty shower gel and deodorant. His hair wasn't tied up and I noticed one side was wavier than the other. I held onto my bike, fiddling with the loose handlebar.

'I think Dan's either got caught, secretly dumped me, moved to Rome or he's in a coma.'

Flint scrunched up his face and shook his head. 'Hopefully, the last option. Come on, let's go back to yours and get you showered. Then you can drive us to Chrissy's and drop me in town later.'

'What about your bike?'

'Don't worry, I'll collect it another time.'

Flint tried to cheer me up on the short cycle ride home, overtaking me, shouting things about my bum from behind and, because he could, he skidded across my path as we arrived at my house.

He fed Bennett and talked to him in the kitchen while I showered, washed my hair and checked my phone. I was obsessed with the productivity of it, or in my case, the lack of any activity or flashes on my screen. I was all about the checking: were there any calls? Was the volume up? Did I have a decent enough signal to pick up texts?

As I came down the stairs, Flint was slumped on my sofa, looking at his phone, his feet dangling off the edge.

'That's an improvement. Feel better?'

'Yep, did you text everyone?'

'Yep. Di is on her way, Nikki and Heidi too, but she said...' He read out loud. '"I want some of Chrissy's food so much, I'll risk indigestion talking about twatface".' He chuckled, then added, 'Jeannie can't make it, but I'm meeting her later anyway.'

I took a deep breath and let the flash of annoyance pass. 'I didn't know you'd invite her.'

'Why wouldn't I?'

'Nothing. You know, I'm not in the mood for Heidi tonight.'

'Well, tough. You two need to start being as you were. You're letting men get in the way. I won't have that. Pull me up, I'm stiff.'

I shook my head. Flint winked and held out his hands. He'd played this trick before. I could never lift him. As I took his hands, he tensed up, making me pull with all my strength. We laughed as I started to slide to the floor in a heap of giggles.

When we arrived at Chrissy's, the whole posse was there, including Chrissy's daughter, Alice. Chrissy had made her signature lasagne. It didn't take a lot of persuading for any of us to drop everything for Chrissy's cooking; this was her legendary dish. The cheesy sauce, the crispy top layer and the garlic. But I didn't feel like I'd be able to swallow a glass of water, let alone my favourite pasta dish. I was just too nervous. I sensed nothing good was going to come from the lack of communication from Dan.

I slouched on the sofa next to Di, Flint pacing the room like a younger Hercule Poirot in a murder mystery, holding a full glass of red wine. Chrissy popped into the lounge, adding things to the dining table, coming back to check that Flint hadn't spilt his wine on her cream carpet. There had been an incident a few years ago when he'd knocked a whole glass of red over and, without hesitation, grabbed a whole bottle of Pinot and poured it on top of the red. He'd claimed it had removed the red stain. None of us were sure, but Chrissy went mental and had since rearranged her furniture to cover the spot.

Di was holding my hand and Nikki was on the other side, patting my knee. I felt like a bereaved Italian wife in a dodgy soap opera, or a widow in one of those mafia films. I should've been wearing a black dress and a veil to hide my heartache, as other grieving widows surrounded me and comforted me with knowing looks. Heidi was texting someone on her phone, sitting cross-legged on an armchair, as Alice brushed her chestnut hair.

Flint ordered me not to cry, asking me to go through my movements with Dan on our last date. Still reluctant to disclose all the details, I offered a brief overview, saying we'd made out intensely. Flint turned his nose up at that and said he didn't like the chat in the car with Dan one bit.

'So, he was down in the mouth when you picked him up, he didn't remember saying he'd always wanted a ginger girlfriend, he then made you stop the car, moaned that he had a shit start to the day, and then asked to start over. Is that right?'

'Yes, but I'm not ginger, I'm auburn.'

'Whatever.' He took a large mouthful of wine, set his wine glass on the dining room table, then continued to stride the floor as if on stage. 'Then he ate like his life depended on it, talked about his kids, and he almost came down his leg in the woods.'

'Grim,' said Heidi.

'Urgh, we haven't eaten yet,' groaned Di.

Chrissy coughed and nodded her head at Alice, who sat humming away. I hoped to god she hadn't heard about Dan all but climaxing under a tree.

'Flint, why can't you like him a bit more?' Chrissy returned with the king of lasagnes and my mates scurried to their seats.

I remained on the sofa.

'I can't, he's a prick.'

'You haven't met him,' Nikki said.

Flint turned the other way, his cheeks reddening. 'So, do we know if he got the text you sent?' he asked.

'What do you mean?'

'Well, remember at the beginning of all this shite, he hadn't read that text you sent? Because of those delivery things that you girls like.'

'Uh huh.'

'Well, has he read your last text?' Flint took over the dishing out of lasagne, starting with his own plate.

Shit. I'd disabled that mode on my phone. Now in a relationship, I didn't need to monitor men's messages anymore. Heidi still sent texts and demanded a delivery report, mocking me for removing the function from my phone.

'Never, ever do that,' she'd said a few weeks back, wagging her finger at me. 'You'll regret it, and remember: he's married and will always have another motive.'

I had regrets. Bigtime.

'I don't know if he's read it, Flint, cos I removed the function from my phone.'

'What a dick,' Heidi mumbled through a forkful of food, rocket salad sprouting from her mouth.

'Guys!' Chrissy shouted. 'Louise. Table. Please.' Chrissy beckoned me to the table.

As I sat down, Flint got up and stood behind Alice, covering her ears like a human pair of headphones.

'Well, you know what you have to do, don't you? Grab your fucking phone, add the read receipt function and send that prat a text.' He planted a soft kiss on Alice's head, leant over Di, picked up many slices of garlic bread and plonked himself back down in his seat.

'Great dinner, Chrissy love,' he mumbled.

Chrissy rolled her eyes, tutting. 'Does anyone have any manners tonight?'

I picked at the lasagne; my friends devoured the rest.

'Come on, you tart, take me to town,' Flint bellowed from the downstairs toilet at 9:45 p.m. He collected our coats and, as he put my scarf around my neck, he leant in and whispered, 'Fancy an old movie afternoon soon?'

I nodded and hugged him tight.

As I said goodbye to my other friends, I paid extra attention to Nikki, gripping her a bit tighter than everyone else. She whispered in my ear that she'd call me tomorrow. Chrissy assured me that whatever happened, everything would be okay, and instructed me to turn my phone off when I got home.

I did as she ordered but, before I did, I re-read the text I'd crafted during dinner.

> Hey, is all good with you? I'm a little worried to be honest. Can you let me know how you are? I'll try you at the weekend Xx

No delivery report. I went to bed with a lump in my throat.

During the mid-afternoon lull at work the next day, I logged into my email account, and there it was – an email from Dan.

Hey, I've read your text. I'm sorry. I'm sorry for everything. I can't talk right now, but I will call you. Things are really bad and I'm in London with Dad at the moment.
 Please don't call me.
 Dan.

CHAPTER 21

That's a Wrap

I was on the way to the outdoor ice rink to meet Chrissy and Alice.

The Carfax Christmas tree, placed with perfection and tradition in front of the clock tower, beckoned everyone to come and take a look. I recalled trips into town with my mum and sister at Christmas time, begging to get closer to the tree, and one year, as my mum gossiped with someone, my sister and I escaped her view and crawled underneath to see if Father Christmas had delivered early. He hadn't, and my mum tugged at our ankles, pulling us out. I feared a stony glare, but as her chum laughed and other shoppers joined in, she couldn't disguise her smile as she demanded we stay put.

It was a Sunday afternoon and the ideal festive December weather: fresh, biting, and the sky was preparing for nighttime to start in a few hours. As the faded blue sky turned to an indigo bruise, the streets were crammed with shoppers of all varieties: loved-up couples, families, and of course tourists, even in December.

I pulled my beanie hat over my ears and walked towards

Castle Street from St Aldates. The plan was to meet the girls in ten minutes for skating at 3 p.m. It was then that my phone started ringing.

Dan.

The call I'd been waiting to receive almost made me want to vomit.

Whatever Dan had to say should be wrapped up in ten minutes. But that wasn't likely, and after all the stuff we'd been through, he owed me more than a ten-minute debrief to dispose of our relationship and move on with his life.

I stopped walking the way I should've been going and went down Blue Boar Street, ducking into the doorway of the little closed haberdashery shop.

'Hi.'

'Hi.'

Silence.

'Where are you?' he asked.

'In town, I'm going ice skating.'

Dan began to laugh. I pursed my lips, determined not to drop my guard.

'Taking up lessons, are we? Learning how to do an axle spin?'

A smile crept onto my face, and I wanted to rip it off.

'Sorry, mum was a massive Torvill and Dean fan,' Dan added.

'No, actually, I'm going on a date.'

He paused. 'Oh.'

I recoiled at my pitiful untruth. 'That was a shit joke, sorry. I'm meeting some mates.'

'Okay, well, I won't keep you then.'

'Dan, honestly…'

'I'm so sorry about the last few weeks. It's been awful. I thought I was going to lose everything. I nearly did, but I'm back in Oxfordshire now.'

I shut my eyes for a second, swallowing the freezing air along with my distress. Quivering in the cold, I once again recognised that I was putting his wish to talk to me before my own needs. In this case, what I needed was a warmer body temperature and to meet my friends, while he wanted to have his say, swoop off, and let me get on with making up new boyfriends.

Decent people didn't do that sort of thing.

'Are you? Since when?'

'Friday,' he replied.

Three days back at home, and he hadn't thought to let me know.

'Louise, it's been awful in my head. I'd say you should try being here, but I wouldn't wish that on anyone.' Dan gave a short laugh. 'It's tricky to explain, but bear with me. I want you to know everything. I owe you that. It was like I was in a tunnel. Not a dark one; there was a light to head towards. I could see everyone I loved in it, but I couldn't turn around or move forward to get to where I wanted to be.'

'Are you out walking? You sound out of breath.'

'Nope, I'm just walking up and down Dad's garden. I find it hard to sit still. Anyway, I lost my appetite, I felt sick all the time.' His voice lowered to a whisper. 'I remember waking up one day in October thinking I was gonna throw up, and that feeling – it's never left.'

I couldn't speak, so I let him continue.

'I was stuck. I mean, every day is the same when you have kids. You're like a robot: making toast, finding gloves that match, refereeing scraps, but one morning something happened. We were leaving the house for school and my chest felt weird, like a giant was standing on me.'

'Christ, Dan, you should've called me. What happened?'

Dan sighed. 'I couldn't breathe, and the kids were there. I collapsed in the hallway, slumped against the wall. Both kids started crying. I was alone. But you know, I've had these sorts of things before, panic attacks. I've never coped with them well. They started after Mum died and I found getting pissed helped them go.'

'Dan, I'm so sorry. I just want to hug you right now.'

'And I can't tell you how much I want that as well. I can almost smell your perfume.'

'Have you seen a doctor?'

'About me smelling your perfume?'

'No, about everything else.' The familiar humour between us reappeared and I swallowed the warmth, knowing I would miss this.

Why didn't I know more about these attacks?

'Yeah, she told me to keep a diary. I've turned into Adrian Mole at thirty-seven.'

I laughed. 'Don't.'

'I am, it's the most depressing read you'll ever set your eyes on. Dear Diary, 8/10 depressed today. Symptoms: crying in the airing cupboard and having the shits.'

We laughed for a moment.

'I told the doctor the whole story. She knows all about you and how you affect me. I told her you were the clarity in my dull life, and I loved every part of you. I told her how we'd met and that it was meant to be. I told her that a conversation with you can make me smile to myself for hours. But then she asked about the future. And that's when I told her what I should've told you.'

I swallowed. 'And?'

Dan coughed to clear his voice.

I traced condensation on the shop window with my gloved finger.

'That the last few weeks, the guilt has been too much. I haven't slept, I'm worried about everything, and I started to hate every choice I was making. My job, my marriage, my house, having kids, and you. I felt like a sad muppet, a cliché, washed up, no life and being controlled by women. Melissa, her family and you. The only woman I wanted to see was my mum.'

'Dan, I had no idea you felt this pressured. We could've talked about it all.' I shut my eyes for a moment, feeling the wafts of guilt stirring in my gut and batting away visions of my own mum.

'I always think of her, that's never going to leave me. I didn't want to make you sad. The other thing is, I've been drinking too much. A few beers when I cooked dinner, then some when the kids were asleep. Then I noticed I was drinking one before collecting the kids from school, to be fake and smiley. But more recently I've been encouraging Melissa to take the kids out for the day, saying I'm working, when in fact I was sitting, drinking, crying, listening to music. You should read those diary entries.'

'Dark,' I said.

'I know. I kept thinking how I'd got myself into this almighty emotional mess. Then work got shit, and busy and then shit again. I wasn't calling people back; I was blanking emails; clients cancelled their work. Some had paid an advance, so I owe them money now. Everything was slipping, all going down, down, down, until I just wanted to lie down, all day.'

I'd had no idea alcohol had become his support, his key to carrying on like normal, and as he spoke, I wondered if I was the mess he was referring to. Did I control him? Tears gave me an answer in the corners of my eyes.

'Dan, why didn't you speak to me and tell me? When we last saw each other, you must have already been so down.'

'I dunno, I thought: here we go again, it will pass. But I was stressed about Christmas, New Year, and thinking of you alone. I didn't want that, but at the same time, I didn't want to be at home either, even with my kids. Can you imagine that? Can you think of how that feels? I hated myself for it. I still do.'

He sniffed and I heard rustling in the background. My breathing slowed down as I pictured Dan crying without anyone to hand him a tissue.

'But things got worse,' he added.

Three weeks ago, Dan had dropped Ben off at school and Izzy at nursery. Then he'd gone home. Rather than attempting any work, he'd opened a can of cider at 9:50 a.m. and carried on. The school had called to inform him he was late for Parent in Class Day.

'I ran up to the school, knowing I looked ropey and half cut. I didn't clean my teeth or look in the mirror. The teachers knew. Ben was so bloody pleased to see me, and I remember walking into the class, asking all the kids to do high fives as I passed. Ben laughed and joined in, but looking back, everyone was staring because a drunk had interrupted.'

'Oh my god, Dan.'

'I know. They put up with me and then cut the whole event short and asked me to see the Head. I mean, how demeaning. Then I was an arsehole to her; I argued until she threw me out.'

'Oh my god, I don't know what to say.'

'Nothing you can say, and there's still more.'

I cringed as Dan told me how Melissa had returned home from work that day. She'd known all about his behaviour after an embarrassing call from the Head, and the jungle drums worked their magic. She'd received texts from parents asking questions, worrying about her and the kids. Melissa called Tim, Dan's dad, and asked him to take Dan away.

This tragic and miserable version of events brought me a flash of something inappropriate – hope. Was his marriage over?

Dan continued. 'So I stayed at my dad's. Hiding away. Dad didn't know what to say, he never does. He made me a lot of bacon sarnies with brown sauce. And then Melissa called me, pleading for me to come home. She wanted one more try. She reckoned she still, you know, loved me and wanted it to work.'

'Oh, right.'

'Louise, hang on. She said if I didn't try to repair the marriage, and seek serious help with my depression, she'd make the move permanent, and I wouldn't have any say over when I saw the kids.'

'She can't do that!'

'She's got the support; I haven't. I'm in the wrong. There's the drinking, but I also know what I've done behind everyone's backs. Melissa said she knew something was going on with another woman but wanted to draw a line under it.'

Draw a line under it?

I inhaled deeply and forced the air out of my nostrils. 'And she wants you back?'

'I guess she does,' Dan replied flatly.

The scale of his sadness seeped through his feeble outpour. Today, his usually upbeat and confident voice that I loved so much sounded crushed. Melissa, his family, his work and I had sapped the strength from him. We'd all had a part to play, but hearing it was difficult to digest.

I wanted to ask how things were now he was home. How much did Melissa know about me? I wanted to know if he still loved me. I wanted to know if he had ever loved me. I wanted to ask if that was us done. The answers to all those questions were reflected in his mood and his absence of words. He'd no plan to fix this and add me into his future again. It was over. I wanted to hear him say it; he owed me that at least.

I decided to ask my questions. 'How do you feel about being home?'

I looked down at my watch. I was now late for ice skating.

'Not great. It's amazing to see my kids, I can't believe how much they've grown in two weeks. At Dad's, I used to picture them and pretend I could feel their cuddles. It got me through each day. But I feel like I'm in a cage now that I'm home. My in-laws are here all the time. I'm not allowed to pick my kids up from school. I'm not allowed to be alone with them. I'm being watched and the only place I'm relaxed is in the bog.'

His voice wobbled, fading out, and my heart cracked down the middle. I knew how not being the ever-present dad must be stripping him of the joy in his life, never mind what it was doing to his confidence.

'Does Melissa know about us?'

'I think she does. I'm not sure she cares that much, but she said something the other day about my "relationships with the school mums". She doesn't know your name, but I'm on a dog lead now. She wants to know where I am all the time.'

I braved it. 'How does this work for you and me?'

'I can't see you anymore.'

'Not even in a while, when things have calmed down?'

'I can't, I can't risk losing my kids and a place to live. I can't even work right now. I've lost clients. Big money. I can't lose anymore.'

'Except me, I suppose.'

'Please don't push me, I can't do it anymore. I just can't.'

I cried. I didn't care that he could hear. He sniffled down the line too. I'd never experienced mutual weeping before. Of course it had to be with him, didn't it? Another first for us.

'I think you should go and have fun with your mates now.'

'Fun with my mates?' Snot flew out of my nose. 'Are you serious? How can I have fun after this? I love you. Do you still love me at all?'

'What good will that do, saying I still love you?'

'I want to hear you say it, if you mean it.'

'Louise, just...'

'Did you ever mean it?'

'Of course I love you. I did then and I do now. You made everything right when nothing was fucking right. You showed me that I could feel loved and be happy again.' He sighed. 'It's like, you smiled at me that night and a change was coming, like everything was going to be new. I knew it was going to be okay after years of it not being okay. But when I thought I'd lost everything, the kids, money, home, well... you and I became unreal – a fantasy. What I nearly lost is my reality, and I can't live without all that.'

But he could live without me. I was irrelevant.

A cry escaped despite the free hand that lay firmly across my mouth. I could have screamed to be held by him one final time, but we'd never get that.

'Louise, I've got to go, and I think you should too. I think it's best if we don't speak for a while. It would hurt us both too much, but before we go, just remember, I did love you.'

I had no words.

'Louise?' I could hear his shallow breathing. 'Shall I text you in a few weeks? Are you there? Oh shit, are you still there?'

'Bye, Dan.'

'Bye,' he croaked, and the line went dead.

CHAPTER 22

'Tis the Season to be Melancholy

I didn't enjoy the ice-skating event. Even the sight of Alice attempting to skate on her Bambi-like legs, her rosy cheeks glistening against the white glossy floor, failed to bring a smile. Nikki and Chrissy frowned at me, their eyes filled with concern.

'Yes, there is something up, but I can't talk today. Okay?'

I didn't need to tell them. They knew.

Chrissy busied herself with Alice, and Nikki ran off to get drinks. She returned with a hot chocolate the size of pint glass, the squirty cream cascading over the sides.

'Drink this,' she ordered.

I wanted to run away and throw up. Nikki remained at my side, her arm linked with mine as our eyes followed the skaters. This rhythmical and graceful display was oddly calming.

Over the next few days, I managed to go to bed, get up, go to work, and repeat. I spent the week after my chat with Dan crying in private. I checked my phone all the time, but there was nothing. I jumped when it beeped, and leapt when it didn't, but deep down I knew it would never be him again.

The week before Christmas, my mum reminded me I'd agreed to host Christmas Day lunch for my family. She recalled that, way back in October, when life was still good and I could focus on how to make bread sauce from scratch, I'd agreed to everyone coming to my house. Mum would bring the turkey, my sister the pudding and I'd get the veg, roast potatoes, pigs in blankets and some kind of starter. A few weeks ago I'd considered if the timing was right to introduce Dan to my family.

Mum texted to check I had written a food shopping list.

```
                                        Yes, all sorted.

When are you going shopping?
Don't leave it too late,
there'll be nothing left.

                            I'm going on Saturday. Flint
                                        is helping me.

Oh gawd, he won't ever be up
in time. What time are you
picking him up? Can't you go
with that Chrissy? She'll
know what cranberry sauce is.
```

I couldn't tell Mum that Chrissy had not only already bought her Christmas veg, but that she'd chopped, cooked and frozen them in November.

My little fibre optic Christmas tree blinked at me with its flashing lights. They were the only clue in my house that it was mid-December. My tree was egging me on: "come on, it's nearly Christmas". I flicked through my mobile after reading

Mum's final text, reporting brandy butter was not for Dad – it gave him indigestion – and asking if I owned cling film for reheating the turkey. I was scrolling through my mobile, and I gawped at a photo Dan had sent me of him a few weeks ago, leaning on a bar, looking fit in a suit. It must have been taken before we'd met, before all the crap in his life exploded. I scrolled and found a photo of him and the kids all sticking their tongues out, not at me, but for Mummy. We didn't have a photo of us together and neither did he have one of me.

When Mum finally gave up, insisting on bringing a packet of bread sauce just in case, I braved calling a friend. I'd had so many missed calls from them all. Nikki and Chrissy would have given them the heads up, so in response, I sent them all the same text.

> I can't talk now, but I will soon. I'll be okay.

A few days passed and I was ready to chat. I selected the first person I wanted to speak to – Flint – but I paused. He was loved up now and maybe not the best option. I wanted his negativity, strong presence, and his hugs, but it was Christmastime. His first with Jeannie. I'd leave him for a bit. Heidi was next on the list, but first I would assess what sort of mood she was in. I wanted to tell my friends he'd done it, and I would get all the cuddles from Di and Chrissy. Nikki would be at my front door in a flash, but tonight I needed something negative. Someone to spit Dan's name out and reassure me that everything would be okay. That person had to be Heidi.

My call went to voicemail. I left her a croaky message.

'Hey Heid, it's me. Call me back when you can. Please.'

She called back a minute later.

'Sorry I didn't pick up,' she panted down the phone.

'Where you been?'

'Gym. Hang on, let me turn the music down.' *Last Christmas* faded fast in the background. 'I met a fit guy tonight. Walking into the changing rooms, he appeared, asking if I'd forgotten my towel. I cringed. He was holding it like a dirty nappy or something.'

'It might as well be. I've seen your gym kit, remember.'

'He was so fit – blue eyes, a blond sweaty quiff. I didn't want to claim the towel; I'd blown my nose on it.'

'Wow, you meet *men* at the gym.'

She laughed heartily. 'I know, check me out.'

Heidi went on to explain that she'd dismissed the towel as not being hers and flirted with him. He'd flirted back, saying he liked her bench-pressing technique and asked whether she liked Body Pump. She'd lied, saying yes, and asked if he was always this dedicated to fitness, especially so close to Christmas, and shouldn't he be out in the pub. He'd asked her why she wasn't out in the pub either. They agreed to train together two days later.

'But why were you out of breath when you answered your phone? He's not there, is he?' I asked.

'No! I wish, but no, the bloody gym called saying they'd found my towel. It was labelled, so the fit guy knows that rag was mine!'

Heidi had labelled all her gym kit when she went on a yoga weekend, something she was now regretting.

'Yeah, but you know, we all sweat. This is a great start. He's seen you at your worst and everything,' I said.

I could hear Heidi running a tap in her kitchen.

'So, you okay?' she asked.

'Nope.' I started crying before I could utter another word.

Heidi threw questions at me. 'Is it Dan? Is he okay? Did he end it?'

She didn't need to know more, but it was only natural for her to want the meat of the story. How else could we tear him apart and plot his premature death in the coming weeks?

Surprisingly though, Heidi didn't judge him. Nor did she question my sadness. Instead, she listened.

When I reached a natural end, she asked, 'So, I know you're heartbroken, anyone would be, but what now?'

'Nothing, that's it.'

'He said he'd text to see how you are, but he doesn't have the right to ask now, does he?'

I'd anticipated the wind of change at some point, but this was earlier than I'd expected. 'I suppose... it's hard to stop all contact with each other in a situation like this. If none of this had happened, we'd still be plodding along.'

'Hmm, I don't think that's fair on you. Or him, I suppose. It would be like picking at a scab. I'm not sure I want you to bleed again.'

'I know. I just... I can't not hear from him again, Heidi. And what if maybe, when all this dies down, this is the end of his marriage?'

'But you can't think like that, darlin'. It's over, even if it's only for now, and things change later. Right here and now, it's over.'

She was right, she was so very right. But I so wanted her to be wrong.

We finished chatting. The tears, lack of food and overthinking had given me a headache. I nipped into the kitchen to make myself a cup of tea and feed Bennett. As I waited for the kettle to boil, I remembered all the times I'd stood in this kitchen with Dan. But he'd never be here again; it was over. Well, for him maybe.

I didn't feel like it was over in the slightest.

🌷

I'd asked Heidi to tell everyone about the breakup, like a round robin of shit news. Throughout that evening, my phone caught fire. They were all magnificent. Chrissy became motherly and invited me round for dinner and sleepovers. Di asked if I wanted to move in with her for a few days; she offered me a massage and emailed me quotes to spur me on.

Nikki sent a poinsettia to my office. I snuffled tearfully at the delivery lady as I signed for it. That was Nikki's style: no words, simply a striking red plant sent with her love that I grappled with on the packed bus later that day.

Flint's approach had a style all of its own. He called as soon as he'd heard and insisted we drink red wine, but I said no and went to bed. The next evening, he turned up, not taking no for an answer.

'It's the best medicine for heartbreak,' he said.

The very notion of necking red wine on the limited calories

I'd consumed made me feel sick, but it was nearly Christmas, so I tried my hardest to get into the festive spirit. Flint bought a tray of Indian snacks and, as he loaded them onto an oven tray, moaning about the layout of my kitchen, he talked about Jeannie. They'd argued this week, about everything.

'But I don't want to go into it. I'm looking after you tonight.' He shut the oven door, then turned to face me.

'I'd like a distraction. Why are you arguing? Shouldn't you be making up with her instead of being here with me?'

Flint smiled and folded up the tea towel he'd just flung down. 'I want to be here. You're *my* distraction.'

'What a pair we are.'

As the food heated, we located my naff Christmas CD collection and finished adding some tinsel to my feeble tree, wearing hats from a box of crackers I'd found in the cupboard. I found myself enjoying the evening, and as the wine diminished along with our energy, Flint located my copy of *Holiday Inn*. We got into our familiar positions: me on the sofa, Flint sitting in front of me, in between my legs as I plaited his hair.

'Give my shoulders a rub, would you?' he asked.

Cautiously, I massaged the back of his shoulders and his neck. I'd done this before, and it's not like I hadn't noticed his muscles, but as he made appreciative sounds, a smile appeared on my lips. I found myself liking how much he was enjoying it. Even more than Jeannie's back rubs, perhaps? Should I squeeze deeper, would he like a softer stroke…?

I patted his shoulders in conclusion, clocking the heat coming from my cheeks. 'Okay, you're done.'

Bennett claimed Flint's lap, and I could hear his gentle

purr, along with my pulse thumping in my head.

'You sure it's okay to crash here?'

I jumped up. 'Sure, I'll go and get bedding.'

I went upstairs and returned with duvets and pillows for him.

'What do you think he is doing now?' Flint asked.

I shrugged my shoulders, vexed that he had mentioned Dan. 'He's probably asleep. It is half eleven on a Wednesday night.'

'Yeah.' Flint frowned. He eyed me making up his bed and then dived onto it. 'You do know he's probably missing you just as much, right?'

I didn't answer. I knew more was coming.

'I'm sure he's relieved to be back with his kids and in his home, but he'll still wonder where you're at. He knows what a top girl you are. He knows you'll be snapped up pretty quick. And you know what? Even if you feel like shit, never let that prick see it. Got it?'

I started to cry.

Flint was sitting up now, cross-legged. He beckoned me with his hands; I'd seen this move before – he meant business with his cuddles. I sat next to him on the floor, our backs leaning against the sofa. He put his arm around me, and my head flopped onto his strong shoulder. I continued to sob, my tears falling onto his t-shirt. He squeezed me tight and kissed the top of my head as I clung to his waist.

'What if I never meet anyone again? What if I never kiss anyone again? What if I never meet a man like Dan again?'

'What? First of all, you will, I know it. Kissing, the same, and as for not meeting a man like Dan, well, that's your Christmas present all wrapped up, love. All I can add is that I hope he has a fucking shite Christmas, which I'm sure he will. He won't even be able to have a shag, or a shandy if he's off the booze. And you know what? If he calls or texts, and that's a big if, can you do me a favour?'

I nodded.

'Don't answer, and trash any texts please?' To stress the point, he put his hands together, closed his eyes and prayed. 'That's all I want for Christmas from you, okay?'

We held each other's gaze. Flint's hand moved to touch my face, but he pulled back. Then he wiped some of the emotional mess from my cheek with his thumb. I held onto my bottom lip, keeping the tears in. Outwardly, I looked helpless, my face covered in mascara and tears, and my contact lenses were so dry they could snap on my eyeball. Inside, I wasn't any better. I was broken; plagued by what was going on under Dan'd roof. Melissa had him. I didn't have him. She didn't deserve him, but I did.

I nodded and nestled into Flint's shoulder, sighing with comfort.

It was the only Christmas present I really needed.

PART TWO

CHAPTER 23

Let's Not Talk About Hairdye, Babies or Sex

Christmas was finished and the new year celebrations forgotten. We were midway through January 2007 and I was doing the best I could to forget I'd met Dan.

He sent me a text two days before Christmas. My insides filled with flitters whenever I saw the little unopened envelope on my mobile.

How are you? I miss you.

I didn't reply.

I found bizarre means of coping without Dan in the new year.

When in complete isolation, I found talking to myself was almost comforting, functional and wise. I sat in my sitting room and sounded out my feelings, like a non-commercial Alan Bennett's *Talking Heads* monologue. If walls could repeat what they'd heard, what a sad little BBC commission that'd be.

I applied coping mechanisms my friends could unknowingly assist with, and it kept everyone off my back. I sold the idea that I was saving dosh during the lengthy winter nights, so we hung out at Chrissy's house, made stews and played boardgames with Alice or decamped to Heidi's, ordered takeaways, watched *Friends*, *Sex and the City* and *Big Brother*. We listened to music at Di's – Pet Shop Boys, Motown, Sybil, Carole King, Dina Carroll and Barry White, singing loud enough to wake the dead, adding some West End musical soundtracks to the mix when we felt like it. Chrissy was always up for a musical recital, out of tune or not.

And Flint. He declined our invites. We were all aware that he was making a big effort with Jeannie, but I was gutted he wasn't around much. I couldn't be selfish and demanding, but I missed him. One night at Heidi's, we had a chat about his absence.

'It shouldn't be an effort though, should it?' Di said.

I shrugged.

So did Heidi. 'Don't ask me. In fact, don't ask any of us, he's the only one with someone. He must be doing something right.'

I didn't want to think about Flint doing anything right with Jeannie. It gave me odd feelings I didn't like, and I already had enough of those about Dan.

Leaving Superdrug during my lunch hour one afternoon in February, the bitter wind whipped my face as I gave my loose change to Mindy, one of the local homeless sleepers. The coins tinkled in her wicker basket. I smiled as she mouthed "thank you".

I walked off, making a mental note to buy her a cup of tea next time. My phone started ringing in my bag.

It was Dan.

I threw the phone back into my bag and covered it with a packet of tissues. I walked on. The phone was still vibrating and ringing. My heart was beating fast. I wanted to pick up, but I knew I shouldn't... but I missed him and his voice. I missed his humour, his everything. I dipped into an alleyway near The Covered Market and pulled out my phone for a second, looking at his name flashing. I should have hit the dismiss call button.

'Hello, stranger.'

My answer was chipper, but I quickly glanced around me, checking my friends weren't following me. I'd promised Flint I wouldn't take this call, and picturing his soft expression at Christmastime made me hang my head in shame as I answered.

'Hiya.' Dan exhaled. 'It's so good to hear your voice. How are yah?'

'Um, confused. You?'

'Um...'

'Why are you calling?'

'Dunno. I know I shouldn't, we said we wouldn't, but I miss you. Is that wrong?'

'Yes, well, not really, I am very miss-able.'

He laughed. 'I miss chatting to you. I was sitting here last night thinking... we didn't get a chance to say goodbye.'

'No, suppose not. That was more you than me.'

'It was so rushed and I wish we'd said goodbye properly.'

'That would have made things more difficult.'

'I suppose.' Dan paused. 'I'd liked to have seen you, though. It seems wrong that we didn't celebrate what we had.'

'A dumping party, you mean? You know they aren't a thing?'

'I'd have got the chance to kiss you goodbye.'

'Kisses aren't part of breaking up.'

'Suppose not.' He sighed.

The conversation moved on and we skilfully managed to avoid discussing his marriage, kids, or anything else personal to him. Dan had met a new client that morning and she'd mentioned a Maggie O'Farrell book she'd enjoyed. Dan had recalled that I rated her books, and the meeting had gone a bit tits-up after that. He couldn't believe how much the name of an author he'd never read produced vibrant and urgent thoughts of me. Before thinking it through, he'd dialled up.

'So honestly, how've you been?' Dan asked.

It was my turn to sigh. I wanted to stay focused and closed off, but I buckled when he asked how I was doing. I'd always loved sharing everything with him.

'Just getting on with life, but it's hard. I never thought I'd miss a person so much. You and I went from full on, to full off. My head doesn't cope well in these situations without warnings.'

Dan laughed. 'I think of things to tell you every day, pick up my phone and put it down again. The number of texts I've created and then deleted is madness. I go to bed sometimes, to replay our times together. I can almost hear your laugh when I'm alone in my room.' His voice wavered.

I wanted to ask what the sleeping arrangements were, but was distracted by the speed at which our simple chats had resumed. It scared me. What was more pitiful: being in sync with someone who wasn't your wife, or not being in sync with the woman you walked down the aisle with in the first place? No time to debate that crap now.

'I have some good news,' he said.

'What's that?'

'I am off parole. As of today, I can collect my kids from school without my mother-in-law in tow. How good is that?'

'Ah, that's excellent news.'

'It's hardly a normal life though, is it? I mean, the past six months have been anything but normal.'

'I know. We just have to get through it, though.'

He sighed. 'I'm not sure how. I've never had to do this; forget someone so extraordinary.' Dan coughed through the crack in his voice. 'I'm trying to get over someone who I didn't want to break up with. That's fucked up.'

'Well, I guess it will take time. Although I think answering this call has already set me back a step or two.'

'I'm sorry, I thought it might help us both.'

'Maybe you should've asked first. I don't think I'd have agreed to it.' I winced. Being hard as nails with Dan didn't come as naturally to me as it should.

'Oh.'

'Anyway, I bought hair dye today.'

'Wish I could see the result.'

'It's called Cherry Red.'

'Cherry Red. That sounds pretty.'

'I hope so.'

Dan didn't reply for a beat. 'Cherry – that's a nice name for a little girl, isn't it?'

I was stumped.

'Fuck, I'm not saying I want more children here, I just... if we'd had a child, a girl I mean. I've been thinking all sorts of crazy stuff – things we didn't do. Hope you didn't think...'

'Look, it's okay. I've had those thoughts in the past, but you are where you are. I also know marital sex will be back on, especially when it's not available elsewhere.'

'Come on, really, it isn't.'

'It's fine. Look, let's not talk about hair dye, babies or sex. You should talk about that stuff with Melissa and I'll find someone else to discuss baby names with.'

Dan remained silent. He needed to hear that my future didn't have a slot for him. My life was unmapped before me, but I was going to be with someone else now. A woman like me possessed potential to meet and fall in love with a decent, available man who would cherish me as much as I did him. If only my own battered heart would catch up with this masterplan.

'So, any plans for the weekend?' Dan asked.

'Flint and I are cooking a roast on Sunday for Heidi, not much else. You?'

'Swimming lessons, gymnastics lesson and a birthday party, I think.'

'Aren't you the active one. Do you have your party outfit ready?'

'It's the kids...' His voice flattened.

'I know, I was joking. Trying to um, you know...'

'I know.' Dan sighed. 'Anyway, I'd better get back to it. Call you later.'

'What?'

'Well, if that's okay…?'

I took a breath in. Was it okay? Making new promises to be in touch with Dan without knowing how this was going to pan out? Before, there had been the boxes, the rules, the point of it all. Yet now? Could I do what I liked? This could be dangerous. Did I want to hear from him so soon?

It was most certainly very much not okay.

'Yeah, course it's okay. I love you. Speak soon.'

CHAPTER 24

A Roasting

Flint arrived at noon with five overstuffed carrier bags.

He barged through my front door, dropping everything onto the kitchen counter. He didn't even say hello.

'No Heidi, then?' he asked instead.

'Morning, by the way.'

Flint plopped a kiss on my cheek. 'Morning.'

He stood, hands on his hips, staring at the bags almost in wonder. He looked like a celebrity about to begin on *Ready Steady Cook*.

'Come on, let's unpack it all.'

'You okay?' I asked. 'You seem a bit stroppy pants.'

'Yeah, fine. Looking forward to showing off my cooking to you.'

It was our anti-Valentine's Day lunch. Well, mine and Heidi's. Flint was planning stuff with Jeannie and Di had a date with a chap who trained horse jockeys, but Heidi's gym/towel bloke had gone AWOL and so, to keep our spirits up, Flint had suggested he cook us a roast.

As we navigated my small kitchen and started to unpack,

we periodically bumped shoulders, hips and bottoms. He removed a bag of carrots from my hands, took me by the shoulders and guided me out of the kitchen.

I laughed. 'It's my kitchen, you know.'

'Well, I'm in charge. You can bugger off.'

I turned the heating up and sat on the sofa when Flint called to me from the kitchen.

'Too early for wine?'

I got up again and faced him in the kitchen doorway. 'Nah. Just a little one though.'

'That's my girl.' Flint pulled the cork from a bottle of red and handed me a half-full glass.

The rest of the afternoon couldn't be described as balanced in the drink department. We went through all the supplies.

All the reds.

Three bottles of the stuff, and Heidi took a punt on a box of Merlot… it wasn't her best idea.

'Shit, this stuff was meant to be continental.'

Flint laughed, taking a swig of one of his delicious bottles. 'I think you've either been ripped off, love, or you're tight and bought cheap shit. That stuff's is only good for stews.'

Flint cooked rare roast beef, crispy roast potatoes – doused in I-didn't-want-to-ask-how-much fat, carrots, parsnips, homemade Yorkshire puddings and red cabbage that I hadn't yet learnt how to cook without it tasting vile. He even made his own gravy – it was all so mouth-wateringly tasty that Heidi and I spent the entire meal grunting during every mouthful and complimenting Flint until he told us to shut up.

'It's a bloody roast, for god's sake.'

'But it's so good, Flint,' I said, putting my cutlery down for a moment.

'I might have to marry you if you keep cooking like this,' Heidi added, ramming a roast potato into her mouth.

My eyes darted to Flint, who was already looking at me. I blushed, shifting my gaze back to my plate as I picked up my cutlery and carried on eating.

'No way, woman, your manners need improving. Did you know you have gravy on your chin?'

Once we'd finished, I washed up, leaving Heidi and Flint chatting in the living room as they selected the music. Folding the tea towel up, I congratulated myself for not mentioning Dan, then instantly felt guilty. I could definitely call myself successful at being an utterly crap mate now. *Bravo, Louise*. I was becoming an expert at lying to my friends. Remarkable what made me proud these days.

The low winter sun started to set, the curtains were drawn, and I lit some candles as we talked about Nikki coming to stay in a few days. Heidi settled down on the sofa, Flint resting on the floor, his head on my beanbag, Bennett flirting with him. I returned to my seat on the armchair. With only the shit wine left, which was going down too well after my bread-and-butter pudding, I enjoyed the tipsy, cosy feeling.

My phone bleeped from on top of the bookshelf.

I ignored it.

'Want me to get it?' Heidi asked.

Shit. 'Nope, it's okay, I'm too drunk.'

'It might be Di.'

'Leave it, it's alright.'

Heidi sat up and reached over to grab the phone. I could feel Flint staring at me. Heidi looked at the phone, rubbed her eyes in disbelief and glared at me, her eyes cold as ice. With swift force, Heidi threw the phone at me.

Flint ducked, shielding himself from a possible phone landing at his face. 'Hey, easy.'

'It's him. Dan is texting her. Is this the first one?'

'No...'

'Were you expecting him to text you today?'

'No! Listen, this is all new, okay?'

'No, it's not *new*.' Heidi's volume went up a notch. 'It's old news and it's fucking boring. Please tell me you and him and not back on?'

'Course not.'

'So, what's the point?' Heidi sat up cross-legged, her eyes stern.

I took a glug of wine. 'Um, it's difficult to explain.'

Flint got up and walked to the kitchen. 'I think we need more crap wine for this.' He returned with the box and offered a weak smile just for me as he poured. 'Go on then,' he said.

I explained about Dan's out-of-the-blue call and how satisfying it was to speak to him. I'd missed him. He'd missed me. We had a connection, a spark, a something. I looked at both of them. We'd moved positions – Flint was now sat next to Heidi on the sofa and I was sat cross-legged on the floor with Bennett. They looked like a team – the anti-Louise-and-Dan team.

Silence.

Heidi got up, walked past me, pausing at the doorway to

the hall. She slammed her hands on her hips.

'I'm not listening to any more of this. Ever. I can't. I can't hear you talk about him like he's bloody Mike Skinner or that bloke from The Kooks. Well, maybe he could match them, I dunno. I've only met Dan once and he's okay in a I'd-chat-to-him-in-the-post-office-buying-stamps kind of way, but I can't hear you big him up anymore.'

'When did you last buy stamps?' Flint asked, smiling as he reclined in her spot on the sofa.

'That's not the point, and *she* knows what I'm talking about, don't you?'

Heidi's eyes bulged. She was clearly expecting a response.

'See, she can't even argue back, she knows this is a waste of time. He's still dicking around with everyone: his wife, you, and probably someone new. Did you even think of that? He's a serial dicker!'

Flint chuckled.

'Don't you laugh. I'm not sure why you're finding this amusing, because you should be backing me up here and not her.'

Heidi scoured the room for her bag. It was right there, under her nose, but she was so steaming drunk she couldn't find it, let alone drive home.

'I'm going. Come on.' She beckoned to Flint.

Doing as he was told, he sat up, wearing a frown, not ready to call it a night, but drained his wine and stood up, stretching his arms above his head.

'Calm down, Heidi. We've got to call a taxi, and don't you think we should all talk a bit?' He sauntered over to her and put his arm around her shoulders as she struggled with her puffer coat.

'Nope. I'm getting the bus, it's not late. You coming?'

Flint let out a heavy sigh and they both looked down at me, still sat like a naughty toddler at their feet. My cheeks were roasting with emotion; salty tears covering my lips.

'Look, you go and huff off, I'll meet you at the bus stop.' He tried to shove her out into the hall, but Heidi wasn't done.

'One last thing. When are you going to stop being happy with the leftovers, hmm? I'm sorry you're crying, I really am, but I'm too angry to be huggy and nice about it. Maybe tomorrow I will be, but just so you know, tonight I've never been so pissed off with you, but mainly I'm sad for you. Really fucking sad.'

Heidi and her alcohol fumes exited, slamming my front door closed and promptly waking Bennett from his slumber on the beanbag.

Flint pulled me up from the floor and held me for a minute as I sobbed into his hoodie.

'What a fucking mess,' he mumbled into my hair.

'I know. We didn't even have seconds of the bread-and-butter pudding I made.'

Flint pulled away. 'Hey, back up. I mean you; Dan; you two speaking again: that's the mess. Does the guy have any morals?' Flint perched on the edge of my sofa. 'Look, I'd better go after her, but listen to me. Never mind him, what about *you*? You're lowering yourself to his level. You gotta take a look at yourself and what you deserve.' Flint stood up and put his parka on. 'I expected more of you, I guess.'

He reached the front door, then turned back to face me.

'One more thing.'

'Go on, hit me,' I said, wiping my teary face on a tea towel.

'If it's alright with you, I'm gonna take the bread-and-butter pudding to share with the lads at home. We can't see it go to waste, can we?'

CHAPTER 25

Book Club Flop

Heidi collected her car the next day without popping in to say hi. Totally unheard of.

Six weeks on and I still hadn't seen her. Things were bad.

Speaking of bad, Dan and I had spent the past month or so calling and texting, but had made no plans to meet. The thrill of seeing his name flash on my mobile was as strong as ever, but it was like opening one of those deformed KitKats. The ones without the wafers. You get them sometimes and, although you should be excited about the thick chocolate being there in all its glory, you want the wafer. The wafer is what makes it and that's what you want.

I wanted Dan and I wasn't getting him.

Were we friends? Did he want me back? Would I ever see him again? Was he "being good" at home until he could escape and begin Dan and Louise round two? His texts certainly indicated he missed me and cared for me, but was it actual love?

I wasn't brave enough to ask him these questions, and he never discussed the future. I didn't want to hear the answers anyway. My friends had all the questions and didn't wait for the genuine answers. Their opinions were the answers: I heard them all in their fullest and finest form one Friday night.

Everyone had decided to head round to my house after work for a girls' night in. Flint was, in his words, "making things right" with Jeannie. Since the roast lunch slanging match, he'd been attentive and was spending a lot of time checking up on me. We'd brought back old film night and initially I'd invited Jeannie, to get to know her a bit, but after Flint had said she was "busy" more than a few times, I'd given up asking. I liked this time with him; I needed him, but Jeannie was missing her boyfriend and I had known Flint would need to do something about it eventually.

Di and I had been banging on for ages about planning a book club and Nikki was due a visit, so it was great timing. Di had sourced a book club list from the library, added some Richard and Judy bestsellers onto it and emailed us the list to digest. She'd asked us to pick our favourite, and for our first meeting, we were to discuss *The Time Traveller's Wife*.

With Easter fast approaching, I had noticed everyone around me had a spritely spring in their step, knowing summer was on the horizon. Even my moody bus driver had perked up; he'd morphed into a most welcoming human these days and regularly commented on the magnolia buds pimping up our bus journey to work. Jasmeet flaunted vases of chubby tulips on her desk, and just the promise of scoffing chocolate in the form of Easter eggs on warm bank holidays was a welcome thought.

After we'd filed off the bus, carrier bags full of calories, we meandered the short journey to my house, nattering, bottles clattering. Di almost skipped alongside me, not coming up for air, swinging her bag for life. She and I were catching up on *Lost*.

'I just don't think it can get more complicated.'

'I know, I want to keep going with it. I'm addicted, but I don't think I have the brain for it.'

Di linked arms with me. 'Well, if you don't, neither do I. Tonight, after we've chatted about the book, we could try and figure it out.'

Before I could agree, Chrissy interjected, 'Do you really think wine will help you figure that show out?'

I unlocked the door for all the girls to pile in. Nikki was parked up outside my house and she waved her sunglasses at us as she opened the boot. Everyone helped her with her overnight bag and alcohol contribution, then barged into my small kitchen and fought for space to dump their wares: pizza, share-and-tear breads, dips, charcuterie meats, Monster Munch and those little M&S tubs of cakes that a person can eat outright in one sitting. And, of course, wine.

While my friends took their shoes off, stroked Bennett, and made themselves at home, Nikki pulled me into a tight squeeze. No words. We'd used them up on the phone, discussing Heidi and the roast row. She smiled at me as she took a bottle of rosé out of a carrier bag, along with some posh crisps and a huge tub of sour cream. *I'm glad this one is here*, I thought.

We sat in the garden, Belle and Sebastian drifting out from the living room, munching on crisps and dips, enjoying the wine too quickly and laughing about our days at work. As the sun started to go down, we were packing up to go inside, and Di asked how Dan was. I gulped. Nikki and I exchanged glances.

I walked into the kitchen to get more wine and shouted from inside the fridge, 'I need more wine to talk about him with you lot.'

'Eh?' Nikki shouted.

I walked back into the living room. 'You know what I know. It's doomed. It's a fuck up.'

'He's a shady ratbag,' Chrissy sneered.

'Look, can we start the book club thing? Shall I put the pizzas in the oven?' I asked, desperate to put a full stop after Dan.

Di rushed out of her seat to fetch the book in question, clipboards and paper.

We managed one hour of hilarious and fully intended intelligence, pretending to talk book. Chrissy got pissed and admitted she'd not read the book; in fact, she'd returned it to the library and swapped it. After that, the pretence collapsed, the wine ran out and the volume on the stereo went up. Di mentioned Dan again and, now a bit pissed and wanting to share my side of the story – not the Heidi version they may have been privy to – I went for it.

They nodded, sometimes with mouths open. I could almost hear Chrissy saying "are we here again, really?". I noticed Nikki's head flitting from left to right, as if she was sat watching centre court during a Wimbledon match.

'So, what do you think?' I asked.

Chrissy was first up. 'I think he needs to leave you to get over him. He shouldn't be doing this. You barely got the chance to get over him last time and here he is again.'

'I know,' I said, fiddling with the ring on my finger.

'Anyone think it's kind of romantic?' Di asked. 'They can't keep away from each other.'

'No, it's not,' said Nikki. 'He's preventing her from meeting someone decent. And he broke her heart.'

I clocked Chrissy's glance at Di, her blue eyes full and ready to burst.

Di winced. 'Sorry, maybe I shouldn't have said that.'

'No, you shouldn't. Sticking your nose in is what she needs,' Chrissy said.

'Is it?' I asked.

'Yes. You need a bit of reality now,' Chrissy continued. 'He's wasting your time and using your good nature to make him feel happy all over again. He needs to fucking find happiness at home, not with you. Or he needs to leave his wife.'

Nikki twirled her stud earing and avoided my gaze, but I wasn't cross with her. I wasn't arsy with any of them, but they'd drilled into my exposed raw nerve. Unfortunately, I was incapable of being rational or confronting reality when it came to Dan. I still loved him, and I'd have done anything to cling to whatever leftovers he offered me.

But I couldn't share that with my mates.

As the evening drew to a close, everyone left, except Di. I noticed the eye contact across the room and watched as they gathered their things and scurried out. I could imagine their thoughts. They wanted to get the hell out of here, to avoid catching the weird and failed romance vibe. Nikki was having a shower while Di washed up and I dried.

I broke the quiet between us. 'How do I stop him from abusing my kindness?'

Di turned to look at me, soapy hands dripping back into the washing up bowl. Her expression was soft and kind, but she frowned. Was Di the right person to ask this question? I could feel the emotions of the night, mixed with the wine, bringing hot tears to my eyes.

She turned away and carried on washing wine glasses. 'Do you think it's a case of him being the right man for you, but that you met him at the wrong time?'

'Yeah, I do. But I can't control the timing, can I? So, really, I should let him go.'

'Yes, you should, but you won't. I know you, remember? There's some kind of pull between you two. I suppose that's love. Is it?'

'Yeah,' I replied, looking down at the tea towel I was wringing between my hands. 'It's our version of love.'

We carried on washing and drying as I tried to find the words to explain how I felt.

'Listen, I know this sounds nuts, but just bear with me,' I said as I finished drying the last glass. 'Love... it's kind of like fruit.'

'Eh?'

'Hear me out. Some love is like a freshly picked strawberry, beautiful and ripe and strawberry-shaped. The very sight of it makes you want to take that delicious first bite. And then other love looks like an oddly-shaped, quirky supermarket strawberry that maybe isn't the best colour, but when you bite into it, it still tastes good. And that's still love, just a different version of love.'

'Well, aren't you the philosopher?' Di's laugh was kind.

'Oh, it's the wine talking.'

'It was beautiful, Louise,' she continued, wiping down the sides. 'So, you and him, if it is real love, real for him and real for you, it'll work out. Is that what you believe?'

'I think so.'

'You'll wait for him?'

I nodded.

She dried her hands and hugged me, saying nothing. The act in itself meant she wasn't quite with me on this, but had no way to tell me without crushing my hopes.

Di collected her things to go and run for the bus, but before she unlocked the door, she pulled a dogeared novel out of her bag and handed it to me.

'Nearly forgot. Now who's pissed? I found this in a charity shop the other day and thought you might like it. It's meant to be funny. Maybe it'll make you laugh and see things a bit more from his side.'

We hugged again and she left.

I looked down at the book. *Tales of a Shit House Husband*. The word "shit" was crossed out, but a replacement wasn't added. Maybe seeing his perspective would be useful, but for now, I needed sleep.

CHAPTER 26

Fuck that Fucking Facebook

I'd invited myself over to Flint's place with Nikki the following day. Flint was helping me with a small car repair. He'd ordered some windscreen wipers for my car and agreed to fit them. Flint often said he'd help with these kinds of tasks, but when I wanted to pin him down and try to fix a date and a time, he always tried to worm his way out of it. Over the years of our friendship, I'd decoded this behaviour to mean that, although he'd said he would help, he'd quickly realised he wasn't sure how to do it, but of course he couldn't admit to that, at which point the regret would creep in. Fortunately, it appeared windscreen wipers were within his remit, so I was in luck.

I needed some uncomplicated time with two of my favourite people, who I hoped weren't going to make me feel like shit, or give me judgemental, sly looks. Flint was gentler these days. It was the side of him I needed, but that he seldom showed.

I still missed Heidi. We'd communicated by text since our row. Surprisingly, our chats weren't frosty, on the short side maybe, but all the same okay. I asked if I could come over to her flat one Saturday afternoon.

She'd replied:

```
Don't push it, I'm still not
ready to see you yet.
```

Followed by another text full of kisses.

On the drive over to Flint's, Nikki and I chatted about men, our exes, and our disasters.

'Our situations are different. One was a smooth operator about his deceitful behaviour and the other was a complete knob head, but both need lessons in morality. That's not our job now. It's someone else's shit to clear up.'

I nodded in agreement. Nikki and I had been for an upbeat Sunday morning swim and managed forty lengths of breaststroke. I'd attempted to show Nikki how I did backstroke, but we'd kept laughing at my zig-zagging performance.

Flint was waiting in the driveway for us, and got straight to work taking the mick out of us both for nothing in particular and repairing my car. To show off, he opened the bonnet, fiddled with oil levels and screen wash, then cleaned parts of the car with a rag before wiping his forehead with his arm.

His face was flushed and he was looking pleased with himself. 'There. Fancy a cuppa you two, before you go?'

'Oh, go on then.' I smiled, nudging Nikki. 'Told you he's handy.'

We headed off inside. In the past, Flint's shared house had always been disorganised and smelled like a mix between teenage boy, unwashed clothes and long-forgotten bananas. But today, I noticed the boys were keeping everything in fairly good order. The barbecue was sparkly and prepped, awaiting the first use of the year; the lawn was free of weeds and recently mowed, and they'd cleared up the bike paraphernalia. It looked less like a student gaff and more like a house belonging to grownups. My Flint appeared to have transformed into an adult man.

'Would you like me to grow you some little plugs?' I asked him. 'I have some tubs you could put them in, here.' I stood up and walked to an area against the fence that would attract a decent amount of sunlight.

I turned back to face Flint as he nudged Nikki in the arm. She had a wide grin on her face.

'Firstly, I don't know what a plug is, apart from the thing that lives in the sink, and secondly, if you're talking about a flower or something that needs to be looked after, then there is no chance of me keeping it alive unless you're planning on doing it for me.' He grinned and put his shades on. 'Thanks for the offer, though.'

I pulled a face at the pair of them and walked to the end of the garden. As I leant on the little rickety gate, gazing out onto the immaculate rows of hard graft in the allotment behind Flint's house, I noticed a carrier bag of spring cabbages hooked over the corner on the frame. It was customary for the gardeners to leave gifts of carrots, spuds, or rhubarb for the boys, and I adored this community. I knew Flint liked it too, and that he knew damn well what a plug was. I was envious of this secret place, this noiseless, structured and soothing little world at the end of his garden. I waved at an elderly couple I recognised. The man stood upright from digging, clutching his back as his wife pointed with a smile at the tunnel thing she had just attached to the ground.

The spring sun had assertively pushed its way through the clouds that morning, the transparent swirls battling to keep their place in the sky. Flint lived on a quiet street for Cowley and you could sense it was Sunday morning. The neighbours Flint never encountered were likely to be students or professionals, sharing houses and still hiding in their beds, hungover. In the distance, I could hear a lawnmower humming, a woman shouting "get down!", and kids giggling. Flint passed me a packet of Malted Milks as I joined them at the patio furniture.

'So, has this one filled you in on the creepiest relationship since Katie Holmes and that freak Tom Cruise?' Flint said.

Nikki spat her tea out while I remained po-faced.

'Oh yes, she has,' Nikki answered, wiping tea from her chin. 'I don't think we should go on about it too much. Let her make her own bloody mistakes.'

I gave her a look. 'Thanks. 'I'm fully aware you all think I shouldn't be speaking to him, but I am, so there.'

'Fair enough. What a fuck up that was, or should I say, still is.' Flint cast slanted eyes in my direction, sitting back in his seat and stretching his long legs onto the arm of my chair. He took a slurp of his tea and added, 'What are you getting out of it? Hanging onto him like that, like a flea sucking on a shabby old farm cat. All of this is preventing you from meeting anyone else. You're getting desperate.'

I stifled a half-hearted laugh at the idea of Dan being a flea-ridden cat, before letting out a dramatic sigh. 'I am desperate.'

I recoiled at saying it out loud and sunk deeper into my chair. It was bearable to live with these opinions about myself, but to hear Flint label me like that was deflating.

Flint sighed, sitting upright in his chair. 'I think we need a night out, where we all get pissed and you have a shag.'

Nikki clapped and sat up. 'Yes!'

I rolled my eyes. 'Really?'

'Yes, really. It's time for you put some slap on, get that foxy little smile of yours out of the loft and climb back on the horse. You need someone who deserves you, even if it is just for one night. Because that motherfucker is wasting everyone's time. His time, his wife's time, my time and most importantly, your time.'

'He's right, Louise,' Nikki added, grinning.

'Yeah, he is, but I have to be ready to cut Dan out of my life first, and that hasn't happened yet.'

On our way back from Flint's, Nikki didn't beat around the bush asking about Dan.

'Do you ever get tempted to look him and his wife up on Facebook?'

'Yes, but I'm scared he'll know or see me looking. I'm a little frightened of Facebook.'

Nikki laughed. 'Me too, it's like an armchair detective tool. I could look him up for you though.'

'Thanks, but I sort of think I'm better off not seeing his face.'

'Or hers. But if you saw them together happy and loved up, you might get over him a bit quicker, and it could be like Facebook therapy.'

'Or I might see signs they are on their way out.'

'True.'

By the time we got home, I had agreed to Nikki's plan, and

I quickly put together some cheese and pickle sandwiches as Nikki logged onto her laptop and waited for it to boot up. While Nikki chatted about a new shampoo she'd recently tried, I found swallowing my food difficult. As well as my mouth being as dry as a Ryvita, there was a zipping in my tummy. No food was welcome here.

Nikki jolted me out of my daydream. 'What's his surname again?'

'Christie, they are both Christie.'

She typed his name in first, and as she hit enter, I faced away from the screen. I panicked. What if his face appeared, or he caught me out and pointed a finger at me? Searching for him in this way felt comparable to peering through his letterbox.

'There we are. That's him, isn't it?'

Of course it was him. Seeing his beardy, green-eyed handsome face, and his glasses – albeit in a dorky and dated photo – still made my heart leap out of my chest. He was attractive and playful, and I still wanted him. It was quite ridiculous. I missed him so much, and I quickly realised that seeing his face was a dreadful idea.

I slapped the laptop shut.

Nikki jumped back.

'No more.'

'Don't you want to see more photos? Or some of the wife? There were a few folders—'

'Nope. I can't.'

'Ah, love, I hope I haven't upset you by showing you his face, but it's there now, if you want to take a look in private.'

Private snooping – exactly what I was afraid of.

CHAPTER 27

Bossy in Glasses

Nikki offered me some advice before she left, and insisted I repeat it back to her. It was like being in my French oral classes at school.

Do some gardening.
See your mates.
Snog a bloke on a night out.

Chrissy had her own offerings. Dan being quiet was progress, in her opinion. She wanted to build on this.

'Let's call this Phase One of the Dickhead Detox.'

I wasn't sure when I'd signed up for this experience, but I doubted a refund would be an option.

To be fair on my insufferable mates, they hadn't been as stern with me as they should've been. The name "Dan" should have been banned and any tripping down memory lane forbidden. They were bored of me, bored of him and bored of it all. Chrissy attempted to keep me in check, lacking any kind of subtlety, snooping for signs I could be meeting him. If that had looked likely, I think she would have taken full responsibility that her tailor-made course was not working and expel me from Dickhead Detox altogether.

As Nikki had instructed, I tackled the weeds that were getting out of control. My brain had drifted off in the sunshine and I was lulled by the methodical process of weeding. I savoured the sight of my yolky primroses and clusters of bluebells when my mobile shattered the peace, ringing from the patio, making me jump out of my skin and drop the trowel.

Dan.

'Hello, where you at?'

He spoke with a strange tone I couldn't quite place.

I returned to the lawn, flopping onto the grass to lie on my back, admiring my next-door neighbour's lilac bush hanging its rich purple flowers over my garden fence.

'I'm in my garden sorting my tools out. You?'

'Oh, you know, working hard, staying out of trouble, wishing I could get into trouble with you. Thought I'd call before I, well, we go on holiday tomorrow.'

Great. There *was* something up.

'Where are you going?' Somewhere dangerous and life threatening, I hoped.

'A caravan in Devon, nothing flash. Melissa thinks we need to get away.'

Does she now? 'Sounds nice.'

'Yeah.'

The conversation lacked something – an energy – and I didn't know where it was heading. Hearing about their family holiday made me want to puke.

I willed him to change the subject to anything but his bloody life. Even our non-existent sex life would be preferable.

Insanely unhelpful to both parties, but it had somehow become an essential chunk of our conversations these days. The last time we spoke, Dan had recalled the afternoon when we gave each other love bites on our arses.

How odd that our sex life was now a nostalgic want and I was satisfied with that. I *needed* to know I still aroused him; but where did I think that'd get me? Mutual masturbation was the new thing. Dan always got horny and had a wank afterwards. His texts provided the details from his imagination – the position we did in it; the garden or bathroom; if I was wearing the red bra he liked.

I told him about the book Di had given me. We laughed about some of the chapters, which were, as I suspected, so very comparable to his own life. The endless piles of washing, homework battles, the hideous mother-in-law and the flirty mums on the school run.

'It does sound like my life, and I have to say, it's a relief there're some other poor sods out there suffering under the rough end of the stick.'

'You should start a union. I'd help you. I could do your admin, filing, answer your calls wearing my glasses.'

Dan sighed. 'Please, don't Lou, that isn't fair.'

'Would you like me to tell you off with my glasses on?'

'Stop it, you know I always want you in your glasses.'

We laughed and then paused for a moment.

'Or you could read the book. I'd lend it to you if I could see you, but hey, I can't. Do you want to know the author's name?'

His reply was brisk. 'Post it to me.'

'You sure?'

'Yeah, why not?'

'Because your wife could see it.'

'She's not interested in any post of mine, and if you sent it this week we'd be away on holiday when it arrived. I normally sort through the post anyway.'

'If you're positive, text me your address.'

'Will do. It doesn't sound like a bookish book, but I kind of like that you've touched it. Is that odd?'

'Yes, it is.'

'Thought so.'

After we hung up, I was puzzled by his address disclosure and confused as to why, after all this time, he may as well invite me in for a cuppa. What was next – family barbecues, kids party invitations, threesomes in the spare room? Was he too trusting, or was he naïve to believe this wouldn't cause him a headache?

Dan texted me later on.

```
The thought of you in your
glasses was too much today. I
hid in the office for a spot
of light relief.
```

I focused on whether he would be sharing a bed with Melissa. Would they hold hands on the beach? Were they officially back together? It was an unhelpful trio of questions by any jealous ex's standards.

Maybe this holiday was for the best – I needed a break from Dan and his horny texts. Our conversations offered nothing but resentment and possessiveness, along with what I could only guess might be grief. I'd lost my boyfriend in the form he was to me. I had a new version of him in my life and I wasn't sure I wanted to carry on knowing this shaded-out Dan.

As I tidied my bedroom on day five of Dan's holiday, I found the book he'd asked me to post. I located an envelope big enough, wrote his address on the front, and wrote a message inside the front cover.

Dan,

I thought of you when I read this book. I hope you laugh at the points I did and can share a few of the funny bits with the kids.
Louise
Xxx

I felt something shift in my chest. It wasn't going to be a breeze, but I was on the move. I wiped the tears away as I cycled to the post office and hid my red eyes behind my sunglasses as Timmy, my lovely Jamaican postmaster, chatted away. We always laughed when I visited there, but today I couldn't manage to socialise with him. He asked if he could take the package away from me and I firmly replied, *yes*, he could, he could absolutely take it away.

It was time for me to remove all reminders of Dan from my life, starting with my house.

CHAPTER 28

Barbecue Sauce

Purging all things Dan proved easier said than done.

I found myself getting lost in my memories, and the happiness they provided was pathetic. These moments became my new relationship, my new obsession, my life. I recalled those cheerier times when everything was novel and invigorating. Having the comfort of my memories was like a date in itself.

Obviously, that was bullshit, as Chrissy reminded me.

We chatted on the phone as she hid in her pantry. Alice was doing her head in, and Chrissy wanted to motivate me to do anything but mope. She had a plan to hatch.

'Look, like any dodgy pill from the 90s, the come down from the high is unavoidable.'

'Eh?'

'Stop popping your Dan pill. The down moments of realising that he's a no-go are crippling you.'

The sound of tin cans being replaced clunked in my ear. 'Are you arranging your food cupboard?'

'Yes, it's very therapeutic.'

'Maybe I should do the same. I start the day out okay but

then I think about him, and before I know it, I'm repeating the whole process again and again. It's like the headfuck version of physical self-harming.'

'You *are* self-harming. You need a physical challenge and I'm suggesting cleaning. It's part of my Dickhead Detox.'

I was dubious at first, but Chrissy was right. I was making progress. I put Super Furry Animals on, blaring out their latest album while I attacked my kitchen, then the bathroom, and I then got to grips with the living room. I shredded, cleared cupboards, filled binbags and thrust them in the dustbin. The physical act of clearing and loading into my bin forced me to come to terms with some basics: I was doing away with Dan, and it was surprisingly uplifting. I really didn't think it would work, but as the clutter disappeared, my world came back to me and I found myself emerging from a fog.

Chewing things over, I realised something new in a snap. I wasn't disposing of anything owned by Dan.

He hadn't left a coat here, or a pair of pants, spare shoes, a t-shirt, deodorant, and he never once asked for a drawer here to store anything. Why would he? He'd rarely stayed over.

I stomped into the kitchen, opened the cupboards, the freezer and then the fridge. I couldn't find one food item he'd bought, eaten, or suggested I buy. The same in my bathroom – no Lynx Oriental or Head and Shoulders for Men or even that lemon and lime shower gel he favoured.

The only item he'd brought into my house were the condoms, and that said it all.

What the hell were we? I couldn't locate one love note saying something adorable. In fact, I didn't know what his handwriting even looked like. I huffed and puffed around my entire house, and it was like Dan had never been inside. You could even say I'd made him up in my head; he was a production of my needy, delusional imagination.

Dan was like a modern-day geezer version of Lord Lucan or Harry Houdini, or that canoe bloke that vanished. There were more of these disappearing types than you might think.

He'd left nothing, absolutely fuck all, not even the slightest imprint on my physical life. And I felt fucking shitty about it.

Enraged, I called Heidi.

'I'm working,' she answered.

'Yeah, I know, but I'm fuming.'

'With me?' she whispered.

'No, Dan.'

She sighed. 'I'm going to the car park, keep talking.'

Still on shaky ground, I didn't really want our first big chat to be about Dan, but I needed her. I told her about my clean up, and Dan being like Harry Houdini, the canoe man and Lord Lucan.

'I'm not sure I'm following you,' Heidi said, panting.

'He vanished. Dan has vanished. When you have a boyfriend, they leave their crap around, don't they?'

'Yes, they do. Men can be quite messy.' A siren passed her and quickly faded into the distance.

'They stay over and want showers, they want to shave, spray deodorant or trim their nose hair.'

'Do they?' Her panting had stopped now.

'Or they cook for their girlfriends, get a takeaway, buy those potent mustard or chilli sauces that I don't like, and men leave them here. I mean, Dan loved barbecue sauce, but I hate it.'

'Hmm.'

'There's no barbecue sauce here! I mean, if my house was forensically scoured, they wouldn't find a hair from his head, not even a pube, or any of his skin.'

'Ew.'

'I know.' Thrusting my frustration out, I exhaled. I needed to get my words into the open, but my mind was a rambling mess. 'All the time we were together, he never left a bloody thing here or brought anything inside my house that he wouldn't take with him. What was that all about?'

'He didn't want to be traced there?' Heidi said.

'He wasn't wanted for murder. No. I have the answer.'

I paused for a moment. Tears were flowing down my cheeks.

With horror, it dawned on me what this was. He'd never seen us as a couple. We weren't the same in his head as we'd been in mine.

※

Thankfully, we were all going out the next night. I needed to get absolutely wasted.

In the early part of the evening, I was everyone's pet project, the aim being to get Louise laid. If a half decent bloke walked past our group, Heidi shoved me square into them. Some took it well and it created a bit of banter, but one guy was mardy. I mean, of course he was – I'd spilt his beer.

'Oi love, sort it out.'

'Sorry,' I mouthed, flashing a smile.

'Whatever.' He shook his head as he walked away.

'Why didn't you stick your tits out, for god's sake.' Heidi nudged me in the ribs. 'They're your best two bits.'

We went to the Zodiac – the best music venue in Oxford that switched to a half decent club when the band and the groupies left. We paid our £5 to get in and began climbing up the flight of stairs taking us to the music. I could feel the baseline deep in my chest. Memories of nights gone by appeared in my mind as I made my way up the dark staircase, the sticky floor and glass crunching under my feet. The black matte painted walls were covered in posters detailing my weekends gone by – a pissed-up timeline of gigs and nights that left me with patchy specifics.

Everyone aimed for the bar except Di and me. We swayed our way to the toilets but didn't enter until we'd finished dancing to *Shut and Let Me Go* by The Ting Tings. We clutched each other, already feeling the body heat from other dancers rammed around us. You could count on the eclectic tunes here – one minute you'd be jumping to Reef and then James Brown would step in. Inside the toilets, the posters on the walls were peeling. There were nine cubicles, two without doors but still occupied, the loo roll had run out, and there was no soap or hot water. The occupants gossiped loudly, fluffing up hair or smudging eyeliner with index fingers in the filthy mirrors.

The beer had taken control; so had the tequila. The short walk from the pub hadn't muted my pissed-ness and I was now more on board with flirting, with anyone. I walked off to find the others. I found them near the bar, chatting, faces shiny from smiles and sweat. Flint chucked his hoodie at me. Chrissy had pulled a guy with a shaved head, wearing a brown donkey jacket with leather shoulder pads. The coat was undone, his arm draped over Chrissy's shoulders, and he was so buff he wore just shorts and lace up boots to complete his look.

Then the unforgettable intro to Curtis Mayfield's *Move on Up* stopped me. I flung Flint's hoodie back at my friends and raced back to the dance floor.

I waved my arms above my head, squeezing between the dancing crowd, singing every word. I flung my head left and right, motivating my damp hair to stick to my cheeks. My fringe had long given up; it'd mutated into two halves pinned to my forehead, enjoying its own freedom.

A lad appeared before me, singing the words into his beer bottle. I leant in closer to form a ridiculous duet. As Curtis sang the words "bite your lip", we sang to each other face-on and burst out laughing. We bumped hips, smiling, and as the tune ended, I noticed his cuteness. About my age, he wore tight skinny jeans with a faded checked shirt, not tucked in. He wore a pencil tie that made me think of the mod look, The Jam and Paul Weller in the 80s. I liked that. His light brown hair was modelled on one of the Gallaghers. At this point in the evening, I couldn't work out which brother it was, and I didn't need to. I would kiss him. He could be interesting.

Boogie Wonderland by Earth, Wind and Fire ended and somehow *Let's Push Things Forward* by The Streets began, and it worked. We continued singing but now we were up close. I attempted sultry dance moves, tugging at his tie. He made his move and kissed me. The heat emanated from his cheeks, his lips wet and beery. We stopped moving, held onto each other and continued to snog as dancers bumped around us. I thought I heard Flint shout something about Jeannie, asking me to look at a text, but dizziness and music took me and I wasn't sure what I could hear and what was in my beery imagination. I dragged my Gallagher away from the dance floor to stand against a wall. He grinned at me, cheeky; he had a dimple on his left cheek. I leant in, grabbed his head and pulled him in. He had one job to do. He knew his place tonight, and he just got on with it. It was a promising start.

Some moments later, he ran to the loo and Heidi appeared.

'Have you been spying on me?' I asked, touching my lips self-consciously.

'Yep, he's fit. You aren't allowed to leave here without his number. I'll check. We'll all frisk you.'

I extended my middle finger at her. She returned the gesture and danced herself back to the bar.

He could be my methadone, I thought. The replacement to take me off the addictive high that I must not want anymore.

I didn't ask for his number, nor did he ask for mine. He kissed me hard with one hand holding onto the back of my head. I nodded to some seats in the bar area, and he returned with ciders, squeezing in next to me in a booth with other drinkers. The table had a mosaic top and I picked at the tiles as my distraction fired questions at me. It made me recall the day Dan prepared a list of his own for me and how we laughed. I didn't want to be the interviewee in this scenario.

Pictures of Dan were swirling in my head and I shut the lad up with a kiss that I couldn't be arsed with. I closed my eyes and, my imagination jaded, I pictured Dan sitting next to me, watching, judging me kissing another man, nudging me in the ribs and asking me "does he kiss like me?".

The Gallagher lad didn't kiss badly, but he wasn't for me. I tried to enjoy the next kiss that I found myself in. I stroked the Gallagher lad's smooth face. Things were absent from this moment: a beard, stubble – and suddenly I realised it was all a big mistake.

When I got back at 2:30 a.m., more than tipsy, I downed a pint of water, took out my contact lenses, slurred to the cat and slumped into my bed. Clean sheets welcomed me to sleep. I'd made progress.

Other men were available. I just had to want them.

CHAPTER 29

A Bit Icky

I staggered to the bathroom for a pee about 9:30 a.m. the next morning. Squinting through my hangover, my head pulsated with every breath. I went downstairs and made tea. I ran my tongue over my teeth; there was a glaze of bad breath, stale beer and mouth-open sleeping. Necking a pint of water first, I returned to bed with my tea before locating my mobile and switching it on, hearing the flurry of drunk and hungover texts from my friends ping in. Brunch was on at Di's.

I showered, turned up the radio to full volume and even sang a bit. I got dressed, no makeup needed, a little spritz of perfume. I'd expected to spend the night tossing and turning and unable to sleep, what with the booze mixed with thoughts of the Gallagher snog, but despite my hangover I ended up having the best night's sleep I'd had in months.

As I let Bennett out into the garden, I passed the landline and noticed it flashing.

'You have one new message,' the answer machine lady said. 'The caller called at 7:57 p.m.'

The message was from Dan. His voice broke as he spoke.

'Hi, Louise, it's me. Just to ask you not to call me. Text or call. Things are really bad here. So bad. Melissa found the book. You've no idea what sending it to me has caused. She knows stuff. I'm begging you, don't call. Please. I am begging you again. Bye.'

Fuck.

I played the message a few times before I left home. I didn't delete it, dialling 1471 to find out which number he'd called from. It was another landline in Stapleford. All very strange. I scribbled it down and took the bit of paper with me.

I was shaky upon my arrival at Di's house, and far too skittish to eat. As I was normally the first in line for any food queue, it wouldn't take one of them long to sense some shit had hit the fan.

Di let me into her house, wearing a flowery apron. Muffled chattering and *A Grand Don't Come for Free* was coming from inside. On walking into the living room, it became obvious the charming brunch scene she'd wanted to create was destroyed. Smoke and steam billowed out of the kitchen, revealing an occasional glimpse of a figure moving around in the murk. It was Flint opening the oven and taking a tray of sausages out in Di's pristine kitchen. She appeared next to me. Her face was lightly pink and she wiped the sweat from her brow with a tea towel. She forced her way into the kitchen, vanishing into the smouldering fumes.

Offering to assist would have been unhelpful at this point, so I sat on the floor with the girls. Chrissy was animated as per normal after a night out, but Heidi was huddled on the sofa under a blanket, texting someone on her mobile.

'Dan's wife knows about me and him.'

Someone muted the music.

'What!' everyone said in unison.

I explained about the voicemail, truly believing this was the most fascinating part of my story, but the fact that I'd posted the book to his house was all my mates wanted to chat about.

'You did what?'

'Why?'

'Really?'

'Can't we talk about the fit bloke you snogged instead please?'

I tried my best to justify my actions. This audience was not on my side.

'Well, I needed to do that one last thing. I mean, I did promise him. I thought he'd read the book and bin it. I don't think this whole situation is putting me in a good light.'

'Damn right, there is no such thing as a good light regarding you and Dan,' Heidi said. 'It's all so dark you might as well be down a mining pit.'

I looked around the room, feeling the heat on my face.

Silence.

'Oh, I don't know. I wanted to clear my head, and sending that book helped a bit.'

'Bollocks,' shouted Flint from the kitchen.

'Pipe down in there,' I yelled back at him.

He blew me a kiss from the doorway.

'Look, you should've left him alone,' Heidi continued. 'I mean, sending the book, okay, but writing inside it? I bet he's *fuming*.'

'How come you're on his cheering committee all of a sudden?' I asked.

'I'm not. I think what you did is a bit... icky, to be honest, and tells me you were trying to get him in trouble.' Heidi screwed her face up to demonstrate her point.

Chrissy spoke next. 'Hang on, he offered his address and asked for the book, we can't forget that. He did this before with his landline number. He's quite the prat.'

'Thanks, Chrissy, I knew you'd remember that. Plus, it was your idea to clean, causing me to find the book and post it.'

'You can't blame Chrissy,' said Heidi. 'It's icky.' She turned up her nose.

We discussed the answer machine message, and what I should do – nothing. We questioned why Dan had called my landline. Nobody had the answer. Chrissy, super detective that she was, called 192 and asked about the number. The helpful BT man confirmed it was a payphone in the town hall, in Stapleford. Again, we discussed why the call was made from there. My friends made fun of him running around his town, locating a phone box that worked, but I just felt sad inside. He was my sort of boyfriend and it disturbed me to think of him so hopeless and frantic.

We briefly dissected my mini spectacle over a terrific feast of sausages, bacon, baked beans, eggs, mushrooms, toast, and more toast with mounds of butter. Di decanted jams and marmalades into ramekins and old teacups, and hers were filled and refilled seemingly endlessly. It was a mad house as we discussed the chaos of the night; it had been the knees-up we all needed.

We concluded that fresh air along the canal was due, and off we went. As we left the house, my phone, which I'd planned to leave at Di's, pinged.

It was a text from Dan:

```
Did you play my voicemail?
```

I read it out and Flint pushed me out the door, slamming my phone on Di's stairs.

'My god, that guy is a nutter.'

🌷

I didn't reply to Dan, following the direct instructions from my mates. Besides, how could I reply when he'd asked me not to? No, silence was best. But what if Dan was anxious that perhaps I hadn't heard the answer machine message loud and clear? Should I reassure him that I'd played it seven times? I pottered around my house, read, painted my nails and watched *Dawson's Creek*. Eventually, I realised I needed Nikki – she'd know what to do. I sent her a text.

She replied:

```
Leave him.
```

God, this was a head fuck.

I woke up for work the next day, fed Bennett, scoffed some breakfast, and heard my phone ringing from my bedroom. I ran up the stairs but it stopped as I reached it.

Dan had called.

What was this new game? Feeling uneasy, it crossed my

mind that Dan didn't have his phone anymore and it was in fact Melissa setting a trap. I ignored the potential trickery and sent him a text from the bus.

> Hello, answer machine message received loud and clear. I won't call or text you anymore, but I'm here when you need me.

I thought the text showed care and respect for whatever deep shit he was in. I received the delivery report. I packed my phone away in my bag and relaxed into my seat, feeling I'd done exactly the right thing.

My morning was busy covering our receptionist due to sickness, and at 1:30 p.m. I strolled out to lunch.

I ambled out into the sunshine and took my lunch to Christchurch Meadow, walking through the iron gates towards the grassy area, led by crowds of tourists ambling down the wide gravel path. There were neat and maintained lavender bushes to my left, and in front, a portion of lawn so fastidiously cared for and respected that the *Don't walk on the grass* sign was always going to be redundant. As I approached the meadow area, I admired the wild hawthorn trees and cow parsley filling the back of the flowerbeds. I managed to find a spot away from some foolish students acting out some scenes from floppy books and a couple arguing over a couscous pot. Admiring my new nail colour, sprawling on my tummy after

I'd polished off an egg and cress sandwich, an apple and some tomatoes, I opened my book.

My phone rang.

It was Dan.

'Hello,' I answered.

'Thank god you picked up. I called you this morning, did you see? You never replied.' His voice was unsteady and sped up.

'You asked me not to, but I texted you.'

'I know, but then I thought, what if she never saw the message flashing and Bennett walked over the phone and hit delete.'

'I always see the message flashing and I told you in my text I heard it.'

Did he know how mad he sounded?

'I wished I'd asked you to let me know if you received it, but I couldn't risk Melissa seeing me text you and I got all twitchy and I haven't slept.'

'What happened? Please, take a breath and calm down. I haven't got long to talk to you.'

Dan explained that when they returned from their holiday, the neighbour had put the post on the kitchen table. Melissa had sifted through it while Dan sorted out the kids. She had separated the post into three piles; apparently – a fact I wasn't aware of – the kids opened all big packages that arrived to the house. They loved to do it, and if they didn't there was a tantrum. So, there, in the kids-to-open pile, had been my book.

Izzy had opened it under the beady eye of her mummy. Of course, the title had caught Melissa's eye, so she'd grabbed the book and read aloud my message.

Dan had hid in the loo as she asked him through the door, 'Dan, who is Louise?'

He'd opened the door to find Melissa standing there, the book in her hand as she nodded for him to follow her upstairs.

'So, what did you tell her?' I swallowed, hoping the dryness in my mouth would fade away. Instead, my heart banged in my ears.

'That you were a school mum who'd left the area, and you had a childish crush on me.'

I tried to gulp, to allow me to take a breather, but my spit was like sand. I didn't want to talk to him anymore. Hanging up would prove I was bigger than him; it would show him the excuse he'd offered to Melissa was an insult, and we were over. *So* over.

'Did she believe you?' I asked instead.

Dan laughed. 'Yeah, she did. Only after more questions though, like whether I'd seen you recently, what you looked like and who your kid was. I thought on my feet and invented a year five boy and just hoped she didn't dig about too much.'

I remained silent.

'How funny is that? I said she was a no one and the book could go in the bin,' he concluded with another surge of laughter.

'Hysterical. In fact, so funny I can't thank you enough for making me laugh so hard. Fuck's sake Dan, are you serious right now?'

'Louise—'

'I'm afraid I'm not done. You called me a childish no one

and you think that's funny? Well, it's not, it's hurtful and cruel. You couldn't have thought of another way to describe me?'

'You know what, maybe, but I was shaking inside and panicked.'

My breath halted. I held onto my belly – a thousand moths had taken flight, wavering there. I sealed my lips tight. I couldn't move them. All I could see were the faces of my friends shaking their heads at me, and for me.

Suddenly, I couldn't hold the rage inside anymore. 'Is the book in the bin?'

'Of course it is.'

For fuck's sake. 'Is that how you see me?'

'What do you mean?'

'Do you see me as a hopeless mum who has a crush on you?'

'No, because you aren't a mum, or local, and I don't think what we had was a crush, do you?'

'I meant, do you see me as a no one?' I wished I was a smoker – I needed a hit of instant calm.

'Course not,' he replied, his volume going up a few notches. 'Come on, have a laugh, will you? I was stressed at first, but talking it through with you, I mean, we covered it up, and I think, as long as we lay low for a bit, things can go back to normal.'

'What the actual fuck, Dan? Back to fucking normal? I was anxious for you! All the calls, texts, and me stuck here not knowing if I could respond. I thought something really bad had happened. You said as much! But now it's all a bit of a laugh, a real hoot. Well ha fucking ha. This isn't a bloody game to me.'

'It's not a game to me either, and can you stop shouting please?'

I'd forgotten my surroundings and glanced around me. The couscous couple had given up on their fight, clearly finding the one I was having much more interesting. I felt like I was burning inside from his absurd explanation of his cover up. In fact, he was right: giving each other a wide berth was the best idea he'd had in ages. I couldn't stop the tears now. I picked up my bag and emptied the contents onto the grass. I needed a tissue.

'I'm not sure you can ask anything of me right now, but I agree on the laying low. Absolutely no calling.'

'Well, for a bit and then we can get back to it.'

'Hmm, not sure.' I wiped a tear from the end of my nose with my sleeve.

'What do you mean? Are you crying?'

'Um, yes, of course I bloody am.' My voice reached a screech. I didn't have a tissue. I picked up a Morrison's receipt and blew my nose on that.

'Oh shit. I don't know what to say, I thought you'd laugh with me.'

I sniffed. 'I don't know what you find comical these days, but nothing about this is funny.' I screwed up the Morrison's receipt, realising it wasn't mine. Grim.

'I'll miss you, though. I still love you.'

'Uh-huh.'

'You didn't say you love me.'

'I do love you. I've always loved you, Dan. That is not in doubt, but right now I... I don't know. I feel like us and our reality is kind of shit.'

We hung up our phones and I glanced at the time. *Crap* – I was going to get a bollocking for being late back to the office. I picked up my things and ran back to work. After unlocking my locker and shoving everything inside, I pulled out my compact mirror. My eyes were swollen, I'd rubbed my mascara off and I needed to blow my nose again. I rooted around the locker for a tissue but had no such luck, so instead I located some powder and patted some around my nose and eyes.

Someone was watching me.

Jasmeet was there to my left, sitting at her desk, clearly not listening to annoying Tom showing her something on her PC. She stood up, pulled a tissue out of the box on her desk, marched over to me and handed it over. Before she returned to her desk, she put her hand on my arm and squeezed it. I swallowed back the tears and, in my head, thanked the universe for Jasmeet and her kindness.

CHAPTER 30

The Cover-Up and Cocktails

My mood was twisted and warped. I veered from tears to anger, then to resentment and spite. I couldn't see change coming, and the terrifying part was that I didn't care how dented I became inside.

In public, I berated Dan. I belittled him and slagged him off. My friends were willing participants in this part of the grieving process. They liked this nasty, furious version of me who swore too much. This Louise liked drinking – a lot – and was cranking up the nights out and only stopping drinking when we collapsed.

One night I'd mixed too many coloured and flavoured ciders that resulted in me being sick up the wall in a toilet cubicle with Heidi. I couldn't remember it, but we spoke about it the next morning, in bed with tea watching *Hollyoaks*.

'I had to stay over; you were trying to take your contact lenses out in the back of the taxi. You thought you were in your bathroom.'

'Don't.' I cradled my head, as if that would eradicate the truth.

'The problem being you drank two bottles to my one.'

In private, I mourned Dan. I listened to music about lost loves, which made me cry so much I had a headache, then I stopped eating proper meals. I kept my true feelings away from everyone. I wanted to see him, touch him and kiss him. I wanted to smell his smell, make him tea in my kitchen, drive to our bus stop to pick him up and chat shit with him. I wanted to drop him off in our usual spot and watch him walk off before turning down a little lane where he'd always perform a comedy salute. I missed that.

I wanted to resume our lengthy evening phone calls when his wife was working late. Where we'd start the conversation after the kids' bedtime, simultaneously clear up after our dinners and end the call cleaning our teeth.

I couldn't stop snooping on him; Facebook handed me the new version of my boyfriend on a plate. This kind of unusual contentment, having a sort of shadowy, hologram edition of Dan, felt better than nothing at all.

I spent an evening with Chrissy, lying in her back garden on sun loungers and drinking non-alcoholic beer. I watched as butterflies landed nearby then fluttered off. One of the best parts of my friendship with Chrissy was the ease of ceaseless nattering or serene silence, both equally as nourishing. We rolled like that.

'Heidi filled me in about Dan and you – the cover up,' Chrissy said, causing me to roll onto my side to face her.

'I guess you could call it that.' I sniffed, adding, 'I thought Dan would stand up to his wife and say: "That's it, I don't love you, I love that Louise girl who wrote in the book. She isn't a nobody, she's my new somebody and I'm leaving".'

Chrissy turned and looked at me, her expressionless silence saying everything and nothing.

'What do you think?' I asked.

'It won't happen yet, but it might. Leaving her, I mean. The cracks are forming and he's not strong enough to fix them.'

I finished the remaining beer from my bottle as Chrissy continued.

'But why should you care what goes on? He's not in your life now, at his request, I might add. Remember that. When he's single, which he will be, let him call you. But I guarantee you and your life will have moved on. You won't even take that call.'

When I left later that evening, I said goodbye and she hugged me tight.

'Do nothing,' she said.

As I drove home that night, the May evening sky was a joyful blurry pink, and a horizontal rope of cloud floated in my eyeline. I thought of my next plan of action. Chrissy's advice sat with me and pinged around in my head.

And for once, admittedly only for a short amount of time, I did absolutely that.

♥

Flint invited as many people as possible over to his place to celebrate his birthday.

Things were rocky between him and Jeannie; in fact, Flint was cagey about whether it was completely off or not. None of us could seem to get any information out of him. Heidi had tasked me with having another go.

'Call him. Ask what to bring for the party, and for god's sake get more juice on those two. You are the only one who can dig deep with Flint. We have to know if he's single or not. I have a queue of superfans in my office waiting to step into Jeannie's little ballet pumps.'

A jolt arrived in my tummy. Flint had superfans? Of course he did. He was a funny, kind, good-looking guy in his thirties with a stable job. What woman wouldn't want him?

I called Flint. I had Heidi's mission on my mind, but I also wanted to know for myself. Were he and Jeannie over? This vital information was suddenly more important than the required provisions to bring to the party.

'So, to clarify, everyone brings a bottle of spirit and a recipe for a cocktail they can make. We drink the supplies down and go to town for more drink and dancing,' Flint explained.

'Got it, but you've avoided my questions about Jeannie. Why isn't she coming? You need to tell me what's going on.'

'Why? I want to have a good birthday and not dwell on it.'

'But we always talk about this kind of stuff and you haven't mentioned her for ages.'

'Haven't I?'

'No, and something's changed between you two.'

'Yeah, it has, and I remember now, I did try and talk to you but you were snogging that dude on the dance floor. And anyway, I'm not speaking about it tonight. Don't forget. 6 p.m. Or I won't let you in.'

As I waited for Chrissy to pick me up, I sat with my laptop

balanced on a cushion, my finger hovering over the link to Dan's Facebook page. I wasn't friends with him, but Nikki and Heidi assured me I could look at it over and over again and he'd never know. I clicked, and his profile appeared, along with some new photos. He'd been out the night before at some sort of school reunion. Smiley people, in a pub, nothing flash. I smiled to myself, seeing him in action, laughing. It reminded me of the night we'd met; enjoying his wit and high spirits.

As I hovered on one of the photos, my stomach dropped, the shock making it impossible to flick through to the end of the album. Dan was stood with a tall, pretty girl called Trish, their heads leaning in towards each other, carefree smiles on their faces. I drank in every detail of her, from her long slim legs and rich brown hair to her irritatingly small waist. Her smile was so radiant I itched to claw it off her smug face. Trish wore a skimpy white vest, emphasising her non-existent chest, but she wore a big smile and lots of red lipstick, highlighting her fine set of teeth.

There were comments underneath the photo – apparently, they had been an item back in the day.

Ahhh, back together at last.
Still got it, Dan, mate.
Cuuuuteeeee
I love school reunions. What a love story.

After that, I raced through the photos with the velocity and resolve of a rookie private investigator. Wherever Trish was, snap, Dan was there too. I went back and forth over the images and hesitated on some, looking for evidence – of what, I wasn't quite sure. I asked out loud the questions only Dan could answer, the main one being: what the hell was going on?

Then something caught my eye. Something I didn't like. My breath became uneven. It could be nothing, but it could be something. My heart rate sped up and I could hear it beating loud in my ears. Trish, her hand placed on Dan's knee under the table, her kilowatt fucking Cheshire cat grin lighting up the fucking scene. It was laughable, but I couldn't stop myself hovering over the likes, clicking into the comments. Dan and Trish had liked this one, and there was one comment.

XXXXXXXXX

Written by Trish.

Fuck.

A car horn blared me back to reality.

Flint's birthday. *Shit*.

I slumped into Chrissy's car, unable to make eye contact. Di and Nikki were already in the back, early Kings of Leon booming from the tinny car stereo. I was the last pick up.

My bottom had just touched the seat when I yelled, 'Drink!'

I'd forgotten my vodka.

I ran back into the house, sighing as I reopened my front door. Staggering a little, I leant against the wall, frozen to the spot.

I took a few deep breaths, bending forwards to hold onto my knees, saying out loud to myself, 'You can do this.'

I slammed the front door and started my evening again, and when I sat down in the car for the second time, the girls cheered as I waved the vodka.

It was 8:34 p.m. and there was not a hint of us departing from Flint's place. The boys had everything organised. Most of the activity took place outside. Heidi joined the smokers, especially as weed was being passed around somewhere near the shed.

One of Flint's colleagues was telling me an unwanted anecdote while I sipped a sweet, sickly drink. I couldn't recall who'd made me the cocktail, but they'd plopped a plastic knob straw in my glass. As I swayed to Womack and Womack, I caught Flint staring at me as he opened beer bottles for friends. He slammed the bottle opener on the barbecue, his eyes slanting in my direction.

I mouthed "what?" at him. He took a swig from a beer bottle, shaking his head. I giggled as Flint began to multiply. Christ, how close was he? To avoid any sermons from him, I wobbled inside to refill. The ingredients were laid on the dining room table positioned next to the wide-open patio doors. Nikki guffawed as I swiftly passed, like I was a floating hologram headless ghost. The ice bucket was empty, the citrus fruits had been used and the ends remained on the chopping board, looking left out. I estimated we had another hour, max, before supplies were sent for, or we went out to the pub.

I couldn't be sure how many cocktails I'd downed but it wasn't going to end well. In between being over-friendly and bubbly, I thought of Dan. He'd have been great fun, gossiping to anyone, doing his one-man comedy show while making drinks. And he'd sneak tiny kisses onto my cheek when I wasn't expecting it.

But in real life, Dan would not be doing any of those things, at least not with me. Instead, I'd already positioned Dan and Trish in my mind as a couple. In my head, he'd already gone down on her.

Heidi was calling me. I turned around to locate her, but she was already there, her nose touching mine. I giggled again.

'Louise, I'm not clearing up your sick tonight. Slow down. You look wankered.'

Someone burped and laughed in my ear.

The burp was all mine.

Flint spoke. 'Louise, come on, sit down. You're not only belching like my Uncle Bazzer, but your eyes are glazing over.'

Where'd he come from?

Flint attempted to steer me somewhere. I resisted and looked up at him, tipping my head backwards. I cracked up again and pushed his chest away from me. He came back, but I wagged my finger at him, staggering away.

I went to the toilet and sat there, door locked, wondering how I'd got there. Not the toilet, of course – to this point in my life. Was this it? Back to being alone. Was happiness something I could now reminisce about? Like the good ol' days at school, the Miss Selfridge lipsticks, or a pack of six Creme Eggs. Those were things to remember, and they were stored in our memories as evidence.

So, of course I called Dan. It was the logical thing to do, sat on the loo seat, soused and not giving a flying fuck. His mobile rang and rang, then went dead. I tried again, holding the phone so close, my nose poked the screen as I pressed the buttons. The same thing happened. I called again with the same result after three rings. I didn't care how I came across. I had to know who Trish was. So what the hell, I did it again. This time, the call went straight to voicemail. He'd switched me and my absurdity off for the night.

I took a deep breath and slurred into my phone, 'Hi, it's me. Where are you? We need to talk. I need to talk to you. I need to know what you've been up to. I know all about her, that girl. Call me back.'

Someone rattled the door handle.

'In a minute!' I shouted.

I got up, my head swimming alarmingly, and snuck out of the bathroom, making my way downstairs to sit on the wall outside. My bum hit the uneven brickwork, my brain deciding at that moment to start up that nauseating spinning sensation. As other revellers walked past me, laughing and starting their night, I accepted I did not need more alcohol.

Swaying gently, I got my mobile out again, struggling with what felt like an extra thumb and four swollen fingers to type in an approximately accurate text version of my verbal message. The need to have my own words heard mattered more than the aftermath of shit I would have to clear up.

Back inside, Flint's mate, Stewart, placed a drink I didn't want, need, or ask for, in my hand. I necked the orange and coconut concoction at speed. If I slowed down, the drink would come straight back up.

So I carried on.

❦

In the morning, I mercifully awoke in my own cosy bed and not slumped against a curb or a layby somewhere, like my body was trying to tell me I was. Groaning, I scanned the clock next to my bed. 8:01 a.m. For a moment, this confused me as I patted my face, trying to work out where my glasses were, until I realised my miraculous twenty-twenty vision meant I'd slept in my contact lenses.

I rolled over to one side of my bed, attempting to sit up and put my feet on the carpet. Bennett was hungry, repeatedly jumping up and down from the bed to the floor.

I was ruined.

I stood up, straightened my body and walked like the Tinman from *The Wizard of Oz*. With each step, a feeling of discomfort vibrated and rattled around in my head. I needed water, but first I needed to be sick. I moved quickly to the bathroom and smelt the vomit in my toilet. Oh shit.

I was then sick, on top of my own dried-up sick.

Afterwards, I wiped my face with a flannel, rubbed some toothpaste around my teeth and gums, then sampled a few sips of water. I knew my hungover body well enough at my age: if I could keep that down, tea would also stay down. I sat on my bum and descended the stairs that way – gingerly and one by one. I made a brew and returned to my bed to hide out from humanity for the rest of my days.

I awoke two minutes later to my mobile ringing somewhere in the bedroom. I looked at the clock. More time had passed than I thought: it was 12:02 in the afternoon. My contact lenses were still in.

The ringing stopped. I grumbled, flopping back into bed, closing my eyes against the light of a day I didn't want to engage with. The wretched thing started up again. I huffed and cursed as I located it under a pile of clothes. There it was, peeping out of my handbag. I picked it up, but it rang off; I'd missed it again.

Dan was the caller.

I downed the cold tea next to my bed. I even enjoyed the yucky layer that had thickened on the top. There were seven texts on my phone, all from my friends. I didn't open them. Another text arrived and changed the unread texts to eight. This one was from Dan.

```
What the hell is wrong with
you? Calling me last night?
Do NOT call me back. Or text
me. I will try YOU again.
```

I closed my eyes, exhaling. Even that routine bodily function hurt. What the hell had happened? Did I call him? Why would I have done that? I checked my call log and gulped, my pulse quickening. My sent texts caused nausea to roll in my belly. What on earth was wrong with me?

People didn't do this shit.

I hunched down in my bed and wondered who of my friends would have the energy to help me put this together. I couldn't think alone; my brain was suspended and out of order. I felt like I had one of those little computer timers placed inside my head, and every time the sand drained clear, someone turned it over again.

🌷

My morning was not productive.

I sent Dan a text, saying sorry. Sometimes less is more and

all that.

I called Heidi. When she picked up, she answered with a grunt.

'McDonald's breakfast?' I asked.

'Nope. Can't even think.' She hung up.

We texted each other instead, arranging a takeaway at my place later.

Next up: Flint.

I shelved a normal Sunday swim in favour of driving with some breakfast to Flint's. After all, it was his birthday. I thought helping him to clear up would be a distraction, but also, as I couldn't remember anything after the orange cocktail. He could help fill in the gaps.

I rang the bell, the door opening as if by a ghost. I walked inside and Flint sat on the stairs in his shorts, looking at me.

'For you.' I handed him the brown paper bag of McDonald's naughtiness.

'My angel,' he croaked, snatching the bag and walking into the living room.

We scoffed burgers and fries dipped in curry sauce, not making a sound. He spilt some burger sauce onto his chest, hooked it up with his index finger and licked it.

We spent the whole afternoon on the sofa finishing our milkshakes. What a mate. I loved being hungover with him. If I'd been with Chrissy, she'd have Alice to tend to and I'd find the commotion too much to handle. Nikki and Di liked to dissect the details, and Heidi offered nothing, but after last night, I couldn't kickstart my brain at all. That was what getting shit-faced does to you. Unwanted repeats of the calls I'd made to Dan replayed in my mind and all I could do was close my eyes, as if by lowering the shutters of my eyelids it would all be forgotten.

Flint fell asleep at one end of the sofa, while I stared at the TV watching *Roman Holiday*, sneaking secret peeks at him as he slept. Flint's arms were folded across his chest and his mouth was stuck in a peaceful pout. I smiled.

He stirred when I came back from the loo. He rubbed his eyes like a little toddler.

'I'm cold,' he murmured.

'You should go to bed,' I mumbled, sitting down next to him.

'We should go to bed?' he asked, sitting upright to face me, his eyes wide.

'What? No! I said you should go back to bed.' My face was flaming red hot heat.

'Christ, I thought you were making me a birthday offer.' Flint's lopsided smile softened, and his cheeks reddened.

I smiled back, our eyes lingering longer than perhaps was entirely necessary.

I didn't see *that* coming, I thought. Was this something? It was certainly new. My phone beeped from my bag.

'That will be Heidi. If she wants some Chinese food, you in?'

Flint nodded. He leant his head on my shoulder as I unlocked my phone. I could feel Flint's breath on my skin. I shivered and smiled.

The smile evaporated.

The text wasn't from Heidi. It was Dan replying to my

"sorry" text. I winced as I read it.

```
You should be, and I said don't
fucking text me, stupid.
```

Before the tears forced their way through, my heart shattered, and I lost all the colour in my face. How could he speak to me like that? I'd made one mistake. One episode that may have caused him some earache. Prior to that, I'd done everything he asked. Every fucking thing.

'What's up?' Flint asked, peering at my phone.

I turned to face him, the tears cascading down my face. I couldn't look at him, but by now, after all this time, he must surely have realised what I was capable of. I had never wanted my lovely Flint to know the real me.

I went for it. I told him about Trish, the calls, the text.

He got up and paced around the living room. He sat down in the armchair and got up again. His silence spoke his thoughts. He had every right to be fuming with me.

'Flint, say something. I feel sick.'

'So do I. You know, when are you going to give this mess up? And before you answer, the right thing to say would be now. The chasing, the moping, the wondering. You have to give this shit up.'

I looked away and stared at my hands, leaving his chocolatey eyes looking uncharacteristically pointy and razor-sharp.

He crouched down in front of me. 'Go and call Heidi, Chrissy, Di, anyone, even wonder boy himself. I'm not listening to you anymore. I'm going back to bed.'

'Flint, I'm sorry.'

He was walking out of the room as he shouted, 'Yeah yeah, happy fucking birthday to me.'

I wiped the tears away and sat in my car, my hands trembling on the steering wheel. Before I could even doubt anything, I dialled 141 and called Dan on his landline – the number I said I'd never call.

Melissa picked up after three rings.

'Hello?'

'Hi there, I wonder if I could speak to Dan Christie, please?'

She sighed. 'Yeah, who's calling?'

'Um, Miss Brown. I'm a client.'

'Okay.' She sighed again and called his name.

I closed my eyes tight, hearing footsteps, shuffling and muffled voices. I imagined Melissa passing him a cordless phone as he sat on the sofa with his kids. They could be in their PJs at this time. He'd feel horrified and would know it was me, Melissa glaring and observing him from the doorway as he answered my call.

'Hello?'

'Hi, it's me. Please don't speak, I'm sure you don't want to, so please listen.'

'Yes, hello there, how are you?' he answered in an upmarket accent that, for a second, made me smile. And then I remembered myself.

'I'm sorry about calling you last night, really sorry, but there's no need to call me stupid. Your last text broke me and—'

He cut me off. 'Yes, that's fine, not a problem. Do you think we could resume this tomorrow, as it is Sunday night? Say 9:30 a.m.?' Without waiting for me to answer, he added,

'Brilliant, we'll speak tomorrow, and thanks for calling.'

The line went dead.

There'd be consequences, and I understood that what I'd done would cause Dan to be enraged, and rightly so. He had issues, and his mental health was probably compromised. But I didn't care. Hurting him as well as myself was the aim.

As I drove home, my breathing was unsteady, and my heart zipped about. I went to bed panicked, feeling that although I'd made those choices knowingly, I wasn't sure I'd understood what the result of those choices would be. Fuck, I didn't even understand who I was anymore. The emerging new role of stalker was custom made for me, like those made-to-measure curtains I couldn't afford.

I'd morphed into a person I didn't like very much. The woman I would have critiqued and made jokes about with my friends. I was the sad, forlorn and isolated character in a film that the viewers jeered at, especially the men.

I was the woman men wouldn't date because she was nuts. I was the woman other women avoided becoming at all costs.

I batted the steady stream of tears away and stashed my phone in my wardrobe, frightened of it and the power we had between us. I couldn't bear the sight of it.

When I arrived home from work the next day there'd been no interaction from Dan, and I falsely and foolishly thought I'd got away with any aggressive comebacks from him. As I locked up my house, going off to meet Heidi at the gym, I noticed the landline flashing: a sort of Scooby Doo baddie robot in the room, staring at me with its red beady eye. I took a deep breath and hit play.

'Leave you a message? I'll leave you a fucking message. Never EVER call my house again. Never EVER call me again. I never want to see your name on my phone EVER. Now fuck off.'

CHAPTER 31

Who is Trish?

A man had never told me to fuck off before.

I replayed the message, eventually deleting it. How could I store this audio as the only record I had of his voice? I could still feel the venom he spat at me, hitting my cheek as I replayed it in my own head.

Not only was Dan furious with me, but it would also seem he didn't like me very much anymore, and I understood he'd never want to see me again. When we'd parted ways at Christmas, despite it being absolutely the right thing to do for him, our affection, our mutual respect and the desire to be together was strong enough to adjust and tweak how we stayed in touch. I was woeful and sad that I'd repulsed Dan, and that any further interaction with him would be harmful to both of us.

I had to contend with Jasmeet as well; she was poking her nose in. I used to think she was my boss, but she was quickly becoming a supportive older sister, just with less hang ups about me pinching her perfume or getting into trouble with our parents.

I tried desperately to tuck away my woebegone demeanour at work. Since the locker tissue incident, I'd given Jasmeet a wide birth as much as I could – given she was my boss. I'd taken to dropping a brittle smile at her every now and then when I caught her eye, in an attempt to trick her into thinking I was flying high.

Big mistake. In between clients, she tapped me on the shoulder.

'Can I have a word?' she asked, standing behind me.

I turned to face her. 'Yeah, sure.'

I blushed. Not sure why; it wasn't as if I was still on the Dorothy Perkins website looking at dresses. If she'd approached me three minutes earlier, that would have been a different story.

I followed her to the stationery room, and she pulled the door closed.

'Um, everything alright? Am I in trouble?' I asked. I noticed my voice was almost a whimper.

I mentally mapped out any potential errors I'd made. I had to be steps ahead of Jasmeet and plan some excuses. Had I made mistakes with clients? I knew I'd scanned documents upside down and not rotated them (one of her pet peeves), and definitely had been known to slope off to the loo when regular, difficult clients walked into reception. Oh god, did she know that I'd accidentally-on-purpose put my gramps' birthday card in the post out-tray to avoid queuing for stamps?

'Oh, nothing work-wise. Well, not really. Look, I'll cut to the chase. I'm worried about you. You seem flat.'

'Oh.' I sighed. I was comforted that there was no immediate disciplinary.

'Can I help? I know its cos of that guy, who, FYI' – here she performed her little rabbit ears signs – 'I wouldn't go to the trouble of introducing me to. At least, not until he behaves like less of a prick.'

'Oh.'

'Yes, oh. I hear things. I know everything.'

I swallowed. 'Okay, but you sound like my best friend Flint.'

'I like him already. So?'

'I'm sorry, I might cry.'

'That's alright. I've come prepared.' She pulled a pocket packet of tissues from her sleeve.

I told her about the phone call, the lies, him, and the mess I'd caused when I was pissed. Jasmeet didn't speak and she didn't frown, but I couldn't hold her gaze. If I did, she'd see the mortification, and I was ashamed, totally fucking ashamed.

'You know the right thing to do. You need to get rid of him, but that doesn't happen overnight, does it?'

I shook my head. Tears were now falling.

'But you can look after yourself until you digest him and all the crap that he brings with him. That's a bit grim, but you know what I'm saying.'

I sniffed and smiled. 'I know.'

'So do it, get some help, find a therapist. This is Oxford; we've all those counsellors training at the university. The mental health world is huge here and you are worth it, right?'

'I hadn't thought about it.'

'Well, you help people all day, now help you. Promise?'

'Alright, I'll think about it. Is this because, you know, my work is getting rubbish?'

'No, this is friend to friend, woman to woman etc.' She did her little bunny ears again.

'Thanks, Jasmeet.' I placed my hand on her arm.

'Okay, let's get back out there. You go and get a cuppa first though.'

We walked down the corridor, and when Jasmeet hugged me, it was like a mug of creamy hot chocolate. I liked her perfume; it was musky with a hint of vanilla. She oozed care for me and, until then, I hadn't known how much I'd needed it. Jasmeet turned to enter the office and I went the opposite way to make a drink.

Before I lost sight of her, she shouted, 'Don't buy the 70s-style print dress. I'm not sure it would take your cleavage.'

She really was like a big sister, in all ways. That or a mystic witch.

A week or so later, Dan called me a few times and I ignored him.

I pictured Jasmeet wagging her finger at me. I didn't take the call. On the third occasion, I picked up. I caved. Jasmeet wouldn't necessarily approve, but I considered speaking to him as moving on. I needed to say goodbye.

Shaky and apprehensive about hearing his voice, I took a deep breath and hoped I could keep this brief.

'Hello?' Anxiety was closing up my gullet. I attempted to swallow the lump in my throat.

'Hi, it's Dan.'

'I know.'

'I thought you might have removed my number. How are you?'

He was onto me; I hadn't removed him, but had renamed him. He was now logged as "Fuckwit" on my phone.

'Alright. You?'

'You know, not good. I want to say I'm sorry for how I shouted at you last week. You pushed me to it, but I'm so sorry I spoke to you like that. That's not me.'

'Accept it was you.'

'That's not fair.'

'Maybe not, but if the cap fits.'

Dan sighed deeply. 'I don't even know why I called you that name, I'm so sorry. All I know is I felt pushed about and I can't cope.'

I noticed Dan's tone was devoid of his usual intoxicating warmth.

'Everything at home is worse than ever,' he continued. 'The arguing, the shit holiday. I slept on the caravan sofa that was fit for toddlers, didn't get any sleep and then your book arrived. And that added a layer of crappiness I didn't expect.'

'You asked me to post it.' I raised my voice and wanted to add more, but he spoke over me.

'But calling me late at night, I didn't ask for that. I think Melissa has been suspicious before, but me hiding my mobile and turning it off, then Miss Brown calling on a Sunday... I mean, Miss Brown?'

I said nothing. I rubbed my face. Dan's words and tone

shrunk me in size.

Dan started to speak in a softer tone. 'Are you okay, really?'

'No, and I didn't say I was okay.'

'Sorry, that's right, you didn't. I'm so sorry it's got like this.'

I wiped tears away from my cheeks using my palm. 'By the way, who's Trish?'

Dan laughed briefly, then explained that she was a girl from secondary school he'd fancied. All the boys did, but she'd singled him out. It was one of those urgent crushes when you're fifteen and the hormones rule the brain. They'd snogged in school, at the chippy, and everyone had known they were sort of seeing each other, as you do at that age.

'Like a *Wonder Boy* moment, when you smile for an hour or something because the girl you want wants you back.'

'Ah, those were the days.'

'Innocent, right? As the story goes, I invited her to my house to wow her with my records.'

'Which ones?' I asked, laughing.

'REM, Public Enemy and De La Soul. I even laid them out in a specific order. Mum had changed the sheets and the house was all mine.'

'And?'

'I waited for her after double Chemistry, but she never turned up. Next day she said she'd forgotten. I went home and wept into my vinyl.'

'God, it sounds like an episode from *Grange Hill*, and I'm not sure vinyl should get wet.'

Dan blurted out a loud laugh.

'Was that the end then, with you two?'

Dan explained he'd never slept with her, but admitted he wished he had. There had been numerous chances and he'd wanted things to be special, but she didn't see it like that.

I asked if he'd kissed her at the reunion.

'No, I didn't.' His voice was a whisper. 'I was happy to see her though, I won't lie, and there was a second where I thought about what would have happened if we'd got together. She's just the same, except miles away from what I want.'

'What do you mean?'

'Dunno, but when you're fifteen, you want girls as they are and you don't care about the bigger picture, do you? You don't care what they know, whether they're clever or funny. The hormones tell you everything you need to know. If a girl is fit, that's it. But when you meet someone like that later in life... well, I found her a disappointment.'

'You could call that snobby, or you've grown up.'

'I know, but she doesn't read books; she laughed when we talked about politics, said she's never voted, and she watches things on TV like *Wife Swap*, that *Ramsay's Kitchen Nightmares* bollocks and probably liked *Big Brother*, but I didn't ask. But I could have kissed her, and I wanted to, but then everything went weird. Like I was cheating on you.'

'That happened to me, a few weeks ago. I kissed someone else.' I held a few breaths.

'Did you? I didn't know that,' Dan croaked.

'Yes, I did.'

'I'm having visions I don't want.' A few beats passed and Dan added, 'Remember when we first kissed? There was that invisible connection with us. I thought snogging Trish was tacky almost – a bit gross. She was very up for it and then I didn't want to. She probably thought I was a tease, but I couldn't tell her I wanted to be with someone who wasn't Melissa. Not that that would have bothered her, but you see another difference. She was really out there and well up for it, but when I met you, it was sort of, um, innocent, wasn't it?'

'Yes, it was.' I pressed my fist to my lips and closed my eyes.

'I compared her to you.'

I didn't reply, the tears rolling down my cheeks.

'My mind didn't fancy her mind. You see, I'd still like to kiss you. But hey, look at the bleeding mess I'm already in. Kissing someone who isn't my wife.'

'I'm sorry, I don't know what to say.'

'It's okay, I know I'm sort of throwing stuff at you.' Dan paused. 'We're about more than kissing. I'd still like to be with you. I think about that promise I made you, about moving in. I'm gutted that's not a plan anymore. I wanted to wake up with you, clean my teeth with you, go food shopping and argue about the bill. I wanted to cut your lawn and sort that lock on your back gate.'

I could only cry as he shared his want for the ordinary, humdrum life we could have created if we'd met in another lifetime. I had to accept, and he did too, that it would be better if we hung up.

I told him that.

'I suppose.'

'I think it's the only way. I've got to get over you, Dan.'

'I know, but I want to know how you are, I need to check you're alright. I can't bear the thought of not being there for you when you need me.'

'But you can't be there for me. We haven't physically seen each other for what feels like a hundred years. That's not helpful.'

'True, but what about if you meet someone else? I want to make sure he's good enough for you.'

I walked out of my living room to locate some kitchen roll. I was curious to know why he considered himself more suited to assessing future men in my life. I hadn't achieved success yet and how he could place himself as the chief evaluator of future boyfriends was beyond me. I pictured him with a clipboard and a checklist, ticking off his own faults.

'I want to stop waking up knowing I still love you, Dan. Does that make sense?'

'Yeah. It hurts, but yeah.'

Yes Dan, it sure does hurt.

CHAPTER 32

The Incoming and the Outgoing

A month or so later, I walked home from work in the mild early-autumn wind.

I'd been to The Old Tom with Flint and Heidi, Old Speckled Hens all round. After-work drinkers filled the place up, but we had secured a table outside, enjoying the last few hours of sunlight. Flint and Jeannie were no more. It was a clean break – so he said. No details were offered on Flint's end; she'd kept the kitten, and it all seemed very simplistic. Either that or he was hiding something. Since the split, we'd checked in on him and there were impromptu invites flying about, which he always accepted.

But as he'd sat down and taken a decent gulp of his ale, he'd said, 'Don't grill me about Jeannie. I'm done. Let's make plans instead.'

So we'd found ourselves discussing our unintentional, but nevertheless very much there, summer weight gain. The three of us had decided to embark on some swift changes, but something odd had also happened that afternoon.

Very odd.

The walk home alone had come about for two reasons. One: it had be an impressive start to the new health regime, and two: there were new feelings to process my end, and I had needed to get out of the pub to do that.

Heidi had started it all by announcing, 'My belly has got to go.'

'Mine too.' I'd peeped down at my prominent tummy, squirming.

Heidi and I had talked about hormones, sugar and booze being our enemy. Flint had stayed quiet for this part of the conversation, smiling at us – his bestest girls.

Then he'd lifted his hoodie up and said, 'I'll join the fat gut club.'

As he'd rubbed his tanned tummy, I'd gazed at him and found I couldn't stop. I'd stopped listening to him; the small gathering of hair dappled around his belly button was far more interesting. I'd taken stock of his large, tanned hands moving in circles across his torso. They were becoming gardeners' hands, *doing* hands, and a thought had entered my mind – what could his doing hands do to me?

I'd heard Heidi cackle. Flint had said something back.

I'd started imagining his strong thighs. I'd wanted to touch him – stroke his tummy. It was a little paunchy, and historically I'd have reached over and pinched him, or it, but I couldn't be that incredulous around him somehow. I hadn't known I was still gawping at his body until Flint waved his hand in front of my eyes.

'Hey, you can stop admiring me now.'

I'd slapped his hand away, not making eye contact. He'd

pinched my flaming cheek, and I'd aimed my weak smile at the beer mat on the table, but when I'd looked back up, his eyes had shimmered back at me.

I'd listened as Flint and Heidi discussed food groups, exercise classes and the amount of water we should be drinking. I'd stayed quiet, finishing my ale, before making the decision to walk home. Would Flint's tanned body vanish from my mind during this walk? Who cared? I had visions of where Flint would place his hands first and I was grinning like a Cheshire cat.

As I walked, my mind soon drifted to work – I'd taken on some additional responsibilities and was now a Senior Case Worker and part of the management team. I was allocated a small crew to look after, permitted a special login code to distribute work, and I attended management meetings, looking important. But mostly, I carried out my staff's performance meetings and they all said I was the most attentive manager – ever. They often popped a packet of Minstrels in my pigeonhole.

Jasmeet had morphed into my cheerleader and encouraged me to go for the job. She'd cornered me at the scanner one afternoon, handing me a piece of paper. Was she for real? I'd thought at the time. Seriously, asking me to scan something for her when she was right there? I'd looked at the document she held, and it was a printout of the job ad.

'I want to see your name in the shortlist.'
'Oh.'
'Not "oh". You say, "yes, I'd love that".'
'Yeah, sure, I will, um.'

She'd leant in and said quietly, 'And you never know who will be successful, eh?' before striding off, her shoulder-length deep brown locks keeping up behind her.

❦

My journey home was nearing its end, and I was listening to Scott Mills through my headphones – I laughed out loud at the section of "Laura's Diary".

As I approached my house, some long legs were stretched out, blocking the path to my door. I couldn't identify the visitor yet, as the rest of the body was hidden by the green wheelie bin, but as I walked closer, my heart started thudding as if it were trying to tunnel out of my body. Some kind of premonition was making my skin shiver all over.

I was right. It was Dan. After all this time.

I swallowed, my feet refusing to move. Jumbled thoughts fell over each other in my desperation to come up with something witty and cool. All I could manage was a silent gasp. I must have made enough noise to penetrate his own stillness, as he looked up.

Our eyes connected, bolts of electricity vibrating through my body.

Before I could gather my thoughts, he was up on his feet, standing to attention. He appeared like an unruly boy who had unravelled all the loo roll. Now face to face with him, I looked away as he spoke, using the need to find my door key as an excuse to break eye contact.

'Hey... hi...'

I moved past him to put the key in the door and turned back to face him.

'I take it you're coming in?'

He nodded.

I stuck the kettle on, fed Bennett, and asked Dan if he wanted tea, but noticed he had taken his shoes off, hung his coat up and sat down. These habitual actions startled me. A few months ago, he'd told me to fuck off, and yet now he appeared to be making himself at home and acting like a named person on the council tax bill.

His eyes slammed into mine, gripping me in an intense hold. I sensed something would happen if I didn't shift. Something that involved shoving hands down pants – that kind of thing. I went into the kitchen and he followed, watching me from the doorway.

'Is it weird being back here?' I asked.

'Yeah, but it's like being home or something. I never thought I'd set foot in here again and there were times I didn't want to come back, or see you, but every little bit of this place is like a happy memory, like a photo.'

I remained quiet, determined not to go along with this. I squeezed tea bags and focused hard on the process.

He continued, 'I remember the first time I walked in – do you remember? – and I noticed that hippy door bead thing you've got hanging there, and I thought, what the fuck has she got here? It was like walking into my nan's flat in the 80s, but I loved taking it all in. Scanning the room. I knew I didn't have long. Does that make sense?'

Done with the tea making, I turned round to face him,

leaning my back against the counter. I knew what he meant; we were never meant to go the distance, have the babies, enjoy middle-aged Med cruises and laugh at our false teeth.

'Totally. Like it was all going to be a memory someday?'

'Yeah, you got it.'

I handed him a mug of tea and looked at him, considering a sip. We moved into the living room and Dan sat still with his head in his hands, massaging his temples. The steam masked his expression and I tried to figure out why he was here. He looked different too, but I was also different – or at least, I was changing. I had a new job, a new health plan and had dirty thoughts about Flint's hands. Something was going on, but still, if you sliced me in half like a stick of rock, I'd be a fucked-up mixture of question marks and love hearts. Dan caught me staring at him and then I noticed what was unusual about him – he was a wreck.

There were so many physical disparities. Dan had clearly lost weight; it was noticeable in his jaw, neck and shoulders. It was obvious something was going on, or had been going on, or that maybe everything that had happened to him since we'd met had caught up with him. His beard was overgrown and sad-looking. One of my favourite things had been to stroke that beard, but I suspected it wouldn't smell of the lemon and lime shower gel he favoured. His hair was dishevelled with rogue strands springing out like little branches attached to his head. His curious green eyes that darted about and wanted to know everything, eyes that sparked up like a fag lighter when he looked into mine, were now muted and didn't mask the sadness I detected. His fingernails would have given Chrissy a hernia with the lingering dirt.

'Why are you here?' I asked.

Dan spoke slowly at first, not looking at me as he explained. 'It seems I am having a bit of a breakdown.'

I nodded.

Dan's pace picked up. 'I woke up thinking it was you I needed to see. So much has happened. I called your office and found out what time you left and waited for you here. Life was flat again, and I was getting those panicky feelings. The GP has given me some medication, but it hasn't kicked in yet. I guess I'm in one of my tunnel times. I can't see any light, Louise, none at all.' He paused to frantically clean his glasses. His eyes were brimming with tears. 'It is a fucking mess.'

'You look so...'

'Fit?' Dan suggested, struggling to laugh through the tears.

'Well...'

'I know, I look rough. Probably because I sleep in my office. And at the weekends, I sleep in a Portakabin.' Dan winced.

'A what?'

'A Portakabin. I went to the pub and I got chatting to these builders. When they left, it was me and the gaffer on the lash. I explained the shit at home and he passed me a set of keys. I said to him, "Mate, you misunderstand me. I'm not that kinda guy". But he offered me his office. "As long as you are out by 6 a.m. Monday morning, when the crew arrives, the place is yours on the weekend". It's like my own little bedsit, without the bed.'

'What do you sleep on?'

'The floor. In my sleeping bag.'

'What about a kitchen?'

'There's a kettle and a fridge, plus I eat at home with the kids anyway. I go to bed when they're asleep.'

'Christ, Dan, what about a toilet?'

'Ahh, well that's the negative bit. The Portaloo is locked, so I've made my own or I go to Sainsbury's.'

I sighed, shook my head and continued to look at him.

I touched my cheek. A sneaky tear had landed there, making its way down to my chin. How much blame could be portioned to me here? Was I to blame?

Unquestionably, a part of his current anguish was now a responsibility of mine. A charge I'd rejected at the beginning of our relationship, instead claiming, as the single woman, that I was the harmless party, a free agent and able to make any old decision I chose. Had I enhanced the troubles in his life? It had always been up to him to manage them, but Dan didn't have the strength to do that, and here, before me, were the consequences.

Dan came over to the sofa and he held onto me. He laid his head in exhaustion on my shoulder. I held him back, and he mumbled sorry over and over again into my hair.

'We both should be sorry,' I said, but he didn't answer. Instead, we chose to remain as we were, snivelling and leaning on each other – providing a covering of humility that warmed and consoled us.

Dan inhaled as he snuggled in deeper. 'I've missed your smell.'

Now was the time to draw a line. I pulled away, shoulders back.

'Do you have someone?' Dan asked.

A few beats passed.

'Sorry, that's none of my business.'

'No, it isn't, but I don't. Well, sort of. Maybe.'

'Are you happy with him?'

'I don't think you have the right to ask me that.'

'I just want to know if you're happy, that's all. I just... I wondered if there was any chance you might still love me.' The last word caught in his throat.

I shoved my head into my hands, my elbows pressing into my knees. I was afraid to look at him; scared of what I might do or say. I squeezed my eyes tight, took a deep breath and remembered it all. The lack of promises, the intense love, the wife, the angst, the kisses, the texts, oh, and his library.

I spoke from behind my fingers. 'You know, you absolutely broke me and my heart, Dan. I'm quite confident you could never fucking fix that.'

Here was the man whose death I had comically plotted with friends, while simultaneously living out our marriage in my deluded head. When I was at my lowest, I had hoped he would forever be in dismal chaos for leaving me. Talk about fucked up. I never knew if I was coming or going, and as Chrissy perceptively quoted once: "god, do you even know if you are Martha or Arthur?".

No, I did not.

Dan interrupted my thoughts as he sobbed gently. I heard him sniff and wipe his nose on his sleeve. I didn't look at him, hugging my IKEA cushion instead.

Finally, I asked him, 'Surely you can't think that arriving

here, after all this time – uninvited, by the way – wondering if I love you, will draw me back in again?'

'I don't know. I hoped there was still a chance. I've been so fucked up and I miss you all the time...'

'But you don't,' I yelled, standing up. 'How can you miss me? I mean, this is the first time I've seen you in months, and from where I'm sitting, you just need a fix of something, anything, to take away the agony in your life, and you think, "Oh yeah, I'll go see Louise and fuck her over again." Well, not this time. I have nothing left for you. My headspace is full of my new life, my future boyfriend, and none of it includes you.'

'Okay.' Dan got up and walked out of the living room.

I sat back down.

He stopped at the front door and started to turn the latch, then changed his mind and walked back to me. He paused in the doorway of the living room.

'I came here to tell you I've left her, and I've left the kids. It is a mess, but I can do it all with you by my side. I know that now. Melissa wants a quick divorce, so I'm moving to my old man's place tomorrow, until I can get sorted. I didn't want to say goodbye to you, I wanted to see where we were. But I can see it *is* goodbye. I'm just too late.' He wiped tears away with his palm and inhaled. 'And before you think it, I wasn't for one second expecting to move in here or anything like that. I just needed to see your face.'

I got up and walked over to him, hanging back; knowing how vulnerable I still was. I looked into his face, a sight so unshakeable and ingrained in me that his features would always be imprinted on my heart. His green eyes, just about visible through the bloodshot sheen, stared back at me. Right at the same time, we moved to hug each other and held on tight. So tight. No words.

Odd that we should reach for each other at the same time today, when at no other point in our relationship had anything happened with that same kind of synchronicity.

CHAPTER 33

Here We Go Again

I awoke to soft, October sunshine drifting through a crack in my curtains. Ignoring the rumbling in my belly, I faced the soundtrack of my day.

The radiators were performing their start up clicking sounds. Panic swirled around my body as I hit rewind on last night, and my remorse seemed to have its own intro.

What had I done? I should feel on top of the world – I'd done it, I'd finally got rid of the illegal squatter in my brain.

But I could have had him.

I could have Dan all to myself.

I sat up, rubbing my face with my hands and walked into the bathroom. I looked at myself in the mirror as the tears fell.

I padded to locate my phone, typing out a text to Flint. Before I hit send, I placed the phone down, considering. I wanted to see Flint, to tell him about Dan. Yes, this was important, but it was Flint's face that flew into my head. Had I not received the unwanted guest, would I be layering up my fantasy thoughts about Flint? I felt like I was cheating on him.

I sent him a message.

> Breakfast? My shout? I have
> news x

Damn right X

I took him to a nearby builder's café. It was a plastic chair, mismatched mug, leaky teapot and Mellow Birds type of place. In silence we stood in the queue, staring at the menu on the wall. A warm arm encased my sagging shoulder and brought me into him.

Leaning my head against Flint supplied a sense of understanding. A few years ago, Flint would have ribbed me, teased me and brought jokes into my misery, but this hug told me he'd outgrown that, that he was here for me, for the good and the bad.

We scoffed, nattered, reviewed sections in the tabloids, pointing out the shite journalism. The Klaxons played from a radio on the counter. Whenever I caught Flint's eye, talking about nothing important, I noticed his gaze was almost questioning, executing a slight squint, but I could sense there was a good deal of content not being said across that table, maybe even a whole conversation we needed to have, one that could wait.

Flint pinched my black pudding and, in return, I stole his butter. Monday to Friday, this familiar establishment would be traditionally and happily full of men who could lift, dig and fix, yet today we were surrounded by absolutely no plumbers, painters or bricklayers. Instead, we were joined by a group of loud lads in their twenties, talking about their night before. One chap received boos and cheers for arriving later than the rest, walking the walk of shame to the counter, red as a cherry tomato when he placed his order. An elderly couple smiled at the banter, but a family with a baby in a carrier, heads down, eating their food rapidly, didn't say a word.

When our plates were collected and there were no more distractions, I told Flint everything. I didn't cry, I just spoke and he listened. As I concluded, cradling my mug of tea, Flint spoke.

'Well done you. It's over, you're free.'

I nodded, not believing a word.

After I dropped Flint at home, I went to the Co-op for cat food. I ambled down the aisles, my basket buoyantly swinging with emptiness. I'd been around the shop three times before I remembered what I needed. I lingered in a walkway near the biscuits, picking up chocolate digestives and Tunnocks teacakes. Feeling frustrated, remembering I needed milk, I stuffed the biscuits back on the shelf and barged into a lady in a blind spot near the milk. Saying sorry, I picked up a two-pint carton, grabbed some cat food and queued. I stared around at the activity, the lights, the beeps, and I felt a nudge on my shoulder.

'Excuse me, your go,' said a man behind me.

I didn't thank him, let alone acknowledge what he'd said.

As the teenager scanned my items, I looked down and realised I'd made a mistake: I had chosen chocolate digestives, but I wanted the teacakes.

'Hang on, I've made the wrong choice.'

To the annoyance of my fellow customers, I ran back to make the swap, paid and left.

Sitting in my car, I started to panic. What if I'd made an even bigger mistake? Had I made the wrong choice? Suddenly terrified, I texted Dan, but he ignored me. I followed it up with a chaser.

> Did you get my text?

No reply.

> Is it too late for me to change my mind, please?

I called him, but he cut me off after two rings.

Then came the silence and I fell into the all-encompassing madness I was used to. The following day, I executed my long-perfected act of hiding my true feelings from absolutely everyone. My colleagues probably assumed my gloomy mood was linked to the building works on Cowley Road, making my bus journey ridiculously long.

Only Flint knew of my visitor, and nobody knew about my panicked change of heart; my re-entry into stalking; the shame of it.

Who *was* I?

What was I *doing*?

In the privacy of my own home, I was cruel to Dan, and ultimately to myself. I sent him texts that were clearly not for him, to provoke him, to alert him that I was still breathing.

They were simple in their content.

> Did you want pepperoni on
> your pizza?

> Can you make it 6.30 to pick
> me up please?

It became a dark addiction, tormenting us both, the very act of sending him these "pretend" texts showing Dan that I was still thinking of him; that I wasn't sure I'd made the right choice. I also butt-dialled him, on purpose, of course. Out driving with the stereo on or walking to work. Sometimes he'd answer, or the call would go to voicemail. I guess he could have looked at this pointless, unwanted and intrusive contact as a sort of crap news report that Louise was living her life, thanks very much, even without him in it.

I thought it showed I still loved him. Someone *not* on the edge of a breakdown would almost certainly disagree.

Dan eventually texted back.

Please leave me alone. Don't
call me.

I didn't get how we could go from "come here, I've left her, I want you" to that kind of empty communication.

I fumed around the office, making sarcastic comments to my colleagues and clients. I was slamming doors, not caring if I jammed the photocopier – leaving it for someone else to fix. One afternoon, I walked outside on my tea break. This was unheard of and not permitted. I didn't give a crap as I walked around the Clarendon Centre in a daze.

I needed help. Where had the thoughts of Flint's hands disappeared to? Why wouldn't they return?

After two months of insanity, I made a decision. I would call Dan and say goodbye properly. This wasn't the way to end things. He'd missed my calls and texts, and so to ensure he answered, I added 141.

He answered, but the moment I started to speak, he hung up.

That night, teary and alone at home, I made countless calls to Dan using 141, hiding my identity to anyone else but him. He slashed all my calls.

If we'd been sparring with swords, wearing tights and cloaks, we'd both have fallen on the floor by now, saturated in sweat. Our mutual weariness of everything would be making certain, once and for all, that we remained where we fell. But before walking away, we'd glance once more time at each other, shaking our heads in disbelief. How had it come to this? I'd never done such awful things; this was the most odious moment of my life.

I was hollowed out.

The next day, I received an email from Dan. He'd helpfully sent me a link to the Thames Valley Police website about how to report a nuisance call, and plainly explained that if I called him again, he'd utilise said link.

PART THREE

CHAPTER 34

The Hobnob Diet

Something was buzzing and ringing in my house. Again and again. It was daylight, yet I was in bed. I didn't know the time, and I kept the duvet pulled over my head.

Eventually, the level of noise was too much.

It was the doorbell.

I got out of bed, lacking any spirit, and opened the bedroom window.

'Let me in; don't make me shout louder. I've got a homemade curry and four pakoras from Chrissy here to share. I suggest you open the door if you want half.'

'I'm not hungry,' I yelled back.

'Well, I am, and I've bought beer, so don't be a selfish cow.'

It was Flint.

I opened the door, and he paused before he dumped the food in the kitchen.

'Well, well, well, what a mess you look.'

'Thanks.'

'Go and have a shower, you'll put me off my food.'

I inspected my reflection in the hallway mirror. My hair

was matted in knots, my complexion blotchy and dry, and I couldn't remember when I'd last washed, or cleaned my teeth. My diet had consisted of strong sugary tea and Hobnobs for days.

Knowing Flint and Chrissy had gone to such efforts to cheer me up spurred me upstairs to the bathroom. Avoiding all my friends' texts, calls and emails was one thing, but steering clear of a Chrissy curry, delivered to my door by Flint... well, that was something I couldn't pass up. Nor did I want to.

As I rinsed shampoo out of my hair, Flint shouted outside the bathroom, 'How long? Shall I heat up?'

'Yeah,' I yelled.

I walked into the kitchen and Flint was bustling around, the microwave pinging, plates clattering, and the smell was divine. I hugged his waist from behind, wrapping my arms around his strong middle.

'Hey, I'm busy here.' He didn't turn to face me.

I clutched tighter.

'I'm sorry,' I murmured into his back. 'I'm so, so sorry.'

He turned around, holding a wooden spoon, and as he set it down, he pulled me into him, resting his chin on my head.

'I know. I know.'

I didn't cry as he held me. The love, security and affection he supplied without question brought all the other shit to a standstill. It all melted away.

We took our food into the living room, and he asked me what'd happened. I shared the email Dan had sent; the weird doubts I'd had, and the much bigger regrets I'd experienced by stalking Dan.

'I just hid away for nine days, not wanting to see anyone.'

'Smelling like a street dog,' he scoffed. 'And you've lost weight.'

'The Hobnob diet.'

'Tragic.'

'I... I called into work sick. I know that's bad, but...' I took a swig from the beer bottle, already lightheaded.

He shrugged and turned up his nose. 'It's to be expected. Easier to hide and wait for the police to arrest you here. Imagine if they had arrived at work... Jasmeet's face.'

I paused, fork midway to my mouth.

Flint laughed, taking a mouthful of beer, then chuckled again and choked. He took his plate off his lap and put it on the coffee table, while I jumped up and slapped him on the back. I couldn't stop laughing, my laughter quickly catching up with his, and every time we took a breath and paused, giggling, we caught sight of each other's eyes and roared again. I grabbed a tea towel from the kitchen, handed it to Flint as he nodded in thanks, and we carried on laughing.

Wiping a tear from his cheek, Flint said, 'Seriously, Louise, you really know how to get into some crap, but that threat from him is bang out of order. It says more about him than you, right?'

'Maybe. It's had the desired effect, though – shocked me into not calling again. But honestly, when I read his email, I threw up. Even now I want to hide my face when I think about it.'

'Well don't think about it then. I like your face. Even like that.'

He picked up his fork and tucked back into his food again.

'He made me crazy. I've never behaved like this before. It's like Katie Melua said. "Being close to crazy and being close to you" – or whatever the words are. I just can't be anywhere near him again.'

'Correct. Listen, I think you should go back to work tomorrow, cut the sad, mopey songs, and just play fucking Oasis albums for a week. Take *that* prescription, will you?'

'Sure thing. I've run out of SSP days, anyway, and I don't think the GP will give me a sick note for I'm-getting-over-my-married-arsehole-boyfriend disease.'

'Probably not.' Flint smiled. 'You're going to be fine. I can feel a change coming.'

I returned to work the next day, a little uneasy, but happy to be in the world again. My world. Flint had helped with that. Especially the previous night as we talked our way through *Breakfast at Tiffany's*, drinking tea and polishing off my stash of hobnobs.

I'd planned on asking for a back-office job to do; I wanted minimal contact with the public. In the past, when management asked for volunteers to unpack the Housing Benefit forms, or reorganise the stationery, most of my colleagues, myself included, had looked at the ceiling, willing for someone else to raise their hand. Today though, that was exactly the kind of task I needed.

I found Jasmeet after our morning briefing. I needed to tell her I wasn't alright.

Jasmeet frowned when I asked if there was any work I could do in the cupboard. 'Not a lot; nothing urgent. Are you okay? We need to do your back-to-work paperwork.' She peered down her glasses at me.

I burst into tears in the lime green painted corridor, colleagues passing by us, looking away and hot-footing-it anywhere but here.

Jasmeet guided me to her office.

'What happened?' she asked, shutting the door.

I told her everything, every single detail. I didn't miss anything as she boiled the kettle, made tea, and we drank the tea. Only then was she entirely in the know.

'Christ, Louise, you don't do anything by halves, do you?'

Jasmeet had been married to her husband for thirty or more years, and despite starting off as an arranged marriage, it was clear that they loved one another.

'Nope. I've been such a fool. You don't know how lucky you are to have Mo.'

'True, and I do love him, but I didn't love him straight away. How could I?'

I sniffed. 'How long did it take for you to love him?'

'About ten years. Definitely after kids, but when I heard that friends of mine in arranged marriages had been cheated on, you know, properly done over, I realised that I had a good one. Mo tells me everything. And you know what?'

I shook my head.

'He is terrible at keeping secrets. He couldn't keep an affair to himself. Plus, I said I'd make him eat meatball pasta out of his bollocks if he cheated on me and the kids.'

I believed her.

'Want to hear a secret? I do envy you guys. I wish I'd played the field a bit, you know?'

'What for?' I asked. 'It's lonely out here, no one to play with.'

'Ah, but you get to try the goods and sift out the ones you want to hang around with.'

I wiped my face with the wet wipes Jasmeet handed me and looked at my hands. I couldn't look her in the eye.

'It's all a fucking mess.'

'You both are, you and him, if you don't mind me saying. I do know one thing, though. I don't see you as an issue girl. He's sort of brought this side out in you. We can remove that.'

I stayed quiet as my chin trembled.

'You're strong, clever, and customers don't pull the wool over your eyes. So why is he succeeding?'

'I don't really know,' I admitted.

Jasmeet got up from her side of the desk and went to the window. Below the windowsill, stacked on the floor to the height of her hip, was a neat pile of brown boxes. She ripped the brown Sellotape off the top box and took out a flyer.

'Here's this morning's job. These leaflets need to be distributed to the usual places and the rest need to go in the general stationery cupboard. But first, keep this one for yourself and call them.'

I glanced down at the flyer Jasmeet slapped on the desk in front of me. It was for a local mental health charity called Talk to Me. They were promoting a new out-of-hours telephone service. You could arrange five calls from the staff if you were suffering from a sudden change in your mental health or supporting someone suffering.

'You need to make this call, Louise. I'm not saying you're mentally ill, but your man might be, and as we know from our job, there's a point when you get dragged down with your loved ones. I reckon that point's getting a bit too close for my liking. Don't you?'

I nodded. Fresh tears were brewing.

'Thanks, Jasmeet.' I stood up and she gave me a strong hug.

I unpacked all the leaflets, distributed and delivered them where they needed to be, then logged onto a PC in a quiet area and followed the link to the Talk to Me website. I registered for a call and sat back in my chair, reading the acknowledgement on the screen.

We will assess your contact request and aim to get back to you within three to five working days. But should you or your loved one require urgent attention, please call the emergency services. Do not await our call.

CHAPTER 35

Hannah

I didn't wait for long to be rescued. The initial call from Hannah arrived unexpectedly, two days after I'd sent out the online SOS.

Hannah had an accent from Newcastle or thereabouts. I didn't clarify, but I was sure I had the area right. Her soft voice was reassuring to listen to, not that she said all that much. I overshared, but she didn't mind. She explained how this worked, like the Samaritans for members of the public who met the criteria: an acceptance that they had mental health worries, or their loved one did, but that they didn't want GP support, just someone to talk to.

Hannah explained, 'You've ticked a fair few boxes in the assessment. For example: "I've started doing new things, like talking to myself at home, missing my bus stop and crying when I lock myself out of my PC at work. In general, acting like a weirdo. Plus, I have an ex-boyfriend who's falling over the edge and dragging me with him". You might recall these are your words from the online form, they aren't my opinions.' Hannah laughed but I could tell she wasn't laughing at me, more like with me.

I squirmed at my openness. 'I am a woman on the edge.'

'I'd say you are ready on the starting blocks,' she said.

I told her about the relationship. She explained how we'd get the best out of our limited time together – honesty. Hannah was not quite the same as a Samaritan; she could offer some practical advice, and my mental welfare was at the heart of our chats. Knowing already that I could trust her, I told her I'd never felt this way about another man. She asked me why not.

'Um, it felt so right with him. Like it was meant to be.'

'Except it wasn't right. There's a lot that's very wrong, and I'm not judging, by the way.'

'I know, I've tried to look at other men, fancy other men. I mean, I did snog a guy, in a club. Nothing came of it...'

'Anyone else? No dates or anyone else you think about?'

Flint's face popped up in a flash. His laughter from the other night, his tummy, choosing to joke with me and not eat his pakora. I brushed it aside for a bit.

'Um, not really.'

'What do you mean?'

'Well, I don't know about him. I mean, there's someone I care for, but we're friends. Always friends, yes, that's right.'

'Maybe he's never been able to get in, you know, past the "Dan" wall.'

'Oh.'

'Just a thought.' Hannah laughed. 'How does it make you feel if I suggest you change your number and cut all contact with Dan?'

'Wow, I don't know.'

'Could you think about that, and maybe next week, you could have a list for me? A sort of pros and cons list.'

'Okay, I can do that.' Biting my lip, I figured the pros list would be humiliatingly limited.

In our third session, we discussed some homework she'd set: how many times I'd contacted Dan in the last week, and if there had been any communication at all, whether fake or not. I couldn't lie.

Hannah asked me to write it all down as I went along. She called it my "lurker diary", and said I should have it to hand so we could chat about the attempts I'd made to speak to Dan and what had brought me to that ludicrous point – again.

'Well, I called once but I haven't texted him at all. And the call was genuine – if he'd picked up, I'd have spoken with him. I wanted to talk to him, but I didn't even hide my number,' I said, smiling to myself with pride.

'Well, that's a massive improvement. What did you do to distract yourself?'

I feared she might not trust me when I answered – it was simple really.

'Well, the notebook was at the ready and I don't want it to be too full. Full of shit notes like: "sent a text at 12:02" or "hung up when he answered this morning". Those aren't things I should be proud of. It's like a shitter version of my teenage diaries, and trust me, they were bad enough in the 80s. Does that make sense?'

Hannah laughed. 'It does.'

'It's like the action of making the call or sending the text was shameful enough. You add the deed of writing it down, and, well, it's mortifying.'

'It's good you feel like that. Progress.'

We chatted about these tricks and how they must be my normal default from now on, for my welfare obviously, but also to avoid getting arrested. At night, trying to get to sleep, I would lay in bed worrying about all sorts of scenarios that made me sweat.

I imagined sleeping in a prison cell, on those mattress-free beds, without a pillow, wearing a bad outfit, and calling my parents for my one and only telephone call, who in my mind then claimed I was a wrong number instead of their firstborn.

I thought about going to court and all my friends jeering down at the judge when he boomed, 'Take her down.'

I thought fearfully, egocentrically, about this too often; thinking about any of those circumstances was terrifying. But I guessed that was Hannah's aim: for me to see my wrongdoing. Constantly thinking of the man who'd dropped me from a fantastic height in the first place was also very wrong. I was angry with Dan, but it didn't mean I felt better hating him.

But I also had to despise calling him and hanging up.

I discussed my worries with Heidi and Di after a Hannah session. I was bloody scared, but to my surprise, they laughed.

'Why would you rot in jail?' Heidi asked.

'This is a serious matter.'

'Yes, but the police haven't been involved so stop thinking of criminal stuff. You're a nutty ex-girlfriend and, to be honest, it takes one to know one. Dan was a nutjob.'

'That's a bit harsh,' Di replied.

'Don't protect him!' Heidi exclaimed. 'Let's go back to prison talk. I reckon you'd be employed to do the laundry and wash all the prison attire and towels, using those massive washing machines.'

'Do you think I'd start smoking out of boredom and stroll around in the yard with my new prison friends?'

'Yep, and you'd get into scraps with some of the inmates and have lesbian fisty fights and loads of affairs.'

In session four, Hannah came into her own. I'd have liked to go for a drink with her; she was that kind of girl. I trusted her experience and the way she explained how people suffering from mental health problems were in agony most of the time and, most likely, they didn't know how to stop the pain. They needed outside help and care from family and friends. But most of all, they needed to want to get better. I explained, weeping, that I'd be there for Dan; be all of that; that I wanted to guide him to get the help he needed.

'That might not be what he wants, though. He may see it as you meddling in his life. I know that isn't nice to hear, but it's the truth. He might see you as part of the biggest problem in his life. Even if he was unwell before, and it sounds as if he was, meeting you has induced a lot of negative feelings.'

'I'm just so shitty with him. I have to walk away.'

'Well, I can't make that decision for you.'

'I know. But Hannah, you know it's hard to do that. He doesn't seem to have anyone who has his back, you know? And I do. I always would.' The emotions filled my throat; it was like I'd swallowed concrete, making it a task to breathe.

'I understand, but he knows where you are, right? He

found you when he needed you a few weeks ago, but now he doesn't need you. It's that simple in his head. He's confused, and you can't help him with that.'

I listened.

'You see, the thing is, anyone suffering from a mental illness is always going to need looking after, and your wants and needs may have to take a back seat.'

'I can do that.' My voice was cracking like a teenage boy.

'Louise, I have a duty to do all I can to ensure your mental health gets better. I think you have all the support you need: you are streetwise, have lots of friends who are willing to support you and you are emotionally intelligent. I'm not concerned about you in the slightest. I can recommend that you have some space from Dan. Without that, you could face becoming as low as he is.'

'Fuck,' I whispered.

'I know.'

'Fuck.'

'I don't want that for you. Why would you want to be like that, live that life? As heartbroken as you'll be, and probably are right now, space is the answer.'

'Space. Right, okay, space.'

'He needs space too,' she added, 'and he needs to let in his chosen support, if that's what he decides to do. I don't think you should be his help, nor will he want your help.'

'So I'm not his chosen person?'

'Only he knows that, but I don't recommend you waiting to find out. Think about being someone else's chosen person. How does that feel?'

CHAPTER 36

Chicken Wrap Meal

Hannah was spot on. Dan didn't want *or* need me.

It felt so final.

At times, straight after the Hannah sessions, things were unbearable for me, and I couldn't fathom it – that I'd never see his face again, or hear his voice. Dan remained as a 2D version that I could view online, if I dared to risk a prison sentence.

At first, for a brief time, I missed and craved the things I'd never have with Dan. I hankered after domesticity with him – bickering because one of us forgot the tinned tomatoes, or arguing over whose turn it was to empty the hoover bag. It was mysterious to me, that all the things I grieved for were not wedding days, anniversaries and romantic dates. I ached to do his ironing, watch him drive my car and bake him a birthday cake.

Before Hannah, the pain of tormenting myself was as much a part of my life as collecting my contact lenses from Specsavers; it was what I did, what I'd become. However, moments came later that summer when something clicked into place, and thankfully, I recognised that there was an emotional gap between Dan and me. I hardly knew how or when I'd got there. I didn't have an epiphany moment; it wasn't that clear cut. But stopping the fake calls and accepting the things I'd miss about him could only mean one thing – I was finally getting over him, and all of my friends were there for me. Especially Flint.

I spent a lot of time in the spring and summer months gardening with him. At first, he and I worked on planting vegetables and tubs in his garden. Then Di gave us a project – she wanted a vegetable patch. She'd started dating someone and her free time was cut into bits. Flint and I took over and she was endlessly grateful for our help. We planned our days of weekend gardening; trips to Homebase or garden centres to fetch supplies. He provided bottles of squash or flasks of tea, and I always made us sandwiches and sometimes the cakes he liked: Madeira, fruit cake and lemon drizzle.

'What's happened to us, Lou? Sarnies, hoeing and wearing gardening gloves.'

'I know! I love it, though.'

'Me too, and I never thought I'd say that, especially the glove wearing,' Flint replied, waving his dirty gloves near my face.

'That's a little weird and pervy.'

He grinned, carrying a huge pile of cuttings to the bin. 'Yep.'

Flint would accompany me and the girls to the outdoor swimming pool, to read the paper while we swam. He tried his best to make me laugh by hooting his critique of my front crawl from his reading position, or he'd hide my bag in a bush. But mostly Flint and I found happiness by making each other laugh, reading horoscopes out of trashy papers, hatching plans for our futures, or simply sitting in silence with ice lollies. Our days of focusing on being on the lash were fading into a new phase that I liked. It was a little blurry and vague, but welcoming all the same.

Flint didn't bring Dan up, but sometimes I did. He set one rule: I was allowed to talk about Dan for a certain amount of time. When Flint first introduced this regulation, he gave me seven minutes or so. I ended up crying, and he held me as I wept onto him. But as the weeks and months passed, Flint reduced the time to one minute and I rarely mentioned Dan, until one afternoon as I helped him load his car up with his tools.

'Isn't it great how we don't talk about Dan anymore?'

'Well, it was until you just did.'

'Oh, come on, you know what I mean.'

'I do. I'm proud of you.'

'Thanks, I feel as if I can breathe again. Though I do miss those seven-minute cuddles from you when I would cry on your shoulder and make your t-shirts all wet.' I nudged him in the ribs.

'You miss my cuddles?'

My neck flushed. 'Yeah.'

'Oh.' He shut the car boot and juggled his car keys from hand to hand.

This open flirting had been happening a lot with Flint. I liked seeing his cheeks glow when I leant across him, grazing my boob somewhere on his body. I liked knowing I was blushing when we both went for the same tool in the shed.

'Well, there are always cuddles spare.' He grinned as he got into his car, reversed out of the parking space and blew me a kiss as he left.

I would have preferred the hug.

※

The most treasured part of that summer came during a visit to the allotment that backed onto Flint's place. We drove there once a week to get advice, pinch ideas for our respective open spaces and very often came home with a bag of goodies, but it was the camaraderie, friendship, kindness and laughs from the other gardeners that kept us coming back, week after week. They named Flint and me "the young team", and always asked us to help with a bit of digging or lifting. They were my new people, and Flint and I fitted right in.

One Sunday evening, I was so happy, I didn't want to leave.

'Come on, time to go,' Flint said, getting up from his cross-legged position opposite me.

Everyone around us was packing up, exhausted but fulfilled from a day tendering. He threw the remains of his tea onto the grass. Maggie was the only gardener with us and was packing up her flask, smiling at us.

'Can I stay here just another hour?'

'You can do, on your own.' Flint winked at Maggie, pulling me up from the deckchair.

We collected our things and walked to Flint's car, and as we yelled and waved goodbye, Reg, from the far side of the allotment, shouted, 'Ta rah, lovebirds.'

Flint and I locked eyes, grinning, and I wasn't sure if it was right to feel quite as glorious and full of sparkle as I did in that moment. Smiles from Flint these days were as comforting and as pleasing as warm butter on a toasted crumpet.

My friends were happy that I was happy. Nikki stopped worrying, Jasmeet was back to being bossy and hardcore with me and everyone wanted more nights out. Chrissy was on the pull and Heidi was big on encouraging me to be less like Charlie Dimmock.

'I'm nothing like her. I've always got a bra on, haven't I?'

'You gotta keep the standards up: more mascara, perfume and lippy. Less dirty fingernails and twigs in your hair.'

Flint had his own opinion.

They came round my house to help me put a print up in my bedroom and I provided a chilli con carne as payment.

'I'm not sure about the makeup, but how do you feel about finding a new bloke?' he asked as he put his pencil behind his ear.

'Yes, I agree, a whole new man with a mate for me,' Heidi added, rooting through my nail varnish collection.

I busied myself with perfecting my bed making, fluffing up my pillows and smoothing down edges. 'I think I need a whole section of nothingness for a bit.'

'For how long?' he asked, a bit too quick.

'Oh, I don't know. I've not made a spreadsheet or planned it or anything, I'm taking one day at a time. I want the next relationship to be just right, and less chaotic.'

'Well, don't take forever. You don't want to wake up with an old, haggard pussy. Men won't go near that.' He wrinkled his nose.

I nudged him. 'How do you know what a haggard pussy looks like?'

He shrugged back, packed up his drill bits and winked at me, his cheeks a little rosy. He looked like a naughty little boy.

I grinned back at him, my skin prickling with pleasure.

To keep everyone happy, including myself, I went out drinking with Di and Heidi on Cowley Road. Nothing wild, just some grown up bars with cocktails, and we concluded our night with food. The day was warm and sticky for late September. We were looking at the menu attached to the window of a kebab shop. The Blu Tack couldn't hold it in place and I held a finger on the corner of the sheet to stop it flapping about. I already knew what I wanted.

A souped-up Saxo slowed down in front of us, lads hanging out of the windows like dogs, but instead of long tongues on show, there was a white arse positioned in the passenger seat window. He pulled his butt cheeks apart and his mate yelled, 'Give him your finger.'

Heidi refused to come inside the kebab place. 'It's too hot,' she said.

She held one of those little fans, sulking, her other hand on her hip, forever stylish, while drunk men eyed her up before they entered the shop. When it became our turn to place our order, I opened my mouth to say hello and the friendly server spoke first.

'Let me guess – chicken wrap meal, not southern fried but the "nice" stuff, crispy lettuce and a teeny bit of cheese?' He even did the little rabbits' ears when he said "the nice stuff", which made me laugh.

Di ordered a hummus pitta thing and Heidi wanted chips and cheese. We paid and waited outside in the cooler air.

'That's so sad he knows what you want,' Heidi said with a snooty lift of her nose.

'Is it? Why?' I asked.

'It just is.'

'I don't think it's sad,' Di said. 'This is the best place to eat late on Cowley Road. Fact. If you're to be friendly with any kebab place, best to be this one.'

'It's semi-healthy here as well,' I added. 'They have fresh salad.'

We stood for a few moments, Di checking her phone. I noticed a group of young girls walk past, very tipsy and holding onto each other. They were in their early twenties, shoulder-length poker-straight hair, all wearing a variation of denim hot pants and baby doll tops and some were wearing hats or headbands. They were fashionable duplicates of each other.

'You know what I think? I don't think it's depressing or anything like that.'

'What?' Heidi asked.

Di stopped looking at her phone.

'I like the fact that I like what I like. I like that I've found the yummiest food to eat after my night out. I like that I return here again and again; it shows I'm loyal. I've learnt a shit load about myself in the last two years, and you know what? I've discovered I like a lot about myself. I'm loyal and I'm alright.'

A lone pisshead bumped into me as he aimed for the door and interrupted my flow.

'Not so long ago, you might remember, I didn't even

know who the fuck I was. I was a nobody, who believed in a somebody, who should have been the nobody.'

'Hear hear,' Heidi said.

'Imagine if we didn't have all the crap jobs, the pathetic men, the pointless shags and the ridiculous bosses; we wouldn't have lived, would we? How can we feel alive if we haven't lived a life, shit or not? I mean, I'm not being a bitch about those young girls up there, but I am glad I've got my life, or I could end up like them, replicas of everyone else, and I don't want to be like everyone else. I like wearing jeans and gardening.'

The girls gripped me and offered a tight squeeze as I finished slurring my words of wisdom. Then, we strutted off like the Sugababes, linking arms, homeward bound.

Life was going to be okay. I'd made my way onto a restored road, with the assistance of clever clogs Hannah. Plus, these two and all my other mates would be there for more arm linking, chicken wraps and hand holding, even if other men – like Dan – popped in and out of my life.

That's when I got it: I'd discovered that another person living on the same planet as me would never be able to completely ruin my life. I wouldn't permit it, and I'd come to realise that nobody would have the power to crack me ever again.

I'd probably always love Dan. I didn't like him or respect him, but I couldn't ignore the impact of our relationship on who I was now. I had been completely rewired by his questionable and deceptive love, and I had often wondered if I'd ever return to my default setting, the one my parents had lovingly shaped and fashioned me into, before I'd accepted that it was okay to change.

As we looked left and right to cross the road, we spotted the young twenty-somethings gawking into their phones, waiting at a bus stop, and a loud male voice behind us shouted, 'Ladies, your food!'

We ran back to the doorway, tottering on our unsteady feet and laughing so hard we could hardly breathe as Heidi shrieked, 'We're coming!'

🌷

Things seemed to have evened out; I'd squared it all up.

Then I was thrown a curveball. A test. Big news.

Jeannie had contacted Flint – she wanted a reconciliation.

He asked all our friends for immediate advice, but not me. Chrissy dropped it into conversation after spinning as we walked down the stairs with our beetroot cheeks, my headband soaked and my fanny numb.

'She wants to get back with him? What for?' I asked, holding onto the banister for dear life.

'Cos she loves him. Or she liked his collection of bicycle pumps. Maybe he's filthy in bed? I don't know.'

A jolt landed in my chest – visions of Flint and a bed.

We pushed the double doors open and cool air welcomed me. I wobbled alongside Chrissy, my legs shaking from spinning and the Flint news.

'Aren't you pleased for them?' Chrissy asked, unlocking her car.

I shrugged, and Chrissy stared at me.

'I don't get why I'm the last to know, that's all.'

The answer was no, I was not pleased for them. I was clear on what I wanted: to see him, to check he was okay and find out more details. If he needed my support and advice, I was his woman, ready and available. I owed him a lot.

Who the hell was I kidding?

I had to know if he was still single. I couldn't dilly dally anymore. I recalled the regretful feelings over Dan – that had been bad enough. But this was Flint, the high voltage feelings in my tummy told me, and I had to know.

I wasn't sure what to expect, but I went to see him. I was scared to find out. Was Jeannie going to be there with her neat blonde bob making a stir fry in the kitchen? Would they be in bed together already? Whatever the case, I had to know, so I went straight after the spin class, sweaty and stinky.

His housemate answered the door. 'Yeah, he's in. Well, he's in the garden. He's just fitted a water butt.'

I walked outside and Flint came out of the shed holding some tools.

I marched straight up to him.

'Hey, Chrissy told me. Why didn't you tell me about Jeannie? Everyone else knows. Are you okay? Can I help?' I placed my hands on my hips, staring at him.

He copied me, hands on hips, grinning. 'Yeesh, so many questions. Do you want a drink and a sit down? You look like you need one.'

Flint opened himself a beer and filled me a glass of tap water. I glanced at my reflection in the oven. My headband was wonky, my face was still vibrant red, and this morning's mascara was now centre stage on my cheeks.

We sat on deckchairs facing the allotment in the October evening sunshine. I tipped my head backwards to absorb the last drops of sunlight onto my skin, as Flint told me he'd never loved Jeannie and shouldn't have dated her for as long as he did. I glanced sideways at him. His shades masked his eyes and he too looked up at the sky.

'I disagree. You tried, and that's a grown-up thing to do. It didn't work out, that's all. How is she?' I twisted the rings on my fingers.

'Not speaking to me now. She said she still loved me but always felt like she wasn't my number one priority.'

'How can she say that? You were good to her, and you did everything she wanted. You even provided a kitten!'

Flint laughed. 'I know, I miss that kitty. It's a bit weird, but women are strange.' He laughed, crossing his ankles and then uncrossing them.

I slapped him on the arm. 'We are most certainly not *all* weird.'

'She said she wanted to check if things were the same.'

'What do you mean?'

'She said I loved someone else.'

I gulped. 'Oh, really?'

'Yeah, really.'

We sat in silence for a bit and then Flint offered a keen wave to some of the gardeners in the allotment. He walked over to his rickety fence and yelled something.

My heart thumped and I fiddled with my headband. I gazed at his strong shoulders, noticed he'd cut his hair, and that he wore odd socks. He laughed with Maggie and Dennis, a true and genuine interaction. They handed him a bag of garden goodies; he shook Dennis's hand with such respect, my heart burst with admiration. Sitting back down, Flint turned to face me.

Had Jeannie known about Flint and me before we had?

'You know what? I don't even feel sad about Jeannie. Just relieved. Does that make me a twat? I tried to be nice about it.'

I squeezed his hand, leaving mine on top of his. To begin with, I wondered if that was the right thing to do, but then it became clear that it was the only thing to do. In fact, removing my hand from his was something I could never do now.

'No, I think that makes you a decent bloke. You were honest.'

We didn't speak for a few beats.

'I know what I want now,' Flint said softly, staring ahead of him. 'Well, I mean, I know who I want. Who I've always wanted.'

I met his gaze, my eyes brimming as he nodded at me, smiling. I nodded back, a massive grin on my face.

Flint picked up my hand, kissed it and held it in his lap.

It was then that I knew I loved him, but no longer as my friend. The feel of his lips on my hand made my heart whoop in my chest. Yes, I'd had those emotions before, but this was new; enthralling yet safe, intimate, and so hot. Previous feelings I'd felt with other men were situated happily on the middle of a staircase, but mix in the emotion and warmth that covered my body when Flint kissed my hand... well, that just made me want to sprint right to the top.

In this moment, Flint carefully unfolded me. He'd known me crumpled, messed up and fucked up – feeling like I'd never feel aligned again. But here, in the glorious twilight, I was unblemished and ready for him.

For us.

Flint went away to Manchester the next day for a month. We spoke every day, but now it was torture not to hang out with him, to not touch him and learn about him in a new way. We agreed that October evening to see how things were after a month apart. I wasn't convinced at first, I wanted it all now. I wanted all of Flint and I tried to persuade him as I said goodbye at his door.

'I'm not going to beat around the bush anymore,' he told me. 'I don't want to fuck this up. I'm not saying I could fuck anything up with you, but I really don't want to risk fucking it up. Do you get me?'

'That's a lot of fucks, but we'd never make a mess of things, I'm sure of it. Don't you even want to kiss me goodbye tonight?'

Flint took a deep breath and moved closer to me, almost pinning me against the wall. He pointed his finger at my nose and tapped it.

'I do, but I think we should wait.'

'I can't,' I whispered, unable to move at all.

'If I kiss you now, I'll have to take you upstairs and have you, and have you *hard*. No questions. I want you. I've wanted for you for far too long, and I want it to be better than a that-will-do fuck, especially with you in your sports bra and that wild spinning hair.'

'But I can take the bra off!' I protested.

Flint shook his head, biting his fist.

'Not even one kiss?'

Flint covered his face in his hands and murmured, 'My god, woman, no more.'

We laughed and held each other. I inhaled his deodorant, his shed and the outside air. How had I never noticed how sexy he smelt?

We parted with politeness, and he kissed me on the cheek. His lips lingered there, and I held onto his hands.

'I don't want to leave you,' I whispered.

'I'll be here. I'm not going anywhere.'

I drove home wildly confused and deliriously happy, grinning and singing like I was in a musical. I started to get undressed when my phone bleeped. Flint had texted me.

```
You know I said I wasn't going
anywhere? Well, I am - I'm
going to Manchester for work,
remember?
```

```
                You aren't. I pinched your
                              train ticket
```

```
I can't believe how happy you
make me. PS - yes, as you
might expect, I had a speed
wank.
```

CHAPTER 37

The New Us

It was December. Christmastime.

Nikki and I were out after work, on a very loud and boozy night. She'd come to stay with me for a few days and her beady eye was on Guy, one of my newest team members.

There was no stopping her. It was hilarious to see her working her arse off to get his attention. She was wearing her new jam-red Christmas jumper, with two little moving Christmas puddings positioned as humongous nipples. It was working a treat on poor Guy, given its tackiness and tendency to draw the eye of anyone she was speaking with straight to her tits. Her huge breasts bounced about, causing the puddings to bob around like they were simmering in saucepans of water. Guy never stood a chance.

I found myself looking around All Bar One and admiring the view. It wasn't my first choice as a place for after-work drinking – maybe I was showing my age – but I had to admit, a sizable effort had been made in the sparkle department. Fairy lights filled the room, framing a huge fir Christmas tree in the middle of the bar area, and the staff were smiley and not at all bah humbug. I couldn't see out of the steamed-up windows but thought how jolly and welcoming it must look from outside.

The only dampener was that Flint wasn't there. A sharp pang shot through my heart as my stomach flipped over, thinking about him. Despite speaking daily whilst he'd been away in Manchester, I now knew he was back in Oxford, but I wasn't expecting to see him tonight. There was a Christmas drinks thing he couldn't get out of. Neither of us wanted to be parted anymore, but I no longer held any anxieties or pathetic worries that he wouldn't show up or text me. I trusted him. This was Flint.

Shakin' Stevens' *Merry Christmas Everyone* came on, a secret favourite of mine. I smiled as I remembered family Christmas parties, my nan bopping around the living room with me, holding both my hands; my mum's legendary homemade trifle and the big spoon that she served it with, the whole family waiting eagerly for the slurp as she dished out each portion. We would festoon the house in paper chains, as well as tinsel; my dad always moaned as Mum secured the shimmering garlands to every wall, draping them extravagantly over our school photos.

The lady behind the bar interrupted my reflections. 'What can I get you?'

'Spritzer please.'

I looked for Nikki, to check if I needed to add a beverage for her to my round, but she was sitting on Guy's lap. He didn't look as terrified now and his hand was holding onto her bottom as she tied golden tinsel around his neck. I waved some colleagues goodbye as they sauntered out.

I paid for my drink, leaning my back against the bar to sip my wine through the straw. This'd be my one for the road; I would get the 11:07 p.m. bus home.

As I congratulated myself on my wise choice, there he was. His smile carried an assurance that beckoned me and urged me to join him.

Wearing redundant office attire, sleeves rolled up, top button undone, showing me a sexy amount of chest hair, he stood alone. Before I could question my legs, I walked over to him.

'I take it you were looking at me?'

'No, sorry, there's a clock over your head,' he replied, deadpan.

I pretended to walk away, but Flint took my arm. He turned me back towards him, and we both smiled, then burst out laughing, going in for a tight squeeze. No nerves.

God, I'd missed him.

We chatted for an hour or more. I missed my 11:07 p.m. bus and waved Nikki and Guy off. Every now and then, Flint would brush my fringe out of my eyes or shield me from a passer-by. Or I would laugh at something he said, leaning in to playfully hit him on the arm, my touch lingering. Of course, we knew everything about each other, but tonight we talked random shit and it was first-class first-date material. The seamless way we chuckled and nattered was now new and exhilarating. It was like someone had opened big red velvet stage curtains in front of our friendship and ta dah! There we were, Louise and Flint. I could picture our future as an empty picture frame, relishing in the joy that it wouldn't stay like that for long.

We'd decamped to a nearby table and found ourselves next to a group of pissed people, making up very un-PC Christmas rhymes. They were idiots and their performances were full of moronic content. Flint nudged me after one specific comment and leant into me. As he whispered into my ear, warm shivers landed on my shoulders.

'Did you hear that?'

'Oh yes.' I rolled my eyes.

Then he said something so cute, I almost kissed him.

'Can you remind me to talk about that on our third date please?'

I grinned widely, nodding.

Flint walked me to the nearest taxi rank, and we joined the queue. I didn't want to leave.

'Wanna share a taxi?' he asked.

'We don't normally do that; we live at opposite ends of town – remember?'

'I know, but I can't leave you to go home alone. Look, I'm trying to impress you here, to be gentlemanly.' Humour flickered in his eyes.

'Ah, got you.' I shuffled closer to him.

'I'll share a taxi with you on a few conditions,' Flint said.

'What's that?' I asked, linking my arm into his.

He faced me, raising his index finger. 'One, you text me when you get inside, so I know you're safe. Two, no funny business in the back of the taxi. I'm a rule player.' I reeled at Flint remembering The Rule Book conversations I'd bored him with so many times. 'And three, I pinched this bit of mistletoe from the bar. Now, no pressure, but I'm going to stand here for five seconds regardless of whether you give me a Christmas kiss.'

He stood there, holding the mistletoe, and I laughed.

I just laughed and laughed at him, his coat undone even though he was shivering, his eyes closed, lips puckered up, trying not to laugh.

He opened his eyes and gave in, laughing with me as I attempted to get close to him.

'No, no, no. You had your chance.' He put his hand up to bat me away.

'Please?'

'Nope.' He crossed his arms across his chest. 'I'm gutted.'

I grabbed the sides of his coat and yanked him in. 'I promise you won't regret it,' I said, his face inches away from mine.

He leant down, and as we smiled at each other, I could feel his warm breath on my mouth.

Then, finally, he kissed me.

He tasted of beer and sea salt, from the snacks we'd eaten earlier.

It was bliss.

I managed to go home alone that night, but to this day, I don't know how. Flint called me and we chatted through the night from our beds, and in the morning, we chatted again. We didn't know how to handle this new us.

Did we have a proper first date?

Did we get on with a relationship?

Did we have a quick bonk or did we plan a weekend of sentimental romance around love-making and three-course meals?

I put this to him as we discussed the vitally important subject of "what the fuck do we do now?".

'Three course meals... very dated, and I'm not really sure it's you and me,' Flint said. 'What's currently troubling me is that you're in your bed right now and I'm in mine – that isn't right at all.'

'I know, but I was offering options.'

'You sound like you're ordering in KFC.'

I giggled. 'Do you want to meet there?'

'No, I don't know. I meant what I said about fucking this up, we both don't want to, but we want it to be memorable.'

'Hmm, how about you come here tonight and we plan to go out for a drink, but see how things, um, develop?'

'Do I bring an overnight bag?' Flint asked.

'Bring a bag? This is too weird, you've never been so polite! You never ask if you can bring fresh pants, you just stay over and go home commando or turn your pants inside out.'

'Well, maybe I won't wear any pants in the first place, if you agree to do the same.'

The inside of my belly bounced about. Now *this* was more like it.

Later that evening, I flapped about for two hours, waiting for Flint to arrive. Applying makeup, sultry eyes, then taking it off, reapplying makeup but more natural this time – another odd thing.

I cooked fajitas and drank a glass of wine. He was on time, and I watched park his car with too much reversing, re-parking, reversing again. This was also odd – one of Flint's show-off things was his ability to drive any car, to any location, on time and not get lost. He could also reverse park with just his little finger.

I opened the front door to him, my body telling me I would either throw up or pounce on him. Instead, I shut the door after him and turned to face him, but he hadn't moved forward enough. We went to kiss hello on the cheek, eagerness coursing through our veins, but head butted each other. More oddness. We laughed with nerves; I fiddled with my hair and Flint entered the kitchen, stirring the wok pointlessly while I opened the fridge, getting nothing out. Slamming the door shut, I turned round to say something, anything, but Flint banged the wooden spoon on the counter.

'What is this?'

'Fajitas, you like them, right?'

'No, not the food, I know what that is. What is this, us? The crap parking, the head butting, and you haven't even noticed me. I thought I'd made an effort.' He looked down at his skinny jeans, a new hoodie I didn't recognise but that I already wanted to unzip.

'Oh my god you have! I can see that, and I like it all so much I don't know what to do. Let's have wine.'

As I poured, I could sense Flint looking at me and my trembling hand. He removed the wine from me and took over.

'I'm not normally this nervous around men.'

'I know you aren't. I know you, remember? And I also remember kissing you last night.' Flint raised his eyebrows suggestively.

I fidgeted with excitement.

I didn't take the glass he was proffering me; instead, I took his face in my hands and kissed him. Soft, yet direct. I wanted to say "enough talking, more of this please".

We kissed with passion against the sink. I could hear the clock ticking and blending in with our moans of gratification. I pulled away from him, Flint's face bemused.

'The wok,' I said and fiddled with the gas switch.

Flint's hands were tugging at my top; his mouth couldn't bear to be apart from mine for a moment. As I snuck my hands under his hoodie and stroked his chest, Flint groaned while I marvelled at how none of this felt odd. It was all exactly as it should be: the skill Flint used to unbutton my shirt without me noticing; how he shook his head before lowering down to softly kiss my breasts; how I said his name in a throaty voice I barely recognised and, best of all, knowing that an entire lifetime of moments like this would follow.

He kissed my neck for a few seconds, then returned to my lips. Wherever his hands touched me, a spark lit up inside that wanted everything to happen between us right that minute.

And it did.

We married eighteen months later.

CHAPTER 38
2015

Later

Flint was nearly forty.

He had some very specific requirements: no parties; no gifts.

'I mean it, Lou. I want to go away with you. No kids. No bloody *Peppa Pig* or *Ben and Holly*. No wet wipes. No bum wiping. No pasta, fish fingers or blackcurrant squash. No pigtails, tutus or dolls. And I most definitely do not want surprise dinners, fake smiles, or to have to mock gasp at a massive forty-shaped helium balloon. I hate balloons.'

I'd rolled my eyes. 'I know that. Is there anything you *do* want?' I'd asked, grinning.

'Anything not on that list, and you. Only you.' He'd leant over the kitchen island and kissed me on the lips.

I hadn't booked a secret getaway to Madrid or Vienna – the two cities we were both keen to visit. Instead, as we sat on the sofa later that night eating prawn crackers, I'd asked him.

'How about Edinburgh?'

He wasn't looking at me. He was taken in by something on his phone.

'Yeah, course.'

'To move there?'

'Yeah, why not.'

'You can wear a kilt to the office.'

'Eh?'

I chucked a cushion at his head.

'Ow.'

'You prat, I'm asking if you'd like to go to Edinburgh. With me, for a weekend. No kids.'

'Not Madrid or Vienna?'

'I'm not sure I can stretch; they're quite pricey.'

'Wherever, I'm in.'

Sizzling romantic moments were not relentless at our age or at this point in our marriage. We needed this break. We weren't on our last legs or anything like that, but since having our children, the neglect hung there between us, along with the washing.

We did very little together as a couple. Sometimes I'd look at Flint across the living room when the kids were in bed and think, *I should take him and proceed straight to a blow job. Or why not strip him here and have a bonk in front of the electric fire, adding* Location, Location, Location *to our sex soundtrack.* But then I'd remember that we had two kids who would be up at 6:00 a.m., and who would always climb into our bed before either of us could instigate morning sex. Which was a shame. I loved and missed morning sex: sleepy, almost-keep-your-eyes-shut sex. It was a primal need that teeth were not cleaned for. With Flint, the hard-on would easily rise most mornings (as was the case for most men), and for me, it was best to grab me early, before the sight of endless lists appeared.

I still loved sex with Flint; it was the same as when we first did it, but better. I'd never had so many orgasms, or felt as sexy. But family life had taken it out of us both. Sometimes, we chose other things over sex, like an England football match on the TV, ironing to an audiobook or escaping the house to see if Morrison's had that thing we really needed. I didn't like it. I wanted something; something to spark us up again and keep us lit. I didn't want our marriage to be another fizzled-out fuck-up.

I'd already hit forty, and Flint had gone to town celebrating my milestone: a day out at a spa with Heidi and the gang, and a necklace from my children, engraved with their names on it. There were flowers and pedicures, and he'd arranged a family party at our house that I didn't tidy up after. In contrast, I was ashamedly yet customarily disorganised, standing in Scribblers at lunchtime the following day, selecting a card to commence his festivities.

I fanned through the "husband" section. Most were smutty and humorous, but I wanted a forty card. I moved away from the rack I was in front of, locating the numbered birthday cards. I'd finished work for the day and started to plan my afternoon in my head before picking up one kid from school and another from nursery. I'd picked up three cards, not absorbing their content.

Trying to pull myself into the moment, I picked up another card. There was a picture of two gorillas on it.

I sniggered and then giggled at the wording. Remembering myself, I looked over my shoulder at another customer, who knowingly smiled back at me; it was commonplace to communally laugh with strangers in this shop.

As I started to pick up another card, I noticed the person opposite me on the rotating rack of cards staring at me. I looked up and froze.

Once I'd realised it was Dan I was looking at, I panicked.

I looked over my shoulder; clocked the customers in the shop; noted them, concerned who was watching. Just the sight of him induced a flush on my cheeks and a thumping in my chest – neither of which were welcome.

Then two odd things happened at once – my breath slowed down and I acknowledged a warm and caring radiance surrounding us.

There'd been a time, many years ago, when the environment around us would've manifested as razor-edged with angular flashes of lightning. But seeing Dan today was strangely reassuring, and in those first few moments it almost comforted me, when ironically, our relationship had been anything but.

'Oh blimey, it's you,' Dan said.

'I know. And it's you. You look... great.'

I meant it. He'd gained some weight, the bags under his eyes had lessened, and he no longer looked haunted. He was wearing office attire: a starched white shirt, dark navy trousers and some kind of jacket. He also carried a man bag with flair.

After the self-conscious smiles, there was a moment; an acknowledgment that there was perhaps a lot to say but, reassuringly, a mutual understanding that we didn't need to offer explanations as to why we were rather quiet.

'So do you, I mean, just the same, but different... I dunno what I'm trying to say here.' He laughed awkwardly.

Customers were moving around us, some shoving, as we fired out polite enquiries, both of us with firm smiles fixed on our faces, though my cheeks ached with the effort. I should be dodging and ducking out of this shop, not engaging in any dialogue with him, but... there was a *but*. There was always a but with Dan.

'Look, I've got to pay for this card,' I said, shrugging my shoulders, not sure if that meant goodbye.

'I'll wait outside?'

'Um, okay. Sure.'

Why, oh why was I thinking of spending more time with him? I took a breath, trying to soothe the feeling that I was doing something wrong. It wasn't lust or desperation that was making me want to stay. I just needed to know that he was okay; that he'd recovered, like I had. I found the pendant around my neck – the one Flint had bought me – and held the names of the three most important people in my life close to my chest.

Back outside, I walked over to Dan as he stood with a cheeky grin. In that moment, I couldn't tell whether the wobble in my knees was from my utter shame at how badly our relationship had ended or because I wanted to bolt in the opposite direction.

'Wow, you look really great. Really, you do.' He hesitated, holding his hand out to me, then let it fall redundantly to his side.

'Thanks. What brings you to Oxford?'

'Work. I'm a creative director now for a firm in Henley, but I've a lot of meetings here. Which is nice.'

Dan explained more about his job. I didn't understand the details, but I tried to diligently nod along while trying to block out the ringing sound in my ears.

'I often wondered if I might see you here. Well, hoped I would. You know, five kids in tow, looking frazzled, wearing your hair up, dropping things and sighing as you picked them up,' Dan said.

'What?' I laughed and instinctively hit him on the arm.

Shocked at the intimacy of the motion, I took a step away from him.

He continued, unaware of my internal discomfort. 'I always walk around the city on my best behaviour, just in case you see me. I've never noticed you, though.'

'That's hilarious.'

'I know, weird, eh? But you've been okay though?' He looked down at his feet, then back up at me.

I glanced around at the passers-by to avoid his stare. 'Yeah, you know. I'm married now, two kids... life's good.'

'Look, do you fancy a drink? We can carry on chatting. I have an hour or so.'

'Um... yeah, okay. Sure, why not.'

He broke into a wide smile.

We walked side by side along the cobbled street and decided on The Grapes. I mentally scrubbed out my to do list and accepted that I'd go straight from here to collect the kids.

We arrived at the pub and paused beside the windows.

The deep purple wooden door was open, waiting for us. Dan nodded for me to enter first and leant over me to push the door. The door knocker was a brass bunch of grapes. Our heads were suddenly inches apart and we both looked away as if we'd seen a top-secret file. More nerves turned over in my stomach.

The Grapes was a dingy little pub, but there was always a seat. Especially on a weekday around lunchtime. We found a table at the back near the kitchen door. The red wine coloured anaglypta wallpaper to my right was as old as I was.

Dan waited at the bar, getting the first round in, while I stacked the beer mats on our table, as if there was to be an imminent inspection.

I calmed down when Dan returned with a large Pinot for me, but as he sat down, the bar staff shouted, 'You forgot your drink, mate.'

Red-faced, Dan jumped up to collect it. Shaking his head as he sat down again, he clinked his glass with mine.

'Old times?' Dan toasted.

'Old times,' I repeated.

The afternoon flew by, and as we chatted, I began to ease into our conversation. It was warming to see a happy and content Dan. We'd found serenity, without the drama, without the mess, without each other. Dan was dating Jennifer. She was a few years younger than him; she didn't want kids and worked in HR. They didn't live together but had been dating for two years. He said she lifted him up out of the shit, and never once looked down on him for having been such a mess in the past.

'She must be good for you; you look so sparkly.'

He laughed. 'Never been called that before,' Dan said,

cleaning his glasses on his shirt.

I told him all about Flint. He asked how we'd got together, about our wedding and honeymoon, but didn't comment, just smiled and nodded. He gulped a mouthful of beer after every smile.

'I'd never have guessed that. You and Flint, I mean.'

'Well, you guys never actually met.'

'I know. I always wanted to, though.'

'Well, I'm glad you didn't. He always wanted to beat you up.'

'I'm not surprised. I was a mess, you know that.'

'Look, it's okay, you don't have to explain anything.'

'I do, I want to. I've always wanted to. I'd like the opportunity to – if you'll let me?'

I nodded.

'After we lost touch, things were dark, lonely and pretty scary. I didn't want to be with anyone. Not even my kids. I can't even remember it happening, but somehow, my dad, brother and a few mates were there, literally every day. Cooking for me, taking me to doctors, therapists and, you know, just hanging out.'

'Wow.'

'I know. I'll never forget what they did. Then, time happened, like it does. One day, I was getting dressed and I saw something different. A future. Like I wanted things again. I mean, all the big things: my kids back in my life, a job and a proper home, but also small things like a decent steak and chips, a pint with a mate and some sand between my toes.

Then I started to laugh, to listen to music, to have fun, you know?'

I gulped down the tenderness I felt for him. 'Dan, I'm so happy you made it. I only ever wanted you to be happy.'

He nodded. 'Same here, for you, I mean. It looks like we both made it.'

'Can I add something? I'm sorry, for my part, you know, the calling and texting you. I'm embarrassed, I...'

'Don't, Louise, I was bang out of order that night and on more than one occasion, but let's leave it, eh?'

I glanced at my phone. We'd chatted for almost an hour. There was more to talk about, more to say. But I had to go home.

There was a bit of me that didn't want to go. Dan batted away my silent protests and bought another round. So, even as another bit of me frowned, I texted a mum friend of mine as Dan looked on, grinning.

'This is a change. Watching you sort out kid stuff.'

'I know – times have changed, right?' I brushed my fringe out of my eyes.

'Yeah. Now you're all about school pickups, snacks – it seems a lifetime ago when that was me.'

'It was.'

We paused; looked at each other.

'Right, one text and a call and then I'm done, hang on.'

I texted Flint to ask if he could collect Meg from nursery. Flint could read me like a book. I flinched, picturing him knowing who I was sat with.

```
Sure shirker, where you at?
```

I explained I was with an old friend and was planning on getting a later bus home. He told me to have fun and signed off with his usual weird emoji. He was busy. He was working. I was busy. I was lying. I wiped the sweat from the top of my lip.

'Right, I can relax.' I sighed and took a long sip of my chilled wine.

I was not relaxed. I was beginning to feel tipsy and nervy. I used to enjoy daytime drinking back in the day, but these days any wine consumed was planned and slotted into my family life. Feeling woozy and not in complete control unsettled me.

Dan was taking it all in his stride though. He stood up to buy a third round, but I insisted. He requested another pint, and I ordered lime and soda for me.

As I waited for the drinks, I turned to my left to see Dan watching me. His observation continued as I carried our drinks back to the table with two packets of crisps secured between my teeth.

'What's this?' Dan asked, picking up my lime and soda.

'Sensible in a glass is what it is.'

Putting my drink down, I sought something to do with my hands. Maybe I should tell him I was feeling like this? Did he feel it? Two hours ago, the sight of him, the conversation between us, was soothing, almost grounding. I'd been up for him filling in the gaps of the years that had passed.

Now, though, the ease had evaporated.

'I'm feeling tense and weird.'

'I know you are.'

'I'm feeling jittery and fidgety.'

He laughed. 'Again, I know.'

'It's just, when I first saw you, I wanted to hear all of your news, but now...'

'Now you don't?'

I rolled my eyes. 'You know what I mean.'

'It's okay.' He grinned; his cheeks flushed. 'Look, I feel the same. My belly's doing somersaults.'

I smiled, but his revelation didn't make me feel any better. It was excruciating to know he felt as edgy as I did.

I fiddled with the trio of rings on my finger. He leant in, took my hands across the table. I snatched them back.

He remained inclined towards me. 'I'm sorry. That seemed the most natural thing to do.'

Neither of us responded and it continued that way for a few moments. He checked his phone while I recovered, fiddling with my scarf.

'Maybe I should go, it's not like I haven't got anything to do this afternoon,' I said.

I sounded jumpy and out of control.

He frowned and nodded.

My heart raced. Nausea came thick and fast with the realisation that I couldn't stay anymore. I turned to him. He stared back. Neither of us blinked.

I swallowed and he mirrored me.

'Are you okay?' he asked, licking his lips.

I shook my head. 'No,' I hissed. 'I'm *not* okay. I can't be here. I'm going to the toilet and going home.'

Hurrying downstairs, I rounded the corner to the ladies, locked myself in a cubicle, had a pee and covered my face with my hands.

Eventually, my breathing slowed down. I washed my hands and dared to look in the mirror – I was flushed pink and exhausted. I sprinkled water on my wrists in an attempt to cool down, pulled on the door and walked out.

Dan was standing there, looking as bemused as I felt. His pupils were enlarged and his gaze was pleading and desperate.

I felt trapped.

I pushed him gently to the side of the corridor, but he came up behind me and held me around my waist, speaking into my ear.

'Don't go home,' he murmured.

'I am,' I replied, my voice shaking.

'I didn't even know I missed you until I saw you.'

I turned to face him, and he continued to hold me.

'I don't want to know if I still miss you, or if you miss me,' I replied.

'I think I understand what you mean.'

He pulled me into his captivating and toxic embrace to kiss me. It was a soft kiss that unsteadied me, until I shoved him away.

'No! No. Please, Dan. Don't do that.'

I placed my hands flat onto his chest and looked down at my feet. He kissed the top of my head and attempted to hold me again.

What had we done? I wriggled loose and walked away from him, running up the stairs to our table. My phone, coat and handbag were on display for pinching. I collected my things and left the pub.

Domesticity overwhelmed me as soon as I turned the key.

'Here's the dirty stop out,' Flint yelled.

I couldn't see him, but I could smell dinner. There were shrieks from the kitchen as my little ones ran into me. I cuddled them, kissed them, sniffed their heads, and knelt to see their little faces beaming at me. Red pen was on Meg's cheek and her pigtails were wonky. Beth's cheeks were rosy as she pointed at her gums.

'Look.' She flicked her tongue at a wobbly tooth.

'Wow, it's really loose. It won't be long, sweetie,' I replied.

Us three girls held hands and walked into the kitchen to find Flint: pots bubbling, extractor fan struggling, Hot Chip blaring, some kind of kitchen rave – exactly how he liked to cook.

He came over to me and ruffled my hair. 'You alright?' he asked, walking away and diving into the fridge before hearing the answer.

I needed to talk to him.

'Yeah, just tired. Can I go upstairs and hide something I bought for you?'

'Of course. We have it under control, don't we girls?'

I sat on the edge of my bed, nauseous. I pulled my mobile out of my bag and with it came suffocating silence. There were no texts, emails, Facebook messages or missed calls that would disclose the betrayal.

Why did that bother me?

That evening, I performed my arse off. We ate our family meal, put the kids to bed and Flint switched his work laptop on for an hour or two. He'd missed some time in the office, collecting Meg from nursery, while I was fending off an ex; not just an ex, but *the* ex. Feelings of shame stabbed me in the gut as my husband headed upstairs to our office. His frown and crumpled expression told me he was shattered, and as a peace offering he didn't know he needed, I insisted on clearing up the kitchen.

Like that was going to cut it.

I put the radio on. Jo Whiley was live. I touched my mouth and held my finger there, where Dan had been, ignoring the bad feelings growing in my tummy with lethal roots.

I busied myself with the dishwasher, washing up and cleaning the hob, trying to focus on the music, but his face and his smile emerged in frequent interludes. I'd run out of housework to do; felt like I was on the run and needed to keep moving. Should I walk to the shop to buy some chocolate? Should I call Heidi and fill her in? Should I tell Flint?

Maybe.

No.

And no.

I popped my head around the door of the office. Flint was sat at the desk, looking defeated. He lifted his gaze and waved me over with his finger.

'I'm too tired, I can't do any more.'

'Then don't. Shall I run you a bath?'

'Mmm, please.'

I kissed the top of his head and left.

🌷

I wondered if my disgraceful behaviour was forgotten. In doing what I'd done, I'd rewound the years. Suddenly, it was 2006 and Dan was keeping his distance from me.

I thought I'd escaped my rotting morals and was relieved Flint wasn't getting a whiff. I was in luck, for a while.

Family life can whoosh you up and pull you in the way you need to go, and it kept me occupied. After a few days, I didn't even feel guilty. I'd rubbed the incident out of my mind so often, the recollection of kissing Dan in the pub was now merged into my other memories of our relationship. If I tried hard enough, I could insert the last cock-up into the file of "shit Dan stuff" and truly forget it was there. I remembered once how Dan had talked about losing his "real", when he thought he might be without his kids and home forever. Well, my family was my "real" now, and the unit Flint and I had fought to create, slogged to thrive in, was the life we both wanted and loved.

Flint was my real and I could never be without him.

Three weeks later, soaking in the bath, kids in bed, Flint out playing football, I was chatting to a friend via Facebook, and as I searched for another friend's trail of messages to copy a link, I spotted a communication from someone new. I hovered over the message.

He'd written to me three days after I'd bumped into him, but since he wasn't one of my contacts, I hadn't seen the hidden message.

Hi Louise,

I hope it's okay to chat here. I didn't have your number.

I've done nothing but think about you since the other day. Thought about how we were together, how I feel about you and how you still make me feel. Man, what have you done to me?

I've been reliving our kiss and imagining looking into your eyes. I'm here again, where I was, all those years ago, hanging on a thread, waiting for you to reel me in.

I have a plan.

We're both with new people, we love them and why should we change that? But then there's you and me. It's big, it's real and it's us, and I don't think it will ever go away. I can't face more time without you, that's the truth.

So, my idea is this. How about we meet once a year, the same day?

We could spend a day together. Without fail, we meet up, do whatever we like, just us two and maybe have a night together. No one can know, nobody needs to know, and it's a secret we keep.

I'm hoping you're smiling as you read this. I've planned it all out in my head.

I never committed myself to you as I should've done and now you've promised your life to someone else, but I still want to be devoted to you. I've always loved you and I can't live happily in this world without you with me in some way. Even if this is the only way.

How about it? Same place, same time, next year? Scribblers? Behind the numbered birthday card aisle?

Let me know xxxx

I closed my eyes, brought my phone to my chest, and sighed. Then, after a few minutes, I clicked on the box underneath his message and started to type my reply.

A few weeks later, a plan was put into action.

CHAPTER 39

It's a No From Me

I looked again at my watch. It was 12:57.

I had to go.

He would be waiting.

I pushed my way through the Carfax body traffic and, as I approached Bonn Square, some rockabilly buskers were doing a pretty good version of *Get Out of Your Lazy Bed* by Matt Bianco. I stopped to check out my reflection in Monsoon's large shop window. I felt good. I was primed for this today and the preparation had been part of it all. I felt exquisitely sexy.

Our book of love was open on this page, and we planned to pause everyday life to make this work. The monotony was halted, just for a bit, leaving us to pan out magnificently.

I marched on, purposefully; confident and eager. When I arrived at Scribblers, I hesitated before I went inside. I could see him milling around, fiddling with his wedding band, picking up cards and putting them down again. His body movements were predictable and familiar. After all these years, I could still predict which hand he would use next, or which way his head would turn. He glanced at his Fitbit and scoured the shop for my arrival. A section of his hair momentarily covered his eyes, and I wanted to smooth it away, kiss his forehead like I'd done a million times.

Then he clocked me and the love beamed between us. I walked in and went straight to him. He placed a soft kiss on my cheek, and I squeezed his hand.

'Funny seeing you here,' he whispered in my ear.

He clutched my hand.

'What are you looking at?' I asked.

'This. Take a look.' He sniggered.

I warmed to the cheekiness he could still pull off at his age.

'Come on, let's get out of here,' I said, pulling his hand as we walked out into the sunshine together.

He paused, poked his nose into the Radio Oxford bag of goodies I'd brought with me and nodded. 'Nice selection, Mrs. I can't wait to tuck into that little lot, and you.'

I smiled up at him, happy that I'd got it right, so right.

Linking arms, Flint and I walked across Bonn Square, ready to embrace our annual day.

The itinerary?

Us.

Just us.

♥

I'm not going to lie and say I didn't think about meeting Dan and what that would look like with us now; older, still horny, but maybe not wiser.

I couldn't thank Dan for much in my life, but the idea he'd

proposed turned out to be exactly what I needed. What Flint and I needed. It was mad, sexy and re-energising. A one-off date with the man I loved having sex with. A crackling, fizzing, horny date. Like old times, but better.

It could have been Dan, of course. Just one day a year to relive it all, feel alive, then go back to reality. Like my annual Pilates trip with the girls. But when I thought about the bare basics written down, I could see the ingredients would never make anything good. It made me recall the time I made a tofu curry for Flint; it just didn't look right. The dish didn't work, and even though I'd tried really hard to make it perfect, it was all wrong.

Just like Dan and me.

My mind had been made up one Friday night. Flint was out with his friends from work, the girls were in bed, the house in order for the next day, so I'd been flicking through the TV channels, until I came across a Channel 4 documentary about marriage. Usually, I would have skipped it, but I was intrigued. The presenter was talking about bumps in the road; how to keep it alive, to avoid separation. I'd settled on the sofa, quickly becoming hooked. The couples they interviewed were honest and amusing about the sex dwindling.

One lady admitted, 'I let him get on with it while I'm imagining Bradley Walsh, or the bloke who renewed our mortgage.'

I'd laughed, then another couple was interviewed.

'We've just accepted we won't have sex till the kids move out. He has a little play every now and then and I get my roots done. It works for us, doesn't it Alan?'

Alan had nodded as his wife smiled, patting her do.

It had been refreshing to know that we were all at it with our marriages. Losing our way, looking around and checking we'd jumped on the right bus. Remembering life before kids, before boredom hit us square in the face. Flint and I may not have had time for lust these days, and we definitely didn't crave sex in the kitchen amongst the remains of fish fingers and Petits Filous, but if someone gave me a time machine, would I go back?

No.

Would I return to that afternoon on the deckchair in Flint's old house share, when I realised that I would love Flint for the rest of my life? Yes, I'd relive that every day if I could. But I couldn't: I had swimming kits to pack and Lego to stand on.

I knew Flint hated how I never properly secured the lid on the kitchen food composter, stinking the kitchen out, and how I always forgot something big on the shopping list. I definitely hated how he reloaded the dishwasher after I'd put anything inside, and I certainly tutted at the way he walked past the stair piles – every day.

But I didn't need to relive the past to remember how much I loved him. I still remembered how Flint and I were at the beginning, before we were lovers; when we were just mates. Then I'd discovered he was the best man I'd ever met, and I'd never stopped believing that. Sure, all the drudgery and grafting had temporarily robbed us of our intimacy, but we'd get back to our beginning, albeit with different hairstyles, more wrinkles and bifocals. I hadn't forgotten. I never would. Flint was my everything. He'd come along, just like that, and made promises to me that he'd always kept. Exactly as I wanted.

That Friday night, I'd picked up my phone, deleted my original reply to Dan, and typed:

Hi Dan,

　Thanks for messaging me, but I wish you hadn't.
　I'm sorry, but I don't think we should meet.
　You have your new life now and I have mine.
　Let's just remember the past; I don't think we could forget it all.
　Take good care of you.
　Love, Louise

There were men everywhere, but they were not always the right man for you. I'd learnt that the hard way.

Some were afraid to admit they cared.

Some had never cared for anyone but themselves.

Then there were those who promised the earth; who, in their heads, honestly believed they were sharing themselves fully, and loving generously.

I suspected their wives might have a rather different take on the matter.

ACKNOWLEDGEMENTS

I have many people to thank for getting my book out in the world, so I'm really sorry if I have forgotten someone. I hope you will forgive me! I've wondered how and who I would thank and I know this list is huge, so here goes.

Firstly, I must mention the gang at Cranthorpe Millner. Thanks for taking a chance on me. I'll never forget the moment I read the email saying you were interested in my book, when it felt like others hadn't been up for it. Thank you to the editors who read my book, your comments always motivated me and cheered me along. Thanks to Shannon for her cover. How you got into my head and plopped all of that onto a book cover is beyond me. And I'm truly sorry for the 328 emails from me about the design, you are now free to hit delete! Thank you to Lauren for listening to all the marketing questions on repeat. A special thanks to Vicky for reassuring me and providing me with relaxing chats when I was quite frankly losing my mind. You are a very calm person. Thanks for everything you've done.

Thank you to all my early readers: Nina, Evelyn, Kate, and others that I'm sorry I've forgotten. I appreciate your critique and time, it means a lot.

A whopping thanks to the professionals who have encouraged me with my writing. Rufus Purdy was the first person I shared any of my writing with. His wit, honesty and positive comments about my work made me stop for a minute and think that I could actually finish the novel. Thanks to Linda Predovsky. You are one of the most generous professionals out there, always willing to help any new writer who is lost and looking for guidance. Finally, to Jennifer – my editor turned guru turned superstar, who basically loved and laughed (in the right places) at my book, just when I was about to give up. Your empowering words and encouraging professional relationship was second to none. I must cite all of the 'real' writers who have chatted with me over the years. So many to mention, so many stalked and harassed by me, but how kind they were: Olivia Beirne, Lia Louis, Holly Miller, Jamie Anderson, Sarah Turner and Beth Moran, to name a few.

Thanks to the ladies what write. Nic Winter for your sound legal advice and for having all the answers; Liz Krause for your generosity, laughs in Barcelona and those dreamy SoCal tones in your voice notes. Thank you to Karen Legge, your support for Louise has been immensely helpful. I truly think you know her like I do. I'm grateful for our mutual friend who unknowingly facilitated our writerly and friendship connection. It was meant to be. Amy Orrell, it's been cool to get to know you and it will soon be your turn!

Finally, Julia, my first writing buddy, my upfront, tell it how it is, mate. Always there with a wet fish to slap me with and a cuddle down the phone. The stars were aligned when we met – thank god!

I'd like to thank my parents and ever-growing family, including the outlaws for generally being around. Mum and Dad, I hope you are proud, but I have a bit of advice: maybe skim over some of the sweary bits and sex scenes, it won't matter all that much if you miss them. Actually... they are needed, sorry about that. Huge thanks to my niece Abigail, who read through the book much quicker than I expected while on holiday and loved it. Big kisses.

The Circle of Truth also need a shout-out: Jo and Lynn, who knew that sipping hot drinks while our little ones were building campfires at Beavers would develop into what we have. Love yah both!

Agent Carter and Dee Dee – thanks for the laughs, memories, music and the tales only we know.

To Jill Jam, as you will always be known in our house – thank you for our mammoth lunch dates and walks and general chit-chat. There is no one I could talk more with, especially when books come up. P.S. Can we place a jam order, please?

And just because I feel a drop of testosterone is required in this huge list of thank yous, how could I forget my Whitton boys? Well, lads, Mummy did it – I hope you are impressed. You can't read it yet, and when it is age-appropriate you won't want to anyway. Neil, I told you I would never give up. Thanks for enabling my dream, thanks for being you and, as always, it's you and me against the world.

Finally, to Gavin, I wish you could be here to read my book, but truthfully, you would have loved the *I Didn't See That Coming* playlist way more. That's a fact! We all miss you.

I have now thanked all the people I know and have met in real life, so all that's left is to thank the fictional writers who have inspired me for many years, and who I've definitely daydreamed about being and knowing. Obvious choices maybe, but still: Anne Shirley, Jo March, Carrie Bradshaw, Emma Morely, Lynda Day. Ladies, I salute you all.

CRANTHORPE
MILLNER
PUBLISHERS

Did you enjoy this book?

Why not leave a review, or email digitalmarketing@cranthorpemillner.com to sign up to our newsletter and receive advance copies of our upcoming titles.

www.cranthorpemillner.com